SPECIAL MESSAGE TO READERS

THE ULVERSCROFT FOUNDATION
(registered UK charity number 264873)

was established in 1972 to provide funds for research, diagnosis and treatment of eye diseases. Examples of major projects funded by the Ulverscroft Foundation are:-

- The Children's Eye Unit at Moorfields Eye Hospital, London
- The Ulverscroft Children's Eye Unit at Great Ormond Street Hospital for Sick Children
- Funding research into eye diseases and treatment at the Department of Ophthalmology, University of Leicester
- The Ulverscroft Vision Research Group, Institute of Child Health
- Twin operating theatres at the Western Ophthalmic Hospital, London
- The Chair of Ophthalmology at the Royal Australian College of Ophthalmologists

You can help further the work of the Foundation by making a donation or leaving a legacy. Every contribution is gratefully received. If you would like to help support the Foundation or require further information, please contact:

THE ULVERSCROFT FOUNDATION
**The Green, Bradgate Road, Anstey
Leicester LE7 7FU, England
Tel: (0116) 236 4325**

website: www.ulverscroft-foundation.org.uk

DAUGHTERS OF LIVERPOOL

Liverpool, 1868: Shrouded in secrecy, Alice Sampson gives birth to a beautiful baby girl. But the former nurse's happiness is blighted by the knowledge that as a penniless unwed mother, her future and that of her child can only be one of shame. Then a knock at the door brings a miracle: she is invited to return to the Liverpool Royal Infirmary and her beloved ward. With the help of her friends and the welcome attentions of Reverend Seed, the hospital chaplain, Alice slowly starts to rebuild her life. Everything is looking up — until her baby's father unexpectedly shows up to claim the child he knew nothing about. Suddenly Alice is in danger of losing everything . . .

KATE EASTHAM

DAUGHTERS OF LIVERPOOL

Complete and Unabridged

MAGNA
Leicester

First published in Great Britain in 2019 by
Penguin Books
London

First Ulverscroft Edition
published 2020
by arrangement with
Penguin Books
Penguin Random House
London

A catalogue record for this book is available
from the British Library.

ISBN 978–0–7505–4812–0

Published by
Ulverscroft Limited
Anstey, Leicestershire

Set by Words & Graphics Ltd.
Anstey, Leicestershire
Printed and bound in Great Britain by
T. J. International Ltd., Padstow, Cornwall

This book is printed on acid-free paper

Josephine Butler (1828–1906) was a pioneer for the rights of women and a social reformer who moved to Liverpool in 1866. In 1869 she became actively involved with a campaign to repeal the Contagious Diseases Acts. These Acts attempted to control the spread of venereal disease through the arrest and forced medical examination of women, whilst men were allowed to continue their activities with complete freedom. By 1871 Liverpool had seen a huge upsurge in women convicted for prostitution as so-called 'moral enforcement' spread to the north. Josephine Butler decried this violation of women and fought for the right of any woman walking the street not to face arrest by the police. She called attention to the idiocy of the Acts in presupposing that every working woman who was found associating, under any circumstances, with a man, and who could not produce a certificate of her marriage to him, was to be called a prostitute.

1

'There is something not quite right in a woman who shuts up her heart from other women.'

Florence Nightingale

Liverpool, 1871

Alice Sampson ran to her small room. Throwing herself down on her knees, she pulled out a wooden box from under the bed. Immediately, she was rifling through the contents. 'Where are you, where are you?' she muttered, pulling out gloves, handkerchiefs, a hatpin, and, at last, a new lace collar. 'There you are,' she cried, grabbing the collar and positioning it as she ran back to the kitchen. 'Sorry, cat,' she yelled as the creature shot off with a yowl when she trod on its tail. And then, at last, she slowed her pace, and came to stand, breathless, by the baby's crib.

'Hello, my darling,' she said, smiling down at the baby girl who looked at her with wide eyes. Alice couldn't resist, even though she was running late, very late; her heart melted as her daughter reached up with her tiny hands. She leant further over the crib, close enough to breathe in the scent of her and feel her soft fingers reaching up to touch her face. Then, she gave the palm of each small hand a noisy kiss, and planted tiny kisses on the tip of each finger

1

in turn, thrilled each time that her baby gave a squeal of delight.

Glancing up to the clock, Alice knew that they definitely had to start moving. 'Come on, you scallywag,' she said, sweeping the baby up, grabbing a paisley patterned shawl from the back of a kitchen chair and wrapping her in it.

No one else was up and about — all of the downstairs rooms, apart from the kitchen, were usually empty in the morning. A brothel was a quiet place at this time of day.

Balancing the baby on her hip, she unlocked the front door and ran from the house, the baby bouncing up and down. Alice knew that she had to move fast. Her friend Maud was getting married today. The two of them were as close as any women could be. The trouble was, Maud was going away today, after her wedding. She was going to America and Alice had no idea when she would ever see her again.

She looked down at her daughter's startled face. 'Sorry, my darling,' she muttered. 'We need to go fast. We can't be late for Maud's wedding!'

Hearing the baby starting to whimper, Alice immediately slowed her pace to a brisk walk and lifted the child up against her shoulder where she could soothe her as she walked along. 'I told you we were going to the wedding this morning, didn't I, Victoria? Maud's marrying Harry Donahue and they're going on a big boat to New York. And Alfred's going with them. You know Alfred, the boy who comes to see you and makes you smile? Yes, you love Alfred, don't you? And you love Maud . . . '

Alice's voice faltered as she felt the familiar tightness in her chest which came every time she thought about her friend leaving Liverpool.

Holding back the tears, she drew the baby even closer to her body and forced herself to keep talking softly to her.

'But at least we've got a roof over our heads, living with Stella and Marie. I know it's not the sort of place I thought we'd be living in. But we've got our own room, all warm and snug, tucked away behind the kitchen. And all the women there adore you, don't they?'

Now the baby was settling, Alice gave a sigh. Thank goodness for Victoria. She couldn't imagine life without her, not now. But then again, if she hadn't fallen pregnant, she'd have been able to complete her nurse training alongside Maud. She would have been working at the Liverpool Royal Infirmary now and living with her friends in the Nurses' Home.

She sighed again, then she started to smile as she looked at her daughter. 'Don't you worry, my darling,' she murmured. 'You may have come along at the wrong time, before I was ready to even think about having a baby, but we will find a way to make things work. We have to.'

Two strides out of the alley, Alice saw a group of rough-looking men at the corner of the next street and tightened her hold on Victoria.

Desperately short of time, she knew that she had no choice but to go in that direction, and she would have to push her way through. These cornermen, as they were called, didn't usually worry her too much. Alice had three brothers at home and she knew how to stick up for herself, with fists if need be.

'All right there, darlin'?' said one young man, coming in close. Alice felt her heart skip a beat. 'How much d'you reckon you should pay for bringing a baby through here?' Alice continued on without looking at him.

'Not so fast now, not so fast,' said the rough voice as he reached his arm out in front of her, forcing her to take a step back. Alice was trapped, she couldn't move, and there was another man next to her. She felt her heart racing and her breath was coming quick as she pulled Victoria even closer. Coming this way to save time had been a big mistake.

'That's a fine shawl you've got there, for your little one,' said the other, his voice barely that of a man. Still Alice didn't look at either of them, all the while planning an escape, readying herself to sidestep, and then run. All that she knew for sure, was that if one of them laid a hand on Victoria she would fight like a tiger to protect her. Any mother would do the same for her child.

The first one leant in and ran a finger down her cheek. She felt the skin of his knuckle, like sandpaper, as he whispered in her ear, 'Well, lovely lady with the red hair, you could give us a few coins, or maybe we could just take the shawl from that baby of yours or maybe we could — '

The lad didn't get to finish his words. A hand grabbed him from behind, almost lifting him off his feet, and threw him aside. Then the whole group of them scarpered.

4

Alice was startled. For a split second, she couldn't move. Then her instinct to run kicked in and she was off, with the baby held fast in her arms.

Hearing Victoria starting to whimper again, she slowed her pace after a few strides and glanced back, trying to make sense of what had just happened. And that's when she saw him: a broad-shouldered man in a thigh-length black coat, walking away from her. Something about his measured stride made her certain that he was the man who'd saved her from the cornermen.

She didn't have time to ponder on the issue and she certainly didn't want to linger on the street, so she turned back and picked up her pace again, profoundly grateful to the man who had stepped in to help her, whoever he was. She'd always been able to fend for herself, but being stopped by the cornermen when she was with Victoria had been a whole different experience. She wouldn't risk that again, ever.

★ ★ ★

Alice had to force herself to stop and take her time crossing Lime Street. It was always so busy outside the railway station, and so easy to be caught by a horse or a carriage wheel.

At last she saw her chance and ran for it, dodging around horse muck as she went. In recent weeks she'd started to feel stronger and quicker. For so long she'd been recovering from childbirth or exhausted from lack of sleep, but now she felt like she could conquer the world.

She could even have walked beyond Liverpool and all the way to the small town in the north where her family lived. Especially now, after what had just happened on the street of her adopted city. Except, they didn't know at home; they had no idea that she had a baby. As far as they were concerned, she had completed her training alongside her fellow probationers and she was now working as a nurse at the hospital.

She was desperate to be at the church for Maud but found herself forced to slow her pace as she manoeuvred between pedestrians. So many people, all moving too slowly. Stuck solidly behind a large woman carrying a basket on each arm, she felt her heart racing again. 'Let me by, let me by,' she muttered under her breath, dancing from side to side in an attempt to get past. She was forced to stop for a moment: there was no way through. Taking a deep breath, she collected herself and then set her sights on the landmark that was St George's Hall. The crowd moved forward, and soon Alice was standing in front of the building, dizzied, as always, by the sheer height of its walls. Instinctively, she shifted her arm to shield the baby, almost fearful that the huge stone pillars that graced the front of the building would fall and crush them both. She'd been in awe of St George's since the day she'd arrived in Liverpool. It had been the first thing she'd seen as she emerged from Lime Street Station with her fresh scrubbed face and a small bag of belongings.

The forlorn cry of the gulls overhead made her move past even faster, that is until she saw one land on the head of Prince Albert as he sat on his horse, immortalized in stone, at the front of the building. She couldn't help but laugh to herself when she saw the great man with a seagull on his head.

'Just look at that big bird on the head of Queen Victoria's husband,' she whispered to Victoria, who was sleeping soundly.

By some miracle the streets were less crowded now and Alice could easily pick up her pace. She was soon at the church — but only just in time. The door was closing, and as she entered, she felt the silence inside the building encircle her like a blanket. On seeing Maud and her groom standing at the altar, Alice feared she was too late after all. She breathed a sigh of relief as she caught sight of a large hat adorned with a red silk flower, which she knew belonged to Eddy, her other close friend from nurse training. She turned to smile at Alice as she walked quietly down and slipped into the pew beside her.

Eddy immediately leant over to give the sleeping baby a gentle kiss. 'Hello, my beautiful,' she said, stroking her cheek. Then, lifting her head, 'Sorry, Alice . . . hello to you as well.'

Alice gave a wry smile. 'Oh, it's all right, I'm used to it now. It's like I don't really exist any more. And now that she's laughing and starting to really pay attention, well, I don't stand a chance, I'm completely bewitched by her.'

'That's just how it should be, isn't it, Victoria?' said Eddy, giving the baby another soft kiss on the cheek, dislodging her hat in the process.

Looking up whilst Eddy fixed her hat, Alice

7

saw the relieved faces of Stella and her mother Marie, further along the pew. They'd left ahead of her, to make sure they were on time.

Directly in front, Alice could see the straight back of a woman with her grey hair piled high: Miss Fairchild, the housekeeper from where Maud used to work before she decided to train as a nurse. And, of course, the small blond head of Alfred, the boy that Maud and Harry were adopting and taking with them to New York.

In the next moment, the Reverend glanced around the small congregation and cleared his throat, and then he began the opening words to the marriage ceremony.

And as the words were said and Alice heard Maud and Harry start to give their responses, she knew that this was really happening. Maud was getting married and she was going away to New York. She felt an emptiness opening in the pit of her stomach and she knew that she would have to fight even harder now to hold back the tears.

As Maud said, 'I will,' her voice quiet but clear, Alice felt a lump in her throat and the tears started to well in her eyes. Victoria must have sensed her disquiet because she was starting to scrunch her face and move her head from side to side, and then she began whimpering. So Alice stood quietly and stepped to the side of the church, turning her back on the couple at the altar and continuing to rock the baby.

That's when she saw a face she hadn't expected to see at the back of the church and she had to hold back a gasp. How did she get in?

thought Alice, looking straight at Nancy Sellers, another nurse from their group of probationers, but no friend of hers and definitely not a friend of Maud's. Nancy had set herself against Maud right from the start and, not only that, she had tried her best to steal Harry away as well. What was she doing here, today of all days? There was absolutely no way that she would have been invited.

Alice looked directly at Nancy and she could see a small smile on her face as she sat alone in the pew wearing a neat blue gown that perfectly matched the colour of her eyes. She knew that Nancy could see her, but it never so much as registered on her face. She just sat, looking straight ahead, her eyes bright and almost burning into the backs of Maud and Harry as they stood at the altar. Any minute now they would be coming back down the aisle. Alice turned back to scrutinize the bride and groom, to make sure that neither of them had seen the unwelcome visitor. When she looked to the rear of the church again, Nancy had gone, as quietly as she had entered — leaving Alice wondering if she'd really been there at all or if she'd imagined the whole thing.

Slightly out of breath, Alice slipped back into the pew, just in time to see the bride and groom kiss, and then they turned to face the congregation. Maud looked radiant and Alice had to admit that her new husband was a very handsome man indeed. She knew from the times he had visited Stella's place with Maud that he was very charming too, but there was always a restlessness about Harry that gave Alice an unsettled feeling. It made her worry for her friend.

But there Maud was, married now, and as she stood with Harry in front of the altar, the pale grey of her gown setting off the dark of her hair, Alice couldn't help but smile. Maud was looking straight at her and Eddy, and they were all smiling.

As the couple started to walk down the aisle, Eddy whispered loudly (she could never do anything quietly), 'She looks so beautiful. Shame he didn't get a new jacket, though, he always wears that old green thing.'

'Shhh,' said Alice instinctively, knowing, as always, that Eddy never meant any harm, but she didn't want Maud to hear. Maud *did* look beautiful, though, with a white silk flower pinned in her dark hair.

And then the wedding party were standing up and rustling around as they made their way out of the pews. The bride and groom had been directed to a table at the back of the church to sign the register and so the wedding guests had a few minutes longer outside the church waiting for them to reappear.

Alice could feel the excitement of the small group. 'Hurrah!' they all shouted the moment Maud and Harry emerged from the church. Miss Fairchild squealed with delight as she and Alfred threw handful after handful of rice.

Seeing how pleased and elegant Maud looked, Alice couldn't help but feel happy for her.

Moving the baby back up on to her shoulder,

still rocking from side to side, Alice wondered what was going to happen now, for her and Victoria. She still couldn't believe that only last year, she'd stepped off a train with her bag packed for a new life as a trainee nurse, feeling such a buzz of excitement, but unaware that there was a baby growing inside her. After just one night with Jamie, one night. How could that happen? Well, she knew, of course, how it could happen — she'd quite enjoyed the happening. But it was so unfair. And she'd never had a word from Jamie. Not that she'd expected it; for both of them, it had been just one night, a way of saying goodbye. She'd been sad to see him go, of course she had, but that sadness was outweighed by the excitement of leaving home herself and coming to Liverpool.

But that one night had changed everything for Alice. In the space of a few weeks, she'd realized that she was expecting a child and she'd gone from being an excited nurse probationer to someone fearful of being found out and needing to hide her growing belly. Knowing, for sure, that she wouldn't be able to finish the work that she'd only just begun.

2

'Women never have a half-hour in all
their lives (excepting before or after
anybody is up in the house) that they
can call their own . . . '

Florence Nightingale

'I saw Nancy at the back of the church,'
whispered Alice, as she stood with Eddy in the
churchyard.

'What?' said Eddy out loud.

'Shh, keep your voice down,' said Alice,
moving a few more paces away from the wedding
party.

'When I got up with the baby, she was there,
sitting at the back, as large as life, with a strange
smile on her face.'

'Are you sure you weren't — '

'I wasn't seeing things. It was her, all right, she
looked straight through me.'

'What was *she* doing there?' said Eddy, almost
to herself, as she followed Alice's gaze towards
Maud and Harry standing outside the church.

'I don't know, I didn't tell anyone — did you?'

Alice saw Eddy's eyes widen and she took a
sharp breath, 'Oh no,' she said.

'Oh no, what?' said Alice, glaring at her friend.

'Well, I might have told Millicent Langtry.'

'Millicent Langtry!' hissed Alice, struggling to
keep her own voice down. 'She's the biggest

gossip around. And Nancy's had her at her beck and call for ages. Didn't you know?'

'No,' said Eddy, looking forlorn, 'I had no idea. Millicent is so slow and she seems so quiet with everything.'

Instantly Alice couldn't help but feel sorry for her friend, and she knew that Eddy would never deliberately do anything to harm a living soul. She didn't always think before she spoke, that's all.

'I'm sorry, Alice,' said Eddy contritely.

'Well, she only came to the church, that's all. Maud didn't see her, so no harm done, hey.'

'I suppose not,' murmured Eddy, glancing over again to Maud and Harry as they clung to each other.

'So that's all right then,' said Alice, not believing herself for one moment. There was no way that Nancy Sellers would do anything without a reason. Why would she turn up and not say anything to anyone? She was up to something, all right.

'Come on, Eddy,' Alice said, seeing Maud smile towards them and beckon. 'Time to get going.'

There was no lingering over the wedding breakfast which was provided in a dark tavern near the docks. Although the whole party knew that they had time to spare, they could hear the sound of the harbour and the cry of the gulls, and it felt as if all the ships were about to leave. So they got through the pies and the pastries in double quick time. And after Harry had downed a good few pints of ale, they all emerged, relieved to be back in the light.

Alfred went straight over to Harry's dog, Rita. She'd been brought by a friend and left tied up outside the tavern. Alice had never seen that dog make so much fuss of anybody. Rita was usually steadfast by Harry's side, but there she was, wagging her tail, making a noise and licking the boy's face.

Victoria squealed with delight when she saw the dog and Alice crouched down with her so that she could reach out a chubby arm and grab the creature's fur. The baby loved the scraggy animal and the dog never growled or snapped even when Victoria gave it a good squeeze with both hands. Alice quickly eased away Victoria's tiny fingers and gave the dog a stroke to soothe her, but Rita was so taken with Alfred that she hardly noticed. When Alice straightened up, Stella and Marie were there. They'd just said their goodbyes to Maud and Harry and were heading back to the brothel to make sure that all was in order for another busy night of trade.

'See you later, Alice,' said Stella, her eyes full of sympathy. 'I know how close you and Maud are, I saw that the first time you both came to see me at the house. You will miss her.'

'I will,' said Alice quietly, 'but this is a wonderful opportunity for Maud, working in New York . . . and she might not be gone for good, who knows?'

'Who knows? Hey,' said Stella with a smile. But Alice knew her well enough by now to be sure that she wasn't convinced. 'Anyway, we'll see you back at the house later on . . . '

Alice nodded and shifted the position of the baby in her arms.

'Come on, Alice,' said Eddy, appearing at her side, tickling the baby and making her laugh. 'Let me carry her for a bit.' Alice handed the baby over and then watched as Eddy swung her up into the air, before settling her on a hip.

Maud turned back and called, 'Come on, you two,' and Harry led the way, easily carrying a large trunk balanced on his shoulder, the dog trotting at his side in a steady rhythm. Alice could see Miss Fairchild dutifully following along behind, her back stiff and her shoulders held square, as she clung to Alfred's hand.

Alice linked her arm through Eddy's as she bounced along with the baby and then she held on even more tightly when they got closer to the dock. It was crammed with people carrying bags and shouting to each other. Alice was trying to take it all in and stay calm when . . . *Bang!* The sound of an explosion echoed around the harbour.

Alice screeched with fright and grabbed Eddy and the baby.

'Eddy, what *was* that?' she yelled. 'It sounded like a gun firing.'

When she didn't get a reply, Alice shook her friend's arm. But then she realized that Eddy was laughing her head off.

'What?' demanded Alice, feeling her face starting to flush with irritation.

'Sorry, Alice, I should have told you . . . to expect it,' snorted Eddy. 'That's just the One O'Clock Gun, the cannon that they fire from

Birkenhead every afternoon. It's a time check for all the ships so that they can set their chronometers.'

'Well, I don't know what a chronometer is, but you could have warned me about the gun,' shouted Alice, over the noise of a horse and cart that were rumbling past. 'I thought we were under attack.'

'Under attack,' murmured Eddy, and she started to laugh even more, then she was grabbing Alice's arm to pull her out of the way of a porter who was pushing a handcart piled with luggage.

'Come on, stick by me,' shouted Eddy, looking to make sure that they didn't lose sight of Harry as he walked ahead.

Alice began to feel even more flustered when they found themselves in amongst another crowd of people. Miraculously, Eddy managed to find them a quiet corner to stand whilst Harry and Alfred went off to find out exactly where they should embark. She even found an upturned crate for Alice to sit with Victoria on her knee. Maud came to stand right next to her, placing a hand lightly on her shoulder, and then she leant down to stroke the baby's head. Alice could feel her friend's joy and pain in that one simple gesture.

Alice opened her mouth to speak but Maud was there first.

'I will be fine, and so will you,' she said in her steady way, continuing to stroke the baby's head. 'And I'll write to you as soon as I can.'

'I know you will,' said Alice quietly. 'It's just that, well . . . '

16

'I know, I know,' said Maud, taking Alice's hand and giving it a squeeze, 'I feel the same.'

Then, holding her arms out to take the baby for one last time, Maud straightened up with her. 'And I'll miss you as well, little one, won't I?' Victoria gurgled and then she put her tiny hand on Maud's cheek. Alice could see her friend whispering to the baby and kissing her and then smelling her hair. And she could see that her eyes were brimming with tears.

'She's always happy when she's with you, Maud,' said Alice gently, 'and she won't forget you.'

Maud kissed the baby's cheek again and then she held her tight against her own body.

'I will be back,' said Maud. 'We don't know when, but I will be back.'

Miss Fairchild had come to stand close and she was talking to the baby. 'Will she come to me?' she asked.

Maud gave Victoria one last kiss and then handed her over.

'Well now, young lady,' said Miss Fairchild, holding the baby slightly away from her body, 'look at you.'

The baby was quiet, staring at the older woman's face.

'She has lovely hair,' said Miss Fairchild. 'Is that a streak of red that's coming in the front?'

'It is, yes,' said Alice, and as she spoke the baby reached out her arms to come back to her mother.

'They never stay long with me,' said Miss Fairchild with a tinge of sadness in her voice.

Alice gave Maud a nudge, indicating that she needed to say goodbye to her former house-keeper. She knew how formal Maud could be sometimes, so wasn't surprised one bit when she saw her friend shake Miss Fairchild's hand.

Alice could sense the loss that the older woman was feeling; she knew that Maud and Alfred were like family to her. So she did not hesitate — somehow it felt right — she put her arm around Miss Fairchild just for a moment as she stood there. It felt strange, to be so close that she could smell the woman's face powder, and the scent of lavender water, and she could feel how straight, how corseted she was. And how she seemed to stiffen further with the contact.

Then, as Alice drew back from her momentary gesture, she could see the woman starting to smile. And then Miss Fairchild was reaching out a hand to stroke the baby's face. Alice held her breath, but she had no need to worry: Victoria was smiling, properly smiling now, at the housekeeper.

'There you go,' she said gently. 'My daughter really seems to be taking to you.'

'This way!' shouted Harry as he reappeared with the boy and grabbed hold of the trunk.

And the spell was broken. Victoria, startled, clutched her mother and Miss Fairchild stepped back, straightening her bodice.

Harry put down the trunk for a moment, instantly concerned that he'd frightened the baby. 'Sorry, sweetness,' he said, taking a moment to stroke her cheek, and then kissing her gently. 'Bye for now, little girl.'

In that moment Alice knew that she'd caught a glimpse of the Harry that Maud had fallen in love with.

'Wait till you see it! It's a fine ship . . . and at least I won't be shovelling coal to stoke the boilers this time,' he said, as he hoisted the trunk back on to his shoulder and strode away.

Alice and Maud exchanged a glance, both bewildered. When did he ever do that? thought Alice, and why has he never told Maud?

The dock was bristling with masts and the whole group were excited because the couple were to cross the Atlantic on a brand-new ship of the White Star Line, the *Oceanic*. It was a paddle steamer, but it also had sails, and there had been much talk around Liverpool about the new luxuries that travellers could expect on board. Alice could feel the buzz of excitement amongst the crowd who were packed on to the quay, many having come just to see the ship set sail.

Alice walked beside Maud, following Harry as he pushed his way through the crowd, and they had their first glimpse of the ship. The *Oceanic* didn't look much different to the other ships as far as Alice could see, and she couldn't help but feel a bit resentful towards it. All she could see was something that was going to take her best friend away from her.

She grabbed hold of Maud's hand, as they were swept along on a wave of excitement with people pushing and shouting all around them. Then they were there, at the departure gate, and Harry was speaking to some man in a uniform. Alice knew there were only minutes left so she grabbed hold of Maud and gave her one last hug.

Alice didn't want to let her friend go, and in that moment she knew that Maud felt exactly the same. The two women clung together. Alice could feel a tightness in her chest and she swallowed hard to control it. But as Maud pulled away, she sobbed, from deep inside. She couldn't help it. Maud took out a neatly folded handkerchief from her pocket, leant in and wiped Alice's tears and then she grabbed her hand and gave it one last squeeze.

'Goodbye, Alice,' she sniffed, before turning to Eddy. Alice watched as Eddy gave Maud a huge hug. She could see how they were both struggling to keep the tears in; Eddy was making so much effort that her face was bright red.

Miss Fairchild had pushed her way through so that she could crouch down and give Alfred a hug as he stood quietly next to Maud, holding him so tight that it looked as though she was squeezing the breath out of him. Eddy had to help the woman up in the end so that the boy could be released. But he didn't run straight off like many would; he stood close to the older woman for a few moments and took her hand, whilst she got her breath back.

Then Harry turned from his conversation with the man in uniform and within seconds Maud was walking up the gangplank holding Alfred's hand. And as she was moving away Alice felt another sob rising in her chest. She didn't even try to keep it in this time; she just let it come.

Maud and Alfred stood at the side of the ship,

waving madly. Alice started to cry even more and Victoria squirmed in her arms and started to whimper. Eddy put a strong arm around both of them.

It took some time for all the passengers to board, but Alice, Eddy and Miss Fairchild were determined to stay right where they were. They weren't going anywhere until they saw that ship well out into the harbour. At last a whistle blew and the crowd stood quietly for a few moments, waiting whilst the gangplank was removed and the ropes were unfastened, and then the ship began to edge away from the harbour wall. A huge cheer went up from the crowd and then people on the ship and on dry land were all waving and shouting out to each other. Alice kept her eyes on Maud's face. As the ship moved away she felt as if something was stretching inside her, more and more as the ship headed further out.

Somewhere on deck a fiddle started to play and a plaintive voice began singing about the leaving of Liverpool. Then there were other voices on the ship and on shore joining in with the chorus . . .

So fare thee well, my own true love,
For when I return united we will be,
It's not the leaving of Liverpool that grieves me,
But my darlin' when I think of thee.

Alice and Eddy let out a sob at the same time as the ship edged away.

They gave one last wave and then continued

21

to watch as the ship eased out into the estuary, the sound of the fiddle growing fainter and fainter. Alice reached out a hand to a woman standing beside her who was weeping uncontrollably. 'It's my only sister,' she sobbed, 'my only sister.'

'I'm sorry,' said Alice, giving the woman's arm a squeeze, and then rooting in her pocket and fishing out a clean handkerchief to give to her.

'Thank you,' said the woman, trying to smile.

When Alice looked back to the ship she realized that she couldn't hear the sound of the fiddle any more or properly make out the shape of Maud. She was gone. Alice stood resolute, wiping the tears from her eyes with the flat of her hand and holding Victoria tight against her body.

Miss Fairchild stood with her hand pressed over her heart, as if she was holding back a pain. And then, seeing the girls, she handed each of them a lavender-scented handkerchief. Alice watched as Eddy gave her nose a good blow on the fine linen. It made her smile, at least, and then she started to giggle.

'What?' said Eddy as she finished with a big wipe of her nose and stuffed the handkerchief up her sleeve.

'Nothing,' said Alice. 'I love you, that's all.'

★   ★   ★

Alice walked back at a steady pace, thinking over the events of the day, saying goodbye to Maud over and over in her head. She couldn't help but feel apprehensive for the new family. They would be out to sea now, across to Ireland and then on the open water to America. She shuddered as she thought about the vast expanse that was the Atlantic Ocean. What if something went wrong? What if the ship sank?

Feeling the baby stirring against her, she immediately switched her attention as Victoria started to cry. Alice felt the surge of milk in her breasts and she knew that she'd have to find somewhere to feed. If she tried to make it back to Stella's place Victoria would be screaming blue murder by the time they got there. The only place she knew where she would be able to sit for a while without attracting attention was in front of St George's Hall. If she sat with her back to the looming building, she maybe wouldn't feel overawed by it, and on a warm afternoon like this it would be full of people.

Alice found a space to sit next to some women on the stone steps right behind Prince Albert's horse. As she sat down, the women smiled at her and then they continued with their conversation, keeping an eye on their children as they ran around the statues and up and down the many steps that led up to the Hall. It was easy for Alice to feed the baby once she had the front of her bodice undone. The large shawl that she used to wrap the baby covered everything.

As she sat, Alice tried to relax and put the sadness of Maud's leaving to the back of her mind. She drifted along with the sound of the murmuring conversation beside her and the sharper comments of people passing by, all punctuated by the intermittent cry of the gulls.

The sudden laughter of two young men walking by, smartly dressed in suits, made her look up. Those two looked happy, not a care in the world as they walked along side by side, chatting. Then coming in the other direction she saw the grey face of an older man, his eyes dead, walking as if in a trance. She looked straight back down to the baby. She knew that something terrible must have happened to him; he looked like somebody who had lost everything.

Alice shifted the baby over to the other breast and then settled back into the rhythm of the feed. The next time she looked up, she saw a girl with blond hair straight down her back, walking slowly, helping an ancient woman with a face creased with wrinkles who could barely walk. The slowness of their pace was almost painful, and the old woman was bundled up in layers of clothes and a heavy shawl. Alice could see by the girl's face that she was desperately worried about the old woman.

Easily passing the old woman and the girl was a man on crutches with a white dog trotting by his side. He looked familiar and as he came closer Alice saw exactly who it was. He'd been a patient on her first ward at the Liverpool Royal, when she'd been a probationer alongside Maud, in what now seemed like a lifetime ago. She remembered him very well; he'd been coming off the drink and full of the shakes and very noisy. He'd been in the next bed to Alfred. How strange that she should see this man again, today of all days. The day that Maud had left for America.

Alice sensed that the baby had finished her feed and was falling asleep. The women next to her were laughing together and then calling to their children. It felt like time to move. As Alice fastened her bodice and then stood with the baby settled on her hip, the women on the steps looked up at her and smiled. 'She looks like she feeds well,' said one of them, 'even though she is so tiny.'

Alice smiled in return and exchanged a few words with the women, and then she was walking briskly past the high walls of St George's Hall without looking up. As she walked, she easily overtook the girl and the old woman. Alice glanced back to smile at the girl, but in that moment, the old lady stumbled and fell on to the hard stone flags. Both women let out a scream.

Alice was straight there, neatly balancing the baby with one arm as she knelt beside the woman who lay groaning on the ground. The young girl was wailing with sorrow.

'It's all right, it's all right,' said Alice calmly, first to the wailing girl and then to the groaning woman. 'Just lie still . . . that's it, and let me have a look.'

The woman still lay groaning but the girl had stopped wailing and was wiping her eyes with the flat of her hand.

'What's your name?' said Alice gently to the woman lying on the ground.

'Ellen Marchbank,' she said, her voice shaky. 'My granddaughter is taking me to the apothecary, me legs are bad.'

'Do you have any pain now, anywhere in your

25

body, especially the hips?'

The old woman tried to move herself, but she couldn't in the big shawl, so Alice started to gently loosen it with one hand, looking at the girl and asking her to help, which she did immediately.

'Now, Mrs Marchbank,' said Alice, when the shawl was loose. 'Tell me, are you in any more pain than is usual for you?'

The old woman stared at the blue sky for a few moments and then she closed her eyes. Her granddaughter drew in a sharp breath and Alice placed a hand on the girl's arm to steady her.

'Mrs Marchbank?'

The old woman's eyes popped open and she started to smile. 'Nah, me body's racked with pain but I can't say it's any worse than it was. It's me rheumatics, that's what it is . . . '

'I'm so sorry that you're in so much pain with that,' said Alice, relieved at least that the woman didn't seem to have done any further damage. 'And I think it's a good idea for you to ask the apothecary for some salts. But can you just try and gently move your legs and arms for me so I can properly check if you hurt yourself in the fall?'

The old woman nodded as she lay there on her back and then she inched some movement from each of her limbs in turn.

'Don't seem any worse,' she said, showing her toothless gums as she smiled. 'And what's more, I needed a bit of a rest, so at least I've got that, and I never thought I was going to meet someone like you today. With your red hair and your blue eyes and your soothing voice, you're just as lovely as my granddaughter here.'

Alice smiled at the old woman. She could tell that it was time to be helping her up. 'Come on, then,' she said, gesturing for the girl to help, before shifting the position of the baby on her hip and reaching down to take Mrs Marchbank's arm. 'Let's get you back on your feet.'

The two of them hauled the old woman up and she lurched unsteadily to her feet.

'Right,' said Alice, 'I think we need to unwrap this heavy shawl completely so that you can move more easily. It did save you from injury, but it might well have been the reason you fell.'

'Righto,' said the girl quietly, helping her grandmother.

The woman still had many layers of clothing underneath, so she was well padded, and she didn't seem to have suffered any serious injury, thank goodness.

'Good job I didn't break me hip . . . I've no money for doctors, I'd be in the workhouse infirmary and that'd be me gone.'

'Don't say stuff like that, Grandma,' said the girl, and Alice could tell that she was close to tears. 'You know I will always do my best to look after you.'

'Try not to worry,' said Alice gently. 'You're doing a good job with your grandmother, I'm sure you are. But when you help her walk, put one arm around her like this, and hold her hand with the other, that's it, like that, so if she stumbles, you've got her. That's it, yes, like that. And if you can find a walking stick for her, that might help as well.'

'You sound just like a nurse,' said the old woman, her face creasing into another smile. 'You should be a nurse.'

Alice thought of trying to explain but then thought better of it, so she just smiled.

'Now,' said the woman, rummaging beneath her various layers of clothing to find a pocket, 'I haven't much money — the Marchbanks have always been poor, dirt poor. But there is a halfpenny here and I want you to have it for that bonny baby of yours.'

'No, no, I couldn't take it, you need it for medicine,' said Alice, shaking her head, but the old woman insisted, pressing the coin into her hand.

'You've helped me today, young lady, and this is for the baby. Right then, let's get going. It'll take us half a day to get where we want to go at this rate . . .'

Wait till I tell Maud about this grand old lady, thought Alice, as she watched Mrs Marchbank and her granddaughter walk slowly away. Then she remembered, Maud was gone. And the sadness of it all struck her afresh.

That evening as Alice sat beside the dying fire to feed the baby with Hugo, the house cat, stretched out at her feet warming his belly, she felt the whole experience of the day wash over her. It already felt strange to be without Maud in the kitchen that evening. But now, as she glanced down to Victoria feeding contentedly, the fingers of her left hand splayed out and gently pressing into the soft flesh of her breast, Alice knew that she couldn't let herself stay this sad for too long. She had a daughter to rear and a whole life of her own that needed to be lived.

3

'Oh, mothers of families! . . . do you
know that one in seven infants in this
civilised land of England perishes
before it is even one year old? . . .
And, in . . . great cities . . . nearly
one out of two?'
Florence Nightingale

The first feed of the day was Alice's favourite
time. After she'd lit the fire in the kitchen stove
and she could sit listening to the spit and crackle
of the wood, she would feel a wave of relaxation
seep through her whole body. This time before
the rest of the house were awake, when it was
just Alice and Victoria, was very special.

She knew it would be Marie up next, coming
into the kitchen just in time for the hotplate to
be ready to take the kettle for their first pot of
tea of the day. She would go first to Victoria,
whether she was lying in her crib or still feeding,
and she would speak to her softly and stroke her
head and then look at Alice and say, 'Good
morning, Mother.' And then, invariably, she'd
look down at the black cat, stretched full length
in front of the fire, not even moving when a
spark came out of the fire and singed his fur.
'Hugo. You lazy good-for-nothing cat,' Marie
would mutter. 'Just like that wastrel of a man
who used to be my husband.'

The rest of the house would be up in dribs and drabs, depending on how late or how busy they'd been the night before. Sometimes they would sleep till the afternoon. Not Stella, though — she was always up and about and always full of life. No matter how tired she was, Stella would always have a smile and a tale to tell from the night before.

So it was strange to see her coming into the kitchen that morning with a frown.

'What's up, Stell?' said her mother immediately.

'I heard last night that the police have closed the Italian woman's place down . . . some are saying it's just the start.'

'What?' gasped Marie. 'Why would they do that? They never have any trouble there . . . '

Stella was shaking her head. 'I know,' she said quietly, 'but it's all part of what the police call their 'moral enforcement' under that Contagious Diseases Act. Now, it seems, they're not just picking women up off the street, they're going into the houses for 'em as well.'

'But what about the girls, Stell — did any of them get away?'

'Well, they say that some escaped through a window, but the rest were taken to the police station.'

'Stupid men,' Marie spat, 'rounding up women like cattle, moving them out of a place of safety. Ridiculous.'

'I hope it's all right with you, Ma,' said Stella, 'but I've sent word with my source that if any of the women want refuge, they can come to us.'

31

Marie nodded. 'Of course, we'll always help out . . . But what if the police come for us as well?'

Stella thought for a moment. 'I think we'll be safe for now, at least. We still have a couple of police who are regular customers.'

'I hope that's going to be enough,' murmured Marie. 'It might be worth having a word with them next time they visit.'

Stella nodded, and then forced a smile in Alice's direction. 'Don't you be worrying, Alice. You're just a housemaid here and I'll make sure that fact is made clear. But if you hear anybody shouting 'police', get yourself into your room with the baby and make sure the door is locked.'

Alice nodded. 'I always lock the door at night anyway when we go to bed, just in case any of the customers come wandering through by mistake. They're often a bit worse for wear.'

'You could say that . . . or that they're just blind drunk,' laughed Stella, but then her face became serious again. 'But that's good practice, Alice, you keep doing that.' She turned to her mother, 'I've asked all the girls to come down for a late breakfast, Ma, then we can get our heads together and make sure we're all prepared.'

By the time the women were assembled in the kitchen, Victoria was sleeping in her crib and Alice was brewing a big pot of tea. Slipping in beside Stella, she sat and listened to the sleepy conversation of the three women who had gathered around the table. This was an early rising for Laura, Lizzie and Marguerite. Even Lizzie was yawning and Marguerite was resting her head, a tangled mass of dark brown curls, on her arms. Stella gave them a bit of time to wake up whilst Marie toasted some bread over the fire, bringing each piece in turn to the table and slipping it off the long toasting fork. The smell of it filled the kitchen, and in no time at all Laura had tied back her dark red hair and was quietly buttering the toast whilst Marguerite stirred the tea and then poured a cup for each of them.

Silence fell for a few moments as the women crunched their toast, then Stella replaced her cup in its saucer and began to speak. Once she'd told them about what had happened at the Italian woman's place, they sat planning escape routes and discussed using the cellar at the end of the hallway as a hiding place. Alice was starting to feel on edge and she kept glancing over to the crib where Victoria slept peacefully.

Marie slipped a hand over hers on the table and murmured, 'Don't be worrying too much, Alice. We women living in brothels always have some threat or other to deal with, but we always manage — '

She broke off as a loud knock sounded on the front door. Marguerite shot straight up from her chair, but the rest of the women sat completely still, their eyes wide.

'I don't think they'd knock at the door if they were raiding,' said Marie, getting up from the table and patting Marguerite on the shoulder as she passed behind her.

She was back in moments, her arm around the shoulders of a black-haired woman with wild eyes and torn clothing. Stella jumped up from her seat, full of concern. 'Valerie! How did you escape?'

'They dragged me out of the house,' croaked the woman, her voice strongly accented, 'but I managed to pull free before they got me in the carriage . . . and I ran as fast as I could.'

Alice knew straight away that the woman must be from the Italian woman's place. She got up from the table and offered her seat and then she went to find a shawl to wrap around the woman's shoulders.

Valerie sat quietly for a few moments and then she looked up and tried to smile. 'I was lucky to have enough money saved up to leave Portsmouth after they first introduced the Contagious Diseases Act and women were made to attend fortnightly examinations for syphilis. Even though soldiers and sailors were free from inspection and openly queuing at the doors of our brothels . . . That's when I began to feel the true injustice of being a woman in a man's world.

'I thought I'd left all of that behind me . . . but now, especially this year, it seems that it's followed me here, to Liverpool . . . and no matter how we try to fight against it, still it goes on. How can they not see that it's a waste of time dragging women off the street and out of the brothels, when men are still allowed to do what they want?'

Stella was nodding. 'I agree, we all know that to be the case, and it does feel like we're getting nowhere, but we can't give up. We have to go on fighting even harder. And in the meantime, Valerie, you can stay with us for as long as you need. We have a spare room upstairs and enough work for you.'

Valerie nodded as she sat with her shoulders slumped and then she lifted her head. 'Without your kindness, I would be back on the street. When I first came to Liverpool I got very sick and I spent some time with the lady who helps women like us, that Josephine Butler. I stayed in her house until I got better. I could have gone there but I know that she has many women at present, and they are sick. I got your word, Stella, from one of the customers, and that's why I came. Thank you.'

'You are welcome,' said Stella.

Alice placed a cup of tea and a thick slice of bread and butter in front of Valerie and then she put an arm around her shoulders and gave her a squeeze. Valerie glanced up and placed her hand over Alice's.

'And you, too, are a very kind lady,' she said.

★   ★   ★

Week by week, every morning, Alice sat by the fire to feed Victoria with the cat at her feet, and then she worked in the house by day, and made sure to lock the door to their room each night. And as the daily rhythm of life continued, there were still reports of working women being picked up from the street as the police continued to impress their policy of moral enforcement. The women remained vigilant and took extra care, only going out at times that they judged low risk. Many customers reported that they'd seen

35

plain-clothes police in the alley, and some of them had vowed to do all that they could to protect the women, if the need arose. However, as time went by, the women of the house got used to their situation, and even though Stella issued daily warnings, some of them began to believe that they were perfectly safe. Certainly, two months on from the raid on the Italian woman's place, it was easy to start believing that the threat was reducing.

They were proved wrong a few days later. When Stella came into the kitchen with a deep frown on her face, Alice knew straight away that there must have been another incident.

'One of the girls is missing. It's Lizzie, she's not in her bed.'

'Lizzie!' gasped Alice, instantly worried for the young woman who loved to come and chat in the kitchen during the afternoons and would sit and play with Victoria.

'This problem is not going away,' Marie announced, following Stella in through the door. 'We haven't heard of any more houses being raided, but women are still being taken off the street.'

'I'd heard that the police were stepping it up, so I think we can be fairly certain that Lizzie has been taken,' Stella agreed. 'She's lived here three years now, and never stayed away without telling us . . . I'll have a bite to eat and then go up to the hospital to see our Ada,' she decided, pulling her dark, curly hair back from her face and fastening it with a yellow ribbon. 'She'll know what to do.'

Alice nodded. She knew that Stella's half-sister, Ada Houston, a senior nurse at the Royal Infirmary, was the best person to speak to. She'd already helped out a few times by using her influence when the women had gone missing.

'Something needs to be done,' said Marie quietly, as she sliced through the morning bread with a sharp knife. 'The police say that what they're doing is moral enforcement, and they're working in line with the Contagious Diseases Act, while men still roam the streets and move between the houses, without question, without inspection . . . Pah!'

She threw down the bread knife and picked up the butter. 'We need to start joining forces, all us women. We need to go and see that woman Valerie told us about, that Josephine Butler. She doesn't just take in women off the streets; she's involved in some kind of campaign.'

'Well,' said Stella, 'despite what Valerie said that first day she came to us, I'm not sure what a posh type like her will be able to do for women like us.' She poured boiling water into the teapot. 'But you're right, Ma, we need to rally support wherever we can. In the meantime, I'll go up to the hospital and see Ada — she might even know how we can contact Mrs Butler. We need all the help we can get. This is starting to feel like a war.'

Marie nodded solemnly.

'Right, that's it, I need to get going,' said Stella, taking a swig of hot tea and grabbing her shawl off the back of a chair.

'You take care, Stell,' said Marie.

'I will, Ma, don't you worry. The bastards won't get me, not if I can help it.'

★ ★ ★

Alice and Marie kept busy that morning, each of them waiting for Stella to come back. They knew that the most dangerous times for women to be out on the streets were the nights and evenings, but who knew what might happen?

When the afternoon came and there was still no sign, Marie was pacing up and down the kitchen and Alice was desperately trying to keep busy.

'She will be back,' said Alice, her voice tight, trying to stay calm for Marie's sake.

Going over to the crib to lift Victoria for her first feed of the afternoon, Alice knew straight away that something wasn't quite right. Her cheeks were flushed and when Alice touched her, she was hot. Her heart started to flutter as she lifted Victoria out of her crib, feeling her writhe against her, and then she was throwing back her head.

Putting the baby back down for a moment, Alice removed her outer layer of clothing and then she went to the sink for a cloth soaked in cool water and tried to sponge her down. But this made her writhe even more and then she started to whimper. Alice couldn't bear to see her daughter lying there in distress; she had to pick her up again.

Sitting down by the stove, Alice tried to feed Victoria again, but she seemed irritable and her nose was snuffly, and she was scrunching her face and drawing up her knees, not wanting to feed at all. And then she started to cry. Alice rocked her and stood up with her, walking up and down the full length of the kitchen, but the cries escalated to a miserable, high-pitched wail that went through Alice's body and made her chest feel tight.

'There, there,' said Marie, rubbing the baby's back, but still she screamed. Her crying had taken over the whole room.

Alice sat back down with her, in tears herself. She tried to put her to the breast again, and this time she did take a little. But within seconds, she was pulling away and drawing up her knees again. To Alice, it seemed like her baby's whole body was burning with heat now. And she wasn't sure, but she thought she could see the beginnings of a fine red rash across her face.

At that, Alice's fear intensified. Her mouth was dry, her heart pounding. She'd grown up in a house where infants had died; every family she knew had lost a child. She had been named after a sister, another Alice, who had died before she was born. What if Victoria was starting with diphtheria or measles or scarlet fever?

Marie was right by her, leaning over the baby. 'What's up with her?'

'I don't know, but she seems really poorly,' sobbed Alice. And then Victoria was wailing again.

Marie laid a hand on the baby's forehead. 'Yes, she does seem hot all right, and it looks like she's got the gripes. But it might be something and nothing . . . Give her to me for a bit, Alice, let's see if we can cool her down.'

Marie took Victoria gently from Alice's arms and within seconds both mother and baby were starting to calm down.

'There there, you little scallywag,' whispered Marie. 'Who's my favourite girl, then? What are you doing to your poor mother, hey?'

As Alice looked on, Marie rocked the baby, her whispered words soothing them both.

'She seems to be easier with you, Marie,' said Alice quietly.

'It's always the way,' said Marie. 'I used to get so worked up when my Stella had a fever, I'd be in a terrible state. But my mother could always manage her.'

But then Victoria was pulling her knees up again and starting to scream. 'What is it?' soothed Marie. 'You have got the belly ache this afternoon, haven't you, little one? Let's try a few drops of brandy on a teaspoon. Can you get the bottle out of the cupboard for me, Alice?'

Alice was straight there, uncorking the bottle as she took it out of the cupboard and then pulling a spoon out of the drawer. In between gripes Alice managed to get a few drops into the baby's mouth. She pulled a face and coughed a bit and then opened her eyes wide. And for a few seconds she was quiet.

Just as Alice started to breathe a sigh of relief, Victoria pulled up her knees again and gave another almighty scream. Alice felt the sound like a sharp pain going right through her heart. She knew that she needed to do something, anything, to try and ease her baby's suffering.

'Right, that's it,' she said firmly, 'I need to go to the apothecary for a remedy.'

'I'll ask one of the girls . . . ' said Marie, but Alice was already grabbing her shawl.

'I know the way and I can tell them exactly what's wrong with her . . . '

'No,' Marie tried to say, but Alice was already gone.

Outside the front door, Alice glanced up and down the alley before descending the step and walking briskly away, towards Lime Street. Out there, away from the warmth and the safety of the kitchen, she felt exposed, and if it hadn't been for the worry about Victoria burning inside of her she would definitely have turned tail and run back to the house. But her baby was sick, she had no choice, she had to go. She glimpsed a movement out of the corner of her eye, a shadow against the wall, and drew in a sharp breath, ready to run back to the safety of the house.

But then Hugo sidled out of the shadow and made his way towards her with his white-tipped tail flicking from side to side. Alice could have cried with relief, so glad was she to see that cat.

'Hugo,' she breathed, pausing for just a moment to give him a quick stroke before making her way out towards Lime Street. When she glanced back, the cat was still trotting after her. 'Shoo, shoo,' she said, waving a hand at him.

Alice was just a few steps out of the alley when she saw the cat shoot past her. In the split second that she was wondering what had spooked him, a thickset policeman in plain clothes and another with a pockmarked face grabbed her.

'Let go of me!' she shouted. 'I'm going to get medicine for my sick baby, let go!'

'We've heard all sorts from you women,' laughed the man with the pockmarked face as they dragged her towards a carriage.

'No, no!' she screamed, fighting like a tiger, but they held her fast, their hands digging into her.

'I have a baby,' she begged. 'Please, please, let me go.'

'That's what they all say. Get in there,' shouted the thickset one as he dragged her into the carriage. Then the other man pushed her in from behind and the door was closed. Alice thought she heard the sound of heavy boots running towards the carriage and a man's voice shouting; it sounded like someone who might be able to help.

But then they were moving, and apart from what sounded like a heavy fist thumping on the side of the carriage and the sound of a muffled voice, there was no rescue for Alice. She felt crippled with despair. Her whole body screamed out for her child. She slumped in her seat, sobbing, tears streaming down her face, as the men sat silent. She had no way of knowing what direction they were taking, but she was certain they would be going to the police station.

It felt like for ever that she was in that carriage, first raging at the men who looked at her with stony faces, then trying to calm herself down and think of a way out. She needed to get away — she was terrified about what might happen to Victoria if she couldn't get back there with medicine.

Dragged out when they reached their destination, she was hardly able to stand, but although she made a valiant attempt to wrench herself free, the men had her held fast. She could see the door of the police station and dug her heels into the ground: she would not go willingly into that place.

'Let go of me, let go of me!' she shouted, still trying to wriggle free as they manhandled her in through the door. But there was no relief from the vice-like grip of the men as they brought her through a packed room and towards a man in uniform who sat behind a wooden counter.

They waited in line behind a poor soul with bare feet and tattered clothes, and Alice stood still and gave the impression that her struggle was over, hoping that this would make them release their grip and she could dive out and run for it. But it made no difference, she was still held fast and fighting off the feeling of absolute despair that was starting to creep over her.

They were at the counter now.

'This is another one we picked up in the vicinity of a known brothel, an alley near Lime Street Station,' announced one of Alice's captors, digging his fingers into her upper arm.

The policeman behind the counter nodded before leaning forward in his seat. 'Name?' he said, his pen poised between thick fingers, lined to the knuckle with black hair.

Alice shook her head, determined not to give

any information about herself. 'I have done nothing wrong, I am a mother who needs medicine for her baby,' she protested.

'What you need is not our concern,' said the man. 'Name?'

'I have done nothing wrong.'

The man sighed theatrically, then he leant across the counter, bringing his face so close to Alice's that she could smell a tinge of onion on his sour breath. 'You were arrested in the vicinity of a known brothel, in an area frequented by common prostitutes,' he hissed. 'We weren't born yesterday, young lady.'

Alice could feel a fine spray of spittle on her face as he spoke, but she did not flinch; she had to keep calm. 'It is also an area near the railway station frequented by many other people, going about their daily business,' she countered.

The policeman scowled at her. 'Yes, but those people have not been seen soliciting outside a brothel.'

Something snapped inside Alice. 'I was doing no such thing. I work as a maid in a house down that alley, I have a child!' she screamed, writhing again now with all her strength, trying to break free from the men who held her.

'You no doubt have a child outside of marriage — that's what you have, a bastard child.'

Alice growled with rage. She would have grabbed him by the throat if her hands were free.

'Take her away,' said the man behind the counter, leaning back away from her and waving his hand in a dismissive gesture. 'Send her with the next lot up to the Lock Hospital.'

'No!' Alice screamed. 'I have to get back, I have to be with my baby.'

But the man's attention had already moved to the next person in line and Alice was being dragged, screaming, through another door to a large room crammed with women. The men pushed her in and she fell, cracking both knees hard on the stone floor. Then she heard the turning of a key in the lock and her heart broke in two.

She crumpled into a heap on the floor, sobbing uncontrollably, unable to think what to do next, aware of the pain in her knees and her breasts, as milk started leaking from her and soaking into the fabric of her dress.

'Alice?' said a woman's voice, a familiar voice.

Alice looked up instantly. 'Lizzie,' she said with all the strength that she could muster, a rush of energy going right through her body when she saw dear Lizzie standing above her. Just seeing a familiar face gave Alice enough strength to scramble up from the floor. And then she felt Lizzie's arms around her and she started to sob again.

'Where's the baby?' asked Lizzie gently.

'She's sick, she's with Marie,' wailed Alice. 'I was going for medicine . . . '

'Oh Alice, I'm so sorry,' said Lizzie, holding her tight, trying to soothe her — but how can you soothe a mother who has been wrenched away from her sick child? It cannot be done.

'We'll get you out of here,' said Lizzie. 'We'll find a way . . . and Marie will look after the baby while you're away. You know that, Alice, don't you? She's an expert when it comes to babies, she'll make sure that Victoria is safe.'

Alice tried to speak but the words wouldn't come out properly.

'Those bastards, though, taking you off the street when you need to get help for your child. You're not even dressed right for a woman of my profession!' Lizzie exclaimed, holding Alice even tighter, holding her together. 'We'll get you out of here,' she said. 'Even if I have to provide free services for all these bastard men myself.'

When the door opened again for another woman to be admitted, Lizzie was straight there, saying her piece. 'That woman there,' she said, pointing at Alice, 'she's not one of my kind. She's a housemaid and she has a sick baby at home . . . '

'Quiet, you,' said the policeman, his face red.

Lizzie stood in front of him, her slim frame looking tiny in front of his bulk. She stood her ground, with her hands on her hips and her fluffy white-blond hair sticking out from her head. Alice felt an ache in her heart, she was so proud of her.

The policeman made to leave the room but Lizzie grabbed his arm. He easily threw her off with a grunt of disapproval, and Alice jumped forward to catch her as she staggered, off balance.

'I won't give up, Alice,' she insisted. 'I'll get you out of here and back to your baby, even if it's the last thing I do.'

'Please be careful, Lizzie,' said Alice. 'I don't want you getting hurt.' But she knew that Lizzie

46

was all that she had, and maybe together they could find some way to escape. Alice needed to hold on to this hope, keep her mind focused on some kind of plan. There was no other way that she could manage the agony of not knowing how Victoria was; for all she knew her baby could be dangerously ill by now. She had to believe that she would be all right, and that there was a way of getting out of this place. Looking down to see the dark circles of milk on the front of her gown, she prayed that it would be soon.

The next time a policeman opened the door, Lizzie tried to speak up again and this time Alice stood by her side, ready to say her own piece if it was required. But there was no chance; there were more police coming into the room and they began to herd the women out in one group.

'Now, Alice,' whispered Lizzie. 'We're going to be taken to the Lock Hospital. This might be our chance for you to break free. I'll try to distract them when I see the right opportunity, and you run for it.'

However, the women were surrounded by policemen, as if they were the most hardened of criminals, and there was no chance to escape as they were marched towards a large vehicle with bars on the windows.

Alice sat on the floor of the carriage, feeling the motion of it as it swayed over the rough streets of Liverpool. She couldn't believe that she'd ended up here, in this situation, completely helpless. As she sat, she started to feel the rage seethe within her. She needed to make a physical effort to contain it, knowing that if she wanted to stand a chance of escape, she couldn't draw attention to herself. She needed to stay quiet and appear compliant.

The carriage stopped abruptly after what seemed like a long time, but Alice had no real idea. Her mind and body were completely taken over by one single purpose: breaking free and returning to her child. The door of the carriage opened and a man's arm reached in to drag the nearest woman on to the street.

'Out, you lot,' he shouted.

Alice waited as long as she could, breathing deeply, readying herself to push through, to run down the street. But as soon as she poked her head out of the door she saw the number of men waiting and she knew she'd have to bide her time. She gulped in some air as she stood in the street, glad to feel the stone flags beneath her feet. Grabbing hold of Lizzie's hand, she steadied herself and looked around. This was familiar territory for her, since the Lock Hospital was right next to the Infirmary. If only someone she knew was walking by, someone who could vouch for her. But there was no one and the women were still surrounded by police. With her head bowed Alice had no choice but to make her way into the hospital.

She held back deliberately as soon as they were in through the door, frantically looking around, hoping to see a familiar face. She held on till the last, with Lizzie by her side, but with dull inevitability she was forced to go with the rest into a large room that felt like a holding pen.

'Right, ladies,' shouted a man's voice, 'we will

be taking you in for examination by the doctor, one at a time.'

Alice heard a murmur of disapproval ripple through the group and then she felt someone grab her arm. 'You first,' said the orderly, starting to drag her out of the door.

'No, you don't,' snapped Lizzie, sharp as a flash and pushing herself between Alice and the orderly. 'She's with me.'

'Step back,' said a policeman, appearing behind the orderly. 'Step back or it'll be a long, long time before you see the light of day again.'

'It's all right, Lizzie,' said Alice, putting her free arm around her friend and giving her a reassuring squeeze.

'Come on, you,' said the orderly, pulling her away, leaving Lizzie standing with her head bowed.

As she was marched along the corridor, Alice looked around, hoping that this might be the chance she was looking for, that maybe she would see someone who could help her.

'Sit there,' said the orderly as he directed her into a small room, indicating the one chair against the wall. As she sat, Alice saw a high, flat couch. Next to the couch was a table and on there, Alice saw an array of metal instruments laid out on a cloth: forceps, a scalpel and a shiny speculum. She knew instantly what the instruments were for and a wave of nausea swept up from her stomach, burning acid in her mouth.

She knew that she had to stay calm and she had to present well to whoever was going to attend her. She took a deep breath, straightened her skirt and tidied the strands of hair that had come loose in her struggle for freedom. Then she sat upright in the chair, trying to look as respectable as she could, wanting to give the right impression, all the while, holding back the anger and despair that she could feel bubbling beneath a thin layer of decorum.

Within minutes, a nurse with a bunch of keys hanging from a leather belt at her waist stood in front of her. 'What is your name?' she said.

Alice felt unable to speak, as if all the words had dried up inside her. All she could do was stare at the bunch of keys on the nurse's belt, as a feeling of dread crept over every inch of her skin.

'Name?' said the woman again, this time more firmly.

Alice looked up to the nurse, straight in the eye. 'My name is Alice Sampson and I work as a housemaid in the city. Previously, I worked as a nurse on the wards of the hospital just next door.'

'Ha, ha,' laughed the nurse, 'I've never heard that one before . . . working at the Liverpool Royal!'

'It is absolutely true,' responded Alice, keeping her voice steady. 'I don't know if you are familiar with any of the staff there, but I worked with Sister Law on Male Surgical and Sister Cleary — '

'Never heard of 'em, never worked in there,' snapped the nurse, cutting her short.

'Well, do you know the assistant superinten- dent — '

'Enough,' shouted the nurse. 'Making up these stories will not help your case. In fact, it will reflect even more badly on your moral character. Do you want to be branded a liar as well as a prostitute?'

'I am not a liar and I am not a prostitute,' spat Alice, straightening up even further on the chair, and glaring at the nurse.

She could see the woman shaking her head.

'I have worked as a nurse. Send someone to the hospital, ask for Miss Houston, the assistant superintendent. She can vouch for me,' said Alice, desperately trying to stop her voice rising whilst her heart pounded against her ribs.

Still the nurse shook her head. And now she was smiling.

'I am a housemaid and the mother of a sick baby,' Alice called out, infuriated by the woman, wanting to get up and punch her.

'The women who end up here say all sorts of stuff,' said the nurse, 'but I've never met one who claims to be a housemaid, a nurse, and the mother of a sick baby.'

'Look . . . I have milk leaking from my breasts . . . Look,' cried Alice, feeling the sheer injustice of her situation welling up inside her now.

'Well, you could have done that with water, couldn't you?'

'You have to believe me,' said Alice, angry now, not able to control herself. 'I need to get home to my baby!' she shouted, standing up from her chair, face-to-face with the nurse.

'Sit down,' ordered the nurse.

Alice stood eye to eye with the nurse,

51

desperately needing to make the right decision. She felt like flying at the woman, pushing her to the ground and then forcing her way out through all the people in the hospital until she was free and she could run back to the house. But she could see that the nurse wasn't for backing down, and she knew that all she could do, for now, was to sit back down on the chair.

'That's better,' said the nurse with a hint of satisfaction in her voice. 'We need to examine you. All of the women that are brought here have to be examined . . . the doctor will be here in a moment. Now, I want you to lie down on this couch.'

'No, I will not,' shouted Alice, her anger breaking through. 'I have done nothing, except have a baby.'

'If you lie down and let the doctor have a look, and what you say is right, then we will let you go.'

'Do you promise?'

'Yes, providing that there are no signs of disease. There may well be something there that needs treating. After all, from what you say, you have a baby and from what I can see, you are not married. How can a decent single woman end up with a baby?'

'Believe me . . . it is possible. I gave birth, that's all. I have only lain with one man for one night, and that is when I got pregnant.'

'We hear all kinds of stories. You will stay here and be examined.'

'No, I *will not!*' screamed Alice, leaping up from the chair and standing with her teeth bared and her hands balled into fists.

The door opened just as the nurse made a grab for her. Knowing that this was her only chance, Alice dived past and then somehow in the confusion managed to dodge around the doctor who was standing in the doorway. He lunged at her but she was too quick for him. She ran down the corridor and then paused for a second, trying to get her bearings, when she heard a voice behind her.

'Alice?'

Alice spun around, her heart pounding. It was Ada Houston, her eyes wide and her mouth open, standing there with some papers in her hand and Lizzie by her side.

'Ada,' she croaked, suddenly overwhelmed and needing to lean against the wall of the corridor.

Ada was straight there by her side.

All Alice could do was nod; she was unable to speak. Lizzie came and put an arm around her, murmuring words of comfort.

Ada motioned for them both to stay where they were and then she turned to confront the doctor who had marched down the corridor with the nurse in tow.

'Excuse me, Dr Anderson,' she said, her voice full of authority. 'I believe there has been a mistake. This woman is someone that I know very well. She has worked as a nurse at the Royal Infirmary; she is of good character.'

Alice saw with some satisfaction the glimmer of surprise in the eyes of the nurse who was now standing next to the doctor. 'Well, Miss Houston, what is she doing here?' said the doctor impatiently. 'These women have been picked up from the street by the police.'

'I don't know, but I do know it's a mistake,' said Ada firmly, standing her ground and holding the doctor's gaze. Alice could hardly bear to watch the transaction; all of her hopes rested with Ada in that moment. She could see the doctor stiffen and pull himself up to his full height and then he was glancing down to a piece of paper in his hand, mumbling something about rules and regulations. An orderly pushed by him with another woman, and he shouted out in frustration.

'For goodness' sake,' he snapped. 'We're overrun with these women anyway. If you can vouch for her, Miss Houston, you can take her with the other one.'

'Thank you,' said Ada, pressing her lips together and turning immediately towards Alice.

'Come on then, Lizzie, and Nurse Sampson,' she said. 'Let's get you both home.'

Alice felt her legs go weak at the knees but she made sure to follow Miss Houston with her back straight as they walked towards the door and the world outside.

Only when they were out into the light, did she start to weaken and almost fell into Lizzie's arms.

'I told you we'd get you out of there,' said Lizzie, grinning. 'I mean, I didn't expect to get out myself, but it wasn't right for you to be in there.'

'It wasn't right for you to be in there either,' Ada said firmly.

Alice felt her breath catching in her throat. 'I'm so worried about Victoria,' she said, 'I must get straight back to her.'

'Victoria is going to be fine, Alice,' said Ada, smiling. 'Marie came out to find me when you didn't return; she brought the baby with her and I was able to check her over. We cooled her down and gave her some medicine, and her fever has started to settle. Who knows what it was that she was ailing from, but she has the medicine now and is going to be fine in a day or two. That little girl of yours is a tough little beggar.'

'Thank you, thank you,' murmured Alice, feeling as though she could collapse with joy and fall down on to the street there and then. But she knew that they needed to get going right away. 'I need to get back to Stella's,' she said.

'Of course you do,' said Ada, rooting in her pocket. 'Let me give you both this letter in case either of you get stopped again. It states that you are known to be of good character and can be vouched for by members of senior staff at the hospital. It's signed by our superintendent, Miss Merryweather — she's with us on this issue and will do all that she can to support the rights of women.

'What happened today was appalling, and we must see that it never happens again. I'll put some thought into it and be along to see you very soon, Alice. We need to think about your future. Now go, both of you, and don't linger . . . '

Alice didn't remember much of the walk back through the city. She clung to Lizzie's arm, her whole body tuned to one thing — getting safely back to her baby.

'Come on,' said Lizzie, sensing the yearning in Alice as they turned into the alley, and they both ran the final distance, arriving breathless on the doorstep as they waited to be admitted by Marie.

'There you are,' Marie almost shouted, her arms around both girls at once. 'And Victoria is so much better . . .'

Alice had already broken free from Marie's embrace and she was in the kitchen by the crib, pulling the cover from the sleeping baby to check her over. Her whole body started to relax when she saw that, apart from two circles of rosy red on her cheeks, her daughter did seem much better.

'She's been taking boiled milk off a teaspoon,' said Marie, following along behind with Lizzie. 'I think she's through the worst of it now.'

Alice collapsed on to a kitchen chair and Lizzie flopped down on the seat right next to her.

'Where's Stella?' they both asked, almost simultaneously.

'Oh, Stell's fine,' Marie reassured them. 'Don't worry, she came back just after me, then she went straight out again to meet some other women in our line of business. We're all struggling at present, we need to stick together.'

'We certainly do,' said Lizzie, slumping forward across the table to rest her head on her arms.

'You two both look done in,' Marie said. 'I'll get you a cup of tea and a bite to eat, and while you're having that, I'll fill the bath.'

'That's sounds like heaven,' said Lizzie, raising her head and trying to smile. 'Alice, you go in first. I'll be lying in that water all day . . . '

Marie brought the tin bath in from where it hung in the back yard and, whilst the two women were eating, she placed it in front of the stove and filled it bit by bit with steaming water from the copper. Even hearing the sound of the water pouring into the bath made Alice start to relax. And then, as Marie brought jug after jug of cold to cool it to the perfect temperature and swished her hand through the water, the rhythm of it made Alice think of home, and bath night. She loved to be in the water.

She couldn't wait to get out of her clothes; they clung to her like a horrible reminder of what had just happened. As soon as she'd finished her tea, she walked through to her small room and peeled off each layer, dropping them one by one on to the floor. Her chemise was stuck to her skin with dried milk. Once she'd peeled the whole lot away, shedding it like a skin on to the floor, she started to feel better.

Then she sat on the bed, enjoying the feel of cool air on her body and rejoicing in the knowledge that she hadn't been forced to submit to some cruel invasion with metal instruments. She shuddered again as she thought about it, knowing that some women would be held down for that to be done to them. Having had a brush with the experience herself, Alice now felt fully resolved to resist the moral enforcement of working women. She would march with the rest

57

in the street if need be.

But, right now, all she needed was to get in that bath and soak away the cares of the day. She took the pins out of her hair and shook it loose, running her hands through it, and then she pulled a blanket off the bed and draped it around her shoulders. As she walked through to the kitchen she could smell the soap and hear the swish of the water in the tub as Marie added more hot.

'Come on then,' said Lizzie, sliding the blanket from Alice's shoulders.

'Ooh, ooh, it's hot,' laughed Alice, stepping in, 'but not too hot . . . ' she murmured as her body slipped beneath the water.

As she lay back, Alice closed her eyes and felt the heat of the water seep right through her body, into her bones. She felt suspended in time, held in a warm embrace. Arching her neck, she made sure her hair was soaking in the water and then she felt the murmur of Lizzie's voice as she told Alice that she was going to wash her. Feeling the rhythmic sensation of the smooth sponge on her skin, Alice knew that she was cherished.

'Sit up and I'll wash your hair,' said Marie softly.

As Alice sat, Marie poured jug after jug of warm water over her head, and then she massaged the soft soap which had been warmed by the fire into her hair. Alice felt waves of sensation coursing through her body.

'Mmmm,' she sighed, 'that is so good . . . '

As the warm water for rinsing was poured over, Alice felt clean, renewed. And then after

Marie had wrapped her hair in a towel, Alice lay back once more, with Lizzie at the side trailing her hand in the water and gently chatting of this and that. The murmur of conversation mingling with the ripple and the drip of the water, until it began to cool.

4

'I do not anticipate that it would be possible ever to have married women in the Service. And it is hardly necessary to add that no woman but of unblemished character can be admitted.'

Florence Nightingale

'What the blazes has been going on?' cried Eddy as she bustled through the kitchen door carrying her nurse's bag. 'I saw Marie out in town when I was between cases, and she said that you'd gone missing yesterday. I was just on my way to treat a bad case of — '

'Shh . . . ' said Alice, pressing a finger to her lips as Eddy stood there in the middle of the kitchen in her district nurse's cape and hat, her eyes wide. 'Victoria's only just gone down. She's a bit restless at the moment, she's been poorly. Come out the back with me,' she said quietly. 'I need to hang some washing out.'

Eddy threw herself down on a wooden bench set against the wall of the back yard, and removed the small round hat that sat skew-whiff on her head. Then, taking the clip out of her hair, she ran both hands through till it stuck out at all angles. As Alice pegged out the washing, big sheets that flapped around her legs in the Liverpool breeze, she told Eddy the full story of what had happened.

For once Eddy was quiet and listened intently to what Alice had to say, not interrupting. Just listening.

'Crikey, Alice,' Eddy breathed, when her friend had finished. 'You had a near miss there. You don't want to end up in that Lock Hospital, I've heard all sorts of stories. And Mr Fawcett, that surgeon who gave us those lectures, he's always in there — you know what he's like. He's the one that you saw here at Stella's that time, isn't he?'

Alice nodded. She still felt hollowed out inside after what had happened yesterday, but once she'd got back home and held Victoria in her arms, nothing else mattered and she had been determined to get on with her work as usual and put the whole thing behind her. But now, picking up on Eddy's concern, she started to feel forlorn. And being with Eddy, sometimes, made her think about Maud and start to miss her — and they still hadn't had any news.

'I hope Maud's all right in New York,' she said, walking over to sit on the bench and resting her head on Eddy's shoulder. 'It will be so strange for her out there. She's never been outside of Liverpool in her whole life — she's never even been to Southport.'

'She'll be all right,' said Eddy. 'And at least she's got Harry and Alfred.'

'Mmm,' said Alice, straightening up.

'Maud will be fine,' Eddy insisted. 'She can look after herself, and me, and you, and Alfred . . . you know what she's like.'

'You're right, of course you are,' said Alice,

starting to smile and then laughing as she reached a hand out to try and straighten Eddy's mass of hair. 'Even though you look like you've been dragged through a hedge backwards, Edwina Pacey, you're usually right about these things.'

'I always look like I've been dragged through a hedge,' said Eddy, laughing. 'And then when I'm in and out of people's houses, I'm wrestling with bandages and stray dogs and children putting sticky hands all over me. Well, it makes it worse than ever. It's a good job I've got this big cape to cover everything up.'

Alice couldn't stop laughing as Eddy continued to show her all the marks and stains on her skirt and tell the story of each one. 'And then, the other day, I was applying a big dressing to a man's leg, just starting to wind the bandage round — you know what that's like. I could have done with someone else to hold the dressing pad in place. Well, I put the roll of bandage down, so I could straighten up the pad, and a dog ran in from the back yard and tried to run off with it. So, there's me, in a tug of war with a dog. And this fella, my patient, shouting and screaming at his dog, and saying ooh, ooh, nurse, it's me leg, it's hurting me leg. In the end I had to unwind the bandage and let the dog have it.'

Alice and Eddy were both doubled over and crying with laughter now. 'I'm so sorry, Eddy,' she said. 'It can't be easy . . . ' and she had to wait to calm down before she could continue. 'It can't be easy, going into people's houses. I mean, it's difficult enough, seeing patients when you've got them all on a ward, but at least you've got some help, you don't have to do absolutely everything by yourself.'

'Mmm, yes, there is that,' said Eddy, wiping the tears from her eyes, but still holding her ribs. 'There is that, but you know what, Alice, I like the challenge, and what I love most of all is being able to be the one to help those patients out there. Some of them have nothing, not even enough food to eat. They are desperate. And once you can get in through the door and they start to trust you, that's when it starts to feel that you're doing something really worthwhile. I mean, I do miss the others on the wards, but you get used to working on your own, and I like it, actually. And you get to know loads of people as well: the people on the street and in the shops; even the men who deliver the coal and the women who sell flowers — you get to know them all.'

'I don't think I could do it,' said Alice. 'I like to be with others and not work on my own. I mean, obviously, I didn't finish the training so I couldn't do it anyway. The only thing I could do now would be to go back on to the wards as an untrained hospital nurse. But they get paid so little and the work is so heavy . . . I might as well stay here as a housemaid.'

'Maybe so. But it doesn't seem right that you have to let all that experience go to waste,' said Eddy straight out. 'We have to find out if you can finish your training — there has to be a way.'

'I'm not sure. I mean, I do remember Miss Houston saying before Victoria was born that if I wanted to go back then I could. And she did say it again yesterday, when she got me out of the Lock Hospital. She said she was going to have a think about things, about what we should do now, and she said she'd be coming to see me. But I'm not sure what she has in mind and, most of all, now I've got the baby, I can't imagine how it would feel to go back to the hospital. I'd have to leave her, Eddy, I'd have to leave her for hours and hours every day.'

'But Alice, with what happened yesterday, you nearly ended up leaving her anyway, leaving her for much longer than hours. Do you really think that it's safe to continue here now? You can't lock yourself up for ever, and what if you get picked up again? Maybe running into Ada yesterday is just what needed to happen if she can help you somehow to go back and complete your training.'

Alice sat quietly, staring at the stone flags and listening to the wet sheets flap to and fro.

'You're right, Eddy,' she said at last. 'You're absolutely right. I need to find a way of getting out of here. But I've no place to live and no money. The only support I have is here . . . If Ada can find a way for me to return to work and finish my training, I'll have a decent income, and that will allow me to keep Victoria with me. So that's what I need to do. I just don't know how I'd manage to make sure Victoria was well cared for while I worked. Even thinking about leaving her for a few hours every day makes me want to cry . . . But I'll wait to hear what Ada thinks.'

Eddy reached for Alice's hand and patted it

comfortingly. 'It wouldn't be easy, but I think that it's the only way . . . Unless your family could help?'

'Forget about that,' said Alice firmly. 'I've kept the baby secret for a reason. They are very strict. Church every Sunday, Bible reading after tea, prayers before bed. They would never accept Victoria. My mother would have the baby sent for adoption straight away, I'm certain she would. I wouldn't even risk going near my family.'

'But what if they turned up to see you here?' Eddy asked. 'Would they ever do that?'

'Well, my mother wouldn't. She writes to me regularly but she can't take time off work. As you know, she runs the family bakery and we supply bread to the whole village and the surrounding farms. There's no let-up in the work, she couldn't take time off even if she wanted to. And my father . . . I wish I could see him, but he's head cowman at a nearby farm. He works every day of the week as well.'

'Right, well, so at least you don't need to worry about them turning up out of the blue and causing trouble,' said Eddy. 'And from what you've said before, the father of the baby, that Jamie, he's gone for good?'

'Yes, he emigrated for a new life and he's still in Australia as far as I know,' said Alice. 'It's a very good job I've got you,' she added, as Eddy put an arm around her and gave her a squeeze. 'But have you always been so strong? I feel like you're squeezing the life out of me.'

'I don't know,' beamed Eddy. 'It's a good

thing, though, really, isn't it? Given I've got a job where I need to single-handedly wrestle with dogs and patients and God knows what on a daily basis.'

'It is good, but you need to make sure you don't kill anyone by mistake,' laughed Alice. 'I don't know what I'd do if you ended up in prison for manslaughter.'

'Oh, you'd be all right, you know you would. I don't know what it is, but since the baby was born, you seem to be more sure of yourself, and stronger. You really seem to have come into your own.'

'Have I?' mused Alice. 'I suppose so. Probably helps not feeling sick all the time and not having to hide my big belly and worry about being found out by one of the Sisters at the hospital.'

'Oh yes, the Sisters . . . ' said Eddy, pulling a wicked-witch face.

Alice laughed. 'I bet you don't miss Sister Law and Sister Fox.'

Eddy didn't reply instantly, which was very unlike her. 'It's strange, isn't it?' she said eventually. 'I'm meant to say, nah, I don't miss that lot, but d'you know what? I do miss them in a strange kind of way. Maybe not Sister Fox — she can be unfair and a bit vicious. But someone like Sister Law, once you get to know her, well, you start to realize, those Sisters live their lives for the patients. It's all about the welfare of the patients, and there's something to be said for that.'

'Mmmm, not so sure about that. When I was on the wards I began to think that Sister Law only lived to have a go at me.'

'Do you think you will be able to go back, Alice?'

'Well, let's wait and see what Miss Houston has to say when she comes down to see me. No good jumping the gun, hey? But you know what, when I start talking to you about your work on the district and about the hospital, I really do start to miss it. It makes me feel that I do want to go back — but only if there were a way for Victoria to be properly looked after.'

'Oh no, what time is it?' said Eddy, jumping up from the bench and hastily pulling her hair back into some kind of shape before plonking the hat back on her head. 'I need to get back out there to the ulcer dressings and the mustard poultices and the consumption.'

Alice reached up to straighten Eddy's hat before pinning it in place, knowing it would probably be skew-whiff again before she even got out of the alley.

'I'm very proud of you, Eddy,' she said, giving her friend a kiss on the cheek.

'And I'm proud of you too, Alice Sampson.'

When Eddy was gone, Alice sat back down on the bench in the back yard and leant her head against the wall. She'd started to think so much about going back to the hospital that she was a bit dizzy with it. And every time that she felt a surge of wanting to go back, she had an opposite surge of thinking that it could never be possible, of not wanting to leave her baby. She was in constant flux.

'Come on, Alice,' she muttered to herself.

'You're thinking too much, think about something else. What will be will be. No sense mithering about it.'

Glancing along the bench, Alice saw a book that Lizzie had lent her; with everything going on, she hadn't even had time to open the first page. She'd always loved reading but all they'd ever been allowed at home were passages from the Bible. And then, last year, at the hospital, she'd read Miss Nightingale's *Notes on Nursing*; but this was the first time that she'd ever been near a novel. She'd been reluctant to take it at first, there was always so much work to be done in the house, but Marie had insisted that she try to make time, telling her that every woman needed more than doing the laundry and feeding babies.

Reaching over and grabbing the book, Alice looked more closely at it, and started to leaf through the pages. It was called *Wuthering Heights* and written by Emily Brontë and she could see straight away that this wasn't something that you'd find in Sunday school. It was something that her mother would have referred to as the 'work of the devil', something that would most certainly lead her astray.

Alice opened the first page with relish.

★   ★   ★

In the end, it didn't take long for Miss Houston to come down to Stella's place to see Alice: she was there the next day. Just as Victoria was finishing her feed there was a tap on the door

68

and then it opened.

'Hello, Miss Houston. How did you get in?' she laughed.

'Oh, your friend Lizzie heard me knock and she was kind enough to let me in,' said Ada, glancing around the kitchen, drawing in every detail.

'Sorry,' she said at last. 'It's just, I haven't ever been to Stella's home before, she always comes up to the hospital to see me. It's nice to see where my half-sister lives. Is she in?'

'No, you just missed her. You know Stella, always busy with something.'

'Of course, well, hopefully I'll see her another time. Please tell her that I called by, will you?'

'I will,' said Alice, getting up with the baby. 'Now I'm just putting the kettle on — do you want a cup of tea?'

'Yes, please,' replied Ada, holding out her arms for the baby. 'Will she come to me for a little while?'

'Of course she will,' said Alice warmly.

'Hello there, beautiful,' said Ada, instantly transfixed by the smiling baby who still had a bubble of milk at the corner of her mouth.

'She's used to going to different people,' Alice told her. 'Living here, she's always enjoying a cuddle with one of the women or spending time with Marie.'

'You are a lucky girl, aren't you?' said Ada, still completely absorbed, as she sat down and balanced the baby on her knee. 'And you've got a whirl of hair on your crown, just like — Like my friend Mary's baby . . . Yes, you have, haven't you? And I could sit here talking to you all day, yes, I could. But I've come to see your mother . . . '

Still Ada didn't show any sign of shifting her attention, so Alice busied herself with the tea, whilst her baby smiled and played on Ada's knee.

At last, Ada looked over to Alice. 'She's still small, like all of those born too early, but she's really filling out now, isn't she? And she doesn't seem to be showing any sign of what ailed her the other day.'

'No, thank goodness. My stomach turned over when I felt her and she was so hot, and she seemed to be in real pain. I panicked. It must have been something and nothing.'

'You reacted like any mother would,' said Ada. 'You were quite right to act quickly; we all know how serious a fever can be in babies. All the mothers in this city know that.'

'I suppose so,' said Alice. 'And with the first, we're bound to worry more . . . '

'Exactly, so you did the right thing. You were just unlucky that the police were waiting outside the alley. What a thing to happen — taking a housemaid off the street simply because she stepped out of the door to get some medicine for her baby. Disgraceful . . . I've written a letter of complaint and sent it to Mr Fawcett at the Lock Hospital and the Police Constable.'

'Have you really?' said Alice, her eyes wide.

'Yes indeed, and I've already had a reply from Mr Fawcett stating unfortunately that we must accept the jurisdiction of the police in the arrest of women off the street, even if they do prove to be former nurses.'

'Typical,' said Alice, wondering if she should share with Miss Houston that she'd seen Mr Fawcett at the brothel, but then thinking better of it.

'Your experience must have been terrifying,' Ada said gently. 'I can't even imagine . . . '

'It was, but I had to get on straight away and look after Victoria, and there's so much work to do here, I couldn't afford to dwell on things. I just needed to keep going.'

Ada nodded. 'I know what you mean, and sometimes it's just best to keep busy and get on with the work. Speaking of which, do you remember I told you that if you wanted to finish the training, I'd try to find a way of you coming back when the time was right?'

'Yes, I do,' said Alice.

'Well, after what happened the other day I've been putting some thought into things and, to be frank, I think you should seriously consider returning to work now that Victoria is old enough.'

Alice nodded.

'You won't have to repeat the whole training programme again. I don't know how you did it, Alice, with all that was weighing on you, but you managed to get through the bulk of it . . . So I've spoken to Miss Merryweather.'

Alice drew in a sharp breath.

Ada smiled. 'No need to be concerned, Alice. Miss M might not know that you are currently lodging in a brothel, but she has a great deal of experience of life. Even before she came to nursing she spent years working with women employed in a silk mill in Essex, striving to improve conditions for them and their children. And a few years ago she even signed a petition for women to get the vote . . . '

'Really?' said Alice in astonishment. 'It's just that she seems so strict and laced up, if you know what I mean?'

'I know exactly what you mean, but trust me, Miss Merryweather is on our side and she will do all that she can to enable any capable woman to return to work and thereby lead an independent life.'

Alice opened her mouth to speak, but Ada continued.

'Yes, Alice, you're a capable woman, and that is why we've decided to award you special measures. If you do another stint on one ward, that should be sufficient. And if you get your qualification, then the salary that you'll have afterwards will be enough to find your own lodgings in an area where you'll be far less likely, as a single woman on the street, to get picked up by the police. Think about it, Alice. You had no chance of fulfilling your potential before. Wouldn't it be good to come back and see where a return to nursing could lead?'

Alice could feel her heart starting to beat a little faster as she thought about her response. She knew that she was interested, but she also knew that she would have to speak to Marie first about whether she would consider looking after Victoria full-time whilst she was at work. She would pay her what she could out of her wage, of course, because it was important to know that her daughter would be cared for by someone she knew well, and trusted.

'I'll have to make arrangements for childcare,' she said, 'but if you're really sure I don't have to start again from scratch, I'd definitely like to come back to the hospital and finish my training.'

Ada smiled broadly. 'That's the spirit,' she said. 'And I've been putting some thought into how it all might be managed . . . '

Alice tried not to look at her baby's smiling face. Even though she was sure that what she was planning was the right thing for both of them, she still felt guilty. It was a strange kind of guilt, though, laced with the excitement of a return to the world of work.

'I've been putting some thought into how it could be managed,' Ada went on. 'I'll get the uniform to you here and I'll supply you with a district nurse's cape and hat so that you can safely make your way back and forth to the hospital without being arrested. God help us if those men become suspicious of a nurse going about her duties. However, I will get a signed letter from Miss Merryweather for you to carry in your pocket, just in case.'

Alice was nodding and trying to smile, but seeing Victoria's big eyes still gazing at her made her feel sorrowful, and momentarily, she was on the verge of tears as she thought about being separated from her.

'Oh, and I've already spoken to your friend,

Edwina Pacey, and she will, of course, do all that she can to support you,' Ada said, standing up and handing Victoria back to Alice.

'One more thing,' she said, fishing in her bag. 'I've brought you this . . . It's a baby's feeding bottle, a new design; I think it's what they call turtle-shaped. The man who sold it to me assured me that clear glass is best so you can make sure it's kept clean, and he also gave me a rubber teat . . . here it is. It will make things easier if you can start to wean the baby now, over the next few weeks, and then Marie can use this to give cow's milk. Just make sure she boils it and lets it cool, that's all. The milk has to be boiled.'

'I will . . . and thank you,' said Alice quietly. She was very grateful, of course, but it had struck her for the first time that she would have to more or less stop breastfeeding her baby. Maybe she could still give her an early-morning and a late-night feed, but for the rest, she would have to hand her over to Marie with this glass contraption. She knew she had no choice and she'd have to accept it, but standing there in the middle of the kitchen, clinging to her baby, she felt momentarily overwhelmed by the sadness of it all.

5

'A woman who takes a sentimental view
of nursing (which she calls 'ministering', as if she were an angel), is of
course worse than useless.'
                    Florence Nightingale

Later that day, Alice sat down at the kitchen table
with Marie and they talked it through. 'Look,
Alice,' said Marie, 'I don't want you worrying
about paying me. I mean, you've worked hard for
your board and lodgings whilst you've been here.
If you can still do a bit of summat to help out
when you can, that should do — '

'No, I want to pay you,' Alice insisted, leaning
across the table. 'We need to have a proper
arrangement, because I know what the work's
like at the hospital. It's exhausting and the hours
are long, so unless I'm on a half-day off, I'm not
going to be able to help you as much as I'd like.'

'Well, then, I suppose . . . '

'Right, that's a deal then.' Alice reached out to
take Marie's hand. 'Things will be tight, but I
want to give you as much as I can out of my
wage. I need a paper and pencil to work it out,
but I know the wage is ten pounds a year, so — '

'You keep back what you need, Alice,' said
Marie, giving her hand a squeeze. 'You know I'm
happy to look after Victoria. Me and her were
made for each other . . . '

The nurse's uniform duly arrived, wrapped in brown paper and bound tightly with a long length of string. Lizzie came through with the package held in her arms, and placed it on the table.

'This came for you,' she said solemnly. 'It must be your new outfit.'

'I think it is,' replied Alice, feeling a little giddy as she picked up the sharp kitchen knife and slit through the string.

'Ooh, dark grey,' cooed Lizzie when the wool dress was revealed. 'Just the thing.'

Alice smiled nervously and took up the uniform, shaking it out. 'Very serviceable,' she said with a glint in her eye. 'Especially with a starched white apron and cap.'

Lizzie started to giggle and Alice was relieved. She knew that her friend had been excited and sad in equal measure about her return to work. She loved to come into the kitchen and chat during the afternoon, and since that day at the Lock Hospital the two of them had become even closer.

'I like the look of this, though,' said Lizzie, running a hand over the district nurse's cape. 'This would look very fine with my new red dress.'

Alice picked up the cape. 'Go on, you can try it on,' she said, handing it over.

Lizzie draped it around her shoulders and pulled it close at the front. 'I've seen the nurses out in the city with these,' she said, smoothing out the fabric with the flat of her hand, 'and I know you're not an actual district nurse, Alice, but wearing this now makes me feel very special, and do you know what, I feel very proud indeed to know someone who is training to be a nurse. I've heard so many stories about the district nurses and what a difference they can make to people in the city. They must have a strong stomach, though, those nurses, some of the things they have to see . . . '

'Not necessarily,' said Alice, thinking how well Lizzie looked in the cape. 'You just have to learn to manage the heaving in your stomach, that's all. You could do it, I'm sure you could.'

Lizzie smiled at her and gave a twirl. 'Nurse Elizabeth Montgomery,' she announced. 'We call her Monty for short, and she can apply a bandage in the pitch dark or on the back of a cart moving at speed . . . she's an absolute wonder!'

Alice laughed out loud, and put an arm around her friend. 'No, seriously, Lizzie,' she said, 'you would make an excellent nurse. Think about the way you looked after me.'

'Well, that may be the case, Nurse Sampson, but currently I'm far too busy entertaining gentlemen of an evening,' laughed Lizzie, slipping the cape off and placing it carefully over the back of a chair.

'And what's this small, squashed item?' she said, as Alice removed the final piece of uniform from the bottom of the parcel.

'This, Nurse Montgomery, is a district nurse's hat. It should be round, but as you can see, it is rather flat.'

'Mmm, you need to get some steam on it,' said Lizzie. 'Then it'll knock back into shape.'

That night as Alice lay in bed with the full uniform hanging on the wall at the bottom of her bed and Victoria sleeping soundly in her crib, she looked from one to the other, and her stomach tightened. The thoughts of 'baby, uniform, nurse, mother' whirled in her head, and even though she was dog tired, she couldn't sleep. It felt as if her mind was still fighting with itself. And then other thoughts, triggered by the dark grey of the probationer uniform, started to creep in. Snatches of memory: crying in the sluice, nausea, feeling that at any moment she would be found out, disgraced. Her head was so jumbled and troubled it felt like the bed was starting to spin.

'For goodness' sake, Alice,' she cried, sitting up in bed. 'You need to sort yourself out.' Then she gave herself a good talking to for a full five minutes, at the end of which, yes, she felt troubled about leaving her daughter, but she knew it was the best thing. What's more, something that she hadn't truly believed was possible was now within her reach, and they'd have the benefit of extra money and security and Victoria would have a mother who was a role model and an independent woman. Of course it wouldn't be easy to return to the wards — she'd need to face her demons from the first time around for a start, and the work would be hard and demanding, and she dreaded having to contend with Sister Law again. But overriding all this was the certainty that she needed to go back, to make something of herself, to prove that she could do it, that she could be a good nurse.

'Remember, Alice,' she murmured to herself as she snuggled down in bed, feeling sleepy at last, 'how excited you were those first few weeks of your training, how you wanted to be the best nurse that Liverpool Royal had ever seen . . . well, now's your chance. And you need to get to sleep because you start back in two days' time.'

★   ★   ★

As Alice walked away from the front door that first morning back to work, she felt as if something inside her was tearing apart. She'd left Victoria sleeping peacefully in her crib, Marie right there in the kitchen watching over her, but somehow, it just didn't feel enough.

What's more, she felt strange in the district nurse's cape and hat, like a fraud, some imposter forcing herself to adopt a role. She had to make herself walk quickly, but her steps were heavy and her heart felt broken. She'd cried after feeding Victoria, feeling ridiculous — most of the working women she knew had to leave their children and go out to work. And not only that, she was privileged to be given a second chance to complete her training, and so lucky that she had Marie who would care for Victoria. She knew all of this in her head, but as she walked, her body was yearning to be back in the warm kitchen, with the baby sleeping in her crib by the fire.

Glancing back before she exited the alley,

Alice saw the cat, Hugo, trotting after her. 'Where do you think you're going? Shoo, shoo,' she said, feeling irritated, wafting her hand at him. Then she started to giggle, despite herself. 'Get back to the kitchen. You're supposed to be a lazy good-for-nothing, not a cat that will follow someone to work.' The cat stopped for a few moments, staring at her, his white-tipped tail flicking from side to side as he weighed up his options. Then he turned and trotted back.

It made her feel better somehow, to know that Hugo was returning to the house. He was part of the cosy kitchen routine that she shared with Victoria and Marie every morning. She wanted him to be there, lying in front of the fire, in his rightful place.

Alice still felt cautious as she stepped out of the alley, but when she was sure that no one was lurking, she continued out on to Lime Street. The ache still throbbed inside her as she moved further away from her baby, but now she actively made herself think about what ward she might be working on and what she might be asked to do on this, her first day back.

Preoccupied with her thoughts, she instinctively found her way through the streets and, in what seemed like hardly any time at all, she was standing at the bottom of the steps that led up to the Nurses' Home and Training School.

Looking up to the heavy wooden door, she felt a flutter of nerves or excitement, she wasn't sure which. But then she had a sense of Maud and Eddy, right there with her, and it gave her a warm feeling. She could even hear Maud's voice: 'Come on, Alice, let's get started.' It was uncanny, Maud didn't even know that she was going back to work, yet just seeing the grand building which housed so many memories made her presence feel immediate.

'Come on then, Alice,' she muttered to herself. 'You can't stand here looking at the door all day, get yourself up those steps.'

She had been told in the letter that Miss Houston had sent to report to Miss Merryweather, and as she stepped through the door and stood on the coloured floor tiles of the entrance, a door to the left clicked open and the superintendent appeared, wearing a large bonnet.

'Good morning, Nurse Sampson, good to see you back,' she said warmly.

Alice found herself blushing and it was difficult to look the superintendent in the eye. Although she'd always felt comfortable talking to Miss Houston about the baby, she was hoping that Miss Merryweather wouldn't start asking any awkward questions.

As soon as the superintendent spoke again, Alice knew that she had no need to worry, about that at least. 'You will be stationed on Male Surgical with Sister Law for the first few weeks. I hope that meets with your approval.'

'Yes,' murmured Alice, trying to stay calm. She knew it could have been worse — she could have been given Sister Fox — but all she could hear, in that moment, was Sister Law's voice, calling through the sluice door: 'Where is Nurse Sampson, that wretched girl . . . '

Alice could see Miss Merryweather looking at

her with some concern, but she couldn't think of anything else to say. She suddenly felt blurry and mixed up as she stood there with the superintendent's bright gaze upon her. She wasn't sure if coming back to work was going to be the right thing after all.

'Nurse Sampson?' said Miss Merryweather.

'Yes,' said Alice, knowing that she needed to pay attention.

'You seem a bit distracted, overwhelmed. Do you want to sit down for a few moments?'

'No, thank you, Miss Merryweather,' said Alice, trying to smile.

'Well, just come with me into the light. I know that today is a big day for you.' The superintendent led the way into the open space of the building. 'Let's just take a few moments before you get back into the thick of it. I like to gaze up to the skylight: it calms me, gives me focus. I often used to share these moments with your friend, Nurse Maud Linklater . . . '

Ah, there she is again, thought Alice, she's definitely with me this morning. Gazing up to the skylight wasn't for Alice — she had too much on her mind for that and she would have preferred to go straight to the ward — but she stood politely beside Miss Merryweather for a few moments. She found herself looking up to the first-floor gallery, where she had lived with Maud and Eddy last year, and it made her think of the final time she'd descended those stone stairs with her bag packed and Maud beside her, not knowing if she'd ever come back in here again. How sad she'd been to leave her small room up there on the first gallery, next to Eddy's. How anxious she'd been about the baby. She had felt desolate that day. Lost.

'Well, now I'm back,' she murmured to herself, looking down to the dark grey uniform that fitted her properly this time around. 'And I'm going to do the best that I can.'

'Are you ready?' said Miss Merryweather, glancing sideways, her eyes gleaming.

Alice couldn't be sure, but she felt that the superintendent had known, in some way, what she needed to do that first morning and she'd stood there just long enough for it to happen.

'I'm ready,' she said.

And even though her legs felt a bit weak as she began to move, she did feel ready now to face Sister Law on the ward, or anybody else for that matter.

Miss Merryweather was walking briskly towards the front door. 'Remove your cape and hat,' she said. 'Hang them here on these pegs by the door, then you can pick them up when you're finished on the ward and you're ready to make your way back to your accommodation in the city.'

Alice did as instructed and then Miss Merryweather pointed to a starched cap that was freshly laundered, waiting on the shelf above the coat pegs. 'This is for you, Nurse Sampson,' she said, standing on tiptoe to remove it from the shelf. 'I folded it myself.'

'Thank you, it's perfect,' said Alice, having never seen such a beautiful cap before. Not even Maud could have folded it like that.

'Oh, it's not just down to me,' Miss Merry-weather said. 'We have a new laundress for the uniforms, a woman called Dolly, someone who Miss Houston knew from the war. She's an absolute marvel.'

Alice pinned the cap in place and then Miss Merryweather straightened it for her. 'Remove it when you come back each day and leave it here, on the shelf. No one will disturb it, but if it does go missing make your way to the laundry and ask Dolly for a fresh one. She'll be able to provide you with clean aprons as well. I've told her that you've had to take some time off for a 'delicate matter' and you've come back to finish your training.'

Alice felt herself flushing pink to the roots of her hair as she followed along behind Miss Merryweather. Somehow it felt worse, to have her situation alluded to in that way. But when she repeated 'delicate matter' in her head, it made her start to smile. There was absolutely nothing delicate about giving birth and then scrubbing floors and washing clothes for a living. Nothing delicate at all.

The superintendent was out through the door now, setting quite a pace. Alice needed to run down the steps to catch her up. As soon as they were through the door of the hospital, Miss Merryweather stopped short and Alice nearly ploughed into the back of her.

'I'm just going along to check on the orderlies and then I'll be doing my rounds,' she said, turning on her heel and looking Alice up and down. Then, fixing her with a bright stare, 'You do remember how to find the ward, don't you, Nurse Sampson?' she said.

And in that moment, as Alice stood there, she didn't know if she remembered or not, but she nodded anyway. 'Yes, thank you, Miss Merryweather.'

'You will feel strange today, Nurse Sampson,' said the superintendent as she walked away. 'But all you need to do is get on with the work.'

Alice opened her mouth to speak but no words would come and her mouth felt dry. She had to force herself to move, to walk towards the ward, and she could feel her heart starting to pound. What if she'd forgotten everything she'd ever learnt? What if she was useless?

As soon as she was through the door of the ward, Alice could hear Sister Law shouting: 'Nurse Bradshaw, did I or did I not tell you to attend to that patient? Look, he's getting out of bed. Go there, now! Hurry up.'

The ward — packed with beds down each side, noisy with patients calling out and nurses flitting up and down — was just as she'd left it. But seeing it afresh took her breath away. She'd forgotten how chaotic it was. Her life at Stella's seemed leisurely in comparison. And then she saw Sister Law steaming down the ward towards her, the white starched cap knotted tightly beneath her ample chin.

'Uh oh, here we go,' she murmured to herself, feeling like a target as Sister moved swiftly in her direction. It's best to stand still, she thought, and take what's coming. It was, as always, impossible to read Sister's expression. Yet seeing her, just as she'd left her all those months ago, made Alice begin to feel that she hadn't really missed much at all. Things were the same here, and this was, somehow, reassuring.

'Ah, Nurse Sampson,' said Sister, her eyes narrowing as she looked Alice up and down, 'you have returned to the fold.'

Alice nodded and tried to smile but her mouth was still a bit dry so she couldn't speak.

'Well, you've lost some weight, I can see that. But you are still pale and your cap is still limp, so no change there, then.'

Alice knew that her cap wasn't limp — it had been specially laundered by the new laundress and folded by Miss Merryweather herself — but if Sister Law said it was limp, it was limp.

'Right, Nurse, let's get you started . . . Go and join Nurse Langtry at bed three. I believe she needs some help with her patient — she's been trying to apply leeches there for quite some time.'

Alice looked across to Nurse Langtry's wiry figure bent over her task, and for some reason, seeing the severe parting of her dark hair peeking out from under her neat cap, she felt a moment of tenderness. She knew that, almost certainly, Millicent had been the one to keep Nancy Sellers informed of everything that was going on, but Alice found it hard to believe that she'd done so intentionally. She might be proved wrong, but it seemed to Alice in that moment that Millicent always appeared to mean well . . . However, the way she was fiddling around with those leeches, it looked like she'd

86

never get them ready to apply.

Just as Alice started to move towards Millicent she heard Sister Law's voice: 'Go on, Nurse Sampson, get moving. As you can see, we're as busy as ever on Male Surgical.'

Sister's voice put Alice on edge and she could see, hear and smell just how busy the ward was. And even though bed three and Nurse Langtry were only across the way, for some reason she was momentarily lost in a whirl. The smell of wounds and the noise of the patients calling out seemed like an affront.

One patient was crying, and then she heard the sound of some poor man vomiting.

That really knocked her, taking her straight back to morning sickness and all the occasions when she'd had to rush to the ward sluice to puke.

'Nurse Sampson!' yelled Sister Law from the other end of the ward. 'Did I or did I not tell you to go to bed three?'

That was it, the spell was broken, something reconnected in Alice's head and she was at last able to move. Taking deep breaths as she strode towards Nurse Langtry, she forced herself to focus.

'Do you want me to do that, Nurse Langtry?' she asked, seeing how Millicent was struggling to fish one of the leeches out of a pot.

'Oh, Alice, Nurse Sampson,' she said, looking like someone had just given her an almighty shock. 'Well, I've been trying to do this for ages, but I can't seem to be able to get them out of the pot. They keep slipping away from me. We need to fix them to this patient's instep, but as you can see . . . '

'Let me help,' said Alice, immediately taking the forceps and grasping the first leech before Nurse Langtry had even finished trying to explain.

'This patient has been very poorly, haven't you, Mr Thomson?' said Nurse Langtry, moving to stand at the head of the bed.

I expect he has, thought Alice, given that he's in a hospital ward.

'And he's had a very bad night, haven't you, Mr Thomson?' Nurse Langtry continued, laying a hand on the man's forehead. 'I think you might have a bit of a fever,' she said. 'I'll just go and get a damp cloth to cool you down.'

'Where's she going?' said Mr Thomson, looking at Alice, his eyes wide. 'She's supposed to be applying some leeches to the instep of my foot. There's a problem with my circulation, I'm in danger of losing me bloody leg 'ere.'

'She'll be back,' Alice reassured him, glancing after Millicent as she made her way slowly up the ward towards the sluice. 'And in the meantime, I've got the leeches ready here. Do you want me to apply them?'

'Yes, just get on with it, will ye?' said Mr Thomson.

Alice had the job done before Nurse Langtry arrived back with a cloth and a bowl of water. Once she'd checked that the leeches were securely attached, she watched Millicent go to the head of the bed, immerse the cloth in the water and then slowly squeeze it out before placing it on the man's forehead. Alice could see that it was still fairly saturated with water.

'What the blazes are you doing, Nurse?' shouted Mr Thomson, grabbing the cloth and throwing it to the floor and then waving away any attempt at further ministration. 'I'm not dying and I'm not overly hot. I've got a problem with me leg, that's all. You've got the wrong patient.'

Alice felt a bit sorry for Millicent as she slowly picked up the cloth from the floor and walked away from the bed. She went after her, thinking that she might be upset, but Millicent appeared unperturbed. She was already stopping by another bed with her bowl of water. It seemed that she was simply looking for another patient who might need to have his forehead wiped.

'Oh my,' muttered Alice under her breath. 'I think there's much more important work to be done here. I need to find someone who works in the same way that I do.'

'Right, come with me,' said Sister Law, striding past. 'There are many beds to be stripped and changed at the top end of the ward. Let's get you back into the work, Nurse Sampson, well and truly back into the work.'

'Yes, Sister,' said Alice with a wry smile. She hadn't thought that she'd end up working with Sister Law on her first day back, but even that felt appealing compared to trotting around after Millicent with her damp flannel.

★   ★   ★

89

Alice felt surprisingly alive as she left the ward at the end of the day. After a slow start she'd got back into the work, and once she was with the patients, trying to do what she could for them, she hadn't been able to worry about anything else. Inevitably she'd thought about Victoria, and she'd had moments when she felt as if a part of her was missing. She'd had to take a deep breath and tell herself that she needed to do this. Finishing her training was the only way that she would have any future for her and the baby, so she might as well get on and make the best of it.

Walking back to the Nurses' Training School to collect her nurse's cape and hat before she made her way through the city, Alice was also struck by how much energy she had, even at the end of the day. The last time she'd made this journey her belly had been bulging out of her uniform, her legs were aching and she'd felt like she just needed to lie down. She'd also been weighed down by anxiety. So, managing the niggling worry over leaving Victoria seemed much easier in comparison.

Seeing Eddy perched on the step waiting for her was also an absolute delight. She ran up to her as though she hadn't seen her for months. Eddy couldn't stop laughing as Alice pulled her up from the step and danced full circle with her.

'I did it, I did it,' she chanted. 'I did the first day!'

'Crikey, Alice, don't let the others see you. They'll all be going off to have babies if they see how glorious you look after a day's work.'

'It was good,' said Alice, her eyes wide. 'I was a

bit slow at first, but once I got back into it I felt like I'd never been away. And I felt better today than I'd ever done last time, because of . . . you know . . . ' She sketched the curve of a pregnant belly with her hand.

'I'm so glad,' said Eddy. 'I've been thinking about you all day. I thought you might come out looking like a wreck.'

'And I've been on Male Surgical — '

'With Sister Law,' said Eddy, 'and you're still smiling!'

'Yes,' said Alice. She started to calm down at last and put a hand to her chest as she became aware of how sore her breasts were feeling.

'Mmm,' said Eddy, seeing straight away how tight Alice's bodice looked beneath the starched apron. 'Good job you'd started reducing the feeds right down and I'd given you those squares of cotton to pack in. Bet you're feeling it now.' Eddy started giggling. 'I wonder if Sister Law noticed that one of her nurses was growing a bigger bosom during the course of the day.'

'Eddy!' said Alice, laughing.

As the girls walked back to Stella's together, each in their district nurse cape and hat, the people on the street smiled at them and some of the cheeky ones even gave a mock salute and called out, 'Evening, Sister.' Alice was amazed.

'I've got used to it now,' said Eddy, 'but it surprised me as well, at first. But then, when I thought about it, the people are bound to be happy with us nurses and what we try to do for them, in the hospital and in their homes. And, another thing, the district nursing service in

91

Liverpool was the very first in the country. They say that William Rathbone set it up because he'd had a good nurse to look after his wife in their own home. After she died, he wanted other people to have that as well. But then they needed more trained nurses, and that's when he consulted Miss Nightingale and the Training School got built. And here we are: me and you and Maud, all part of it.'

'The people are bound to be proud, when you think of it like that,' said Alice quietly, linking arms with Eddy. 'And we are lucky to be a part of it all.'

6

'It can be safely taken for granted
. . . that a thorough hospital nurse
can seldom turn herself to any
other business.'
                    Florence Nightingale

The next morning was hard. Victoria had been unsettled all night, maybe teething, maybe just feeling the separation. Alice had been feeding her on and off since the early hours — she'd also lit the stove, made the breakfast, handed her over to Marie whilst she got her uniform on and got ready for work, then she'd tried feeding her again. And then she'd had to hand her back to Marie, screaming.

'Go, just go,' shouted Marie, above the outcry. 'She'll be all right once you've gone.'

Alice nodded. She had no choice: she had to go to work, she needed to finish her training and she needed the money. Even though she would give a good proportion of her wage to Marie and Stella, there would still be some left over for her to put aside. She knew all of this, but this second morning, her heart was even heavier and her body felt like lead as she headed out of the kitchen.

As the front door clicked shut behind her, she could still hear Victoria screaming. Every nerve in her body felt alive with it, the sensation jangling through her whole body, wave after wave.

Glancing back once more down the alley, with tears welling in her eyes, she thought that she might, at least, see the cat trotting along behind her — but even Hugo had deserted her. She felt truly miserable.

Walking out on to Lime Street, Alice saw two policemen in plain clothes standing at the corner of the next alley. She was certain they were the ones who had picked her up and forced her into a carriage the day she was taken to the Lock Hospital. As she got closer, she felt a shudder go through her body, but she knew that she needed to stand tall and look like a nurse. So, lifting her head, she wiped the tears from her eyes, straightened her hat and pulled the cape around her more closely. Her heart was pounding and she held her breath as she walked by as fast as she could, praying that they wouldn't recognize her.

She didn't dare look at them but she was alert to any movement. Thankfully, they stayed as they were, and all she could hear was the mumble of conversation as she passed by. It seemed that Miss Houston had been right: the district nurse uniform would serve her well. In fact, she even thought she might have heard one of them call out a friendly 'Morning, Sister.'

The relief that she felt as soon as she was at a safe distance helped her to calm down. She knew that she would have to trust that by now, Marie had the baby settled. She had to go to work and that was that.

Alice missed Maud so much as she stood on the ward, whilst Sister Law did the head count and assigned tasks. She always used to stand with Maud on this ward. Looking at the other nurses, she felt set apart, distanced, especially from the two new probationers who looked like friends. In fact, they could have been her and Maud last year. I hope, for their sakes, one of them isn't pregnant, she thought with a wry smile to herself.

'Am I amusing you this morning, Nurse Sampson?' said Sister.

'No, Sister, I was just . . . ' Alice's mind was too tired to have a ready response. 'I'm just happy to be back on Male Surgical, that's all.'

'That may well be the case, but try not to show it,' said Sister, scowling first at Alice and then at each member of the group in turn. Silently, warning them all.

'Right, Bradshaw and Fry,' she hissed, in the direction of the new probationers. 'After your dire performance yesterday, I want you to pay more attention. Start up at the top end of the ward: stripping, cleaning and making up the beds. I will be along to check . . . '

Alice looked over at Millicent Langtry, but she was staring into space, seemingly oblivious to what had just been said. Alice still couldn't believe that Millicent was now a trained nurse. She had no idea how she'd got through the twelve months' training. Maybe because she was always so quiet, she didn't attract any attention. And without a shadow of doubt, Nurse Langtry, in Sister's eyes, had the correct moral character;

she was clearly unblemished.

Unblemished by life, even by thought, mused Alice.

'Nurse Sampson!' called Sister. 'So sorry to interrupt your meditations but we need to start work. You'd better come with me — that way I can make sure that you stay alert and you're properly engaged with meaningful tasks.'

Alice felt like telling Sister that she'd better keep an eye on Nurse Langtry in that case. She'd just seen her wander off absent-mindedly. She still couldn't work Millicent out. Even though she'd been in their set first time round, it was difficult to get a sense of who she really was. Alice knew she was quiet and she always tried to do the best for the patients, but she was so slow with everything, and she struggled to pick up on what a patient's actual needs were, so much so that Alice always ended up feeling irritated with her.

'This way, Nurse Sampson,' shouted Sister from halfway down the ward.

She'd have to remember to look more alert tomorrow morning; she didn't want to end up working with Sister Law every day. And she certainly didn't want to end up with a bad report. She needed to pass; she needed her certificate, the piece of paper that would give her the right to work as a trained nurse. And then she could stay on and work in the hospital or out in the district, whatever she chose to do.

'Nurse Sampson, my word, you are in a daydream today . . . Come with — '

But Sister was cut short as two orderlies came

running in through the door with a patient who was covered in blood, lying on a stretcher. Alice had never seen Sister run, but she took off like lightning, speaking to Michael Delaney, the orderly at the head of the stretcher.

'He was dumped outside the hospital, me and Stephen found him,' said Michael, desperately trying to catch his breath. 'Looks like somebody's put a tourniquet on his upper arm but he's lost a lot of blood. It looks like he might've been stabbed.'

Alice saw Sister put a reassuring hand on Michael's arm, while her eyes travelled up and down the stretcher, assessing the patient.

The poor man was unresponsive and looked, to Alice, as though he was barely alive.

'He is very pale, looks like he's in shock. Take him straight into theatre and put him on the table. You can leave him on the stretcher, he's too poorly to move,' said Sister, her voice clipped, full of energy.

'Right, Sister,' said Michael and Stephen together, already moving up the ward. Alice could see the faces of the other patients, sitting up in their beds. Some of them looked away, one man crossed himself.

'We've no time to lose,' said Sister, turning on her heel. 'Nurse Sampson, I need you to go as fast as you can to Female Surgical, where you will find Mr Jones and Dr McKendrick. Tell them to come immediately.'

Alice ran out of the ward door at full pelt and straight into Miss Houston.

'What is it?' said Ada, seeming to know

97

instantly that they had an emergency.

'We have a man in a terrible state, I need the surgeons,' Alice called over her shoulder as she careered down the corridor.

When she returned with Dr McKendrick, she waited at the ward door for Mr Jones as he laboured along behind. A man of his age simply could not run down the corridor, and Alice wanted to make sure that she got him directly into theatre.

She followed along behind as he walked up the ward and then in through the doors of the theatre. Alice caught her breath when she saw the high wooden table in the centre of the room. The patient had already been positioned and Sister Law was elevating his arm with one hand and pressing a ball of lint firmly over the wound with the other. His whole body was covered in blood and more blood still oozed from beneath the dressing.

Mr Jones was already at the sink, scrubbing his hands. Miss Houston had her sleeves rolled up and was preparing the instruments.

Alice heard the clink of an enamel bowl as Miss Houston placed it ready. 'What do you want me to do?' she said, looking at Miss Houston.

'You take over from Sister, she needs to get back on the ward.'

Alice was straight there, side by side with Sister Law and taking hold of the ball of lint that she was pressing firmly over the wound. Her hands were instantly covered in blood.

'That's right, Nurse Sampson, firm pressure, and you'll need plenty of lint; the blood is soaking right through. As you can see, the poor man has already lost a great deal. Now take his arm with your other hand — that's it, lift it as high as you can — that will help slow the bleeding.' Alice had never seen anyone who wasn't already dead look as pale as the man lying on the table did.

'Observe, Nurse Sampson, the signs of exsanguination: pale skin, blue lips and fingertips, collapsed state, shallow breathing . . . And if you could find a pulse,' added Sister Law, 'it would be rapid and thready.'

Alice nodded. It felt good to be in theatre; last time around she'd never once been chosen to come through the door. She could feel her breath coming rapidly and she was a little dizzy with it all — she had never seen so much blood loss before, ever.

'You are managing well,' murmured Sister Law, placing a stack of fresh lint pads on the small table next to Alice. 'I'll leave you to it now. As you can see, Miss Houston is an extremely capable and experienced nurse, especially in an emergency. Follow her lead and don't be afraid to ask, Nurse Sampson. Always ask.'

'Yes, Sister, thank you,' said Alice, grabbing yet another lint pad.

Mr Jones was next to her now at the table and she removed the ball of lint for a few moments so that he could observe the wound. The surgeon narrowed his eyes and peered closely at it, his nose almost touching the flesh.

'Ah yes, definitely a knife wound, quite a large blade too, and very sharp. It looks like a deliberate slice rather than a stab, as though someone knew what they were doing. Must have caught the brachial artery. Good job someone had the foresight to apply a tourniquet,' he said, nodding to a leather thong around the patient's arm. 'It isn't applied firmly enough, but at least it's done enough to make sure that our man made it as far as the hospital.'

'Do you think we'll get away with tying the vessel and stopping the bleeding?' asked Miss Houston.

'Sadly, no,' said Mr Jones. 'As you can see, the affected arm is blanched; it's been starved of blood for too long. We'll have to remove the limb as well, I'm afraid.'

Alice looked at the arm she was holding. She could see calluses on the hand, a broken nail on the man's thumb. It seemed so personal and so sad that the poor man's right arm would have to be removed. She glanced at his face: he looked middle-aged with thinning brown hair and a stubble of beard, like any other man you might see walking around Liverpool. But this man has been marked out, she thought, and he will never be the same again.

Miss Houston sprayed some liquid over the instruments and the patient's arm.

'It's carbolic acid,' she explained. 'We've found that it helps reduce suppuration post-operatively. It will give him a better chance of survival, that's if he lives through the surgery.'

Alice nodded, trying to take in all the detail, beginning to realize why Maud had been so taken with theatre work. It was sharp, exciting.

'Stand by with the chloroform, McKendrick,'

said Mr Jones. 'We don't want to risk giving it now, but sometimes when they feel the smart of the knife, they start to come round.'

Dr McKendrick nodded; he already had everything prepared. He seemed to Alice to be perfectly calm and she was already admiring the precision of his movements. He and Miss Houston seemed to work instinctively together as they prepared the patient.

First, Mr Jones went into the wound with some forceps, fishing around for the blood vessel that had caused the man to bleed so much.

'Swab,' he shouted, and Miss Houston went straight into the wound with a swab held in her bare hands.

'Got it!' said Mr Jones at last. 'Now let's finish the job and remove the arm.'

Alice felt her heart pounding as she stood ready to assist.

'I'll support the arm,' whispered Miss Houston. 'Can you stand ready to take it from me once it's separated? It won't take him long.'

Alice nodded, not daring to speak and disturb the quiet intent in that room. There was something almost reverent about it.

As the knife slipped through the man's skin, Alice felt her stomach turn and she was suddenly light-headed. She took a deep breath, a tactic she'd used previously in similar circumstances. This was the first time that she'd seen a major operation, and she was keen to see everything. But the more she watched, the dizzier she felt, and then she could feel a cold sweat breaking out on her skin.

'Try to stay upright if you can, Nurse Sampson,' Miss Houston murmured. 'But if you think you're going to go over, sit yourself down over there on that stool — '

It was too late, Alice had hit the floor.

When she came to, she was gazing up at the concerned face of Dr McKendrick. He was smiling at her.

'I'm so sorry,' she muttered, feeling like a complete fool. Stretched out on the floor, no use to anybody. 'Is the patient . . . ?'

'The patient is fine, Nurse, just fine. Mr Jones is closing up the wound; you can watch if you want, but I think you're probably best lying here for a while longer.'

'Yes,' said Alice, 'I'm so sorry.'

'Please do not apologize,' said McKendrick, his voice clipped and well-spoken, but also gentle. 'When I was a medical student in India, I fainted every single time I went into theatre for two weeks. I had to take a chair with me in the end, so I wouldn't cause any trouble. The surgeon was very wise. He knew I would get used to it eventually, and he never turned me away. He told me this: all the best doctors and nurses faint in theatre. They do so because they feel for their patients. I believe this to be true.'

He was probably just being kind, thought Alice, as you are right now, Dr McKendrick. But she smiled up at him and thanked him for his kindness just the same.

She lay on the floor until everything was finished and Mr Jones had left, and then the door swung open and Sister Law was looking down at her, and she almost fainted again on the spot, because Sister was actually smiling. Only for a moment, but to Alice, it was like the sun coming out from behind a black cloud.

'Right, Nurse Sampson,' she said, straightening her cap and making sure that the string was knotted firmly beneath her chin. 'Let's get you up on your feet and then we'll find you a cup of hot sweet tea before you get back to work. Don't you be worrying about the faint — it happens to many people. I, myself, never fainted. Nor did your friend, Nurse Linklater, when she first came into theatre. But we were the exception to the rule. So do not worry.'

Alice tried to sit up; it felt too strange to be lying there on the floor with Sister Law looming over her. She pulled herself into a sitting position and propped herself against the wall. She still felt light-headed, but Sister seemed satisfied that she was making progress: she nodded, then turned on her heel, sweeping out through the door without another word.

Then it was just Alice, Miss Houston and Dr McKendrick in theatre.

'We are applying a stump bandage to the patient's arm,' said Ada. 'This can be a bit tricky, as you can see. First you have to tether it and then the bandage goes backwards and forwards like this, then we need to make sure it's wrapped firm, to help reduce any swelling.'

It looked like a work of art from where Alice was sitting. She was in awe of the bandaging and knew that she'd need a lot of practice to even start to be able to do anything like that. She was also impressed by the way Dr McKendrick held the arm in position and helped Ada with the bandage. She didn't even have to direct him, he just seemed to know what to do. She saw, as well, a moment when Ada's hand brushed his, as she wrapped the bandage around, and caught the look on his face, for just an instant.

Ada, however, was completely oblivious, and only interested in a good bandage. But Alice was sure that she hadn't been mistaken, she'd seen a spark of something. No wonder, she thought, just look at her — all dark, curly hair and bright eyes. He must be a bit older than her, but with his black hair and dark eyes, they were very well matched.

'That should do it,' said Ada energetically, as she wrapped the final loop of bandage and tucked it in. McKendrick was still holding the arm, transfixed by her. She was, of course, still completely oblivious.

Alice gave a sigh. She felt sorry for the doctor — it was easy to see that he adored Miss Houston and it looked as though she had no idea of his feelings towards her. She almost thought about trying to make Ada aware, but just as quickly realized that wouldn't be a good idea. These things had to develop of their own accord, or not at all. Not that she'd had any experience to back up that theory, but common sense told her that was probably the best way.

'Are you fully recovered now, Nurse?' asked McKendrick, coming over to where Alice was sitting.

'Yes, I feel much better, thank you,' she said,

thinking what a lovely person he was.

She made to stand up but lurched a little, and he grabbed her, keeping hold of her arm until she was completely steady.

'Now, Nurse Sampson,' he said gently, 'I did try to sponge some of the patient's blood from your hands whilst you were passed out, but I think you should go now and wash them again.'

Alice looked down — yes, he was right.

'Thank you,' she said quietly, to this man who seemed to think of everything.

'I need to make my way to Female Surgical now, Ada, to catch up with Mr Jones,' he said, once Alice was steady and balanced at the sink.

Ada barely glanced up from the patient. 'Can you send the orderlies in to remove him to a bed on the ward, please, Anil?'

He nodded and then he was gone.

Well, at least they're on first-name terms, thought Alice. Maybe all is not completely lost for poor Dr McKendrick.

Once Michael and Stephen had been in with the stretcher to remove the patient, it was just Alice and Ada left in theatre clearing up. Just as Alice made her way to assist with wiping the table down, the door swung open and Sister Law was there again. 'Good to see you on your feet, Nurse Sampson. Here's your sweet tea,' she said, leaving it on the window ledge. 'Drink it up and then get back on the ward as soon as you can.'

Alice opened her mouth to speak but Sister had already gone.

'It's always so busy out there,' said Ada, smiling. 'I don't know how she does it day after day.' She caught the look on Alice's face. 'Yes, I know she runs a tight ship, but you know what, if I was a patient, I'd want Prudence Law to be in charge of the ward.'

Prudence! said the voice in Alice's head, as she tried to stop herself from giggling. Prudence Law!

'Right, Nurse Sampson,' said Ada. 'You seem to have made a good job of the table. Can you help me wipe down these instruments and put them in a bowl full of carbolic acid? We've started soaking them now in the solution, to reduce germs. We just need to find the bowls . . .

'I'm sorry I didn't get to see you on your first day, Alice,' she went on, 'but in fact I was just coming on to the ward to find you when you came running at me . . . How are things going, and how are you coping with leaving Victoria?'

For a moment, Alice was unable to reply. She felt her breath catch and she was surprised by the tightness in her throat when she tried to speak. The way that she missed her baby was like an empty space inside her; she had no idea how to describe it.

'I am coping, but it is so hard to leave her,' she said eventually, feeling ridiculous as she felt herself turning a deep pink, even down to the roots of her hair, simply because she was speaking about her secret child, here at the hospital.

'It must be hard, I know that. But you have to trust that it will be worth it in the end.'

Alice nodded. 'This morning was bad, she was screaming when I left.'

'Oh dear, I'm sorry to hear that. It's bound to happen, I suppose. That must be a lot to deal with first thing in the morning. But if it's any consolation, Alice, from what I've seen of you today, the way you're applying yourself and getting on with the work, I can say, in all honesty, that you seem to have the makings of a nurse who can finish her training.'

'Really?' said Alice. 'Even though I just fainted clean away, during a routine operation?'

'Yes, really. Even though I manage all kinds of emergencies and can witness any amount of blood in theatre, I fainted too the first time I saw an amputation.'

'Did you?' said Alice, her eyebrows raised. 'Was that here, at the Infirmary?'

'Oh no, it was years ago. I saw my first one during the Crimean War.'

'Oh my goodness,' said Alice. 'Of course, I'd heard that you were out there. That must have been quite something.'

'It was,' said Ada. 'I didn't realize at the time. I was very young, I was swept along with everything but, now, when I think about it, I have no idea how I got through it.'

'Did you work with Florence Nightingale?' Alice asked.

'Not as such, but I worked with some nurses who'd trained under her. And I did get to meet her. Twice, in fact.'

Alice's eyes widened. She'd grown up hearing stories of Miss Nightingale, and she'd had a portrait of the heroine of the Crimea hanging above her bed at home. 'Did you see her tending the patients, with her lamp? She must have been like an angel.'

107

'I didn't see her working on the wards, but, you know, most of that stuff about her with the lamp, it was just stories. I don't think even Miss Nightingale would want people to think of her as just some kind of ministering angel. Yes, the patients were her priority, but that didn't mean she would sit by a bedside for hours on end. She is a very intelligent woman, good at knowing exactly what's required, and at that time, during the war, there were other people to sit with the patients, and other priorities for Miss Nightingale. She was in charge of everything at the hospital in Scutari, completely dedicated to her work and very, very determined. Without her, we wouldn't have nursing as it is today. There wouldn't be any proper training for women like you. We'd still be stuck back in the dark ages with filthy hospitals and incompetent nurses.'

'I see,' said Alice, musing over what Ada had just said. 'So most people don't really have much idea about what Miss Nightingale really did out there.'

'Yes, I think that's probably the case.'

Alice felt sorry, in a way, to lose the image of Miss Nightingale that she'd always had in her head. But then, surely, the real Florence Nightingale was even more impressive. What an incredible woman.

'So did you see your first amputation in Scutari hospital — is that where you fainted?' she asked, starting to wipe down the operating table.

'No . . . I didn't actually work in Scutari. I ended up near the front line. It was, in fact, on

108

the harbourside at Balaklava. I was straight off the ship and dragged over to help an army surgeon. Someone mistook me for a nurse but I'd had no experience whatsoever. I passed out completely. But I didn't have a kind doctor looking after me like you just had. Oh no, the doctor I ended up with was a bad-tempered young man who had no patience with a nurse who couldn't stay on her feet.'

'What a brute,' said Alice. 'From what Dr McKendrick said, many people faint first time, and you'd only just disembarked from a ship.'

'That's as may be, but Dr John Lampeter didn't have time for any of that, not back then — there was a war on.'

'I hope you never had to work with him again.'

Alice saw a slight stiffening of Ada's body, as if something had tightened inside her.

'Well, I had no choice. He was at the hospital where I was working . . . but, do you know what, he turned out to be a very different sort of man after all,' said Ada, plunging her cloth into water and wringing it out with vigour.

By the tone of Ada's voice and the way that she'd stiffened when she'd been talking about this Dr Lampeter, Alice was fairly sure that poor Dr McKendrick didn't stand a chance with Miss Houston. What a shame.

Ada cleared her throat, seeming desperate now to change the subject. 'Have you heard anything at all from that young man of yours?'

Alice shook her head. 'Jamie, nah, that's all over anyway,' she said, turning to check that the door was still closed and they couldn't be

109

overheard. 'All that matters to me now is Victoria,' she whispered. 'And doing this work, here at the Infirmary, so that I can complete my training.'

'Good way of thinking,' said Miss Houston. 'A wise woman, an experienced nurse called Mary Seacole who I also worked with in the Crimea, once told me that there is no better work than nursing. And for me, that has always been the case. There is nothing in this world that I would rather be doing. And for someone like me, growing up near the docks in Liverpool, with my background, I would never have thought that I could have a job like this.'

'Did you never want to marry?'

'Well, no, it just wasn't . . . it was complicated. I may tell you one day, Alice. I think you and I have a great deal in common. But suffice to say, for now, that this is the best life for me, here at the hospital. And I am looking forward to working with many more nurses like you and Maud. And I believe your other friend, Eddy, Nurse Pacey, is doing very good work out on the district: I hear she's something of a marvel.'

'She is that, all right,' said Alice, smiling.

'All finished in here?' called Sister Law, opening the door with some vigour and scowling into the room.

'Yes, Sister,' replied Alice and Ada together, both of them starting to giggle as soon as the door swung to.

7

'A woman with a healthy, active tone
of mind, plenty of work in her, and
some enthusiasm, who makes the best
of everything, and, above all, does not
think herself better than other people
because she is a 'Nightingale Nurse',
that is the woman we want.'

Florence Nightingale

As Alice walked to work the next morning, she
felt different. It did help that Victoria had slept
through the night and that she'd been happier
left with Marie that morning. But there was
something else — she felt a little less heavy
somehow. The pangs that she'd had to endure
whilst she walked down the alley the two
previous mornings seemed to have started to
lessen. If she hadn't got Marie in the house to
look after her baby, she had no idea how she
would be managing. She felt sorry for the
working women of the world who were forced to
leave their children, packed in with many others,
at the home of a baby minder. She was so lucky
to have Marie, it was like leaving Victoria with
family. Better than family, she thought grimly,
thinking about what reception she would have
got if she'd taken her baby home.

So, this morning she felt calmer, her step was
lighter, and as she turned to glance back down

the alley, there was Hugo, trotting along behind her. She stopped briefly to give him a stroke then tried to shoo him back to the house, but today, he seemed to have plans of his own as he skipped past her, heading for Lime Street.

Alice stepped out on to the street, into the bustle of early risers going to work. Today, for the first time, she didn't just need to go to work, she felt like she *wanted* to go to work. She knew that even Sister Law's scowl couldn't unsettle her: she was Alice and she was happy to be back at work.

The morning's work was busy, as usual, but Alice was increasingly familiar with the routine and more adept with many of the tasks than she'd ever been first time round. She was content with her work. That was until she was given instruction to team up with Nurse Langtry. Alice had started to get used to Millicent's style of work, and now that she had got back into the work herself, she could take the lead. So it was all manageable, until Millicent turned to her with the semblance of a smile and said, 'I saw Nancy last evening, she told me to tell you that she sends her best wishes to you and the baby. She hopes you don't run into any difficulties at work this time round.'

Alice couldn't speak. She stared at Millicent, feeling her face starting to burn, not with shame, but with rage. Pure rage. She couldn't believe that Nancy Sellers had found a way of getting to her, even though she had left the hospital as soon as she'd completed her training.

She was on the verge of spitting out her rage,

straight into Millicent's face, when she remembered Maud's words, something she'd said many times: *don't react, don't let Nancy see that she's getting to you.*

Thank you, Maud, thought Alice, taking a deep breath, before forcing herself to smile. 'Oh, that's nice. Please tell Nancy that I send my thoughts to her as well . . . '

Fortunately, because Millicent was so slow with everything, she didn't even seem to notice Alice's red face and gritted teeth. She just smiled and said, 'I will tell her.'

'What is dear Nancy doing now?' asked Alice, using the exchange to glean as much information as she could.

'Oh, she's a private nurse, in a very good part of town. Quite exclusive. She's caring for a gentlewoman who, poor thing, has a painful and chronic condition.'

'Good for her,' said Alice through her gritted teeth, thinking straight away, poor woman indeed, having a nurse who's also painful and chronic.

She made herself smile; she was getting better at this. 'Well now, Millicent, we can't be gossiping all day. Do you want to get on and see to that man in bed five, the one who needs a mustard poultice, and I'll go down the other end and make sure they're all sorted. We need to make sure that everything is in order for Sister, don't we?'

'Yes, we do,' said Millicent, duly trotting off towards the sluice. Alice had no idea why: the poultices weren't in there. What was she doing?

Thankfully, Alice managed to find enough work at the opposite end of the ward and Sister Law was happy to direct Millicent at the other. It made Alice think of last year, when she and Maud were trying to keep out of the way of Nancy. She was back in the same situation, although of course Millicent was just an empty vessel that Nancy saw fit to use. There was no malice in her at all; she had just repeated what Nancy had told her.

And even if Millicent repeated it to others, what could Nancy actually achieve, given that Miss Houston *andMiss* Merryweather both knew that she had a child? In that moment, Alice knew, it was just meant for her, to unsettle her, to let her know that, even though she was no longer working at the Infirmary, Nancy could twitch upon a thread and make Alice feel uncomfortable.

Later that day, Alice was called to attend the man they'd taken to theatre as an emergency the day before, the amputated arm. He still wasn't improving and he'd been a bit restless in bed, moving his head from side to side and muttering.

'Let's give him a small dose of laudanum,' said Sister Law. 'The pain will be acute. Sadly, things don't look good for the poor man, but the last thing we want is for him to suffer even more. And we don't even know his name . . . '

In that moment, Alice could clearly see the care that Sister had for her patients; it shone through the stern face that she showed to the world. This wouldn't do: she was starting to warm to Sister Law. Who'd have thought that would ever happen?

'It's quiet enough on the ward now, Nurse Sampson,' said Sister after she'd administered the laudanum. 'You sit by him, make sure he stays calm, and it's visiting soon. Maybe he'll get someone to see him and we can find something out about him.'

So Alice found a stool and sat by the bed. It made her feel sad to see the man's one arm resting on the sheet. She made sure to sit at the left side of his bed, so that she could hold his hand. The man was restless for a few more minutes after the drops and he was muttering some jumbled words, but nothing that Alice could make out. She held on to his hand and spoke softly to him until he settled. Then she sat steadfastly by the bed, thinking her own thoughts and making up stories about who the mystery patient — a very ordinary-looking middle-aged man — might actually be.

'How is our patient today, Nurse Sampson?' said Dr McKendrick, appearing at the other side of the bed.

'Much the same,' replied Alice. 'But he was restless earlier; Sister thought he might need a dose of laudanum. He seems settled now.'

'Sister was probably right,' said McKendrick, leaning over the bed to look at the man's face more closely.

'We haven't even got a name for him,' said Alice. 'That's another reason Sister wanted me to sit here. It's visiting soon, she wanted to make sure that no one came in without us seeing.'

115

'Mmm, good thinking,' murmured McKendrick, opening the man's eyelids one by one. 'Well, his pupils are reacting to light, so still some sign of life there, but he is very pale, isn't he? He must have lost a great deal of blood. Is the stump satisfactory? No sign of suppuration?'

'No, it looks fine. I helped dress it this morning and there is some redness but no discharge from the wound. And Mr Jones asked Sister to bring out the mercury thermometer and take his temperature.'

'Oh, the new device — did it work? Has he got a fever?'

'No fever . . . and, as Sister said, we could have found that out by laying a hand on his forehead, not messing about with some new-fangled device.'

McKendrick laughed out loud.

'Good point, Sister Law, very good point. Well, let me know if there's any change, will you? Somehow it seems worse, doesn't it, that we don't even know his name. I suppose we are his family now.'

'True,' said Alice, looking back to the man who was almost as white as the sheet on the bed, and then reaching out to take hold of his hand again.

She was still sitting by the bed as the visitors came on to the ward. It felt sad, that no one was there to see her patient. She saw the smiles on the faces of those men who had visitors, it seemed to make all the difference. And although her patient was unconscious, who knows, if a familiar voice spoke to him, he might start to

116

rouse up; it might really help him.

Maybe he simply doesn't have any family, she thought, looking back down to the man on the bed. But surely somebody must know him? She could see by the calluses on his hand that he'd had some kind of occupation. Something that involved lifting, maybe, although his hand was clean, no ingrained dirt around his fingernails. What could his job be? And why would an ordinary working man get stabbed and left outside a hospital? It niggled her, there seemed something not right about it. She'd overheard Michael and Stephen talking about him, and they seemed convinced that he'd been left by the cornermen. They were sure that he was involved in some kind of illegal activity. But Michael, in particular, was famous for his stories, so no one really knew.

Alice looked up again, and this time, she saw a broad-shouldered man wearing a thigh-length black jacket walking in her direction. Instantly she knew him. She definitely knew him, but she couldn't quite place him. Then, when she saw the way that he was walking, his measured stride down the ward, seeming like he owned the ground he walked on, she knew that she had seen him before, just the once. Although she hadn't even seen his face that day, she knew that he was the man who had rescued her from the cornermen, the morning of Maud's wedding. Not wanting to stare and needing to collect her thoughts, Alice looked back down to her patient. But when she saw a shadow fall over the white sheet of the bed, and she heard him draw in a sharp breath when he saw the amputation, she knew that the man had come to see her patient. He was standing by the bed.

She looked up, and her heart jumped.

The man had removed his hat, and he stood looking straight at her, his gaze calm. His eyes were dark, almost black; and they matched his hair, which was swept back from his forehead. He seemed to be waiting for something, biding his time, and for a few moments all Alice could do was stare back at him.

'Do you know this man?' she said at last, breaking the spell.

'Yes, I do,' he said, offering no more.

'Oh, that's good. We need a name, can you tell us?'

'I can — this man is Ray Lloyd.'

'Ray Lloyd,' repeated Alice, looking back down at the man in the bed. 'Do you know what happened to him?' she asked, meeting the man's dark eyes again with her own.

'Not really . . . All I heard was that he'd been found in a pool of blood and brought here, to the hospital,' he said, his voice forlorn.

'Can you tell me anything else about him?' she asked, looking him straight in the eye and starting to feel hot beneath her starched cap.

'He's worked for me for many years, a fine man. He turned up on the docks about ten years ago looking for work, and I took him on. He has no family; we, the people in my business, we are his family . . . I'm very sorry to see him in this state. He's always been such a strong man and a good worker.' As he spoke, Alice saw his head start to bow. He truly was sorry, she thought.

'What kind of work do you do?' she asked gently.

'I suppose you could say that we work in the import trade,' he said as he leant across the bed to look more closely at his friend, holding his hat in one hand and resting his other hand lightly on Ray's chest. Alice caught a whiff of cologne and noticed how well trimmed his black beard was. He was also wearing a gold brocade waistcoat with perfect buttons. He must do well from his import business, she thought, very well indeed, to be able to afford clothes like that.

Straightening up, the man replaced his hat and then fished in his pocket before handing Alice a small card. 'I'll be back in to see him tomorrow, but if anything happens before then you can find me, or someone who knows me, at my business address. Please send word.'

'Thank you,' said Alice, taking the card and noting his well-shaped fingers as she did so.

'Till tomorrow, Nurse . . . '

'Sampson,' she said, 'Alice Sampson.'

'Nurse Alice,' he said, with a smile. 'I hope that you are fully recovered from the incident with the cornermen the other week. I trust no harm came to the baby.'

Alice turned a deep pink, instantly worrying that someone might overhear, but at the same time, his words seemed like a connection, a personal thing, something just between him and her.

'Everything is fine,' she stammered. 'How did you recognize me?'

'The colour of your hair, the shape of your face, and your lovely blue eyes, of course,' he said. 'I hope to see you again tomorrow, Nurse Alice.'

He certainly wouldn't have seen the colour of my eyes from that distance, she thought; he's a flatterer, definitely that type. All the same, as she watched him go, seeing him walk back up the ward in his black jacket, it felt like fate had brought him to her.

She saw Michael and Stephen with their stretcher both turn their heads to stare at the man as he walked by. He seemed to make an impression on everyone.

They were straight down the ward. 'Do you know who that is?' said Michael.

'Yes, he's this man's employer.'

'No, do you really know who he is?' said Michael, his eyes shining with excitement.

'I don't know what you mean,' said Alice, puzzled.

'That's Roderick Morgan, *the* Roderick Morgan, he owns an import business. He came from nowhere, off the streets of Liverpool, and now look at him. Some say he's got the biggest part of his money through smuggling, though,' said Michael, with a glint in his eye.

Alice laughed.

'No, really, I mean, proper smuggling, right under the noses of the police,' he said, with a grin.

'Really?' said Alice quietly.

'Really,' said Michael, still grinning.

'Mr Delaney,' shouted Sister down the ward, 'I

can see you're enjoying passing the time of day, but we do need to move this patient . . . '

I'd best give Sister Law all the detail, Alice thought, glancing once more to her patient and then getting up from her seat and following behind Michael.

'So, he's Ray Lloyd,' said Sister, saying the name slowly and smiling to herself, as Alice stood nodding. 'It is so important to have someone's name, so important. Thank you for that, Nurse Sampson.'

'Oh, and another thing,' said Alice. 'The man who came to see him, his employer, Roderick Morgan, he left this card with his address, and he said to send word if there's any change in Mr Lloyd's condition before he next visits him.'

'Roderick Morgan,' mused Sister, 'I seem to know that name.'

'I think he's in the import trade,' said Alice, feeling her cheeks starting to burn.

'Oh, you do, do you, Nurse Sampson,' said Sister, rapidly back to her usual self. 'Well, you keep your thoughts away from the male visitors and solely on the patients from now on.'

'Of course,' said Alice, knowing that, even though Sister Law didn't mean it that way, it was nevertheless very sound advice for a woman in her situation. She had, however, taken the precaution of memorizing the address on that card before handing it over.

8

'Night Nurses. In my restless nights
my thoughts turn to you incessantly by
the bedsides of restless and suffering
Patients . . . '
Florence Nightingale

Being back out in the world of work was starting
to feel exhilarating. As hard as it remained to
hand Victoria over to Marie, Alice knew that she
was getting better at it each day. As much as she
adored her daughter and everything that she did
was for her, Alice was more able to remember
now that there was a whole other world outside
that door. She was re-engaging with that world
and finding, maybe because she'd been forced to
remove herself from it, that it was all the more
bright and interesting and full of promise, than
ever before.

Walking out that morning, with the cat
trotting behind her, having the privilege of
leaving Victoria with a woman who not only
loved her like her own, but who knew how to
contend with her — play times, fractious moods,
and her crying — Alice felt content, at last, and
excited about the day ahead.

On the ward, however, there had been a
change of plan. One of the night nurses had gone
off sick with a fever. The ward was in disarray
and Sister Law had been told that no

replacement could be found for the coming night.

'You'll have to do it, Nurse Sampson,' she said, looking directly at Alice, who knew by the expression on Sister's face that she would have no choice.

'We don't usually ask probationers to cover the night shifts, but needs must, and I can't ask either of these two, 'wet behind the ears',' she said, pointing at the two new probationers. 'Or . . . ' Alice followed her line of gaze and saw Millicent folding a towel. 'And you know the ward, you've got some nous about you, and you're almost at the end of your training. You'll have to do it.'

Alice nodded, thinking it through. She could go back to Stella's directly, help out this morning, get some sleep in the afternoon, feed Victoria to the brim, then out for the night shift. Marie was always around in the kitchen at night and Alice would give her a bit extra when she got paid for covering the night shift as well. Yes, it could work as long as Marie didn't mind.

The only regret she had, instantly, was that she wouldn't be around for visiting time. Ray Lloyd was still holding his own, there'd been no further change, so Mr Morgan would be visiting again. Well, Alice, it's fate playing a hand, she thought, as she made her way off the ward. There is no way that getting involved with a man like that, or any man for that matter, is a good idea. No way at all.

Nevertheless, she continued to think of Mr Morgan's dark eyes and she could smell his cologne, all the way home.

123

Initially, night duty didn't feel any different from days. Sister Law was still around at the start of the shift, fussing over the detail of the patients with Night Sister. The men on the ward, apart from the poorlies, were all awake and ready for their evening beverage. Much the same.

Once Sister Law had said her goodnights, though, and the ward began to darken as some of the patients fell asleep, that's when the world of the hospital became a very different place.

For a start, you could hardly see a hand in front of your face. There were some oil lamps standing on the table, and lanterns and candles to use, but the ward was so dark. And there were only two staff, herself and the night sister, with a night superintendent on call. When Sister was busy doing her rounds, Alice was expected to do everything else and see to all the patients who were calling out. Until the night shift Alice had thought that the days were exhausting, but this was a whole different thing.

The night sister, Grace Tweedy, was a very quiet woman; Alice had heard a rumour that she'd once been a nun. That was probably true, at least, thought Alice as she knelt to say a prayer with her before the night's work began. Alice had to help her up — she was a fair age and her knees were bad. No wonder, thought Alice, all that kneeling and praying on hard ward floors.

'You should use a cushion, Sister,' she said.

'I need to feel the hardness of the ward, I need to be connected to it,' said Sister Tweedy.

'Even so,' said Alice. 'It can't be good for you, not at your age.'

Sister grasped Alice's hand. 'What a lovely girl you are,' she said, 'thinking of me like that.' Then she was off, limping down the ward, doing her rounds, with straggles of grey hair escaping from under her cap.

'Nurse, Nurse,' called a patient from the far corner. 'I need a urinal, quick, quick.'

Alice grabbed one out of the sluice and went as fast as she could, but in the dark she kept bumping into things and then lost sight of the patient momentarily. She only just got there in time. Thank goodness for that, or she'd have had the whole bed to change as well.

There was no rest at all on nights. Alice was constantly answering patients' calling out and then helping Sister Tweedy turn the poorly patients in bed, shifting their position so that they wouldn't develop bed sores.

When they came to Ray Lloyd's bed, Sister lowered her voice. 'I think we might have to send for his family,' she said. 'I can tell by his breathing, I don't think he's going to last the night.'

Alice felt her heart miss a beat. She'd been sure that fate had played a hand and moved her on to nights, so that she could keep safely out of temptation's way by not seeing Mr Morgan. But now it seemed he would almost certainly be coming to the ward whilst she was on duty.

'Can you hear that? There's a slight rasp in his breath, and the breaths are shallow and more spaced out.'

Alice stood with Sister and they listened together. She's right, thought Alice, his breathing is different.

125

'Now help me turn him, and then we'll see if there's any change.'

The effort of turning in bed made poor Ray Lloyd worse. His breathing was gurgling now, rather than rasping. It was clear that the man was entering his final phase of life.

Alice felt so sad for him, just from the little she knew: he'd no family, who knows what life he'd had, and clearly he'd been attacked by someone. Michael had told her that he'd heard the police weren't interested. They'd said there was no evidence, but he'd thought it was because they knew that some gang was involved and they'd been paid off. Either that, thought Alice, or they were too busy rounding up working women off the streets.

It felt like no one cared. Well, maybe there is one person, thought Alice, and it won't be long before he arrives. Sister had the card, and she'd just been to inform the night superintendent of a change in Mr Lloyd's condition. When she came back, she told Alice that Mr Morgan had been sent for. Alice kept herself busy, but she couldn't do anything without also listening for the sound of his leather-soled shoe as he measured his stride down the ward. She was frustrated with herself and even more frustrated with Sister when she told her to go and sit with Mr Lloyd; she could tell by his breathing that he was coming very close to the end.

'I've already said a prayer for him, and when the Reverend Seed has finished on Male Medical he'll be in here, and he can see the man before he departs this life,' said Sister. 'Now you go and sit with him, so that he isn't alone. We never leave the dying on their own, unless there is no choice, especially if they are without family. And a surprising number of people in this city are without family.'

Of course I'll sit with him, thought Alice. It's the least I can do.

And she felt that it was exactly the right thing to do. In the hush of the night, with the glow of the candles and the lamps around them, in that space between daylight, it seemed like the most natural time for Ray Lloyd to die.

Alice sat with him, gently sponging his forehead with the cloth that Sister had left by the man's bed. Then she held his hand. She was perfectly at peace. Until she heard the sound of a leather-soled shoe on the hard ward floor and she saw the dark, unmistakeable shape of a man coming towards the bed.

Instantly her heart was racing; she was almost holding her breath as the man approached. Then his face loomed out of the darkness, and she could see, instantly, that it wasn't him: it was the pale face of Reverend Seed.

'Hello there, Nurse,' he said, his voice mournful. Alice was taken aback not to see Mr Morgan but instantly glad that the Reverend had come to say prayers for her patient. She felt suddenly overwhelmed and she could feel a sob building in her chest. She got up from the bedside quickly and managed to say, 'I'll leave you to say the prayers, Reverend,' before heading off down the ward and diving into the sluice.

All of the pent-up sorrow for her patient, and

127

the excitement at the prospect of his visitor, burst out of her, in a fit of sobbing. She grabbed a clean towel off the shelf and desperately tried to muffle it. But out it came, and even when she buried her face in the towel and desperately tried to think of happy things, like her daughter's smiling face, she couldn't take it back, it continued to erupt from her body. Her chest was heaving, starting to feel sore, and tears were streaming down her face as she stood in the sluice. When the door clicked open to show the shape of Sister Tweedy, the shock of it, at last, allowed Alice to get back some control. She couldn't stop it completely, but she managed to rapidly convert it into a coughing fit, using the towel to muffle the sound. 'Sorry, Sister,' she croaked, desperately holding back the tears. Sister Tweedy stepped forward and placed a solicitous hand on Alice's arm. Good job I'm on nights, thought Alice; Sister Law would never have stood for this. And even if I was choking to death with a cough, she'd still have told me off, and marched me out of here.

'Oh dear,' said Sister Tweedy, still not cottoning on in the slightest. 'Are you all right, Nurse Sampson, shall I get you a drink of water?'

'No, no, Sister, I'm absolutely fine,' whispered Alice, her voice genuinely hoarse. 'Has the Reverend finished with Mr Lloyd?'

'Yes, I think so,' said Sister. 'Are you able to go back and sit with him again?'

'Of course,' said Alice, wiping the towel around her face to dry the tears, before heading back to her patient and walking slap bang into the solid form of someone standing at the bottom of the bed.

'Sorry, Reverend,' sniffed Alice, 'I thought you'd gone.'

'He has,' said a voice that Alice instantly recognized: Roderick Morgan.

'Sorry, Mr Morgan,' she said, her voice still husky and struggling to keep an even tone. She could see his profile in the semi-darkness, clear-cut against the moonlight coming in through the ward window. He was taller than the Reverend Seed, of course it was him. Alice had a strange ache in the pit of her stomach, her heart was beating like a drum in her chest, and she was glad of the darkness, so he couldn't see the redness of her cheeks.

'I was just coming back to sit with Mr Lloyd, but now that you're here, do you want to sit with him, there, on the stool next to the bed?'

'Thank you,' said Mr Morgan, his voice quiet.

Alice saw him sit and grasp Ray's hand; it shocked her to see the obvious strength of feeling in that one action. They must have been close, she thought, seeing straight away the sadness in the man's demeanour. She was perfectly calm now, able to distance herself and get on with her job. She went straight to Mr Morgan and put a reassuring hand on his shoulder. He turned to her and tried to smile.

'Thank you, Nurse Alice,' he said, 'I'm glad that you seem to be working nights as well as days.'

'I am this week,' she said. 'I'll be on night duty

129

until they can find a replacement night nurse.'

'I see,' he said, turning back to his friend. 'At least he doesn't seem to have any pain, at least there's that,' he murmured. 'I've seen too many die in pain . . . '

Then he fell silent, lost in his own thoughts.

'We'll look after him,' Alice said softly.

'I know you will,' he murmured, turning to smile at her.

'I'm just going to check on the other patients. Shout out if you need anything,' she said. 'I'll hear you.'

'I will, Nurse Alice,' he said, reaching up to pat her hand where it rested on his shoulder.

'And Alice,' he said, as she turned to walk away, 'please call me Morgan, no one uses Roderick.'

'Morgan it is,' she said, starting to feel the beating of her heart again with the sound of his name in her mouth.

Morgan stayed by his friend until the early hours of the morning; he wouldn't take any rest or accept any refreshment. He just sat, lost in thought. Just as the morning light was starting to show through the windows of the ward, Ray Lloyd took his final breath. Alice heard Morgan call and she was there instantly, her hand on the man's shoulder as he sat with his head bowed, shedding tears.

When Sister Tweedy came she said another prayer and then told Mr Morgan to make his way home; they would see to Mr Lloyd and make sure that he was washed and laid out in the proper way.

'A very nice man,' said Sister as Morgan made his way slowly down the ward. 'A great deal of respect for his friend — not many will sit all night. He must be a good man.'

As Alice walked home that morning, she felt tired but also buzzing with energy, and a bit light-headed. She wanted to put it down to having been up all night, busy on the ward, her first night shift, and, yes, a good part of it was that. But it wasn't just that, she knew it wasn't. And it seemed as though fate had intervened yet again, and made sure that she and Roderick Morgan had met once more. To Alice, as she walked back through the early morning streets, it felt like they were on a collision course. She wanted, she needed, for her daughter's sake if nothing else, to steer away. But she knew, there and then, that the way she was drawn to Morgan was instinctive. There was a connection that had started to form on the morning of Maud's wedding when he'd rescued her from the cornermen. He intrigued her, and she knew that her attempts to steer clear were futile. If fate intervened and she saw him again she would have no choice but to follow her instinct.

9

' . . . when the night watch begins at
nine, the wards are dark, except the
Nurse's candle. A spare candle,
unlighted, is always at hand.'
Florence Nightingale

The next day brought another night shift for
Alice and she'd hardly slept. Her mind and body
were completely thrown out. The buzzing
excitement that she'd had going home that
morning had been fuelled by the delight of
seeing Victoria, fresh awake from a night's sleep.
Sitting with her, holding her, smelling her hair,
whilst Marie worked around them, making
some food, tidying the kitchen. There sat Alice
with her daughter on her knee, still with
thoughts of the work she'd done on the ward, of
Sister Tweedy, poor Ray Lloyd, and, of course,
Roderick Morgan, dancing in her head.

The bright daylight was shining through every
window, and although she knew that she needed
to sleep, and Marie was urging her to, her body
wouldn't let her. Only by late afternoon did she
start to feel some exhaustion seeping through
into her heightened state and she was,
eventually, forced to lie down and take some
rest. She was in a dead sleep until two hours
later she sat up sharply, her heart pounding, the
sound of Victoria's cry having pierced her sleep.

Once she was awake, there was no chance of any more rest. She got up, feeling sick and groggy, her head a heavy weight on her shoulders.

Alice still felt groggy as she walked to work. She had no idea how the night nurses managed this day after day. I suppose they just get used to it, she thought, as she wove through the people out on the street, making their way home, or staggering out of the pubs. The world was topsyturvy all right.

Arriving in plenty of time, Alice was heading up the ward when she saw Millicent coming the other way, arm in arm with another woman, someone not in uniform. It was Nancy.

It hit Alice, as always, in the pit of her stomach, when she saw Nancy. As much as she tried not to let her get to her, she still hadn't got full control over it. She knew that she would definitely be able to hold her own against Nancy now, she wouldn't be bossed about by her, but the legacy of that time on the ward, when she was sickly and anxious, still lived with her. Maybe it always would.

Anyway, Alice held her breath and kept walking as Nancy and Millicent passed her on the other side of the ward. Luckily, they didn't seem to have seen her. Glancing back, she was relieved to see that they had almost reached the door. Then Nancy looked back over her shoulder and met Alice's gaze. And she leant in to whisper something in Millicent's ear, still keeping her eyes on Alice before turning away. Alice saw Millicent giggle and then she too glanced back, before the two of them exited the ward, arm in arm.

Instantly Alice was annoyed with herself. She couldn't believe she'd fallen for Nancy's tricks yet again. And seeing her face, with that triumphant look in her eyes, was infuriating. Alice physically shook herself as she walked up the ward, in an attempt to rid herself of the crawling feeling at the back of her neck that Nancy's gaze had left with her. She could still see her face, and she was desperate to free herself of it. Then something struck her: there had been something different about Nancy. She didn't look quite the same, and now Alice was actively trying to recall every detail. She was in her 'going out' clothes, maybe it was that. But no, there was something else as well; her face was a bit flushed, a bit rounder in shape. Just being able to note that difference really helped Alice to distance herself. It made the Nancy that had just walked down the ward not the one that she'd been overpowered by last year. It made Alice remember that Nancy didn't work at the Infirmary now, she was working out in the city, miles away. Alice hoped that the work of nursing a private patient was really suiting her, and that she would never decide to come back to the Infirmary.

'Nurse Sampson,' shouted Sister Law. 'Stop dawdling and get up here.'

Alice almost laughed out loud. It felt a relief to be harangued by Sister Law, to be snapped back into reality. Despite her exhaustion, she knew in that moment that she was really looking forward to her second night shift with Sister Tweedy.

'We've just had a visit from one of your set,

134

Nurse Sellers,' said Sister Law, when Alice reached the top of the ward. 'Do you remember her?'

'Yes, of course,' said Alice calmly, glad that she'd seen Nancy leaving the ward, and that she'd had a chance to deal with her feelings about the woman before Sister brought her up. 'I'll never forget Nurse Sellers.'

'Well, I just wondered if you remembered anything at all from last year. You were always so distracted, so pale and sickly looking, you seemed like you had a lot on your mind,' said Sister Law, her eyes bright and seeking information.

Alice stood her ground; she didn't blush or try to stammer a response. She simply stood, silently holding Sister's gaze.

'You're different now,' mused Sister, shifting her gaze down the ward, before fixing on Alice again with narrowed eyes. 'I can truly see the makings of a nurse, a good nurse at that . . . but you're still pale and your cap is limp, always limp. So don't get above yourself, Nurse Sampson. Even though Sister Tweedy was very pleased with your work last night and she seems to worship the ground you walk on. Do not get above yourself. You still have a great deal to learn and a great deal of work to do. Understand?'

'Yes, Sister,' said Alice, with a straight face, although inside she was grinning from ear to ear.

Alice was prepared tonight. She made sure that she grabbed a pillow off a spare bed to put down on the floor for Sister Tweedy as she knelt for the prayer.

'That does feel better, Nurse Sampson,' she said as Alice helped her up. 'I will try to

135

remember to use it in future. I will be sorry to lose you from the night watch; I think you'll be back on days tomorrow. The night superintendent will be along to the ward later to confirm, but it seems they might have a new night nurse.'

Alice couldn't help but feel a bit disappointed — she was starting to feel at home in the nighttime world — but she did need to complete her training, and there was more experience to be had on days.

On this, her second night, Alice was more prepared for the dark. She made sure to carry a candle with her and take tasks over to the table in the middle of the ward where the oil lamps stood. She was mainly seeing to patients as they called out, while they were trying to settle to sleep. She was busy and didn't have any time to think about how very tired she felt. Passing the bed that had been Ray Lloyd's, she felt a shiver go through her body as she thought about him, the poor man who she had never known, who had died there last night. And the man who had sat beside him — she had been thinking about him all day, she couldn't get him out of her head. 'Well, Alice,' she muttered to herself with mock sternness, 'unless you need rescuing from the cornermen again, you won't be seeing him any time soon, so you might as well forget it.'

The patient in the bed now, a Mr Knox, had been to theatre that day. Mr Jones had removed a large lump from his chest wall, some kind of growth, Sister Law had said. They were hopeful that now the man had come through the operation things would go well for him. But

Sister Law said the growth looked suspicious; it was probably cancer.

Alice couldn't help but feel for the man, who had no inkling of Sister Law's thoughts about his situation. She'd told them as she gave the night report that Mr Knox was a sailor, a good-natured sort who'd worked in ships his whole life. He'd been homeward-bound from Australia, and all that time, the lump had been growing. He hadn't said a word to anyone about it on the outward journey, he didn't want to worry the rest of the crew, but by the time they were heading home, he was struggling to hide it and it was interfering with his work. The ship's surgeon had taken one look, shaken his head, and said he daren't touch it, not out there in the middle of the ocean. Mr Knox had told Sister Law that he'd been desperate to get back to Liverpool. He'd told her that coming home was the slowest voyage of his whole life.

Alice could see that the man was still sleeping off the chloroform; she would go to him later and check the dressing, make sure there was no seepage of blood. And she would see if he could take a sip of water.

'Nurse, Nurse, I need a urinal,' shouted the man from the corner of the ward who she had attended last night. But this time she already had one in her hand. After stumbling about in the dim light last night, she'd made sure to be better prepared.

'Coming, Mr Nugent,' she called, only bumping into one other bed before she got to him in plenty of time.

By the time all the patients were settled and

Sister Tweedy's rounds were done, Alice was beginning to feel a bit heavy in her body and fuzzy in the head. She'd started out the night a bit groggy but still buzzing, and she'd been ready and able to match the level of activity on the ward. She wasn't sure now what was happening to her body, but she had a tingly feeling in her limbs, and she was starting to feel a bit numb.

'I'm just going to check on Mr Knox,' she told Sister Tweedy, her voice a little slurry.

'Yes, Nurse Sampson, good idea. I was going there myself but I need to get some laudanum for Mr Nugent. Let me know if he needs anything for his pain, will you? When he comes round from the chloroform, he might be sickly and he probably won't know where he is. You sit with him, make sure he's all right. I left a flask of brandy by his bed earlier — give him some of that if he wakes up.'

'Yes, Sister,' said Alice, already walking towards Mr Knox's bed.

The man was still flat out and she didn't want to disturb him, so she set her candle down at the side of his bed and then gently turned down the sheet to look at his dressing. That must have been quite some lump, thought Alice, seeing the size of the dressing, secured by a bandage around his torso. I hope it heals up for you, Mr Knox, I hope you do well, she said in her head, as she pulled the sheet back over him.

The stool was still by the bed from the night before, so Alice sat on it, right there where Morgan had kept vigil for his friend. There she was, watching over her new patient, but also thinking about *him* again, and starting to feel a tickle of excitement in the pit of her stomach. How ridiculous, she thought, scanning every detail of her patient's face, trying to dislodge any thought of Morgan with almost physical effort.

She could tell, even though he was sleeping, that Mr Knox was indeed a good-natured sort. The lines on his face told her that he was someone who regularly smiled and laughed. Even as he lay asleep, he looked as if he had a smile on his face. His grizzled chin and his thinning grey hair, swept back from his forehead, matched what she knew: that he was a man in his sixties. His face reminded her of her father. She wondered if Mr Knox was a quietly spoken, deferent man, like Frederick Sampson. Somehow she didn't think so, seeing the arms that lay outside the sheet, covered in tattooed anchors, ships and, on one arm, an exotic bird. And on the other arm, the thin, fading line of someone's name, so ancient that it was illegible in the dim light. Probably some sweetheart from long ago, thought Alice, with a sigh, starting to feel sad for him and then yawning as she made every effort to fight off that fuzzy, heavy feeling that was creeping over her whole body.

Well, Mr Knox, she thought sleepily, I wish you well, I hope you have someone out there who loves you, and I hope you don't mind me sitting by you, keeping watch. I'll just rest my arms on the bed here next to you . . .

Alice had no idea what happened next; all she could think afterwards was that she must have blacked out from sheer exhaustion. What came seemed like a deafening noise that could wake the dead. So loud, or so it seemed to the sleeping Alice, that she shot up on her stool, nearly fell on the floor, and knocked her candle over, snuffing it clean out.

'Sleeping on night duty!' hissed a voice from nowhere.

'Sleeping on night duty,' insisted the voice again, after Alice had righted herself on the stool, desperately trying to make sense of where she was and what she was doing. She could not only feel the breath of the speaker but smell the tinge of brandy on it as well.

'We'll see about this!'

Alice was unable to speak — and what could she say? She had no idea what had happened. And now she could hear Mr Knox groaning in the bed. Although she was terrified by what had just happened, she was, most of all, sorry for any harm that it might have caused him.

She was on her feet now, her mouth dry and her heart pounding.

'Please, please,' she said, trying to focus through the dim light on the shape of the woman next to her. 'Don't make any more noise, I don't want any of the patients to be disturbed.'

'Any of the patients *disturbed*,' repeated the woman. '*Disturbed* . . . what about the neglect, the dereliction of duty?'

'But I — '

'No *buts*, Nurse. You have no say in this. I am the night superintendent, I can dismiss you now, on the spot. You are a disgrace to the uniform you wear.'

140

'Please, please, I need this job,' Alice almost sobbed, breathless now, as the reality of her situation began to dawn.

'You may need this job, but does this job, this very important job, need a thoughtless, incompetent nurse like you?'

'She isn't thoughtless,' piped a voice from the bed. 'She's a very good nurse.'

The superintendent immediately switched her gaze to Mr Knox, as he lay on his bed. She didn't seem to know what to say.

In that moment, Alice, her head still swimming, started to get the measure of the woman: she was tall, with broad shoulders, wearing a high, starched collar and a cap knotted tightly beneath her chin. Her mouth was set in a thin, straight line. She carried a lantern which she held up now to Alice's face.

'The patient speaks highly of you,' she said, 'that might be in your favour. However, I will have to confer with Sister Tweedy as to what our course of action will be. It might be possible for you to be given *one* more chance,' she said, implying that Alice made a habit of falling asleep at her patients' bedsides.

'Thank you, Sister,' breathed Alice.

'I am a superintendent!' snapped the woman. 'And I will be watching you . . . ' She shifted her gaze briefly to Mr Knox again, before stalking down the ward with her lamp.

Alice sat back down on the stool, her shoulders slumped.

'Jesus, Mary and Joseph,' said Mr Knox. 'She's more scary than any of the captains I've ever

141

worked with, and I've worked with some devils, I can tell you.'

'She is . . . terrifying,' said Alice, her voice sounding small. 'Thank you for speaking up for me, and you don't even know me or what sort of nurse I am.'

'That might be so, but I can spot unfair behaviour from a mile away. And I'm not havin' it, not on my ward.'

Alice had been right, the man was someone with a light heart. He was grinning at her now, making her feel so much better, even a little giddy.

'You pay that old biddy no mind,' he continued. 'If she comes after you again, you come straight to Tommy Knox, I'll sort her out.' Then he started laughing and coughing and then he was drawing up his knees in pain. 'Just as soon as I get this blasted bandage off and get back on my feet, that is,' he croaked.

Alice was straight up off the stool. 'Sister left some brandy by your bed. Here, have a swig of this,' she said, popping the cork out of the flask.

'Cheers,' said Tommy, grabbing the flask and taking a hefty swig. But this made him cough even more, and he was starting to cry out with pain.

'I'll find Sister straight away and get you some laudanum,' she said, all thought of whether the superintendent was still on the ward gone from her mind in that moment.

'Thanks . . . Nurse . . . best nurse on the ward,' he croaked, rolling on to his side, trying to get some ease.

Alice was now fully awake, sharp, and determined to get the medicine that her patient needed. Superintendent or no superintendent, she would be doing her duty for her patients.

10

'Streets are miserable places to walk
in during a great part of the year.
Nurses want and unconsciously
crave for fresh air . . . '
Florence Nightingale

Alice burst out on to the street the next morning,
glad to be leaving the hospital and eager to be
home with Victoria. She needed to leave behind
all the difficulties that she'd encountered with
the night superintendent and some of the sorrow
that she was feeling for her new patient, Tommy
Knox. Nevertheless, she knew that she'd be taking
some thoughts of Tommy home with her; she was
thinking of him already.

Even though Alice was completely wrung out
and dizzy with exhaustion, she made herself put
one foot in front of the other and make good
speed towards Lime Street. She managed to smile,
as always, at each and every individual who called
out, 'Good morning, Sister.' She could never risk
betraying any trace of not being a bona fide
district nurse: hers and Victoria's safety relied
upon it.

It seemed to take for ever to reach Lime
Street, and by the time that she did, she was too
tired to pay much attention to the world around
her. Therefore she didn't see the small group of
cornermen gathered near the railway station

until it was too late. Alice had no choice but to walk through them, but luckily for her, they were already involved with a well-dressed man who'd just descended from the train. Not for the first time, Alice wondered why the police didn't put their energies into ensuring public safety rather than driving working women like Lizzie off the street. As she was just about through the cornermen, she saw, out of the corner of her eye, one make a move in her direction. Immediately, her heart was racing. She needed to get back to her baby, not to be held up like this.

But all he did was smile, then doff his cap. 'Morning, Sister,' he said, grinning. Alice could have punched him for giving her such a scare, but she returned the smile, and went on her way as quickly as she could.

Reaching the alley at last, she began to slow her pace. As soon as she turned in, however, Hugo streaked past, his head down and his ears back. Alice had never seen him move so fast. Looking down the alley, she saw the reason straight away: there were police in uniform and one in plain clothes lining the alley, at least three of them.

Alice's heart missed a beat. Immediately she was back, closed in that carriage, struggling against them. She took a deep breath, needing to steady herself. Remember, you are a district nurse, you have just walked through the cornermen with no trouble. You can do this, you are on your way to treat a patient at that address, she repeated in her head. Pulling the nurse's cape more tightly around her and trying to look

145

confident, she straightened her back and walked down the alley.

She held her breath as she walked by, so close to them that she could hear the murmur of their conversation. One of the men who had bundled her into the carriage was there, standing with the rest. She made sure to turn her head away just a fraction as she passed him.

'Morning, Sister,' said the last in line, stepping in front of her. 'Sorry to enquire, but may I ask your business? It's just that we believe there to be a woman of ill repute hiding in one of these properties. I think a respectable woman like you would be best moving on to another location.'

Alice cleared her throat. 'Thank you, Constable,' she said, looking him straight in the eye. 'But I have no concerns whatsoever about visiting the properties in and adjacent to this alley. I have a very urgent case to attend, so can you please let me by.'

'Well now, Sister — '

'I have a letter here from Miss Mary Merryweather, superintendent at the Liverpool Royal Infirmary, giving me full permission to visit these properties,' said Alice, fishing in her pocket. 'I don't think Miss Merryweather will be very pleased when she hears that one of her district nurses has been impeded by the police . . . '

'No, of course not, no, I mean, yes, you go and see to your patient, Sister.'

Alice swept by, before she could be drawn into any further conversation and risk being recognized by the man in plain clothes. As she stood on the step, knocking on the door as if she was indeed a visitor to the house, she could feel her heart pounding in her chest and her knees were weak, and when the door was opened by Marie, she almost fell in.

'What's going on?' she whispered.

'It's Lizzie again,' Marie told her. 'She was out on Lime Street, talking to some of the cornermen, having a laugh, just being herself, you know what she's like. And she saw them coming for her, so she ran straight back here, as fast as she could. They didn't know which house; they've been knocking on doors saying they want to come in and search. But Stella is having none of it — she told them they couldn't come in without the proper papers. Anyway, Lizzie is long gone. She went straight out through the back gate and disappeared into the city, they'll never find her. But Stella's fighting mad and she says if they knock again, she's still not letting them in.'

'Is Victoria all right?'

'Slept through it all, and, as I say, nobody's coming in here.'

Going through into the kitchen, Alice went straight to the crib. In her exhausted state she had to fight back the tears when she saw her daughter's pale, sleeping face and the fingers of her tiny hand splayed out across the crib blanket. Victoria, her beautiful baby girl, sleeping through everything, yet so vulnerable, lying there in her crib. What if the police had broken through the door? What then?

She leant down to give her baby a gentle kiss on the cheek, feeling her warmth beneath her lips and smelling that special baby smell. Straightening up, she had to give herself a shake, to try and waken up. She needed to make sense of their situation, work out what she should do.

'Get your hat and cape off, Alice,' said Marie, already pouring a cup of tea. 'Stell will be down in a minute, you can talk to her about things.'

Alice did as she was told and then gratefully slid into a chair with a cup of Marie's best brewed tea in front of her. She took a sip and rested back, closing her eyes until she heard the sound of Stella coming into the kitchen.

'They're still picking women up from the streets,' Stella said. 'We know that, and since the Italian woman's place was closed down I've known we're at risk of that as well, but I don't think they're coming for us just yet.' She pulled out a chair and sat opposite with her thick, curly hair pulled back extra tight, and her sleeves rolled up. 'There haven't been any other places raided since the Italian woman's and we still have our clients from the police, and even that doctor from the hospital. I think we're safe for the time being.'

Alice gave a sigh of relief. She never thought she'd be grateful for Mr Fawcett being a visitor to the brothel, but now she was. She never wanted to see him here or at the hospital ever again, but she was grateful, at least, that his patronage meant that Stella had some influence out there in the city.

'The other thing is, we've got Ada and Miss Merryweather on our side,' Stella continued. 'And yesterday,' her face brightened, 'I was able to meet with Josephine Butler at last. And what a fine lady she is, too. We were invited into her drawing room to take tea and we had a very good conversation indeed. She goes around the country, giving lectures and speaking on behalf of us working women. In one city, she had to speak to a room full of men — no women or boys allowed. She said it felt strange, and her voice was quiet at first. But, as she stood in front of them, she thought, why not, I can say my piece as well as any man, and these women need my help.'

'What can she do, though, to stop this happening and make us safe?' Alice asked.

'She has influence because of her social standing,' Stella said, 'more influence than any of us working women, and they're organizing protest marches and all sorts. She thinks it could take years but she's determined to see it through, to stop women being picked up off the street and forced to be examined . . . It makes my blood boil, just thinking about it, especially after you were taken, Alice.'

'I'm all right,' said Alice, reaching out a hand to Stella. 'I'm not letting it get me down. In fact, it set me on a new path. Maybe I wouldn't have gone back to nursing without that — maybe I would have left it too long. And after last night — well, I won't go into the detail, but I had a tough time on the ward with a senior member of night staff. But it made me realize just how much it all means to me: helping the patients, doing the work and being able to earn my own money . . . '

'I must admit,' said Stella, 'when you came to see me, that first night with Maud, remember, when you were pregnant and not knowing what to do, I wasn't sure how you would cope with anything. You looked weary and you couldn't stop crying, and then, even when you came back here just before the baby was born, you were like a lost soul . . . '

Alice was nodding. She couldn't fully remember that time, even though it was only last year, but she did recognize herself back then in what Stella was saying.

'But now look at you,' said Stella, beaming at Alice and reaching a hand out to her across the table. 'You have blossomed, Alice, blossomed into a determined, strong woman. Having a baby can do that, for some. For others, it can make them a trembling heap. But you are remarkable, Alice.'

'I'm not sure that remarkable is the right word. Last night on the ward I was definitely a trembling heap, and right now, I am absolutely exhausted.'

'Yes, but the difference is, you can pick yourself up when you need to. Even I can be a trembling heap sometimes, I just let myself get on with it. I know I'll soon be right again. And I am. What I'm trying to say to you, Alice, is this: you have the world at your feet now, you can do this. And when you have your certificate you can get a place of your own, and pay for someone to look after the baby . . . '

Alice was nodding now, with tears welling up in her eyes. 'This is all thanks to you and Marie, for giving me the chance. If it hadn't been for you . . . and now look at me, I'm a trembling heap again.'

Marie put an arm around Alice's shoulders and gave her a squeeze. 'You get yourself to bed, Alice, you're just exhausted. I can look after the baby; you need to rest.'

'I'll be all right,' said Alice. 'And it's best if I stay awake now and sleep tonight. I'm back on the day shift again tomorrow.'

By the time Victoria was waking for her next feed, the women had been chatting and laughing so much that they'd almost forgotten the police were in the alley.

'I'll go and have a look,' said Stella. 'Tell 'em to go and sling their hook if they're still there.' But when she came back, she was smiling. 'They're gone.'

★   ★   ★

'Let me help you with that,' said Alice later that day, seeing Marie busy with the posser over a steaming tub of laundry.

'You go and have a sit down,' said Marie. 'You must be tired by now. I can do this and I'll see to the baby when she wakes up again.'

'Nonsense,' insisted Alice, taking the posser out of Marie's hands.

'All right then, you win,' smiled Marie, stretching her stiff back as she stepped away from the tub. 'This laundry work doesn't get any easier for a woman my age.'

Alice was soon done with the possing and then

151

she was pegging out the washing in the back yard. It was only when she sat down on the bench and rested her head against the brick wall of the house that she began to feel the creep of exhaustion again. She had thought to take some time to read her book — the adventures of Cathy and Heathcliff were waiting — but she was too tired for that. So she rested back and let her mind drift, as she listened to the slow flap of the wet sheets on the line.

Then she heard something else, a scuffling noise, and when she looked up, she saw one of the best pillowcases slowly disappearing from the washing line.

Alice was on her feet straight away, grabbing the pillowcase. Then she saw a girl with tousled hair at the other side of it, pulling with all her might.

'Oi,' shouted Alice. 'What d'ye think you're doing?'

The girl held on tight, so Alice let go, and the girl fell flat on her back on to the stone flags, the breath knocked out of her.

Looking down at the girl, Alice was immediately filled with concern. She was so thin, and covered in grime, her pale red hair dirty and matted in clumps; and now she was crying, the tears making clean white lines down her grubby face.

'Come on,' said Alice, her voice gentle now. 'Let's get you on your feet and then I'm going to find you something to eat.'

She hauled the girl up and helped her over to the bench. 'You're not in any trouble,' she said,

152

'and I want you to sit here till I get back with some food and a cup of tea.'

The girl nodded, still sniffling, and staring at Alice with big green eyes.

Pleased to see the girl still on the bench when she returned with the food, Alice felt an ache in her chest when she saw the look of hunger on her face. The girl was starving — on the streets of Liverpool, in this day and age.

'Why did you need our pillowcase?' Alice asked as the girl shoved bread and jam and cake into her mouth all at the same time.

'I needed to take it to the pots and rags stall and get a few pennies for some bread,' she said, as she chewed and swallowed. Alice had never seen anyone eat like that before; she had never seen anyone so hungry. 'My mam, she sends me out when we've no food. She gets sick sometimes and she can't work and she needs me to look after her.'

Alice felt deep sadness, like a pain in her chest. She couldn't imagine any woman not having enough money to feed her children. Imagine if she couldn't feed Victoria, if she had to send her out on the streets in years to come, just to get some bread for the table. It made her want to weep with sorrow for this girl and all the poor children on the streets of Liverpool. She knew that there were some charities that gave out food and suchlike, but there had to be a better way than this.

'You're doing a good job looking after your mam,' she said, gently reaching out a hand to smooth some of the tangles of dirty hair away

153

from the girl's face. She would have loved to get her over the dolly tub full of warm water and wash that hair with plenty of soap and some disinfectant. She could see how beautiful it was underneath the muck. It would be wonderful to see her crown of curly red hair, and to untangle it. It would be glorious. And with her green eyes, the girl was set to be a real beauty.

'What's your name?' asked Alice.

'I'm Sue Cassidy,' she said, with a hint of pride in her voice. 'And I'm ten years old.'

'Well, Sue Cassidy,' said Alice, 'I tell you what I'm going to do. I'm going to give you some money for food, and I want you to go straight back home with it. And if your mam has to send you out again, you come here to me first. I'm Alice, ask for me, or ask for Marie, she's my friend. I'll tell her about you. I'll make sure there's some money here for you if you need it.'

The girl stared at her. It seemed like she'd forgotten how to smile, but Alice saw that her eyes had started to shine, just a little.

As Alice went in to find the box where she'd put her first wages, she felt glad that she now had the means to help. If Sue Cassidy had turned up some weeks earlier she would have been really struggling. And though she only had just enough, after paying Marie, Alice felt this was a very good way of spending her first few shillings.

Seeing the girl's face as she counted out the coins into her hand, Alice knew that she was doing exactly the right thing. How could any woman, if she is a mother, and she has the means, turn her back on a child who needs help?

'Thanks, missus,' said Sue, putting the coins into her pocket straight away, and then bringing something back out. 'I want you to have this,' she said, 'it's my special find.'

'Very lovely,' said Alice, seeing a shiny piece of metal that had been cut into a circle, probably some attempt to make a counterfeit coin.

'You can have it,' said Sue, 'I want you to keep it.'

'Thank you,' said Alice, taking the special piece without hesitation.

Then Sue was fishing in her pocket again. 'And this one is even more special,' she said, opening her hand to reveal what looked like a heart-shaped earring, bright red in colour. It could be mistaken for a ruby, but Alice knew that you didn't find rubies on the streets of Liverpool. And she'd seen Lizzie with a pair similar to this: it was painted glass in a cheap setting, but lovely all the same.

'I see what you mean,' she said, leaning down to have a closer look. 'It is lovely. That colour would look very nice with your hair and your skin tone. You're like me, pale skin.'

You could be my daughter in a different life, thought Alice, her heart full of concern for the girl who an hour ago she would have walked past in the street, probably without a second glance. There were so many of these children out there.

'I need to go,' said Sue, jumping up from the bench.

'Remember what I said,' said Alice, giving the girl's hand a squeeze, not really wanting to let her go back out on to the streets. She caught sight of the few inches of bare leg between the top of the girl's tattered leather boots and the ragged hem of her dress, and found herself almost in tears. That bare leg seemed to make the girl look even more vulnerable somehow. Then she heard the sound of Victoria crying and instinctively glanced towards the kitchen door. When she looked back, Sue Cassidy was gone.

Alice heard Marie picking up the baby and soothing her and she knew that there was already a bottle prepared. She knew that she could let Marie feed her, she loved to feed the baby. So she stood in the yard with her head bowed for a few moments. And then, seeing the white pillowcase still lying on the flags, she picked it up and smoothed out the creases, seeing at one end the smudge of dirt where Sue Cassidy's hand had held it so tight.

Sitting back down on the bench, with the crumpled pillowcase on her knee, in the same spot that Sue had occupied minutes before, Alice leant her head against the solid wall. She felt the hardness of it behind her, and thought how hard and bare life could be in the city. Staring at the stone flags, she saw a couple of straggly green weeds, struggling to survive amidst the stone and the brick and the soot. And for the first time, in all the months that Alice had been in the city, she actually missed her home in the north. Really missed it, deep inside — not just the homesickness that everyone gets. It was strange to feel it. Her home hadn't always been a happy one. Her mother was a harsh, domineering woman who wouldn't listen to anybody. But at home, they were surrounded by green fields, there were flowers and butterflies, and the air was clear, and just at that moment, with Alice's back-yard perspective, she felt as if the sky at home was always blue and the sun was always shining. She would be able to breathe properly there; Victoria would be able to play in the grass, like she, Alice Sampson, used to as a child. They would both be able to grow together.

But then, Alice knew, her position was impossible. Her family would never accept a child born out of wedlock. Her father would: he was a gentle soul, a softly spoken man who worked as head cowman for a local farm. He would take her, and the baby, if it was left to him, Alice knew that he would. He had cried that day Alice moved to Liverpool. But she knew that he would never raise his voice against his wife, Alice's mother. Jemima Sampson not only ruled the household with an iron hand, but also the bakery which she ran like clockwork. Once, as a child, Alice had wandered in there when the bread was being kneaded. She'd reached up to look in the wooden trough where the dough was mixed and accidentally dropped in the dandelion that she was clutching in her small hand. Her mother had grabbed her and held her by the scruff of the neck, inches away from the oven that was glowing with heat. Alice had never forgotten that day, and she had never wandered back into the bakery again.

From that day, Alice had been fearful of her mother, but as she became an adult, she also

157

began to admire the way her mother worked. Mixing that amount of bread dough every day was tough work, you had to be strong, and her mother kneaded side by side with the men. There had never been any question of Alice going into the family business. She was the youngest and the only girl. Two of her brothers already worked in the bakery and the other, the one most like her father, was also a cowman. There was no work for Alice at home, and so her mother had started making enquiries, first about a position as a housemaid, and then, fortunately for Alice, about becoming a nurse. The vicar's daughter had trained as a nurse, and come back to the village to work as a district nurse. She was a chaste, God-fearing girl, and Alice's mother had been really taken with her and her 'calling'. She'd told Alice that the vicar's daughter was like their very own Florence Nightingale and she thought that following the same course would be a good life for a Sampson girl. She had hoped that Alice would marry early, but it had become clear that wasn't going to happen. Alice knew that the day when Jamie had come to the house, full of excitement about his plans for Australia, her mother had been heartbroken. She'd always had a real soft spot for Jamie, and had often spoken to Alice in terms of 'when you're Jamie's wife'. Sometimes, Jemima had even seemed closer to Jamie than she was to her own sons.

Alice sighed. She didn't like to keep all that had happened since she came to Liverpool secret from her family. It troubled her and she was terrified that one day her mother would find out anyway. And then what? What would she do? Alice knew that the woman was capable of anything. That's why she had no choice. She couldn't even think about telling *anyone* at home.

As she stood up from the bench, Alice caught sight of those weeds again, and a single, lonely tear escaped down her cheek. Too exhausted to cry properly, she wiped it away, and then busied herself, feeling at the sheets to check if they were drying. All she could do was live her life from day to day. Keep working at the hospital, keep helping here at the house, keep taking care of her daughter.

There must be something waiting for me and Victoria, something just for us, thought Alice as she walked back into the house. She supposed that most people looked at her and assumed that she must be hoping that the father of her baby would come back from Australia. But she knew that hope had died out long ago. With the distance of time, even before Victoria was born, Alice had realized that she didn't really miss Jamie that much. And she'd assumed he felt the same — he hadn't even written her a letter from Australia. And now that she was back at work, really feeling part of it this time around, she couldn't imagine having to give up nursing and settle for marriage. No, she definitely didn't want Jamie, she was sure of that, and what's more, she didn't even want him to know that he had a child.

11

'Nursing is said . . . to be a high calling,
an honourable calling . . . The honour
does not lie in putting on Nursing like
your uniform, your dress . . . '
Florence Nightingale

'Nurse Sampson,' called Sister Law, puffing out her chest and standing at the top of the ward with both feet planted square.

'Here we go,' Alice muttered to herself, as she walked up the ward to start her shift. She must have heard what happened on the ward the night before last.

Alice stopped in front of Sister and stood her ground, determined to put her case, to not be bowed down by anything that the night superintendent had reported. Alice could see Sister Tweedy in the background, writing up her night report.

'It has been brought to my attention by Sister Tweedy . . . ' said Sister, pausing momentarily. Alice felt a shock go through her body. Had she been wrong to trust Sister Tweedy after all? She was thrown; now she had no idea what was coming.

Sister gave her a hard stare. 'Don't look so worried, Nurse Sampson. It has been brought to my attention by Sister Tweedy that you have done an excellent job on night duty.'

160

Alice almost fainted with relief right there on the spot. She glanced across at Sister Tweedy, who was still scribbling her report; she could have run over there and hugged the woman.

'Nurse Sampson,' said Sister Law. 'Can I have your complete attention.'

Alice looked back at her, grinning from ear to ear.

'Not *that* much attention,' said Sister with a scowl. 'And as I've told you before, you are really making an impression on the ward. Long may it continue, Nurse Sampson.'

Alice was still smiling — she couldn't help it — and she began to see the glimmer of amusement somewhere behind Sister's mask-like expression.

'As a reward for your progress — again, do not let this go to your head, there is still much to be done — you will accompany me on the ward round with Mr Jones this morning. We need our nurses to have a breadth of understanding and as much medical knowledge as possible, but I don't allow just anyone on the ward round. That privilege has to be earned. You have done well, Nurse Sampson. Be ready to be called when you see Mr Jones on the ward.'

'Yes, Sister,' said Alice, still smiling.

'Now, stand with the rest while I give my report and then get on and make some beds. You are infuriating me, grinning away like that. Stop smiling at once.'

'Yes, Sister,' said Alice, desperately trying to keep a straight face.

She felt very special indeed on the ward round with Sister Law and Mr Jones. She was the chosen one, for that day at least. She felt even more special when they came to Tommy Knox's bed and he gave her a wink — careful not to let Sister see, of course.

Alice was glad to see him sitting up in bed; it looked like he might do well after all. Surely, if the lump had been suspicious, he wouldn't look this well after surgery?

'Now, Mr Knox,' said the surgeon, leaning over to pull aside the dressing which had already been loosened by another nurse, following Sister's direct instruction. 'Let me see . . . '

All was silent around Tommy's bed as Mr Jones made his inspection. Finally, he seemed satisfied and straightening up gave the semblance of a smile. 'It all looks very well indeed, Mr Knox, you should be able to get up and about in no time at all. The stitches will have to stay in for a few weeks, of course, and we will have to be extremely vigilant for suppuration. But so far, all seems to be well.'

'Thanks, doc,' said Tommy, grinning at Mr Jones. 'My ship will be back to sea in six weeks' time; how do you think I'll be fixed for that?'

'We will have to see, Mr Knox, we will have to see, but so far so good . . . ' Mr Jones turned to Sister Law, lowering his voice, 'I'm still waiting for my colleague with the microscope to have a look. He'll let us know if there were cancer cells in that lump we removed . . . '

Alice felt her throat tighten, and she wanted to ask more about the cells and the microscope, but Mr Jones was already moving on to other matters: 'I noticed some redness around the

162

wound. Do we have a recording of this man's temperature?'

'Not as yet,' said Sister. 'Are you sure it is required at this stage, Mr Jones?'

Having no reply from the surgeon, who merely stood looking at Sister with his eyebrows raised, she, in turn, spoke to Alice. 'Please bring the thermometer, Nurse Sampson. Mr Jones requires a reading.'

Alice wasn't sure but she thought she saw Sister roll her eyes as she made the request.

'Don't worry, Mr Knox,' said Sister, seeing the look of alarm on Mr Knox's face. 'This is not a painful procedure.'

Alice went directly to the special cupboard that housed the wooden box wherein lay the new mercury thermometer. She had never been trusted with the handling of it before so knew that she had to be extra careful. As she returned to Mr Knox's bed, she walked slowly.

'Come along, Nurse Sampson,' shouted Sister. 'It's not the crown jewels.'

Back at the bed, Sister instructed Alice to remove the long glass tube from the wooden box. 'Please don't drop it, Nurse Sampson,' she said, with a glint in her eye that indicated to Alice that Sister thought it might not be the end of the world if she did indeed drop it and it was smashed to pieces.

'Insert it into the patient's axilla,' urged Mr Jones. 'The man's armpit, Nurse, his axilla is just a fancy name for the armpit.'

'The other way round: yes, that's it. See the bulb here — that contains the mercury, you can

163

see the silver, yes. The premise behind the whole operation is that the warmth of the patient's body will cause the mercury to expand, thereby forcing the level of mercury up the fine bore of the tube. When the level has stopped moving upwards, that's when we read the temperature. These new thermometers are much easier to use. The other one we had was an unwieldy twelve inches long, this is half the size.'

Alice was fascinated. Once the long glass tube was inserted, she continued to support it at one end and watched it like a hawk.

'It will take five minutes,' said Mr Jones. 'Sister and I will progress to the next patient and then come back to you.'

Alice nodded, still scrutinizing the glass tube. When she looked up, Tommy was looking at it too, his grey hair stuck out at all angles, and then he looked up at her with a smile, showing the one single tooth in his grizzled head. It was a wonderful smile and Alice was so relieved to see him out of pain.

'I never thought I'd see anything like this in my lifetime,' he said, shaking his head. 'Who knows what the study of science will lead us to next, hey? We might have a man on the moon one day, Nurse Sampson, a man on the moon.'

'Thank you so much for what you did last night, Mr Knox,' said Alice quietly. 'You saved my skin.'

'You are very welcome,' said Tommy, with another grin, 'all part of the service, and, as I saw last night, and I know from years at sea, the captain of the ship can be a very tricky customer

164

indeed, if you get the wrong one. Now, our Sister Law, for example.' Alice gave him an anxious glance, wondering what he was going to say. 'At first sight, she might look like the worst captain that anyone could fall under, but, in no time at all, the men would see that she has the best interests of all who sail with her, well and truly at heart.'

'Really?' whispered Alice, looking back up from the thermometer.

'Indeed so.'

'Look, Mr Knox,' said Alice, genuinely fascinated by the thermometer, but also keen to distract her patient before Sister came back. 'The level of mercury is rising.'

'That is wonderful indeed,' said Tommy. 'Just by the warmth of a smelly armpit. I don't even mind if I have got a bit of a fever now, Nurse Sampson, not now I've seen the wonders of science.'

'The level seems to be steadying up now, Mr Knox.'

'Please call me Tommy, and yes, I can see what you mean. You are a woman of science, Nurse Sampson, a woman of science.'

'Are we ready to read it, Nurse Sampson?' enquired the surgeon, reappearing at the bottom of the bed.

'I think so, Mr Jones, the level of mercury is steady now.'

Mr Jones took the glass tube from her and checked for himself, then he made his reading of the markings: 'So that's . . . ninety-eight degrees Fahrenheit, Mr Knox.'

'Is that good or bad?' said Tommy, as the surgeon made to move away.

'Oh, that is absolutely fine, Mr Knox, absolutely fine.'

'That's good then, isn't it, Nurse?' smiled Tommy, as Alice packed the device back into the wooden box.

'It is very good, Mr Knox . . . and I'll be back to secure that dressing for you and rebandage just as soon as I can,' said Alice, giving his hand a squeeze before heading back down the ward to return the thermometer to the special cupboard.

As she was walking back to join the ward round, Alice was stopped in her tracks by the orderlies, Michael and Stephen, coming through with a new admission.

'We've got one man and his dog here for you, darlin',' said Michael, giving Alice a wink. 'Where d'ye want 'em?'

Alice recognized the new admission immediately. He was the army veteran who'd been on the ward last year, the same man that she'd seen walking past St George's Hall on the day of Maud's wedding.

'Mr Delaney,' hissed Sister, coming up behind the orderly. 'Please refrain from addressing my nurses in such a familiar fashion, and stop wasting time. Take this man to bed five.'

'Yes, Sister,' said Michael, and Alice could see him struggling to repress a laugh.

'One moment, Mr Delaney,' she said, holding up a hand when she saw the patient on the stretcher for the first time. The man had his eyes closed, he looked thin and weather-beaten, his hair and beard were long and matted. He was in a poor state. Then she shifted her gaze to the ragged white dog, some kind of bull terrier that was anchored by a frayed rope to the stretcher. Alice held her breath. She was sure that Sister would not allow a dog on the ward, not under any circumstances.

Michael was already muttering, 'He wouldn't leave the dog, Sister, he said he'd rather die in the street than leave the dog. There was nothing we could do.'

What happened next not only flabbergasted Alice, but also the two men holding the stretcher. Sister leant down to the dog, stretched out a hand and gave it a stroke. The dog gave a low growl, but Sister was undeterred, speaking gently to the creature. 'Well, you are a battered old fella, aren't you?' she said, scrutinizing the dog's ripped ear and a fresh tear across his scarred nose.

When she straightened up, the patient had opened his eyes. 'Welcome to the ward again, Mr Swain,' she said, with the shadow of a smile on her face. 'I hope we can help you to get better.'

In that moment, Alice recalled that Sister Law had given this man special attention last year; she'd even made sure he had some money from a special fund to see him on his way when he was discharged. Sister seemed to have a real soft spot for the army veterans.

'I'm afraid you won't be able to keep the dog on the ward overnight, Mr Swain, hospital rules. But you can keep him whilst you get settled. Mr Delaney will take him home tonight and look

167

after him for you, won't you, Mr Delaney?' Sister glared at the orderly.

Alice saw Michael open his mouth to reply, but he seemed unable to speak. In the end he nodded, muttering something about not knowing what his missus would say, but it seemed that a deal had been struck to Sister Law's satisfaction.

'Now take the patient to bed five. And where are his crutches?'

Michael and Stephen were nonplussed. 'I sold them,' said the patient. 'The dog needed food and some man with a bit of money needed crutches.'

'We'll supply you with another pair,' declared Sister, laying a hand on the patient's shoulder.

'Now come along,' she said, as the orderlies sagged at the knees with the weight of the patient, their faces red with exertion.

'We might as well have a look at this new admission,' said Mr Jones, striding after Michael and Stephen as they made their way up the ward.

'Come on, Nurse Sampson,' he called. 'You can observe the assessment.'

It took a few minutes for the dog to be accepting of anyone examining his master, but in the end Michael was able to hold on to him at the bottom of the bed. The veteran had been found collapsed on the street. His right leg had been in a terrible condition for years following a war wound sustained in the Crimea. Alice remembered from last time the violence of the injury, the big chunk of flesh missing from the calf. This time the leg was angry, swollen, and oozing yellow pus on to the clean hospital sheet.

'I don't know if we'll be able to rescue it again, Mr Swain,' said the surgeon. 'We will need to take you to the operating table, and when you're under the chloroform, I'll make my assessment, but you might be waking up without the blighter this time.'

Alice saw Mr Swain nod; he seemed resigned to his fate.

'How do you feel about that?' said Sister Law, as she gently pulled the sheet back over the man's legs.

The patient shrugged and appeared lost in thought for a few moments, but then he spoke, his voice low but well-spoken. 'I have so much pain in that leg every day, I've felt like chopping it off myself . . . but if you can clean it up and save it, I would be grateful. I've heard about phantom pain, from some of those who served out there with me. From what I've heard, the pain can be just as excruciating, with or without the limb.'

'Very true,' said Sister. 'But if gangrene has set in, there might not be any choice.'

'I understand, Sister,' said the man. 'But at least I can report that I have, at last, been able to take your advice. I've stayed off the drink. I went through the shakes really bad, but I had a place to stay in, a boarding house, and I managed to do it without dying. I needed to find somewhere for the dog, you see. I found him on the street about three months ago. He was in a terrible state then — he'd been used for fighting and

169

he'd been shoved in a box and left for dead. I saved him. And once I cleaned up his wounds and got to know him, I couldn't risk him suffering because I was too drunk to look after him. So me and Stanley, we managed to get a room together.'

'Very well done, Mr Swain,' said Sister. 'And he is a fine fellow, isn't he? He's been through the wars, though, you can see that. What's that new wound on his nose?'

'When the leg got worse again and I started to feel sick with it, I fell over in the street, I couldn't get up. Some wild dogs came at me that night, and Stanley fought them off.'

Alice could see that Sister was almost in tears as the man told his story, and Michael, who was still holding the dog at the bottom of the bed, gave him an extra stroke. 'Good boy,' he said. 'Good boy.'

'Let's get you well again, Mr Swain, so that you can continue to look after your dog,' said Sister. Then, seeing that the patient had started to close his eyes, she glanced at Mr Jones and laid her hand on his forehead. 'He's hot, Mr Jones. No need for the new-fangled thermometer this time — the man clearly has a fever.'

Mr Jones smiled at her. 'Let's get him to theatre then, Sister, as soon as we can.'

'You'd best take the dog now, Mr Delaney,' said Sister. 'Keep him in that room of yours until you're ready to go home, find him some food from the kitchen and a bowl of clean water. Oh, and clean up his nose, will you?'

'Yes, Sister,' said Michael, bundling the dog up

170

into his arms. As he walked away down the ward, Alice heard the dog give a sorrowful whine and she saw him looking back at Mr Swain as he lay, insensible, on the bed, never taking his eyes off the man. Poor Stanley, she thought, I hope it won't be long before he can be reunited with his master.

Alice wasn't sure if she wanted the opportunity to go back into theatre again, not after last time, but she was prepared to get the experience if that's what she was required to do. However, the decision was taken out of her hands. Nurse Langtry had been promised the next stint, and given that Alice had already done the ward round it seemed only fair.

'Go and fix Mr Knox's dressing, Nurse Sampson,' said Sister, as she strode away up the ward with Mr Jones in tow.

Alice glanced across and she could see the Reverend Seed was sitting by Tommy's bed. It looked as though they were deep in conversation, and then they were both laughing. He can't be reading prayers, thought Alice, anxious to get on and follow Sister's instruction. She hadn't encountered the Reverend since her night shift, but seeing him now, looking relaxed, his dark hair flopping forward on to his brow, she got a different impression from the one she had in her head. He liked to talk, he could smile, and there was an air of gentleness about him that struck Alice as very kindly.

Very kindly or not, Alice knew that she would have to interrupt them: the dressing needed to be done.

'Sorry to disturb,' she said to them both, 'but I still need to rebandage your dressing, Mr Knox.' She saw the Reverend's face flush red and he shot up from his seat.

'Sorry, sorry,' he mumbled, and then turning to Tommy, 'I'll call by and see you next time, Mr Knox, if that's all right?'

'Yes, any time, Reverend,' said Tommy, and then when Alice got to the side of the bed, he whispered, 'I think the Reverend might have a soft spot for you, Nurse Sampson.'

'Nonsense, Mr Knox,' she said firmly. 'He's just a shy man, that's all.'

'He didn't seem shy when he was sitting chatting to me . . . '

'Right, Mr Knox, let me have a look at this dressing,' Alice insisted, determined to shift focus back to the work in hand.

'Aye aye, Captain,' said Tommy, grinning. 'There's a fella I've seen out and about in the city,' he said, nodding in the direction of Mr Swain as he was loaded on to the stretcher. 'He's been a regular round the docks and in the pubs for many a year.'

Alice wasn't surprised to hear that. 'Now let me just check that the dressing pad is in the right position. If you could just relax back on your pillows.'

The dressing had slipped, exposing the wound. The area looked angry, the skin bright red and puckered with black stitches.

'He was in the Crimea, he's a veteran. Some say he got medals for what he did out there.'

'Really,' said Alice, only half listening as she

172

continued her inspection of Tommy's wound. 'You've lost a good chunk of your tattoo when they removed that lump, Mr Knox.'

Tommy looked down. 'I have that,' he said, laughing. 'That was my first ship, the *Beaufort Castle*. I was an apprentice, only a nipper, when I worked on her.'

'It looks like a very impressive ship, Mr Knox, from the bit that's left,' said Alice.

'Aye, she was a fine ship, a three-masted barque. But I didn't know what'd hit me on that first voyage. As soon as we were out to the ocean, I was sick as a dog for weeks. I cried me eyes out for three nights in a row. Then it dawned on me: we weren't going back, I'd made me choice, I needed to go with the ship. I wish you could have seen her in full sail, Nurse Sampson . . . but she was wrecked in a violent storm off the coast of West Africa in 1828. Most of the crew drowned, and those that survived, they found 'em days later, lashed to the shrouds of the mizzenmast.'

Alice had stopped now, so taken with the story, she'd forgotten to position the dressing.

'But what about you, were you . . . ?'

'Nah, I'd already moved on by then, to work the clipper route to Australia . . . I was sorry to hear about the ship, but some of the crew, well, maybe they got what was coming to them. Maybe they did.'

'What do you mean?' she asked. 'Now, if you could sit up for me, that's it, so I can get the bandage round. That's it.'

'I had a hard time on there, a hard time. Some

of the crew, they'd worked the slave ships. They were hardbitten, violent men . . . They were still working the same routes to West Africa, but they'd switched the trade to palm oil — there was good money to be made from it, back then. I learned a lot on that first voyage, Nurse Sampson: who to trust, who to keep out the way of, and, most of all, when to keep quiet . . .'

'If you could just hold the end of that bandage for me, till I get the next one . . . that's it,' said Alice, appalled to hear that her patient had shared a ship with men like that. 'It sounds like you must have had a terrible time on there. Why did you get the tattoo, then? Surely it just reminded you?'

'It did, yes, that's the whole point, Nurse Sampson. I wanted to be reminded to take great care in choosing a ship and her crew. From then on I always looked for the good in everything . . . That's why when the opportunity came to help with the war effort, I took it. I worked the ships that took that lot, the British soldiers, out to Turkey and the Crimea, during the war,' said Tommy, gazing over at Mr Swain as the orderlies took him through to theatre.

'They were busy years, the 1850s, busy years. Backwards and forwards to Scutari and Balaklava with soldiers and horses and ammunition. We lost too many of those horses, even before they got near to the other side. And I can tell you, Nurse Sampson, once you've buried a horse at sea, sliding it down into the water off a big plank, once you've done that, you never forget it. We used to cry our eyes out each and every time.

Even more than we would if it'd been a soldier or a seaman. Strange, that. I suppose those creatures didn't ask to be out there, they just seemed so big and helpless . . . '

'That must have been terrible,' said Alice, fascinated and moved by what he was saying. 'Now if you could just lean forward for me, I'll tuck the end of the bandage in and then you're done.'

'Aaargh,' groaned Tommy as he sat forward. 'That's giving me a bit of jip.'

'Just for a moment longer, while I get this bandage secure,' said Alice, working as quickly as she could. 'Then I'll get you some more laudanum.'

Tommy nodded grimly.

'One of the superintendents here at the hospital, Miss Houston, she was out there as a nurse,' said Alice, trying to distract him.

'Was she?' gasped Tommy.

'Almost there now, Mr Knox,' she soothed.

'Well, she'll know about it,' said Tommy, at last able to lean back on his pillow and get some relief. 'I bet she still has the nightmares, sometimes, I bet she still hears the sound of the men and horses screaming . . . Those men that we brought back from there, they weren't the same men as we took out. They weren't just maimed from shells, they were different; some of them were silent shadows of the men we'd taken out. They had a haunted look in their eyes.'

'It must have been awful,' said Alice.

'It was for them. Not for us — we had plenty of regular work at that time, the ships did well.

But what it taught me was this: war is a terrible thing, Nurse Sampson. I hope that you never have to live through another, not in your lifetime.'

'I hope so too, Mr Knox,' said Alice, as she checked that the bandage was secure.

'That's a fine job you've done there, Nurse Sampson,' said Tommy, glancing down to his chest. 'A woman like you would soon take to a life at sea, you'd be a real asset. I once had the pleasure of working with a sailor who turned out to be a woman . . .'

Fascinated as Alice was by the story that Tommy was about to tell, she knew that she had to move on to the next patient. Sister Law would be back down the ward in no time.

'Tell me later, Tommy,' she grinned, adjusting his pillows to make sure that he was as comfortable as he possibly could be. 'Now you get some rest, Nurse's orders.'

'Aye aye, Captain,' he said, giving her a mock salute.

By the end of the shift, Alice was exhausted, but satisfied. In particular, she'd taken a great deal of pleasure from ensuring that Tommy had been well looked after: she'd not only re-dressed his wound, she'd spoken up when he needed pain relief, and helped him get out of bed for the first time since he'd come back from theatre. It felt like a privilege, to be trusted with looking after Tommy. She only hoped that he'd be fit to go back to sea when the time came. The way he'd spoken to her, she knew that he was only truly alive when he was out on the ship with the crew. He'd not spoken of any family, just the men on the ships.

As she made her way off the ward, Alice was just out through the door and walking down the corridor when she heard a voice calling her from behind.

She knew who it was instantly: the Reverend Seed. Turning to face him she saw the man stop abruptly, his eyes wide, and then walk slowly towards her, holding out a piece of paper.

As he started to speak again, Alice could see his cheeks were flushed pink. He *is* shy, she thought, and she felt that she wanted to reach out to help him.

'Nurse Sampson, this is for you,' he said, thrusting the piece of paper in her direction. 'I'm hosting a tea for any probationer nurses who are able to attend. You can have tea or your measure of beer or brandy, whatever you want. And there will be cake. I'm still trying to get to know all the people here at the hospital. And Miss Merryweather thought it would be a nice idea to get all the probationers together, especially someone like you, who doesn't really know the rest of the set. So if you can come . . . '

'Thank you, Reverend,' said Alice gently, taking the piece of paper from his trembling hand.

'It's next week, on Thursday, the details are all in there . . . ' he muttered, glancing up to meet her gaze at last.

'I will have a look and come along if I can.'

'Thank you, thank you,' he said, almost bowing, as Alice turned to leave.

I don't think there's anything in what Tommy said, she thought, as she continued down the corridor. He's just a young man who's led a very sheltered life. He's shy with women, that's all.

As Alice made her way to the Nurses' Home she was looking forward to meeting Eddy, as she often did after work, so that they could walk through the city together. But there was no sign of her friend and Alice couldn't help but feel disappointed. She knew that sometimes Eddy got delayed with one of her cases, but Alice was still alive with the day's work and it would have been nice to talk it through as they walked home.

What a good day she'd had; what a relief to be going off the ward without the worry of some incident with a superintendent. It seemed like a whole different world.

After removing her starched cap and apron and placing them on the shelf, Alice went to check the pigeonholes. Maud had told her she would write to her, addressing it to the Training School. She had been checking regularly, anxious to hear the news and to have a forwarding address, but still there'd been no word. She was more than ready for a letter from Maud, so when she saw an envelope with her name on it, just for a moment, she thought that it had come. Then she saw the handwriting, the unmistakeable hand of her mother.

Alice wasn't sure she wanted to open it. There was never any change in the news, and simply reading her mother's words and seeing her writing made her feel anxious, as though Jemima Sampson was breathing down her neck. Her mother wrote every month without fail, and each time that Alice received a letter, she was careful to always send a reply, assuring her family that she was working hard, busy on the wards, doing well. Even when she was heavily pregnant and had just given birth, she still sent the letters, anxious not to give any cause for suspicion.

'You'd better open it,' she muttered to herself, ripping open the envelope before she could change her mind. She quickly read through all the usual information — the weather, the numbers of loaves, how many cows had calved, what the neighbours had been doing. Then, something new jumped out at her. Jamie. Jemima had seen his mother last market day. She'd said that they'd had another letter, he was still doing very well. He was working on a cattle station in Queensland, Australia. He had his own horse and he was earning very good money . . . Why is she telling me this? thought Alice, knowing straight away that the only reason her mother would be doing so was that she still hoped Jamie would come back. She still wanted him as part of the family, as Alice's husband.

'Too late for that, Mother, too late for all that,' she muttered to herself, feeling irritated now, crumpling the letter and stuffing it in her pocket. She reached for her cape and hat and made her way to the door. She'd only just got to the bottom of the steps — she wasn't even properly on the street — when she saw a broad-shouldered figure, standing with his hat in his hand, looking straight at her.

She looked at him, and her heart jumped.

It was Roderick Morgan. What's he doing here? thought Alice, her heart starting to race. Surely he isn't here to see me? But even as she had that thought, the man was striding towards her, smiling.

'Nurse Alice,' he said, looking, as always, as though he owned the very ground that he walked on.

'Hello,' said Alice tentatively.

'Sorry, I didn't want to worry you,' he said, coming close enough now for Alice to see the gold watch chain across his brocade waistcoat. Her knees were beginning to feel a bit weak.

'It's just that I wanted to thank you for looking after my friend, Ray Lloyd. We had the funeral today, and I couldn't help but think of you and the night we spent together in the hospital.'

Alice hadn't entirely been able to keep Roderick Morgan out of her head in the last few days, and she tried to hide her delight in seeing him again.

'Please, Alice, just as a token of my gratitude, I wonder if you would agree to accompany me on an afternoon out. We could take tea somewhere.'

'Well, yes, but not now, I couldn't . . . '

'No, of course not,' he said, stepping close enough for her to smell his cologne. 'I've been in to see Sister Law, to thank her as well, and she told me that you have a half-day off tomorrow.'

How on earth did he get Sister Law to disclose that? thought Alice. He must have hypnotized her or something.

'Yes, I do, but — '

'Well, you could bring the baby along as well,

180

or you could ask Marie to look after her . . . You've probably not had an afternoon out for a very long time, at least not since the baby was born.'

'But how did you know about Marie?'

'I have my sources,' he said, fixing her with his dark eyes. To Alice, in that moment, he seemed like Heathcliff from *Wuthering Heights*. She knew that there was probably no way that she was going to say no to this. It felt like she was under some kind of spell.

'Meet me on Lime Street Station, under the clock, at two p.m.'

'Yes,' said Alice automatically.

'Until tomorrow then,' he said. And then he bowed, replaced his hat and strode towards the carriage that was waiting on the street.

'I look forward to seeing you,' he called, turning to her again before he climbed into the carriage.

Alice stood, unable to move.

She felt rooted to the spot. What had just happened? Should she have accepted his invitation so readily? Could she trust him? The questions raced through her head as she stood, transfixed, watching his carriage move away.

'What's up with you? You look like you've been struck by a thunderbolt,' said Eddy, appearing from nowhere and linking arms with Alice.

'Oh Eddy, it's so good to see you, and you've turned up at just the right time.'

'Crikey,' said Eddy, after Alice had told her the whole story. 'I've never heard of that happening before, but you deserve something special, Alice, you really do. Don't go asking me if it's the right thing to do. I've no idea. If it was me, and I liked a person, I would just go, without thinking about it, but that might not be the best advice. I can be, what you might say, a bit haphazard. I mean, for example . . . '

As Eddy chattered on, the two friends walked back through the city arm in arm. There was no need for Alice to speak; Eddy was more than happy to do all the talking. So, as they walked, Alice was able to think, and in the end, she decided it was all right to accept the invitation and have an afternoon out with a handsome man. She would, of course, speak to Stella and Marie when she got back, see what they thought. But, the voice inside her head was saying, why not, Alice Sampson? It's time you did something different.

12

'A sick person does so enjoy hearing good news: — for instance, of a love and courtship, while in progress to a good ending.'

Florence Nightingale

'You should go, Alice,' said Marie.

'Well, is it all right with you, if I leave Victoria?'

'Of course, she and I were made for each other, you know that. And what's more, you haven't had a single day off, Alice, not since she was born. You're a young woman, a beautiful young woman, and you need to go and enjoy yourself. Even if it is for just half a day.'

Alice tried to keep her excitement under wraps during the morning shift on the ward, but by the time she got to Tommy's bed, she'd already been told off by Sister Law at least three times for smiling.

'You're a ray of sunshine this morning, Nurse Sampson,' said Tommy, with a twinkle in his eye. 'Now I don't know much about anything that goes on, especially on dry land, but I'm thinking that there might be some kind of romance in the air. Something that's happened since I saw you yesterday?'

'I can't be telling you about that kind of thing, not at work,' said Alice, feeling her cheeks flush red.

183

'Maybe so, Nurse Sampson, but I think you've just answered my question. Now you make sure that the gentleman in question treats you with the proper respect, and if he doesn't, well, he'll have me to answer to, Tommy Knox. I'll be on to him straight away.'

'Don't you worry about me, Mr Knox. I've always been able to look after myself, I grew up with three brothers,' she said.

'Even so,' said Tommy, 'you report back to me.'

'Yes, Captain,' said Alice, smiling at his weather-beaten, good-natured face. 'Now, Mr Knox, let's get this dressing done for you, otherwise Sister Law will be down here . . . '

It was a good job that Alice had an abundance of smiles inside her that morning, because when she took down the dressing, she was immediately concerned about Tommy's wound. Trying not to let him cotton on to her concern, she told him that Sister had said she also wanted to look at the wound.

Sister Law pressed her lips firmly together as she leant over the bed, considering the wound on display. Then, looking up, she said, 'Now, Mr Knox, this might not be anything to worry about, but there does seem to be some suppuration. We need to apply a poultice, to see if we can draw it out, but there is a risk that the wound might not be healing.'

'I understand, Captain, I mean Sister,' said Tommy, glancing at Alice.

'Right, Nurse, make up a kaolin poultice straight away. Let's do what we can to rescue the situation, and get out the thermometer, will you, you know how to use it. Check Mr Knox's temperature, and then we have the recording for Mr Jones's ward round.'

'Yes, Sister,' said Alice, covering the wound with the dressing pad, before going to prepare the poultice.

She had the warm poultice applied in no time and then she was there by the bed with the thermometer. Tommy was quiet, preoccupied, as she took his temperature, but he was still interested in watching the mercury going up the glass tube.

'What's it this time, Nurse Sampson?' he said.

'It's one hundred.'

'Mmm, that's higher, isn't it?' he said.

'It is, but sometimes a temperature can be elevated post-operatively, it's all part of the healing process.'

'My word, Nurse Sampson, you are very quick with all this stuff, aren't you? You will go far in the nursing profession, I know you will.'

Sister Law was able to confirm that Tommy did have a mild fever, and she was straight-talking. 'This could go either way, Mr Knox. It might well come to nothing, but if it does progress, as an experienced seaman like you will know only too well, it could mean that you become very sick, very quickly.'

'I understand, Sister,' he said, 'and I appreciate you being direct with me.'

Across the ward at Mr Swain's bed, Alice assisted Sister Law with re-dressing the large wound on the veteran's leg. The man was very

185

sleepy, after a large dose of laudanum, and still recovering from the chloroform as well. Sister told her that Dr McKendrick had repeated the drops many times, just to get the man under, and then topped it up during the course of what sounded like a grim and lengthy procedure to debride the wound, and thoroughly clean it down with iodine solution. What was left now looked like a piece of raw meat from knee to ankle. Alice had no idea how it was going to heal, if it healed at all. But Sister told her that if they'd caught it in time, nature would work its wonders yet again, and the area would heal.

'Remember what Miss Nightingale said, Nurse Sampson: what we do here in the hospital is only to prepare the body for the work of nature. Nature will heal if the body is in the correct condition.'

Alice was so busy, she almost lost track of time, but this meant, at least, that the time sped by, and she was able to beat the constant distraction and switch her thoughts away from the afternoon that lay ahead.

Thankfully, she was off duty on time and running through the streets with her nurse's cape flying behind her, heading straight home so that she could change into her best gown before heading to Lime Street Station. Lizzie had been eager to help and she would be waiting.

First, Alice checked on Victoria — sleeping soundly with Marie sitting by the crib doing some mending. Then Lizzie helped her remove her nurse's cape and hat and pulled her, giggling, into the bedroom. Her uniform was soon unbuttoned and discarded on the bed and Alice was slipping on her light blue gown.

'Look at your hair, what a mess!' cried Lizzie, immediately pulling out hairpins and then dragging Alice by the hand back into the kitchen. 'Sit,' she said, with a glint in her eye. Producing a box of hairbrushes and face paint, Lizzie then expertly set to: combing, brushing and neatly fixing Alice's hair. Then, pulling Alice's chair away from the table, she stood in front of her, studying her face for a few moments.

'Stop laughing,' Lizzie ordered, desperately trying to stop herself from giggling. 'I'm just deciding what to do with you.'

'Not too much,' Alice warned, 'I've never worn any make-up.'

'Oh, you'll look like a painted puppet when I'm finished with you,' teased Lizzie, turning to her wooden box and producing a small brush and a pot of powder.

Alice covered her face with both hands.

'Of course you won't,' laughed Lizzie. 'I can do daytime make-up as well, you know . . . '

So there sat Alice whilst Lizzie applied a bit of powder to her cheeks and some paint to her lips. 'Not too much,' she said. 'We don't want you to look like a whore.' And then, she picked up a stick of kohl. 'Your lashes are pale; this will make your eyes stand out . . . Nah, I think we'll leave it,' she said, after a few more moments of study. 'Your pale face and lashes make your face look fresh and open. And more beautiful.'

Standing back to scrutinize Alice with her eyes

narrowed, Lizzie declared that she was done and whisked a hand mirror in front of her face for her approval.

'Yes,' said Alice, amazed at the difference that a bit of lip colour made. 'Thank you.'

'No time to lose,' shouted Lizzie, pulling her up from her seat and draping the nurse's cape around her shoulders.

'You look lovely,' smiled Marie, glancing up from her mending. 'You go and have a good time. Don't be worrying about the baby.'

Alice ran to the crib and gave Victoria a peck on the cheek, leaving a tiny smudge of lipstick on her soft skin.

'Come on, come on,' cried Lizzie. 'No time for snuggling with babies.' She picked up Alice's paisley pattern shawl.

For safety the girls had planned for Alice to wear the district nurse cape and hat on the way to the station and Lizzie to wear the shawl. Then they'd swap and Lizzie would come back on her own wearing the cape. Even though they were only going around the corner, they knew that they had to be careful. Plain-clothes police were still being sighted in the area. Besides, Alice knew that Lizzie was desperate to wear the cape and hat, even if it was only for five minutes.

At two p.m. sharp, Alice was looking up to the clock on Lime Street Station. As she stood, people swirled around her, some running by, one knocking into her. And then she heard the hoot of a whistle, and a cloud of steam and smoke came billowing across, engulfing her. She couldn't even see the clock, but when the time

188

showed, it was three minutes past two. She was certain, now, that this had been a big mistake. The man wasn't even going to show up.

It was five minutes past two now, that was it, he was definitely not coming. Alice turned on her heel, full of disgust, and bumped straight into him as he reached out a hand to tap her on the shoulder.

'Oh, sorry, I thought you . . . might have said outside the station and not under the clock,' she said, not wanting him to know that she'd been concerned.

'Sorry I'm a little late,' he said. 'I had to see someone, and it went on longer than I expected.'

'Oh no, don't worry about that,' said Alice, flushing pink to the roots of her hair. 'I've only just got here myself.'

'Shall we go then?' he said, and Alice realized that she was still just standing there, staring at him, her heart bumping in her chest.

'Yes, of course,' she said.

'Do you want to take my arm?' he said. 'I thought we could go over the river to Birkenhead Park and take tea by the lake. Is that satisfactory?'

'Yes,' she said, 'thank you.' And as she walked down the steps of Lime Street Station, on Roderick Morgan's arm, Alice thought that she was, most certainly, one of the finest ladies in the whole of Liverpool.

'I have a boat waiting,' he said, as they turned away from the station, and even before he finished the sentence, Alice was sure that she could feel the breeze off the Mersey on her face.

189

He continued to make gentle conversation as they walked, but the words seemed to get jumbled up in her head, and somehow she couldn't concentrate. It felt like she was walking in a dream.

It seemed like no time at all before they were going in through the harbour gate. Alice felt the excitement of it straight away. She realized that she hadn't really seen the place on the day that she'd come here to say goodbye to Maud. She'd been too sorrowful and too distracted. This time she could properly smell the salty air and hear the cry of the gulls. And the closer they got, the more she was caught up in the energy that emanated from the place. She felt excited now; she wanted to see the water and the ships.

'It will be busy today, there's a ship going to New York,' said Morgan.

'Is it the *Oceanic*?' asked Alice.

'It is, yes,' he replied, clearly impressed.

'Oh, it's just that my friend, Maud, she went on that, she sailed to New York after she got married.'

'A wonderful city,' said Morgan. 'I've been there many times. I would love to take you there, Alice, to see your friend.'

She glanced at him sharply, thinking that even in her wildest dreams, no man should be suggesting such a thing on a casual acquaintance.

'When we get to know each other a little better, of course, and that's if you do want to go,' he added, immediately sensing her disquiet.

Alice nodded, satisfied that the man had at

least some foot in the real world. Nevertheless, she had to admit, the thought of going on a ship across the Atlantic Ocean sent a thrill right through her body.

'This is where I work,' said Morgan, waving his hand in the direction of a huge, brick-built warehouse on the harbourside. Alice would have liked to slow their pace a little, to take it all in, but he swept past with her on his arm. She could see the ships jammed in side by side, and when she looked out to the estuary, there were more there, waiting to come in. The unmistakeable buzz of it all, on top of her own excitement, was starting to become a bit too much to bear, so she was relieved when he stopped and asked her to wait for a moment, whilst he disappeared from view, down some stone steps.

As Alice stood with the world of the harbour flowing around her, she had time to get her breath back, and she knew that, even if she didn't get any further, or get to go out on a ship today, this was enough, simply being here, today, with a beautiful man. Even if it was just for one day. She hadn't liked to leave Victoria — she had so little time with her now, with working at the hospital — but Marie was right, a woman needs a bit more in her life than looking after babies and doing the laundry. This was wonderful.

She was still gazing out across the harbour, when Morgan's head bobbed up from the stone steps. 'We're all set. This way, Alice,' he beckoned.

'Down here,' he indicated, waiting to take her hand and guide her.

191

Alice picked up her skirt, wondering what the boat would be like and how many men would be rowing, or maybe it would have a sail . . .

At the bottom of the steps, Morgan told her to stand still, while he leant down to say a few words to a man who sat bobbing up and down in a very small boat. He looked remarkably like Tommy Knox, with his weather-beaten face and grizzled chin. The man was holding an oar in each hand. Alice had been expecting something much bigger and in her mind's eye it had a padded velvet cushion. If this was their boat, she could see that they would be squeezed in and they would be very close to the water.

After Morgan had brought his conversation to an end, he straightened up and offered her his hand. Alice hesitated, and looked him straight in the eye. 'Are you sure that we're all going to fit in there?' she asked.

The man in the boat started to chuckle and he was shaking his head.

'We'll be fine,' said Morgan, still holding out his hand.

'It's just that I've never been in a boat before . . . Does it rock around? Is it safe?'

'Safe as houses,' laughed the man with the oars.

'It's perfectly safe,' said Morgan, smiling and stepping into the boat, which immediately lurched from side to side. 'Come on, Alice,' he said, 'I'll hold it steady for you.'

'But I can't go in there,' she stammered.

'Of course you can,' he said with a grin.

Alice stood momentarily terrified. What if she

fell out of the boat and drowned, leaving her child an orphan? She was still shaking her head, her feet planted firmly on dry land.

'Honestly, Alice,' Morgan said. 'Look,' and he wobbled the small boat from side to side with his feet. The old sailor with the oars was laughing his head off.

'It's more than safe, miss,' shouted the old salt. 'You've no need to worry.'

Alice was terrified, but seeing Morgan, still smiling and reaching a hand out to her, she made her decision; she would go.

'If you're not happy when you sit down, here on this seat next to me, we won't set out. I promise you, we will go back up those steps. But Alice, to go out on the harbour and see the ships from here, there's nothing like it. I promise you, you will love it. And these small boats, they go to and fro all day between the big ships. They're as safe as houses.'

Alice was still frowning, wishing that they were houses, sitting firmly on dry land, but she'd already made her decision. So she took the hand that he'd proffered and stepped down into the small boat. As it lurched, he grabbed her and they both started laughing. But once she was sitting down, side by side with him, she began to feel a bit safer. She did clutch the side of the boat once they started to move, but she soon got into the rhythm of it, and once she could see how the vessel rode the swell of the water, she began to feel proud of herself for stepping into a boat, having never been out on any body of water in her whole life. Wait till I tell Tommy

193

about this tomorrow, she thought, as they made their way across the harbour.

'How far is Birkenhead?' she said, concerned that the small boat seemed to be heading out to sea.

'Just across the river. Don't worry, we'll soon be there. And then when we come back, we'll take the ferry.'

Alice nodded, still holding on to the side of the boat and beginning to feel the warmth of his body as he nestled against her.

She started to smile as his arm crept around her back and she eased herself into a more comfortable position. He gazed at her and smiled in return. 'I think you will like the park, Alice,' he said softly.

Before they reached the other side of the river, the old salt rowing the boat deftly pulled them alongside one of the ships moored at anchor.

'I won't be a moment,' said Morgan, clambering out of the boat and up the ropes at the side. He was back within minutes clasping a wooden box under his arm.

I wonder if that's the smuggling Michael told me about that day on the ward, thought Alice, smiling to herself, as he placed the box carefully in the bottom of the boat and covered it with a tarpaulin.

'A box of the best cigars,' he said, looking up and instantly answering her unspoken question.

'Right,' she said, not sure what else to say.

The closer they got to the other side of the river, the more Alice could see how different it was to the crowded city that they had left behind. There seemed to be more sky, more air somehow. Even before they landed, and Morgan stooped to help her out of the boat, Alice had begun to feel a lightness about her and she sprang out of the boat, catching him off balance. Laughing, they clung together for a few moments.

There was a hackney carriage waiting nearby and, after a few words to the driver, Morgan came back and indicated with an outstretched arm that they were ready to move. As they drove, Morgan told her some of the history of Birkenhead Park, how agricultural land had been bought for public use. Alice could tell by the way that he was speaking, as if he himself had built it, that he loved the place. He even told her about the drains, of stone and tile, that provided all the water that supplied the man-made lake — a lake that contained aquatic plants, goldfish and swans. And the paths were rolled gravel on top of crushed stone and cinder.

'And wait till you see the grand entrance and the pavilion, based on a Roman boathouse, right by the lake.'

'How do you know all of this?' asked Alice, with a smile.

'I have inside information,' he said at first, but then seeing her questioning face he continued, 'my father worked on it. He was one of the navvies who dug out the paths and the lake, and he helped build the stone walls.'

Alice was surprised. She'd thought he was going to say his father had been the architect or something like that. Maybe Michael had been right when he'd said that Morgan came from the streets of Liverpool. Rags to riches.

As they arrived at the entrance and drove through the beautiful curved arch, Alice began to understand why he was so excited about the place. She'd got used to seeing all the grand buildings in the city, and this was nowhere near as ornate. But, for Alice, the line of the entrance was beautiful and it stood out, brilliant against the green, open space. They had nothing like this in the small rural town where she came from. She felt as though they were arriving at the Queen's residence. All she could do was smile, and then she reached out a hand to Morgan, sitting opposite. 'Thank you for bringing me here today.'

She could tell that he was trying not to smile too much but was very pleased by the first impression that the park had made.

Morgan opened the door and descended first, so that he could assist Alice out of the carriage. In that moment she thought that she actually was the Queen; nothing had ever happened to her like this before. The sky was blue, the sun was shining and there, waiting to hold her hand as she stepped out of the carriage, was the most handsome man that she'd ever seen. As she descended from the carriage, her heart was fluttering and when she looked around, it almost took her breath away. There was grass, stretching away in all directions, flanked by trees. And the air was clear, without a tinge of soot.

She felt a bit breathless. All she could do was gaze around her, still holding his hand. Then she heard a jingling sound and when she looked around, there stood a group of donkeys, all saddled up with their tinkling bells and brightly coloured bridles, ready to take excited children on a ride across the park.

Inside, Alice felt like an excited child herself. And as she took Morgan's arm to stroll down the well-laid path, she took deep breaths of the clear air to try and steady herself.

As she walked, she realized that she hadn't really seen any grass or green trees since she'd moved to Liverpool. She had lived in amongst crowded buildings and smoke-blackened brick and smoke for so long, with the few trees being dark with soot, that she'd forgotten how much she'd missed the green fields, and especially the trees. Seeing them now almost moved her to tears.

Their afternoon in the park went by like a dream. Morgan was a perfect gentleman: he took her arm, made conversation, paid her attention. And when they came to the Pavilion, Alice couldn't help but stand back and admire the beautiful structure. Then, as they sat at a table set by the lake and waited for tea to be brought, she could hardly speak. Watching the lazy glide of the white swans on the lake, she thought that she might have found her heaven.

'Where are you from, Alice?' said Morgan, eventually.

'I think you know that already, from your sources,' she said, meeting his gaze with a smile.

'Of course, yes, but I mean, where were you born?'

'Ah, I see,' she said, not seeing any reason why she shouldn't give a full account of the rural town where she was born.

'What do your family think about you having a baby?' he asked.

'Oh, they don't know, they can't know. That's why I'm still here. Well, that, and I need to finish my nurse training. But you know all about that, don't you?'

'Not quite all,' he said. 'I must admit I was rather surprised to see you on the ward when I came in to see Ray. I wasn't expecting that. But I was glad that I could catch up with you, see that you were all right. If the cornermen trouble you again, Alice, just let me know.'

'I will,' she said, wondering what mysterious powers he had.

'And what about you, Mr Morgan?' said Alice, pouring herself another cup of tea. 'What's your story?'

She saw him stiffen a little and draw back in his chair. She sat there waiting. She wasn't going anywhere, she had time to listen.

Just as he was opening his mouth to speak, a voice rang out behind them, 'Morgan, old chap. How are you doing?'

Alice could swear that his face was instantly relieved as he stood up and turned to greet the well-dressed gentleman who was heading in their direction. Morgan didn't introduce her and she saw the gentleman give her a puzzled glance. Their exchange was short and all the while Alice could see that Morgan held his shoulders square, almost blocking her from view.

'That was a . . . business acquaintance,' he said, as he sat back down. 'I've been in the import trade many years. I can't go anywhere without bumping into somebody wanting to know when the next shipment of tobacco or brandy is coming in . . . '

As he rested back in his chair and continued to speak about his work, Alice knew that she wasn't going to get anything more from Mr Morgan about his personal life, at least for today. She could also see that, despite his easy demeanour, there was something in his eyes that told her that behind that smile, he was almost certainly hiding something from her. It didn't put her off; in fact it made her heart beat a little faster. He intrigued her. And as they sat, and he poured more tea, she watched his manicured hands on the fine bone china and then lifted her eyes to his smiling face and it felt like nothing else mattered. She just wanted to melt into him and rest warmly there with her head against his broad shoulder, for ever.

She could have watched him until the evening began to fall and the night closed around them, but in what seemed like no time at all, he was looking at his pocket watch and telling her that they needed to make sure to catch the ferry back across the Mersey.

All too soon they were travelling back in the hackney carriage and then boarding the ferry. And she could see that he looked a little distant now, as if he had other things on his mind. But he was still attentive, still making sure that she was comfortable.

As the shores of Liverpool loomed closer, Alice took a moment to savour the time that she'd spent away from her usual life. She'd missed seeing Victoria but she hadn't worried about her, not once, and she knew that she had never felt such ease with any man before. Even Jamie, who she'd grown up with.

As they arrived back, the light was starting to fade. Alice knew that the day would soon be over but she felt perfectly content. There was no pressure from him, and even though she hardly knew him, she felt secure. The afternoon out had been exactly what she needed. And as she walked along, her arm linked in his, she felt light, as if she was still drifting in a dream or some other woman's life. The life of a lady.

She had asked if they could walk back through the city, to make the day last as long as possible. When they reached the top of the alley, Alice hesitated. She didn't want to be saying goodbye to him outside the blue door of the house and have some customer stepping around them, so she requested that he leave her there.

'As you wish,' said Morgan, glancing down the alley one more time to make absolutely sure her way was clear. And then he was starting to smile. 'I have never met anyone quite like you before, Alice Sampson.'

Alice straightened her back and looked him in the eye, almost hypnotized. It was uncanny. Even after all the years that she'd known Jamie, she'd never felt anything like this. It was like magic.

'Not one, just like you,' he repeated quietly, taking her hand and lifting it to his lips.

200

Alice had to smile and take a deep breath, otherwise her knees might have given way there and then. She felt the tingles of that kiss reach down all through her body.

'Until the next time,' he murmured, and all she could do was smile and make herself walk away from him with her knees weak and her heart pounding. She wanted to look back, desperately wanted to, but she would not. If he meant all of the things that he'd just said, he would be standing there, gazing after her. If he didn't mean it, well, he'd have turned and walked away. Right then, she didn't want to know the reality. In her head, she could see him, gazing after her until she disappeared out of sight.

Today had been exactly what she needed; it had been heaven. But Alice knew that she had to be careful. She was a mother, and her every waking moment was taken up by doing the right thing for her child. Days like this one were for taking time off and for dreaming, only dreaming.

13

'. . . a strong practical . . . interest in the case, how it is going on. This is what makes the true Nurse. Otherwise the patients might as well be pieces of furniture.'

Florence Nightingale

'Ha, ha,' laughed Tommy Knox on the ward the next morning. 'Even I don't like going out on those small boats into the harbour, they're rocking all over the place.'

'Really?' said Alice. 'Well, the sailor with the oars told me that they were safe as houses . . . '

Tommy didn't answer, he was still shaking his head and laughing, but then his face began to crease with pain and Alice knew that she would have to try and calm him.

'It's all right, Tommy, all right, just rest back on your pillows, that's right, now let me have a look at the dressing. Mmm, it looks ready for another change,' she said, keeping her voice steady but immediately concerned by the colour of what she could see oozing from the wound.

'I'll leave you now and go to find Sister. We need to get you some more laudanum for the pain, and we'll see about changing that dressing, when the pain is more manageable.'

'Aye aye, Captain,' gasped Tommy, trying to smile but only able to manage a grimace.

Alice knew that his pain was severe; she needed to find Sister Law straight away.

'I see,' said Sister, after listening carefully to everything that Alice had to say. 'The wound is showing signs of suppuration but Mr Knox doesn't seem to have much of a fever and it isn't showing any sign of healing. It might mean that the lump we removed was indeed cancer and that it is still active.'

Alice was trying to make sense of what Sister was saying.

'We might need to try some other treatments, some lead or arsenic paste, in that case,' said Sister as they made their way to the cupboard containing the laudanum. 'And if that doesn't work then there probably won't be any more that we can do. We've seen these cases before. Unfortunately, all we can do is wait and see. But I'm sorry to say, Nurse Sampson, that things don't look all that good for our Mr Knox.'

Alice felt shaky inside. She wanted to cry, there and then. But what good would that do Tommy? He was lying there on his bed waiting for some pain relief. The best she could do for him was take him the laudanum and do everything in her power to make him comfortable.

Sister Law picked up the medicine but then caught sight of one of the probationers, Nurse Fry, struggling to help a patient out of bed. 'You take it, Nurse Sampson, administer the drops and then let me know when he's settled enough for us to do the dressing.

'Give him a tot of brandy as well, Nurse

Sampson,' she called. 'I've left the bottle by his bed.'

Back at Tommy's bed, Alice was moved to tears when she saw how he was trying to help himself as much as he could. He'd leant back on the pillows, closed his eyes and was taking deep breaths, just like she'd told him.

'But there's no shifting this pain without the laudanum,' he grimaced, opening his mouth to gratefully receive the drops.

'Now take this as well,' she said, offering him a swig of brandy from the small bottle by his bed.

'I thank you kindly, Nurse Sampson,' he said, his face still puckered with pain. 'But can you please remind Sister Law that I much prefer me rum.'

'I'll tell her,' said Alice, trying to smile, but fighting to hold back the sadness of what Sister Law had just told her. 'I'll be back to do the dressing, just as soon as the pain starts to ease.'

'Aye aye, Captain.'

Moving across the ward to Mr Swain's bed, Alice found a similar situation. He was lying, gritting his teeth, with such a look of agony on his face that Alice didn't even have to ask if he needed anything for the pain.

She spoke gently, telling him that she would get something for him, desperately wanting him to be out of his misery. His jaw was so tightly clenched that he could barely speak, and his body was rigid beneath the hospital sheet.

'I wish now I'd told him to chop the bloody thing off,' he muttered.

Alice felt her heart ache for him; he sounded

completely without hope.

She was just about to go ahead and administer some drops from the bottle she still clutched in her hand, when she heard Miss Houston's voice behind her. 'Hold off with those for the moment, Nurse Sampson,' she said. 'I saw this patient earlier and I've asked Dr McKendrick to come and have a look.'

Alice turned, relieved to know that some action was about to be taken. Ada came to the head of the bed, telling Mr Swain that she was sorry that he was in so much pain, then quietly explaining that the doctor would be there very soon to assess him, and there was definitely something that they could give to help him.

Even before she had finished, Dr McKendrick appeared, carrying a small wooden box. He took one look at the patient and then spoke softly to him. 'Mr Swain, you don't seem to be getting much benefit from the laudanum drops that we've been giving. I want to try some new treatment. I have been administering what are called hypodermic injections to severe cases. I use a needle to inject some morphine just beneath the skin. Is it all right if we try this for you?'

'Yes, yes,' muttered Mr Swain through clenched teeth, his whole body starting to shake now with the sheer effort of withstanding relentless pain.

'Hypo means under, and derma is from the Greek for skin, so hypo-dermic,' murmured Miss Houston.

'Hypodermic injection,' repeated Alice, as she

observed Dr McKendrick open the wooden box and take out a glass tube with markings down the side, which had some kind of plunger fitted to it. Then he fished in his pocket and removed a small bottle containing some liquid. 'I already prepared a third of a grain of liquefied morphine,' he said to Miss Houston. 'From what you'd already told me, I felt sure we'd need it.'

Ada nodded.

Then he removed a needle from the velvet-lined box and screwed it on to the syringe. Removing the stopper from the small glass bottle, he held it with one hand and then inserted the needle into the liquid, pulling up the plunger to draw up the liquid. Once he had it all, Dr McKendrick held the syringe up to the light, gave it a few taps and then depressed the plunger a little, until there was a drop of the liquid at the tip of the needle.

Miss Houston moved to the patient's head. 'We are going to give the injection into your right thigh, just beneath the skin, Mr Swain,' she said. 'It should be given to the affected area but due to the rawness of your wound, that is impossible.'

Mr Swain nodded, and then he started to groan with pain.

'Just do it, just do it,' he pleaded.

Miss Houston grasped his hand. 'You will feel the sharp scratch of the needle and then it will sting, but in ten minutes or so the pain should start to wane.'

As she was speaking, Dr McKendrick pulled aside the bed sheet, and Alice saw him grasp some skin on the man's thigh with one hand, and with the other he inserted the needle at an angle, and then slowly depressed the plunger. Once the needle was withdrawn, he massaged the area and then gave the needle a wipe with a clean handkerchief before unscrewing it from the syringe and replacing both parts of the apparatus back in the velvet-lined box.

Miss Houston gestured for Alice to come and hold Mr Swain's hand. She was straight there, her own teeth clenched, as they all stood praying for the man's pain to subside.

'Nurse Sampson, we are just going across the ward to check on Mr Knox,' said Miss Houston. 'We will be back directly. Shout out if you have any concerns.'

Alice nodded, glad to be involved in the whole process, but sceptical regarding the relief that could actually be brought by injecting such a small amount of liquid into a man's thigh.

The minutes went by. Mr Swain was gripping Alice's hand so tightly that it was quite painful, but she was determined to endure it. He was still clenching his teeth and his body was shaking again with the effort. Alice didn't think he could take much more of it. She was increasingly concerned for her patient, and hoped that Miss Houston and Dr McKendrick wouldn't be long with Tommy. She glanced across but they were still speaking.

Looking back down to her patient, Alice could see the furrows of pain etched across his face. She was desperate for him to have some relief. If this injection didn't work, she was beginning to think that he might need to have some chloroform or something.

Then, as she shifted her weight slightly, she felt some relaxation of the grip that he had on her hand, and his body started to calm. This might be starting to work, she thought, beginning to feel a little excited.

But the man's face was still scrunched up with pain. The only thing that she could do was continue to hold his hand. She'd seen what a difference this simple act could make to a patient. It was something that she'd learnt early on in her training. The contact of a human hand was like an understanding between two people. She'd learnt through experience to give the right amount of pressure. Not squeezing too hard or too soft — gentle but firm was always best. It didn't always work. When the pain was excruciating, as in Mr Swain's case, it was impossible to reduce with the touch of a hand. But she still used it anyway, just in case.

She continued to hold his hand until his grip relaxed even more.

'How do you feel now, Mr Swain?' she asked gently.

'Much better,' he said, opening his eyes but sounding a bit sleepy. 'I feel like I'm floating.'

Alice started to smile. She glanced across to Miss Houston and this time, met her gaze. Miss Houston smiled in return. Alice felt like she wanted to tell the whole hospital what had just happened. She couldn't believe it.

'Well done, Mr Swain, well done!' said Dr McKendrick when he came back across the ward. 'I am so pleased that the injection has worked for you.'

'S'wonderful,' slurred Mr Swain. 'Thank you, Doctor . . . ' and then he was drifting off to sleep.

Dr McKendrick gave a small smile, nodded and then told them he was urgently required on Female Surgical. Picking up the small wooden box, he hurried off to his next case.

Alice had let go of Mr Swain's hand and she pulled his pillow into a more comfortable position, making sure that the sheet beneath him was straight.

'That is the most marvellous thing that I've ever seen,' she said to Miss Houston, her eyes shining. 'I didn't think there was much chance of it working, such a tiny amount of liquid like that. And he was in such horrible pain. But what a result!'

'It does work very well, doesn't it?' said Miss Houston. 'I've seen Dr McKendrick use it a few times now and apart from one case where there was very little benefit, the results have been very pleasing. He is an exceptional doctor . . . '

'He is indeed,' agreed Alice.

'All right, Nurse Sampson,' said Ada. 'Now that our patient is out of pain, do you want to help me with his dressing? We're going to try something I learnt out in the Crimea . . . '

'Yes, definitely,' said Alice, full of enthusiasm.

'Mr Swain,' said Ada. 'We are going to remove the dressing from your leg and I will replace it with some gauze soaked in iodine. This will sting quite a bit at first, but you shouldn't feel it too much after the injection. The iodine will clean the leg and help prevent further suppuration. It will promote healing. We can give you some laudanum as well, if required. Do you understand?'

Their patient nodded sleepily.

'Right, Nurse Sampson, if you could run and get me an enamel bowl, a full bottle of iodine, some lengths of gauze and a bandage, we'll make a start. Also, bring a small rubber sheet from the sluice. This will be a messy business, and we need to put it underneath his leg to protect the bed.'

When Alice returned, Ada had donned an apron and she had already removed the soiled dressing.

'What we need to do now, Nurse Sampson, is soak the gauze in the iodine, and then place the soaks along the leg. We could wash it down first but I don't want to spend too long, just in case his pain returns, and the iodine should do the job nicely. When all the soaks are in place we'll bandage, not too tight but firmly enough to hold the dressings in place. We'll need to put double bandages on, to try and stop too much seepage of iodine.'

Alice nearly said, 'Aye aye, Captain,' but fortunately it came out as, 'All right.'

She poured a full bottle of iodine into the bowl, immediately smelling the pungent aroma. And as she added the gauze and submerged it in the liquid, her hands were instantly stained yellow.

'I'm sorry, Nurse Sampson,' said Ada with a smile. 'Our hands will be yellow for a while after this.'

Working together, the two nurses soon had the leg dressed and bandaged. Alice was pleased with the job, and relieved that Mr Swain had slept through the whole procedure. They'd never have got anywhere near him with any of it, if it hadn't been for the injection.

'Right, Nurse Sampson, this dressing will need to be changed every day, for at least three days. Can you do it for me?'

'Yes, of course,' said Alice.

'Speak to Sister Law about his pain relief. If drops of laudanum will manage it, then use that. But by all means, call for Dr McKendrick and the hypodermic injection again if Mr Swain needs it.'

'I definitely will,' said Alice.

She was back and forth between Tommy and Mr Swain for most of the day. By the time of afternoon visiting, Sister Law, concerned that neither of the men had visitors, told her to get herself a seat and sit by one of them, or take turns between the two.

And so Alice found herself there, listening to Mr Swain murmur snatches of disjointed conversation as he drifted in and out of sleep. Sometimes he grimaced but mostly he was still drifting somewhere with the morphine he'd had. Once he was shouting 'Help, help!' and Alice knew that she was glimpsing what could only be a part of his experience during the war, when he'd received his injury.

As she sat, she could keep an eye on Tommy across the ward.

Looking at Mr Swain resting peacefully in the

211

bed, she found it difficult to believe that he was the same patient that she'd nursed last year when she was a first ward probationer. He'd been coming off the drink and he'd had terrible shakes and been very agitated. The nurses had to attend him constantly, sometimes wrestling him back down on to the bed. She recalled that he'd given one of the nurses a black eye. She seemed to remember it had been Millicent Langtry. Poor Millicent, thought Alice, she just can't react fast enough.

'Stop it, Alice,' she muttered to herself, starting to feel a tickle of amusement building.

Mr Swain was still very settled, so she got up from the stool and carried it across to sit by Tommy's bed. He was sleeping, so she just sat quietly. Then, seeing him grimace, she gently lifted the sheet to check the dressing: all seemed to be well. Then she laid a hand on his forehead to check for fever.

'You shouldn't be doing that now, Nurse — are you a nurse?' said a well-spoken but harsh voice from the bottom of the bed.

Alice looked up, startled.

'Yes, I am a nurse,' she said.

'Well, times have moved on. Are you not aware of the new medical thermometer?' said the indignant young man, with thin hair and small, deep-set eyes.

'Yes, of course, but —— '

'Well, in my opinion, it has to be the method of choice for determining fever,' said the young man, raising his chin.

'And you are . . . ?' said Alice, not knowing if

212

he was a visitor or a doctor.

'I am Tobias Stafford, a medical student. I have been placed on the ward to work with Mr Jones, and to keep you nurses in order.'

Really, thought Alice, we'll see about that.

'I see,' she said. 'Well, in my view, having just felt the patient's forehead, I don't think we need the thermometer just yet.'

'All the more reason, Nurse, for me insisting that the instrument is brought immediately, so that we medical men can check.'

'As you wish,' said Alice, not showing any sign of moving from her stool. 'The thermometer is on the top shelf of the store cupboard,' she said, pointing down the ward.

'Yes, but — '

'Sister told me to sit here with the patient and not leave his side,' she said emphatically. She was determined that, unless a patient's life was threatened, she would not leave her stool for an obnoxious young man like Mr Tobias Stafford.

She watched him stride down the ward, his nose in the air.

Out of the corner of her eye she could see him examining each of the shelves in the store cupboard, and more than once he glanced in her direction. Then he was back, huffing and puffing by the side of Tommy's bed with the box containing the medical thermometer under his arm. Alice watched as he removed it from the box with a flourish.

'Right, Nurse,' he said, pursing his lips. 'Watch and learn.'

Alice continued to sit politely and she did

watch, just to make sure that no harm came to her patient.

She saw Mr Stafford open Tommy's shirt and place the thermometer in the axilla, the wrong way round. Alice knew that the bulb had to be in the armpit, otherwise it wouldn't work. She opened her mouth to tell him, but the arrogant man lifted a hand to silence her.

'Watch and learn, Nurse,' he said, gazing across at her with a satisfied smile.

Alice didn't make any further attempt to correct his mistake; she let him get on with it. He would find out soon enough that the thermometer wasn't registering, and she looked forward to seeing his face.

After a few minutes, Mr Stafford glanced at the thermometer. Alice saw him frown, and then he gave a small cough, but still he stood by the bed with his nose in the air.

Alice could see Tommy starting to wake up, and his eyes fluttered open. He saw Alice and smiled at her and was going to sit up when she said, 'Please stay still, Mr Knox. We have a new medical student, Mr Stafford, and he is measuring your temperature with the thermometer.'

Tommy shifted his gaze to Mr Stafford, and then he looked down at the thermometer.

'You've got it in the wrong way round,' he said. 'The bulb needs to be in the armpit so the warmth will make the mercury expand.'

'What, what?' blustered Mr Stafford, his face bright red. 'Of course I knew that, I was just, I was . . .'

Alice couldn't help but smile and Tommy had

a glint in his eye when he looked back at her.

'I was just checking that this nurse knew what to do,' he fobbed, removing the thermometer and replacing it in the box with a click.

As Mr Stafford stalked back down the ward it was all Alice and Tommy could do to stop themselves from laughing out loud.

'I hope he doesn't come anywhere near me again,' said Tommy quietly. 'He reminds me of a wet-behind-the ears officer on board ship, thinking because he's got a bit of training, he knows it all. So long as he keeps away from me . . . '

'Do you want to sit up?' said Alice, still smiling. 'Are you feeling more comfortable now?'

'I seem to be, Nurse Sampson. Maybe this thing is on the mend after all.'

'Maybe so,' replied Alice, her throat tightening as she helped him lean forward and started plumping his pillows.

Visiting was almost over and Alice knew that Sister Law would be back down the ward any minute with further instructions. Whilst she was positioning his pillows to make sure he was as comfortable as he possibly could be, someone tapped her on the shoulder. It was Millicent, speaking quietly and mumbling something about a man who wanted to see her. And then she was pointing down the ward and telling her that he was there, near the door.

Alice glanced up and saw a stocky man in a wide-brimmed hat pulled down over his face. She had no idea who it was.

'I'll just finish here and then I'll go and see him,' she said, glancing down the ward again, but still she didn't recognize him, even though he was now looking in her direction.

'I'll be back to check you again soon,' she murmured to Tommy before walking briskly down the ward.

As she got closer, she could see that the man was staring at her from under his hat, and the lower part of his face looked weather-beaten.

Then he removed his hat with a flourish.

Alice screamed. She couldn't help it.

Standing there, grinning from ear to ear, was someone she had never expected to see again. Jamie!

Immediately, her legs went weak and she almost staggered but was able to force herself upright.

She could hear Jamie's voice, insistent, calling her name, and then he was at her side.

'Jamie,' she gasped, feeling as though all the breath had been knocked out of her. He was broader in the shoulder than he used to be and his hair had been bleached by the Australian sun, but it was Jamie all right. Alice stared at his face, newly lined with creases on his forehead and a furrow at his brow. She was struggling to take it all in.

He grabbed her arm, steadying her.

'Sorry to give you a shock,' he said. 'I got off the ship today, I came straight to see you.'

'But — my mother wrote — she told me you were working on a cattle ranch.'

'Well, I was, and I did do that, but the letters take so long to reach home, probably by the time my mother got that one, I'd already decided to head home. I missed everything much more than

I expected. I missed you, Alice, so much. I kept thinking about you here, in Liverpool, working at the hospital, and it didn't feel right. You should be back home, with your family. I didn't realize until I came here to board my ship for Australia what a place this city is. Full of sin. I know that your mother approved you coming here, but she has no idea . . . That's why I came to see you straight away. I've got a bit of money together, I can take you back home with me. We can be together again — '

'No,' cried Alice instinctively, her head reeling.

She saw him lean away from her and ball his fist. For the first time since she had known him as a grown man, she felt a little afraid.

'I mean, we can't talk about this here,' she said, lowering her voice. 'Sister will be down the ward in a minute. Meet me outside the hospital, when I finish.'

'But can you not just leave now, Alice? I'm back. We can be together. I didn't know till I went away to Australia, but you're all I ever wanted. Come with me, come now. You don't need to train as a nurse any more.' He grabbed her arm.

'Jamie, stop!' cried Alice. 'Please, I need to see you after work, I can't just leave. You must understand . . . '

His shoulders slumped and he let go of her arm. Alice couldn't help but feel sorry for him. He looked exhausted and dusty from travel, as if he was worn out and dried up.

'Do you have somewhere to stay?' she asked.

He nodded.

'Well, go there and clean up, then get some

rest. I'll see you outside the hospital, near the gate. I'll be there by eight p.m. at the latest.'

He nodded again and tried to smile, but all of his energy was gone.

'We'll talk then, I promise,' she said softly.

As he turned and walked towards the door, Alice felt her legs go a little weak. She was still shocked by his sudden reappearance, but what shocked her even more was how relieved she was to see him walking away. He had made her feel scared and empty inside — this person from her home who she knew, but didn't know any more. Someone who, at one time, everyone had considered to be her fiancé. There was no elation, no excitement. All she felt for him was concern, and all she felt for herself now was anxiety that her life in Liverpool and her future career would be compromised.

Alice knew that if he found out she had his child, he would insist on dragging her home to be married. And what's more, in law, Victoria was his child, not hers. She had heard stories of children being claimed, removed from their mothers. She couldn't risk that happening to Victoria. She had to keep her secret from him.

She ran from the ward that evening, praying that Eddy would be waiting for her, wanting to get into the Nurses' Home so that she could speak to her before Jamie turned up.

She quickened her pace when she saw Eddy sitting on the step.

'Quick,' she shouted, grabbing hold of her arm and dragging her up the steps.

'What the heck,' cried Eddy, as soon as they

were in through the door.

Alice was fighting for breath and needing to calm herself down so that she could tell the full story. She clung to her friend's arm, until she was able to get the words out.

'Crikey,' said Eddy, when she'd gasped out her explanation. 'That is unexpected. We all thought he'd gone for good. But are you sure, Alice? Are you quite sure that you don't want to tell him about the baby? Maybe you should take some more time to think about it.'

'I've never felt more sure about anything in my life, ever,' said Alice, calm now and measuring her words. 'Once he'd gone to Australia, I never really thought of him again until I found out I was carrying his child. And then, my feelings were vague. We grew up together, I didn't know any better. If he'd come back before the baby was born, I wouldn't have had any choice, and I was in such a state I probably would just have gone back home with him and settled down. But now . . . my life feels so different. I feel truly alive and I love the work. I'd have to give up everything. I can't do it, Eddy, I just can't, and he won't know any different. I'll tell him I need to stay here and finish my training; he'll go back home and he'll find some other girl to marry.'

'Well, Alice, you seem pretty sure to me . . . But you need to go and tell him now, get it over with,' Eddy said, glancing at the door. 'You go first, I'll follow along behind, so I can keep an eye on things. You'll have to make out that you're living here, inside the Nurses' Home, so he won't be suspicious.'

'Righto,' said Alice, still sure of her conviction but feeling butterflies in her stomach with the thought of encountering him again.

She saw him waiting. He looked up and smiled as she approached and in that moment she was even more sure of her decision. There was no spark, no connection between them. Not like she had with Morgan.

'I can't stay long,' she said immediately. 'They're very fussy about us spending time outside in the evening and we need to have our evening meal.'

Jamie nodded and tried to take her hand. Alice slipped it deftly from his grasp.

'I might as well come straight out and tell you, Jamie,' she said. 'I'm not coming home. I love the work here, my life is in Liverpool now . . .'

She saw him reel back as if she'd punched him.

'But I can't come and live here, Alice,' he said. 'My work is in farming, you know that.'

'I do know that,' she said quietly, waiting for him to realize.

'But that means that we will be living apart.'

'It does, and the thing is, Jamie, the hospital doesn't allow nurses to be married anyway, so — '

'So what you are saying is that you would rather stay here, in this sinful place, with all these people, and the filth on the streets. You want to stay here and nurse sick people in that crowded, horrible ward,' he hissed at her, his eyes blazing with anger now.

'Yes,' said Alice simply, struggling more than

ever to recognize this man who used to be so quietly spoken.

'Do you have any idea what I've been through out there, Alice? I've been robbed and tricked and beaten. All so that I could try and make some kind of a living. All the time thinking that I could get some money together and come back to you . . . '

'Well, I'm sorry for that,' said Alice firmly. 'But when we parted it seemed that you had no real intention of coming back.'

She screamed as he grabbed both her arms and started to shake her. 'Don't you start telling me what my intentions were,' he shouted, his callused hands digging into her flesh.

'Oi,' shouted Eddy, immediately there by Alice's side. 'You let go of her.'

'And who are you?' he blazed.

'I'm a senior nurse at this hospital, and if you don't let go of her I will call the police.'

'Pah,' spat Jamie, releasing Alice and throwing her off balance.

Eddy grabbed her and held her tight.

'You go home, Jamie, just go home,' sobbed Alice. 'Go and make a new life for yourself.'

He growled something in return as he backed away, and then he turned and stalked off down the street without a backward glance.

'He's gone, he's gone,' murmured Eddy. 'And it looks like he won't be back. But just to be on the safe side, once you've got your cape and hat on, we'll leave through the back of the building tonight. I'll be with you every step of the way, Alice, every step of the way. And when you arrive

221

in the morning, I'll be watching and waiting to make sure that the coast is clear.'

★ ★ ★

Alice slept poorly that night. The thought of Jamie had moved into her like some demon. She woke feeling ragged.

'You take care out there today, Alice,' said Marie, as she bent over the crib to kiss Victoria. 'You can never trust a fella who thinks he's got a claim on you.'

Alice nodded. She didn't really think that Jamie would turn up again; he had never had much staying power. Once he lost face with anything, usually that was it. But she would be on the lookout.

As she approached the Nurses' Home she could see Eddy on the step, peering around like some guard on sentry duty. As soon as she spotted Alice she shouted over, 'All clear.'

Alice couldn't help but laugh. Eddy would never be able to keep a low profile.

★ ★ ★

The ward was busy, as always, and that really helped. Alice submerged herself in it, taking even more time than usual to provide the detail of care. Tommy and Mr Swain kept her busy, and they had a couple of new admissions, one of which went straight to theatre for abdominal surgery. He was in the next bed to Tommy and needed regular attention post-operatively. Just at visiting time, as she was finishing a dressing check and trying to get her new patient to take a sip of water, she spotted Tommy waving frantically in her direction. At first she thought that he must need some laudanum or something, but then she saw him pointing down the ward. The visitors were just starting to file into the ward, and leading the way, she was horrified to see, was Jamie. He was glancing from side to side. He was looking for her.

She thought of ducking down by the side of the bed, but she could see the tension in his body; she knew that he would search and search until he found her. Best to step out and confront him, she thought.

'There you are,' he called, striding towards her.

Alice stood her ground and folded both arms in front of her.

He came right up to her, his eyes burning into her. 'I hope that you've been thinking things through, Alice. And you can see the error of your ways.'

'I have not changed my mind, Jamie,' she said, meeting his gaze. Noting again the thickness of his neck, the new roughness of his voice.

'We'll see about that,' he said, grabbing her arm.

Alice caught a fleeting image of the alarm on Tommy's face and then she could hear him calling down the ward, 'Sister, Sister.'

'You need to come with me, now,' Jamie said, his voice breaking.

'No,' she cried, wrenching her arm free. 'I

223

can't do that. My work here is important to me. I told you all of this yesterday. I am staying here.'

'You have to, you will — '

'I will not,' said Alice, planting her feet square, her breath coming fast and catching in her throat.

'Are you still telling me that this work, this stuff and nonsense about nursing, is more important to you than I am?'

'Yes,' said Alice simply. 'I won't change my mind. I'm sorry, but — '

'I'm not having it, Alice!' he shouted, lunging at her, grabbing the starched cap off her head, scrunching and twisting it in his hands before throwing it to the floor.

The ward had fallen silent, apart from one patient who was groaning in pain. Alice was in tears, her resolve broken. She bent down to pick her cap up, hearing at once the sound of Sister Law shouting down the ward, 'Mr Delaney, Mr Walker, please escort that young man off my ward and out of the hospital. Now.'

Alice straightened up, still determined to stand her ground. Then she saw Jamie start to make another lunge for her; she knew by his face he was going to drag her off the ward if need be.

'No!' she shouted.

In that moment, she saw a figure step between her and Jamie. It was the Reverend Seed.

Jamie must have been shocked to see a man of the cloth standing in his way. For one moment Alice thought that he had given up.

Then she heard his voice. 'Step aside, Reverend.'

'I will not,' said the Reverend firmly.

224

Jamie tried to push past him, but the Reverend stood his ground, shielding her.

She heard Jamie growl and then the Reverend ducked down, as Jamie threw a punch.

Immediately, the Reverend straightened and neatly planted a punch, right on Jamie's nose.

He staggered back; his nose was bleeding. And Michael and Stephen were straight there, one at either side of him.

'Well done there, Reverend Seed, I never would have thought you could use a punch like that,' said Michael as he and Stephen dragged Jamie off the ward.

He shot Alice a glance as they led him away; she saw the fury in his eyes. He looked like he wanted to kill her.

Alice tried to steady herself but her heart was pounding and her hands were shaking as she stood there holding the crushed cap, desperately trying to make sense of what had just happened. She felt as though she'd been hit by something very heavy.

'Thank you,' she said to the Reverend. He didn't seem to know what to do with himself now. He didn't know what to say.

Sister Law was straight there. 'Bravo, Reverend Seed,' she said. 'Where did you learn to box?'

'Oh, at school,' he said, almost apologetically. 'I never thought I'd ever need to use it, though. I hope I did the right thing?'

'You did indeed,' said Sister, turning to Alice, who was trying to pin her cap back in place.

'As for you, Nurse Sampson, I don't really know what has been going on, but can I suggest that you sort out your domestic squabbles outside the walls of this hospital? Are you clear?'

'Yes, Sister,' Alice said, trying to steady her voice and still attempting to pin her cap back in place.

'Leave the cap for now, Nurse Sampson,' said Sister Law. 'Get yourself a new one tomorrow morning.'

For a moment, Alice didn't know what to do with the crushed cap. She was standing in the middle of the ward, holding it.

'Give that to me,' said Tommy. 'I'll keep it safe for you till the end of the shift.'

Alice felt heartened by the man's kindness and as she walked to the side of his bed her legs began to feel steadier. Tommy gave her hand a squeeze. 'You can tell me if you want, Nurse Sampson, but you don't have to say a word. All I can say is, from what I saw of that young man yesterday and what I've just seen now, he's best away, well away.'

Alice handed the cap over to him and then she held his hand for a few moments. There was no need for either of them to say anything; all she needed was to feel his understanding of her situation. When she looked up she saw the Reverend Seed waiting quietly at the foot of the bed. He gave her a small smile and then nodded his head before turning on his heel and walking down the ward.

'Now that's a decent fella for you,' said Tommy quietly from his bed. 'And he packs a fair punch as well . . . who would have thought it.'

Alice smiled at him, then she took a deep breath and forced her shaky legs to take her down the ward to help a patient who was struggling to get out of bed. The man thanked her and then he took her hand as she stood by to make sure that he was steady enough to move.

'Don't you worry, Nurse,' he said. 'If that fella comes back lookin' for ye, we'll all be after 'im.'

'Thank you, Mr Latimer,' she said, starting to smile. And when she looked back down the ward she could see all of the men who were well enough to pay attention, looking in her direction and nodding their heads or offering a small salute.

14

'The nurse must have simplicity and a
single eye to the patient's good.'
Florence Nightingale

Alice gave a wry smile as she left the hospital
that evening. It was no surprise, after the day
that she'd had, that it was raining. Carrying her
ruined cap in her hand, she trudged the short
distance to the Nurses' Home. She felt nervous
coming out of the safety of the hospital, even
though Michael and Stephen had checked for
her that the coast was clear. But she was
determined that she would not give in to Jamie.
Even in the few hours since the shock of seeing
him again on the ward, she'd started to build up
more strength, convincing herself that she was
ready for him, if he tried anything else. And she
knew that, if he dared to take one step inside the
Nurses' Home, Miss Merryweather would soon
see him off. She wouldn't allow any man into the
hallowed space that lay behind that heavy
wooden door.

Safely through the door, Alice walked straight
to the open space. She had never done it before,
after a day's work, but she remembered how
Maud had found peace, looking up to the
skylight. The light was fading now, but Alice
gazed up, needing to stand where Maud had, if
nothing else. Trying to get some comfort. And

maybe she would have found some peace there if she hadn't been in the path of other nurses and probationers also coming off duty. She'd picked the wrong time; all she could feel was jangled, as she stood there with them streaming past her and climbing the stone stairs up to the galleries.

As she stood, one or two spoke to her and said goodnight and she saw Millicent Langtry drift past without seeing her. And then someone tapped her on the shoulder.

Alice froze, and then switched round, half-expecting to be confronted by Jamie again.

'What the heck is up with you?' said Eddy. 'You look like you've seen a ghost. Ah, you've seen him again, haven't you?'

'Yes,' said Alice. 'He came to the ward . . . '

And as she told Eddy the story her voice never faltered.

'We need to be even more careful with our comings and goings now,' said Eddy firmly. 'For example, we'll keep going out through the back. And you keep your head down in the morning when you're coming in. Can you not wear a wig or something, cover up that flame-red hair of yours?'

'Not really,' said Alice, starting to smile. 'Just imagine me turning up with my district nurse's hat perched on top of a wig. Even if Jamie didn't see me, I'd probably be picked up by the police.'

'True,' said Eddy. 'Well, we'll just be vigilant, and I'll be waiting for you out front again in the morning, and every morning until we know that the coast is clear. Maybe we could wrap you in a large shawl, give you a walking stick or something.'

Alice was giggling now.

'Let's get you back home to Stella's,' said Eddy, taking charge. 'I don't want you roaming the streets on your own. But rest assured, if he does come near, I'll give him a black eye to add to his busted nose.'

Alice couldn't help but laugh. Eddy was exactly the person she needed right now. It was wonderful to feel so well cared for and protected as they made their way through the city. Even so, when they were in amongst the crowds and she caught sight of something out of the corner of her eye, she imagined it was somebody lunging at her, and felt the shock all through her body.

'I'll leave you here, if that's all right. I need to get along and see my family,' said Eddy, as they stood outside the blue painted front door.

Alice nodded, and then put her arms around Eddy, 'Thank you,' she said. 'I don't know what I'd do without you, Edwina Pacey.'

'And I without you, Alice Sampson,' replied Eddy, giving her a kiss on the cheek. 'Now, I'm not moving from this step until you go through that door.'

As soon as Alice was in through the door, she heard the sound of Victoria, whimpering a little, sounding a bit tired. The sound ran through her and pulled on the knot of anxiety inside her. She could feel tears welling up as she stood there, taking deep breaths, trying to compose herself before she went through to the kitchen.

'Alice?' called Lizzie from the reception room, getting up from the purple velvet settee that she favoured to come through to the hallway and put an arm around her. 'Alice, what is it?'

Alice slumped against her, unable to speak.

'Come on, come through to the kitchen, let's go and see Victoria,' said Lizzie, gently leading her through and then helping her remove her cape and hat.

'What is it?' said Marie, turning with the baby in her arms.

Stella looked up from the table. 'Alice?'

'He turned up on the ward again today,' she said, 'and tried to drag me away . . . '

'What?' said Stella.

'No!' said Lizzie, speaking at the same moment.

Marie simply walked towards her and handed her the baby.

Alice buried her face in Victoria's hair, breathing in the scent of her. She stayed like that for as long as she needed, and then she sat with her, picking up the spoon from the table that she liked to play with and a doll that Marie had made for her.

As Alice sat back in her chair in the warm kitchen, the same room where her baby had been born, she started to feel some calm seeping back into her body. And when it was time, she put Victoria in her nightdress and then she sat and rocked her in front of the stove, like she did every night. Just rocking her and watching Hugo flick his tail as he lay there in front of the fire, his black fur speckled with brown singe marks.

'How that cat doesn't go up in smoke, I'll never know,' said Marie, looping an arm around Alice and giving her a squeeze. 'Lazy good-for-nothing moggy.'

And then Alice sang the lullaby that was their bedtime ritual, watching as her daughter's delicate eyelids fluttered towards sleep.

When the baby was sleeping, Alice still held on to her, rocking from side to side, not wanting to put her down, not yet. When her arm was stiff and aching and she could do no more, she walked through to their room behind the kitchen and settled Victoria in the crib which Marie had moved through for her.

Alice knew that she had to rest. Slowly she removed her clothing, savouring the feeling of freedom that came when she wore just a loose shift. Then she took down her long red hair, carefully placing the hairpins on the small chest that stood against the wall. She sat on the bed and brushed through her hair, feeling like a child again herself with this, her own bedtime ritual.

The 'baby' of the family, she'd always been allowed to sit on her father's knee as she brushed her hair, and as she'd sat, he'd told her made-up stories about the cows and the sheep on the farm, giving them names and all kinds of adventures. Until her mother would glance up to the clock, give him a nod, and it was time for bed. Then they would both scramble up the stairs, her and Frederick Sampson, in his stockinged feet, still smelling of the warm breath of the cows that he tended. As she sat now, alone in her small room, she missed her father. She missed him so much, it felt like a pain in her chest. And she wanted him, and only him, to know about his granddaughter. She wanted him to come and see her. But it felt like that would never happen, not now.

Hearing the baby snuffle, she leant over the crib once more, her hair falling around her face and surrounding her daughter. Leaning very close, she listened to the steady rhythm of her baby's breathing and then she was whispering to her; vowing that she would never give her up, no matter what happened.

'You are my daughter, Victoria,' she murmured. 'Mine.'

★   ★   ★

The next morning, Alice stepped gingerly out of the alley, not only alert to plain-clothes police but also on her guard in case Jamie was lurking. As she made her way to the hospital she drew in a sharp breath on a number of occasions when she caught a glimpse of a brown jacket or a man with the same way of walking. She had to give herself a stern talking to, and try to put the events of yesterday out of her mind. She couldn't let anything get in the way of her work at the hospital, not now that she was only weeks away from completing her training.

When she arrived at the Nurses' Home, Eddy was there again, as promised. 'All clear,' she shouted as soon as she saw Alice. 'All's well.'

Once Alice had reached her and they were both standing on the steps, Eddy said reassuringly, 'He's probably gone back home this time, Alice.'

'Probably,' said Alice, glancing around her, even as she spoke. 'Anyway, thanks, Eddy, you

233

get yourself off to work.'

'I'll see you this evening,' shouted Eddy, instantly on the move. 'Try not to worry.'

'I'll try,' murmured Alice to herself, as she turned to go up the steps. Then, remembering that she needed to get herself a new cap from the laundress, she swore under her breath and ran in through the door. Grabbing the squashed remains of her cap off the shelf, she set off running, but then had to run back to leave her cape and hat on the hook.

'Oh God,' she muttered under her breath. 'As if I'm not in enough trouble with Sister Law as it is, without being late.'

Grabbing the squashed cap again, she ran to the laundry, where she hoped she would find the laundress ready and waiting to meet her requirements. As she approached, she could see steam pouring out through the door. Once inside she made out the shape of a huge mangle in the corner and there were baskets of laundry stacked up. But there seemed to be no sign of a laundress.

'Hello, hello,' she called, starting to feel a bit desperate.

'Hello there,' said a tall, broad-shouldered figure stepping out from the fug of steam. 'What can I do for you?'

'I'm so sorry,' said Alice. 'I had an accident with my cap yesterday and I need another one urgently.'

'You wait there, young lady,' said the woman, her sleeves rolled up to the elbow. 'We'll soon have you sorted.'

Alice handed over the cap. 'This is a very sorry-looking object,' said the laundress, putting it aside and already taking a hot iron to press a new one. 'You must be the nurse who had some trouble on Male Surgical yesterday — is it Nurse Sampson?'

'Yes, that's right,' said Alice, amazed, as always, how news travelled around the hospital.

'Well, there you go, Nurse Sampson,' said the laundress, expertly folding the new cap. 'And if he comes back to bother you today or any other day for that matter, you send for me. I'm Dolly. I'll sort him out.'

'Thank you,' said Alice, grinning at the huge woman who stood before her and remembering that Miss Merryweather had told her that the new laundress had served in the Crimean War with Miss Houston.

Alice ran from the laundry and down the corridor to the ward. Arriving with seconds to spare, she joined the group of nurses already standing at the top of the ward with Sister Law. She'd been seen arriving late, she knew she had, but there was nothing she could do.

'A word,' said Sister Law, after she had allocated the morning duties.

Here we go, thought Alice, bracing herself as Sister Law puffed out her chest and pulled her shoulders square.

'Yesterday was an absolute disgrace, Nurse Sampson.'

'I know,' said Alice, her head bowed. 'And I'm so sorry.'

'Typical of a member of the opposite sex,' said

235

Sister. 'Throwing their weight about, thinking they know best. I will not have that on my ward.'

Alice looked up and Sister leant forward, her eyes shining. 'If he comes on my ward to cause trouble for you again, Nurse Sampson, he will have me to answer to. I didn't know the full story yesterday, but Mr Knox and Mr Delaney were able to furnish me with a little detail and I now have a clearer understanding of your situation. I will not have any young woman bullied or abused on my ward. Do you understand?'

'Yes, Sister,' said Alice.

'Now, get on with the work, Nurse Sampson. Let's get these patients sorted out.'

Alice went straight over to Tommy's bed. Sister had told them all during her report that Sister Tweedy had had some increased concern for him overnight. The wound was oozing even more, and he was still in a great deal of pain.

She stood by the side of his bed and spoke to him gently, but he was sleeping very soundly after a double dose of laudanum. She would make sure that she was around when Mr Jones came to review the patients. She needed to know more about Tommy's situation.

Mr Swain, on the other hand, was sitting up in bed, looking quite chipper.

'That pain doesn't seem to have come back with the same intensity after that injection. I just needed some laudanum drops this morning. Sister is very pleased with everything and she said that you will be doing the dressing for me again today, Nurse Sampson. Is that correct?'

'Yes, it is,' said Alice, looking forward to

managing the whole thing by herself this time.

She made sure that she collected all the materials for the dressing and that the rubber sheet was in place to protect the bed linen before she started.

'Now, as I'm on my own today, Mr Swain, please could you hold on to your leg for me, support it whilst I get the iodine soaks in place? Yes, like that. That will do nicely. Thank you.'

Alice couldn't help but notice the long scar down her patient's arm, cutting through an unusual tattoo — it looked like a black swan.

'That's my war wound,' he said, noticing her interest. 'Well, that and the leg. I got this one, on the arm, first. We were fighting hand to hand and I slipped, couldn't hold my ground. My opponent was quick, he came at me with his bayonet. I thought I was dead, but I managed to push him off and, well . . . Anyway, I didn't notice that he'd ripped clean through the sleeve of my tunic. And not until I saw the blood dripping from my hand did I realize that he'd sliced me, right down the arm. Once I saw that, my legs went a bit weak and the men had to drag me back to safety.'

'Did you go to one of the military hospitals?' asked Alice, as she soaked some more gauze in iodine.

'They stitched me up in the field hospital, then they shipped me down to Scutari, packed on to a ship with hundreds of others. That's when I met Miss Nightingale for the first time.'

'Did you?' said Alice, her eyes wide.

'I did, she came to meet all the new men

coming in on stretchers. She had a look at the arm and gave some instructions and that was it. I didn't see her again till I was hit in the leg.'

'So, how did that happen? I thought that Scutari was hundreds of miles away from the front line.'

'Oh, yes, it was. But they sent me back up there, to the front line, when the arm was healed . . . and — that's — when — I got hit by a shell . . . Sorry, Nurse, that bit's more painful than the rest.'

'Bear with me one moment, Mr Swain. Last bit, then we'll get the bandage round. You rest back now, just keep your leg bent like that. That will do . . . So what happened then, with the leg?'

'I was unlucky. We were days away from the fall of Sevastopol, sitting it out in the trenches, waiting for the Russians to start retreating. But there was a lot of shelling in those last few days. We were bombarded. A shell came; my mate, right next to me, he was hit full in the face, he died instantly . . . And I got caught. The leg was wrecked, well, you can see the extent of it. They almost amputated it there and then. But there was a surgeon, a Dr Lampeter, and he made the decision to salvage it. I only met him briefly. He was a man of few words and he looked like he could be a bad-tempered bugger. But whatever he did that day, it made all the difference.'

Dr Lampeter, thought Alice, I'm sure that's the one that Miss Houston told me about.

'Anyway, they shipped me back to Scutari again. And I got really sick that time, burning up with fever. I thought I was going to die. They carried me through on a stretcher, and another surgeon was straight there. I can't remember much about it, but he seemed very keen to chop the thing off. And by that time, I didn't really care. They could have put me to sleep for good, there and then, for all I cared. But Miss Nightingale appeared beside me; she seemed like an angel with her calm voice and the attention that she gave me. They put the stretcher down on the ground and she knelt down beside me. Even though I was barely with it, I'll never forget her face. She inspected the leg and told me that the nurses would clean up the wound and then they would dress it daily and see how it went. The doc was not happy, not one bit. There seemed to be some kind of argument going on, above my head. But that woman, she stood her ground. She saved my leg, did Miss Nightingale.'

Alice felt tears welling in her eyes, as he came to the end of the story. 'That's incredible, Mr Swain,' she said, wiping her eyes as she turned away from his bed to collect the enamel bowl stained by iodine. 'You should write a book about it.'

'I might just do that, Nurse Sampson,' he said. 'And I'll give you and Sister Law a mention for saving the bloody thing, yet again.'

'Well, it's down to you as well, you know,' she said. 'And you're doing very well this time, Mr Swain. We hope to see you discharged very soon.'

'That's good to hear, Nurse Sampson ... Shame about Tommy, though,' he said, nodding in the direction of the opposite bed. 'He's had a terrible night.'

Just how terrible the situation was for Tommy, Alice was unaware of until Mr Jones pulled them aside for a private discussion before the ward round. Sister had selected her and Millicent to accompany them, plus the new medical student, Mr Stafford.

'What do you think about Mr Knox, Sister?' said Mr Jones quietly, gazing down the ward towards Tommy's bed.

'Well, sadly, there is still no sign of the wound healing, his pain is unmanageable at times, and his chest sounds a bit rattly. He seems to definitely be presenting as someone with cancer that has moved to distant sites. The tumour on his chest wall was very large.'

'I'm afraid that you are right, Sister. I have a result back from my colleague with the microscope. Sadly, the tumour did contain cancer cells. We could start local treatment with arsenic, but I think we will be far too late to make any difference. And it is probably not worth causing toxicity. Sadly, I don't think there is any possibility of cure . . . ' said Mr Jones, his voice sombre. 'Only a post-mortem can establish the fact, but I think he almost certainly has cancer in the chest cavity.'

Alice felt her whole body shudder.

'Are you sure, Mr Jones? Is there no chance that he might recover?' she asked, tears starting to well in her eyes.

'No real chance,' said Mr Jones, and Sister was also shaking her head.

'Surely this is all part of the work, Nurse,' said Mr Stafford, almost tutting. 'Is that not so, Mr Jones?'

Mr Jones turned on his heel to face his medical student. 'My dear fellow,' he said, 'this may well be all part of the work, but this is a man's life we are talking about here. Nurse Sampson has every right to feel concern for her patient.'

Alice didn't care about Mr Stafford or his pompous opinions; all she wanted was for someone to say that Tommy was going to pull through. But it seemed there was absolutely no hope of that.

After the ward round, she went back to Tommy's bed. Mr Jones had answered his questions in the best way he could. He'd told him that they thought it was the cancer, that things wouldn't get better. Alice didn't know if she wanted to talk to him about his condition or not, she thought it might just make her cry. But she wouldn't avoid him, that was for sure. So there she stood, by his bed.

'Well, Nurse Sampson,' he said. 'This is a bit of a mess, isn't it? There's me thinking I might be getting out of here and there's Mr Jones looking at me with his sorry face and more or less telling me I won't get better.'

'I'm sorry, Tommy,' said Alice.

He reached out to take her hand. 'I still can't believe that when my ship heads back out to the ocean, I won't be sailing on her. I won't be sailing ever again. I've got a different voyage to be going on, if you know what I mean.'

Alice could feel the tears brimming in her eyes, but she took a deep breath and stood her ground, right by her patient. If she started weeping it wouldn't do him any good; he'd just

241

be comforting her, and he might not want to talk to her again for fear of upsetting her.

'Is there anything you need to do, Tommy, anybody you need to see or make your peace with?'

'Well, I want to see my mate, Davy, again. We've sailed together many a year, and I'd like to spend some time with him, talk over the old days. He's as close to me as any family. He's been in a couple of times and he'll definitely be here before the ship leaves. Apart from Davy, there is nobody else.'

Alice stayed put, as Tommy gazed into space, seeming miles away. 'The worst of it is not going with them when they set sail . . . and it's strange, when the doc started to tell me the news, I drifted out of meself somehow. I was standing on the deck of a clipper ship, somewhere off the coast of Australia, and the lads were all around me. And I could hear his words but all I could feel was the darkening of the sky, like when you know a storm's coming. It felt like, once, when we were out on the ocean, we saw the world go dark, in the middle of the afternoon. Everything stopped and the world was black as night for the best part of five minutes. All we could see of the sun was a ring of fire, around where it had been. I can hardly describe the feeling of dread, and the silence that fell. The captain told us we'd witnessed an eclipse of the sun, but to us lads on deck, it felt like a glimpse of the end of the world . . . '

And then Tommy started to cry, silent tears at first and then sobs wracking his body. Alice had no idea what to say; there were no words. She stood by his bed and held his hand, tight. Her heart felt like it was breaking for him. She saw Sister Law pass quietly by the bottom of the bed, giving Alice a nod of approval and then carrying on her way. Alice knew that even if she had been ordered to another duty, she could not have moved from that spot at Tommy's bedside.

Eventually, he stopped sobbing and she could see him starting to look around the ward. Alice pulled out a clean handkerchief and offered it to him.

'Thank you, Nurse Sampson,' he said, 'you are the finest nurse in all of the world.'

'And you are the finest patient,' she said, not knowing what else to say. 'You get some rest now, Mr Knox, and if there is anything at all that you want or that I can do for you, just let me know.'

'Aye aye, Captain,' he said, still dabbing at his eyes with her handkerchief.

★   ★   ★

Leaving the ward that evening, Alice felt drained of everything, and almost forgot to follow Eddy's instruction and check that Jamie wasn't lurking. She hadn't the energy to run. Just as she stepped outside she heard someone calling her name, and looked around to see the Reverend Seed trotting after her.

'Nurse Sampson, Nurse Sampson,' he said, a little out of breath. 'I just wanted to remind you of the probationer nurses' tea tomorrow. I

243

wondered if you will be able to attend?'

'I'm so sorry, but I have an afternoon off, and I have some business to attend to,' Alice said, not able to tell him that all she really wanted to do was spend time with her daughter.

She saw how disappointed he looked; he couldn't hide it.

'I trust you are fully recovered from the incident on the ward?'

'Yes, I am. And thank you so much for stepping in like that,' she said, surprised to be feeling a little sorry that she wouldn't be able to attend the tea that he'd arranged. After he'd intervened to save her from Jamie, she'd started to develop a new respect for him.

'Was that young man . . . was he someone that you have an understanding with . . . ?'

'No, nothing like that, not now . . . ' She was starting to feel a little uncomfortable with the direction of his questioning. 'Sorry, Reverend, I do need to go. I have a friend waiting for me, please excuse me.'

'Yes, of course, Nurse Sampson,' he said, giving a small bow and then turning to trot back to the hospital.

Alice sighed. It all seemed too much for her. She just wanted to be left alone, for ever.

Walking on a little further, she could see Eddy standing outside the Nurses' Home. She was so happy to see her.

'All clear,' shouted Eddy.

Alice couldn't help but smile. Eddy never could keep under cover or do anything quietly.

She started heading towards her but was

startled by a movement.

'I see you've had a good day,' said Roderick Morgan, stepping out from nowhere, right in front of her.

Alice gasped and jumped back, thinking, for a split second, that it might be Jamie.

'Are you all right?' said Morgan, his face full of concern.

'Yes, of course. Sorry, I thought you were someone else, that's all.'

Alice could see past him to Eddy, who was making all kinds of gestures as she stood on the steps. Alice had no idea what she was trying to communicate.

'I was wondering, Alice, if you wanted to meet me tomorrow, on Lime Street Station. I seem to remember you said that it was your afternoon off?'

'That would be very nice,' said Alice, instantly feeling guilty because, for him, she would forgo time with her child. 'But I will have to ask Marie if she'll have the baby, so I can't say for sure.'

'No matter, I will be there at two p.m., under the clock. If you come, you come, if not, I will be disappointed but we will meet some other time.'

'Yes, all right,' said Alice, catching a glimpse of Eddy still gesturing behind him.

Morgan gave a small bow and then went on his way. Alice struggled to keep a straight face and she could see Eddy holding her ribs to stop herself from laughing.

'Is that the one who took you to the park?' asked Eddy, out of breath, still trying to control herself.

Alice bundled her in through the door before she told her anything and then they both started laughing.

'Yes,' she admitted finally.

'And I saw Reverend Seed trotting after you when you were coming out of the hospital . . . Alice Sampson, who will be next on your list?'

'Shut up, Eddy,' said Alice. 'The Reverend Seed is just a shy man who doesn't know how to speak to women, and the other one, well, it's far too soon to be sure of what's going on there.'

'But, nevertheless, Nurse Sampson, the dark, handsome stranger is the man of your dreams.'

'No, nothing like that . . . '

'Well, why are your cheeks all flushed pink, Nurse Sampson? And even though you are exhausted, your blue eyes are sparkling. Aren't they, aren't they?' teased Eddy.

'Shut up, Eddy,' said Alice, starting to laugh again.

'Oh, and I have another surprise for you,' said Eddy, producing a letter from her pocket. 'Da-dah! A letter from Maud, at last!'

'Open it,' said Alice, grabbing Eddy's hand. 'And read it to me whilst I get myself changed.'

Eddy unfolded the letter and began to read.

'Dearest Eddy and Alice,

I am sorry it has taken so long to write. It took more time than expected for us to secure permanent lodgings and I needed to be sure of an address before communicating. I am pleased to report that all is well.

246

The work at the Women's Infirmary suits me very well indeed and I'm spending as much time as possible in theatre, there is so much to learn! It felt very strange at first to be working with women doctors and I am very fortunate indeed to be here with some of the first to obtain a medical degree. Elizabeth Blackwell, the British doctor, the one that Miss Houston's friend contacted, is no longer here, she has moved back to England; but her sister, Emily Blackwell, is a fine surgeon and she takes charge of the hospital. There could be no better experience for me.

Our patients are, for the most part, women from reduced circumstances. And I'm sorry to say that there is a great deal of poverty on the streets — very much like Liverpool. This is set to continue as immigrants from all over the world continue to pour in. New York is a modern city and it is expanding rapidly, new buildings everywhere. And they have just started building what's called a suspension bridge over the East River — the huge New York and Brooklyn bridge will be the first in the world to be constructed in this way. There seems to be so much possibility here, hence the reason why the Women's Infirmary has been given room to grow.

Alfred is doing very well at his new school. He says it isn't equal to the Blue Coat but it will do well enough, and we now have access to a public library, so I can borrow extra books for him if need be.

Our lodgings are clean and satisfactory. The landlady is of Irish descent and has spent some time in Liverpool before her move to New York. She is a very generous woman and Alfred has taken to her very well indeed.

I hope that you are both keeping well, and, Alice, don't wait too long before you make plans to return to the wards and finish your training.

I think about you both every single day as I walk to the hospital. Please write soon and let me know how you are doing.

I miss you both very much indeed.

Your loving friend,
Maud'

'She'll be so pleased to know that you're already back at the hospital,' said Eddy, folding the letter and pushing it back into the envelope.

'She will,' murmured Alice, lost in thought. 'Funny she didn't mention Harry, though, not once,' she said, standing ready to go, in her district nurse's cape, a crease of worry between her eyes. 'Don't you think that's odd?'

'Mmm, that is strange. Maybe she just forgot,' said Eddy, scanning the street before linking arms with Alice.

'Forgot that she has a new husband?' murmured Alice as the two women walked arm in arm out into the evening.

15

'The nurse must always be kind, but never emotional. The patient must find a real . . . centre of calmness in his nurse.'

Florence Nightingale

Alice walked to work the next morning thinking of her patients, especially Tommy. He was never far from her thoughts. Seeing a sudden movement to her left, she drew in a sharp breath and stopped in her tracks, drawing the nurse's cape more tightly around her. It was just a man rushing to work, he didn't look anything like Jamie, but she was, as always, alert. A woman brushed past and gave her a concerned glance. Alice forced herself to smile and then picked up her pace again, telling herself she would be safe, she would be fine. And as soon as she saw Eddy smiling and waving from the steps of the Nurses' Home, she knew that was the case, at least for now.

Walking down the corridor to the ward, she allowed herself one thought of her afternoon off. She would only be able to see Morgan for ten minutes, but it still made her heart beat a little faster. Marie had some business to attend to so she couldn't mind the baby, and Alice knew that she couldn't take Victoria with her, she just couldn't. Besides, with the possibility of Jamie lurking somewhere in the city, it was probably

249

best that she didn't spend too long out there. It did occur to her that the railway station might not be the best place to meet — after all, Jamie could be moving through there. But she had to believe that Eddy was right, that he had probably headed straight home after the incident on the ward. Surely, if he'd still been in the city, he'd have tried to confront her again by now, wouldn't he?

They were busy on the ward, and the time flew by. It was late morning before Alice was able to get anywhere near Tommy's bed, but when she did so, he had some news. Sister had spoken to him that morning and suggested that he consider making a move, whilst he was well enough, back to the Sailors' Home. She'd told him that the district nurse could see him there to do the dressing and make sure he had a good supply of laudanum, so there was no reason why he couldn't go and spend time in the place that had always been his home during his periods on dry land.

'I almost have me discharge papers, Nurse Sampson,' he said. 'And you can come and see me there if you want. I'll send a message to my mate, Davy, he'll come and fetch me.'

Alice knew that seeing patients after discharge wasn't advised, and the couple of times she'd been asked previously, she'd politely declined. However, this felt different. She had got much closer to Tommy than any patient last time around, and she knew that she would be worrying about him and needing to know how he was getting on.

'I will come to see you, Mr Knox,' she said quietly. 'I would like that very much.'

★ ★ ★

Alice was waiting on Lime Street Station, beneath the clock, at two p.m. sharp. She knew that he would be there this time, there was absolutely no doubt in her mind. She stood with her back to the station, gazing at the clock, and when she turned around at exactly the right time, he was walking towards her, and her heart jumped.

'I'm so sorry I can't stay, I can only say hello,' she said, breathless.

'I understand,' he said, with a glimmer of disappointment clouding his eyes for a moment. 'I am glad of any amount of time to see you, Alice,' he added, reaching out to take her hand. 'Even though your hand seems to have turned yellow.'

'Ah, yes,' said Alice, starting to giggle. 'I forgot about that. It's just iodine, that's all, from a dressing that I did this morning.'

'A sign of all the good work you do on that hospital ward, Nurse Sampson,' he said, stooping to kiss her hand.

He straightened and looked directly at her, his dark eyes shining. And in that moment, as they stood beneath the station clock, they were enveloped in a cloud of steam. Alice felt him step close, she could smell his cologne, and then his arms were around her and she was kissing him. The steam made them cling together even more tightly and the clanking of metal and the whistle of a train simply added urgency to the moment.

As the steam cleared they started to draw

251

apart, and Alice could see that he was, for once, slightly ruffled. It took a few moments for him to collect himself.

'I'm sorry that you have no time today, Alice, but we will meet again soon.'

'Yes,' she said, glancing up to the station clock. 'But now I need to go straight away. I promised Marie, and she has been so good, looking after Victoria for me.'

'Of course,' he said, stooping to kiss her stained, yellow hand one more time. 'I have some business to attend to for the next week or so, but I will be back to see you as soon as I can, and we will arrange another afternoon out, if that suits you?'

'It does suit me,' she said, smiling as she turned to leave, still able to smell his cologne.

As Alice walked away, she had no way of knowing that she'd been seen by someone walking through the station. Just as the steam had cleared, a woman had instantly stopped in her tracks and watched them, her eyes narrowed. It was Nancy, a large shawl wrapped around her, covering most of her body. She was watching the couple so intently that she was completely oblivious to other passengers bumping into her and needing to step around her.

Alice would have been troubled if she'd seen the knowing smile that Nancy gave as she went on her way. It would have unsettled her. But fortunately, she had no idea. The passengers, the steam and the noise of the railway station were no more than a wondrous haze to her in that moment.

＊　＊　＊

Thoughts of Morgan beneath the clock on Lime Street Station stayed with Alice for the rest of that week as she looked after Victoria, went back and forth to work, worried over her patients, and helped Marie with the work of the house. She carried the memory of that special moment with her, like a shiny token.

The week went by quickly and it seemed like no time at all till she walked on to the ward and found Tommy sitting up in bed and smiling. 'It's all arranged, I'm going home,' he said, as Alice came to check his dressing and administer the laudanum drops that he was now having regularly, at least three times per day.

'That's good,' said Alice, glad that arrangements had been made. Even in the last three days she'd seen more changes in him. He was losing weight, his chest rattled more, and he seemed to have a yellowish tinge to his skin.

'What do you expect?' he'd said to her, when she'd been worrying over him. 'I'm not exactly in my prime and I'm only bound to get worse.'

There was nothing Alice could say except, 'Well, you still have some life in you, Mr Knox, and I want to try and make sure that you get the absolute best out of it. You don't even seem to want a tot of brandy any more, could you not even manage that?'

'I wish I could,' he said, 'but it doesn't taste right, Nurse Sampson, it tastes sour. It's difficult to explain. And more often than not I feel sick now as well.'

'Well, let's see if we can get you some ginger root or some arrowroot, that might help. I'll ask Sister Law.'

Tommy was smiling at her and reached out for her hand. 'Look, Nurse Sampson, I don't really think you need to do that. I'm not saying I'm giving up or anything, but all I seem to need at present is a regular dose of that,' he said, nodding towards the bottle that she held in her hand. 'The rest I can deal with. And, yes, there is life still to be lived, but it will be short for me. Thank goodness. Even without this cancer, I'm not someone who can be left on dry land. I need the sails full and the ship cutting through the water, the taste of the salt on my lips . . . '

'I know,' said Alice, giving a small sigh. 'But at least when you go back to the Sailors' Home, there will be other sailors around, and you're very close to the docks. Maybe they could carry you down there.'

'And chuck me in,' he laughed. 'I wouldn't mind that, not now.'

'Don't say that,' said Alice, her face serious. 'Let's wait and see how you go . . . '

Tommy glanced down to his thin legs beneath the sheet and shook his head. 'They used to call me Tommy Strength when I was a young man. At one time I could lift a hundredweight clean above me head,' he said quietly. 'Now I can hardly lift a cup of tea . . . '

Alice didn't know what to say in return but she reached out and took his hand.

'Well now, Nurse Sampson,' he said, rousing himself after a few moments. 'I can see Sister

Law glancing in our direction, so I suggest you get yourself over there to our Mr Swain — he's probably next on your list?'

'He is,' said Alice, 'but are you sure you're all right?'

Tommy nodded and then he started to smile. 'Wait till you get a good look at Mr Swain, you'll have a shock.'

'Why?' she said, creasing her brow. 'Is he . . . ?'

'Oh, he's fine, but wait till you see him.'

Alice was straight across the ward, and it was a good job that Tommy had warned her, because the man looked so different that she probably wouldn't have recognized him. His hair had been cut and his beard was gone. He was clean-shaven.

She looked back over at Tommy, her eyes shining, and then back down to Mr Swain. She never would have thought that he was such a handsome man under all that hair. It must have been years since he'd had it cut.

'They did it first thing this morning. Sister Law arranged for the barber to come in, special,' mouthed Tommy across the ward.

'Stop that chit-chat and come here, Nurse Sampson,' shouted Sister down the ward. 'I need you to show Nurse Bradshaw and Nurse Fry how to apply a poultice in the correct way.'

Out of the corner of her eye, Alice could see Tommy quietly laughing. He never failed to be amused by 'our Captain' as he called Sister Law.

Alice was happy to help the new probationers. She'd seen Millicent making a move in her direction earlier, and she certainly wanted to avoid getting involved there. She simply could not work with the woman. It wasn't just her association with Nancy, although that wasn't easy — she had to be so careful what she said, and she couldn't mention Maud, not after Nancy turning up at the wedding — but it was also Millicent's different pace of work. She was still so slow, even though she'd been qualified for months. Eddy had joked that Millicent would be best suited to work in the mortuary, and it had made her giggle at the time, but glancing back down the ward now, Alice thought that it was true.

Standing by a patient's bed with her head bowed, the severe central parting of her hair peeking out from beneath her cap, Millicent looked strained. She was clutching a handkerchief in her thin hand and appeared close to tears. Alice couldn't help but feel sorry for her. There was no doubt that Millicent truly cared about the patients on the ward, but that didn't mean she had the right qualities to be a nurse. If I was a ward sister, I'd be having a word with her, for her own sake as well as that of the patients, thought Alice, as she made her way to assist the probationers.

'Right, you two,' she said, smiling at Nurse Fry and Nurse Bradshaw. 'Follow me, and I'll show you how to prepare a kaolin poultice.'

Alice was finding that she enjoyed working with the first warders. She'd already been able to help them with their bed-making technique; even though her own hospital corners weren't ever straight, she'd found that showing them the right

256

way to do things and giving lots of encourage-
ment really made a difference to them. And
these two, they were close friends as well outside
of work and they reminded her so much of her
and Maud.

★ ★ ★

The following day, Tommy was all set for
discharge during afternoon visiting. Alice had
been given the task of making sure his belongings
and bottles of laudanum were packed, as well as
a note for the district nurses, carefully written by
Sister Law and sealed in an envelope. She'd been
hoping that Eddy might be his district nurse, but
she was working a different area at present. That's
a shame, Alice thought. I think those two would
get on together very well indeed.

'My mate, Davy, he's comin' for me. He's
bringing a carriage right to the door of the
hospital,' said Tommy, smiling, but also fidgeting
with his hands on the bed sheet and glancing up
and down the ward.

'You'll be all right, Tommy,' said Alice. 'And
I'll be out to see you tomorrow, if I can. I've got
a half day.'

'I would like that very much indeed, Nurse
Sampson,' he said. 'We can give you a proper
sailors' welcome.'

There was no mistaking Tommy's friend as he
strode down the ward, a broad-shouldered man
with hair bleached by many years of salt and sun.
Alice headed straight back to Tommy's bed, to
make sure that everything was in order. She

could see how the men were together, laughing and holding on to each other — they were obviously close.

Davy looked up as Alice approached, and then he stretched out his arm to shake her hand.

'You must be Nurse Sampson,' he said with a big smile. 'I'm David Hall — that's my official title at any rate. I'm sorry I haven't been able to come in and see my mate here more often; it's just, we've been busy getting the ship ready to go back out.'

'It's good to meet you now,' said Alice. 'And Tommy has told me a few stories about you already. Is it true that you got a job on your first ship by walking the full length of the deck on your hands?'

'It is,' laughed Davy. 'I couldn't do that now, not with my bad back. Did he tell you the story of how we got together, me and Tommy?'

'I don't think so . . .'

Davy launched straight into the tale of how he, being the ship's carpenter, had just painted an area on one of the lower decks, when the second mate came along: 'You remember him, Tommy, Mr Prendergast, in his navy-blue coat with shiny brass buttons? He was always checking, always on to us.'

Alice could see Tommy starting to laugh already.

'Well, I'd just slapped the last of the paint on and he comes along asking if I've stirred the paint. We need this job doing, get on with it! And he plonks himself down on the wooden ledge full of wet paint. He was going to sit and make sure I did the job.'

Tommy was wheezing with laughter now.

'Well, I didn't know what to do. I'd be in lumber straight off, I knew I would, so I froze. But then Tommy comes down the ladder, he sees what's what. And he says, 'Mr Prendergast, I need you to come and check the main mast, we need an expert eye.' So up he gets, and we both see a big stripe of white paint all the way down the back of his jacket. He has no idea. Tommy winks at me, and it was all I could do to stop myself from cracking up laughing. And off they walk. You said, didn't you, Tommy? That *not one* of the ship's crew let on about the paint. Prendergast wouldn't have found it till he took his jacket off. But do you know, he never said a word about it. He just turned up the next day with a brand-new jacket.'

Tommy was still laughing. Alice was glad that he'd already taken his drops.

'So that was me and Tommy, from that day on, sailor and ship's carpenter, mates for life, eh, Tommy?'

'For life,' repeated Tommy, grabbing hold of Davy's hand, tears springing to his eyes.

'I'll just check with Sister that you're ready to go, Mr Knox,' said Alice, wanting to give the two men some time together. 'I'll be back in five minutes.'

When she came back, Davy was sitting on the bed, and as Alice approached, he wiped his eyes with the flat of his hand and jumped up.

'I'll get the orderlies to bring the stretcher for you, Mr Knox,' said Alice, knowing that he was far too weak to walk any distance.

'No, you won't need to do that,' said Davy, taking a large rag full of dried paint out of his pocket, to wipe his nose. 'I'll take 'im . . . You just carry the bag for us, miss, and we're ready to go. Your carriage awaits, sir,' he said, sweeping Tommy up from the bed and striding off with him down the ward. Alice trotted along behind, trying to keep up.

Davy wouldn't let the driver move the carriage until he was sure that Tommy was completely comfortable. He'd brought a pillow and a ship's blanket along to make sure. 'I help out with the injured men sometimes,' he said, by way of explanation. 'We don't have any nurses on board ship, we lads have to do everything.'

Alice was impressed by the expert way he positioned Tommy; he really seemed to know what he was doing.

Reaching in to the carriage, Alice wished Tommy well. 'I'll be in to see you tomorrow. And the district nurse should be along later today. Don't forget to take the drops!' she called as Davy closed the door.

She felt sad when she walked back on the ward and saw Tommy's bed, empty. She went to it and stood for a few moments, as if paying her respects.

'You have done an excellent job with Mr Knox, Nurse Sampson,' said Sister Law, appearing at the other side of the bed. 'And he will be well looked after out there by the district nurse. Now, let's get this bed stripped and cleaned down. We have another patient waiting to come in.'

Less than an hour later, Alice saw Mr Stafford

there, at the bed, with the new patient. It made her smile, at least, when she saw the medical student take his pocket watch out with a flourish and grasp the new patient's wrist, pursing his lips as he checked the man's pulse. The man in the bed was flat out and looked poorly — Mr Stafford would be struggling to find a radial pulse.

Alice almost went over to check the patient herself, but then another man was shouting from the top of the ward: 'Nurse, Nurse! Quick, I need help . . . ' And she was away to her next duty. She never did get back to see the new patient, still in what she thought of as 'Tommy's bed'. She was up and down all over the place for the rest of the shift. And then she needed to check Mr Swain's dressing — the bandage she'd applied had started to unravel. And then the day was coming to an end.

Alice was almost last to leave the ward, but once out through the door, she started to pick up her pace. She didn't want to be too late going through the city and she knew that Eddy would be waiting.

A voice called to her from behind, 'Ah, there you are, Alice.' A voice she knew only too well.

Alice froze instantly. She knew exactly who it was. Nancy.

She turned to look, not wishing to engage with the woman, but feeling that she probably should try and find out what she was up to. Nancy stood in the corridor, her body wrapped in a large shawl, her arm firmly linked in Millicent's.

'Yes?' said Alice, taking a few paces towards her.

'Dear Alice,' said Nancy, 'I just wanted to make sure that you knew, that's all . . . '

'Knew what?' said Alice, trying to stay calm but impatient to be on her way and quietly infuriated by the tilt of Nancy's chin.

'Oh, that you know he's married,' said Nancy, taking a few steps and then leaning in towards Alice, her eyes alive with it.

What? thought Alice, her mind clutching at fragments. 'Who is married?' she responded, meeting Nancy's gaze evenly, as her heart hammered in her chest and her mouth started to feel dry.

'The man I saw you with on Lime Street Station . . . Roderick Morgan.'

Alice saw her blink, just once, after she'd said his name, and she hung on desperately to herself, still looking Nancy in the eye. Her mind careered all over the place. *Married?*

'He and his wife and child, they live in a big house on Princes Road,' continued Nancy.

A wife? A child?

Something inside of Alice snapped. 'Of course I know he's married,' she almost shouted, gulping down the lump in her throat that was threatening to stop her breathing. 'Everybody knows that,' she said, turning away with tears stinging her eyes.

'Well, that's good, nobody wants to be made a fool of, do they? Especially someone like you, who has a child of her own to look after,' Nancy called after her.

Alice stopped in her tracks, turned on her heel, and walked straight back to Nancy. She could feel her cheeks burning red and she must have looked like a fire-breathing dragon because Nancy was visibly shocked as she leant in, face-to-face.

'None of this is any business of yours,' she almost spat. 'Where I go — who I see — and most of all, anything to do with my daughter — is none of your business.'

Nancy leant away and glanced down to the floor for a moment, but then she was straight back. 'Well, let's hope that Mr William Rathbone, the patron of the hospital, doesn't get wind of it . . . I mean, you think you've got the senior staff in your pocket, Alice, but you haven't got all of them. There are still some with influence, some who would be able to cut short your dream of becoming a trained nurse.'

Alice opened her mouth to speak, but she had Maud's voice in her head, telling her *not* to let Nancy see that she was getting to her, *not* to show *any* reaction. Just in time, thanks, Maud, thought Alice, taking a deep breath. Standing in the corridor, it was way too risky to continue with this particular conversation. Nancy wouldn't even need to bother feeding in some kind of rumour to Sister Law or God knew who else, not if Alice herself started shouting about it in the hospital corridor.

As hard as it was to swallow it down, Alice glanced away and took another deep breath, and when she looked back and saw Nancy afresh, standing there wrapped in her shawl, smirking, deliberate, she knew, in that moment, that she could rise above all of this. Nancy meant nothing to her now. She didn't work at the hospital, she had no power over her. What's more, Alice knew that she didn't need to say anything more, not if she didn't want to. So she tried to smile. It was probably a very crooked smile, but she did her best, and then she turned, as calmly as she could, and simply walked away.

With every step that she took, she felt her own power increasing and she knew that whatever Nancy did, from now on, she had no hold over her. Even if the worst came, if Nancy somehow managed to get some rumour or complaint to the highest authority, Alice knew that she would be ready to retaliate. And what's more, she had the support of Ada and Miss Merryweather and even Sister Law. In that moment of elation, as Alice strode away down the corridor, she felt like she could manage anything. As for Roderick Morgan, well, she would speak to him all right. As soon as she got the chance, she would definitely be speaking to him.

16

'One of our sisters told me that she
had often learnt more from her
patients than anyone else.'

Florence Nightingale

'What's up with you?' asked Eddy, immediately up on her feet, when she saw Alice marching towards her.

'He's married,' snarled Alice, glancing back before she spoke just to make sure there was no chance Nancy was in hearing distance.

'Reverend Seed?'

'No, Roderick Morgan!' said Alice, grabbing Eddy's arm and pulling her up the steps to the Nurses' Home. 'Nancy just took great pleasure in giving me the news.'

'Nancy? How did she know?'

'I'll tell you everything when we're walking,' said Alice. 'Millicent Langtry will be here in a minute, she was with Nancy. I don't want her overhearing.'

Alice poured out the story as they walked through the city, holding tight to Eddy's arm, not letting her get a word in edgeways. Alice talked and talked, almost shouting sometimes. Too furious to even cry one tear. She was livid.

'Married!' shouted Marie and Lizzie, together, when she walked into the kitchen, her face like thunder. Hugo shot past her with a yowl, his ears

265

laid back, close to his head.

Still Alice could feel nothing but fury. Then, after she'd poured the whole story out again, she started to feel like a fool. How could she have been so stupid? Especially when she had a child.

She felt like marching straight down to the docks in the morning. She still remembered his address from the card he'd given her, and which warehouse he had waved his hand at, saying that's where he worked. She started planning it in her head. She would go there early, before going to the ward. But he wouldn't be there at that time, *he'd be at home in his big house with his wife and child.*

The fury that Alice felt was alive inside her like some beast. Well, maybe she could go in the afternoon — after all, it was her half-day. But she wanted to make sure she saw Tommy at the Sailors' Home first; he had to be her priority.

Alice's fury carried her through her shift on the ward the next morning. She worked like a whirlwind. All her duties were finished and she was able to leave the ward for her half-day, on time. 'My word, Nurse Sampson,' declared Sister Law. 'You've made our heads spin this morning!'

As she walked out of the Nurses' Home after collecting her cape and hat, Alice stopped dead in her tracks. She saw the carriage first, and then she saw *him*. She wouldn't have to march down to the docks after all.

She saw him straighten and give her a curious look as she started moving towards him at some pace. Driven on by fury, Alice had no control over herself.

266

He had a crease between his brows and his eyes were questioning as she paused, square, in front of him, and then she slapped him, hard, across his face. Her instinct had been to punch him with her fist, but at least she'd been able to take back a little control and avoid that. She could easily have broken his nose with the amount of feeling that boiled inside her.

He reeled back, clutching his face. Alice saw his driver start to climb down, saying something, but Alice couldn't hear anything for the noise in her head.

Her hand stung, but the pain felt astonishingly good. She was calmer now, calm enough to speak.

'You are married,' she spat. 'And you have a child.'

'I, I, was going to — '

'No, you weren't going to tell me,' she said. 'You were going to lead me on, toy with my affections, play some kind of game!'

'No, Alice, no, I swear — '

'I don't care, you can swear all you want to whoever you want. But I never want to see you again, Roderick Morgan.'

At last, Alice was starting to feel better, like she'd hawked something up and spat it out. Now she could breathe again. She felt no compunction to say anything else. She simply pulled her cape more closely around her and then turned on her heel, leaving him there, where he stood, with an angry red weal starting to show across his left cheek.

$$\star \quad \star \quad \star$$

Alice had seen the Sailors' Home before — everyone in Liverpool knew the tall building on Canning Place, with its ornate towers and mullioned windows and the sandstone liver bird above the entrance. It was a place where returning seamen could receive their pay and find safe, clean board and lodging whilst they were ashore. Eddy had told her once that her father, who worked as a carter on the docks, had witnessed Prince Albert laying the foundation stone for the building. She claimed that he'd spoken to the Prince, but Alice wasn't sure about that — Eddy had all sorts of stories.

Anyway, although Alice had seen the building, she'd never been up close. She hadn't stood in front of the ornate wrought ironwork of the gate and she had never imagined that she would, one day, walk through the door. This place was very much the preserve of men.

'Excuse me, miss,' said a porter, appearing in front of her. 'Oh, I'm sorry, Sister.'

'I'm here to see a patient,' said Alice confidently. 'A Mr Knox.'

'Yes, of course,' said the porter, showing her through to the space inside. It was immediately wonderful to Alice. The central hall was triangular in shape, narrowing down towards one end, like a ship. The place was laid out in galleries with iron balustrades, each decorated with dolphins and mermaids and twisted ropes. Gazing up from the ground floor, she counted five galleries, and it was light in there. The roof of the central hall

268

was a huge skylight, giving the impression that the building was open to the skies.

'This is incredible,' she said, turning to the porter, almost breathless.

The man was smiling; Alice could see he was very proud of the building. 'It is,' he said, gazing up to the galleries. 'It's a magnificent building: designed by John Cunningham, same man as built Lime Street Station; and opened in 1850 for the benefit of the sailors of the world. But we nearly lost it all in a great fire just over ten year ago.'

'Really?' said Alice, still gazing up to the galleries, seeing how open the structure was. She could see that the fire would sweep right through. 'That must have been terrible,' she said, approaching the porter as he motioned for her to follow him towards a cast-iron staircase.

'It was. One man died wedged under these stairs,' he said as Alice started to climb after him, up the iron treads. 'Trapped by debris, his bones broken, burned and scalded. They pulled him out, but he was dead within the hour.'

Alice felt a shiver go through her body and she took a deep breath as she continued to follow him up the staircase.

The porter stopped again, halfway up, and looked back at her. 'Sorry, Sister, but Tommy's on the very top floor. Bit of a climb, I'm afraid.'

'That's all right,' she said, slightly out of breath and wondering how on earth Davy had managed to get Tommy up the stairs yesterday.

As they continued to climb, the porter called back over his shoulder, 'Aye, he's in cabin forty-two, top gallery . . . That's where the fire started, in that cabin. Ash from a lit pipe falling on the bedclothes. The men up there, they had to break through the iron windows and crawl out on to a stone ledge to wait for ladders. They were crying out to those below. Some as naked as the day they were born.'

Alice paused for a moment and took another deep breath, starting to feel heavy in her limbs as the man continued with his commentary. 'Did they get rescued?'

'Oh, aye, they got down the ladders. Some had burns but most lived to tell the tale. There were only two deaths that night. It could have been a lot worse.'

Alice nodded grimly, following the porter along the gallery. She was glad for the wrought ironwork of the balustrade and grateful for the beauty of the mermaids and dolphins. At least they were able to lift her spirits before she went in to see Tommy.

She was so distracted that she almost ploughed into the back of the porter when he stopped abruptly in front of a door. 'This is Tommy Knox's cabin,' he said, tapping on the door, and then continuing on his way.

'Come in,' she heard faintly through the door.

'Nurse Sampson,' croaked Tommy from his bed, 'welcome aboard.' And Alice did feel that she might be on a ship. The small room was exactly how she would have imagined a ship's cabin to be: a simple, boarded space with a cast-iron bed, one chair, and a cupboard, fixed to the wall.

'Well, this is very nice,' she said, pulling the

chair from the side so that she could sit by his bed.

'It feels like home to me,' he said.

'Your voice is hoarse, Tommy,' she said, leaning forward to scrutinize his face. 'How are you feeling?'

'Oh, don't worry about that,' he said. 'It's just that I've been talking to the fellas, that's all. They gave me a good homecoming and we've had a few tots of rum.'

'Just take your time,' said Alice, seeing that he was getting out of breath as he spoke.

'Some of 'em have already gone back to sea, I won't see 'em again.'

'I'm sorry, Tommy,' she said. 'That can't be easy for you.'

He just shrugged and then rubbed a hand across his face. 'Anyway, Nurse Sampson, you'll be pleased to know that the district nurse has been in and Davy's been lookin' after me. He even brought me a bottle of mixture to help the cough,' he said, pointing to a thick glass bottle on the small cupboard.

Alice swivelled round in her chair and picked up the bottle, full of brown liquid.

'What is this stuff?' she said, removing the stopper and giving it a sniff, and then reading the label: 'Cough Syrup . . . contains Alcohol, Cannabis, and Chloroform.'

'It seems to be loosening up me chest,' he said.

'Mmm,' said Alice, eyeing the bottle suspiciously. 'You need to be careful, Tommy, about these remedies from quack doctors. It might be loosening up your chest but you don't know

271

what other harm it might be doing.'

'So?' he said, starting to laugh, his chest rattling along with it.

'You're not dying just yet, Tommy,' she said. 'If you were, you wouldn't be laughing like that.'

'I suppose so.' He coughed, then leant over the side of the bed and spat up some dark phlegm into a bowl.

Alice handed him a handkerchief to wipe his mouth. He had a stack of clean ones by the bed.

'They are really looking after you here, Tommy,' she said.

'They are that,' he said, more breathless now from the effort. 'I just don't want to be a damn nuisance, that's all.'

'You're not a nuisance,' said Alice, patting his forearm. 'I could see how Davy was with you; he and the others really want to look after you.'

'Well, hopefully, it won't be for much longer. I can feel it in me bones. And, as you can see, my skin seems to be turning yellow.'

Alice looked closer. 'Ah, yes,' she said quietly.

'I know what it means, Nurse Sampson, and I'm not afraid. I've seen so many men pass away both on board ship and on dry land. I know the score and I'm not afraid, not of the dying. I just don't want it to drag out too long, that's all.'

'Well, I don't really know how much time you've got, but I can see you're sitting up, still drinking a bit, so it might be longer than you're expecting.'

'I hope not. I'm starting to feel more than ready for my final voyage. The sooner I'm singing with the mermaids the better.'

Alice gave a small sigh. She felt frustrated by the inevitability of everything that was happening to him and even more frustrated that there didn't seem to be anything that she could do to help him.

'Are you all right, Nurse Sampson?'

'I am, it's just that, oh, I don't know, you just don't deserve this, that's all. And I wish I could do more to help you.'

'I'm well looked after here, Alice — it is Alice, isn't it? And I can call you that, now we're not under Sister Law's eagle eye?'

'Yes, that's right,' she murmured, trying to smile.

'Davy has a couple of weeks left before they set sail, he'll look after me. And thank the god of the high seas for this place; I've been putting money away in the savings bank here for years and now I've got enough to settle my bill at the hospital and to pay for the district nurse. I've already told her what I want when the time comes. I want her to open the window so my soul can leave. Davy and the fellas will see to the rest and make sure I get a decent burial.'

'Oh Tommy,' said Alice, holding back a sob. 'I don't know how you can talk about it like that.'

'Well, I've had a long life, and I've lived it well, Alice. I've seen the world. My time has come, as it will for every one of us. So I don't want you worrying. I just wanted to see you one last time so I could thank you for all that you did for me on the ward, you really looked after me. And if you open that top drawer, behind you, I've got something to give you.'

'No, honestly.'

'Just do it,' he said, with a glint in his eye. 'You'll see in there a small cloth bag, that's it, give it to me.'

'These scissors have travelled with me on every voyage,' he said, sliding out a pair of ornate-handled scissors in a solid silver sheath. 'They were me mother's. I was only a nipper when she died, but I knew to get these in me pocket before they took 'em with the rest when they came to lay her out . . . I want you to have them, Alice, they're my lucky scissors.'

Any protest that Alice felt like mustering was silenced when she saw his face. His eyes were shining with tears.

'Thank you, Tommy,' she said, reaching a hand out to take them. She held them for a moment and ran her fingers over the carved decoration on the handles. 'I will treasure them.'

'And, Alice,' he said quietly, almost whispering now. 'I want you to do something for me. When you look up to the night sky and see the stars above, think about me sometimes . . . I don't know if there is a god, but if you're ever out on the ocean, you must look up to the stars and see the heavens in all their glory. So many stars you can hardly put a pin between 'em. That's what makes you think, there must be something . . . and maybe I'll be up there with the rest of the crew.'

Alice held back a sob, as she nodded and reached out for his hand. 'I will do that for you,' she said, feeling a stillness in that small room, like something holding its breath. She didn't want to break the spell.

Tommy was lying back on his pillow now, his eyes closed.

As Alice sat, she felt perfectly calm inside. There was nothing more important than what she was doing, in that moment, sitting quietly, holding his hand. She knew that he was ready now, he'd made his peace with the world and he was ready to go.

'I'll get some rest now, Nurse Sampson,' he murmured. 'Davy's taking me up to the roof tonight. From up there you can see the docks and the river and the Welsh mountains beyond . . . '

'I'll leave you now, then,' she said. 'Thank you, Tommy . . . I'll come back and see you next week.'

'No, Nurse Sampson,' he said quietly. 'Let's say goodbye now.'

Alice swallowed hard. 'I'll only say goodbye if you promise to ask the district nurse to let me know if you want to see me again, and also to let me know when you've left us.'

'I promise,' he said, opening his eyes and giving her a crooked smile. 'Goodbye, Nurse Sampson.'

'Goodbye, Mr Knox,' she said quietly, letting go of his hand. And then there was nothing more to do but leave the room.

Alice had a lump in her throat as she gently closed the door behind her. Walking to the balustrade of the galleried landing, she held on to the rail for a few moments to collect her thoughts. As she stood, she became aware of murmurings, other voices, from behind the closed doors of other cabins.

When she looked down to the ground floor, she saw a young man looking up at her. He gave her a wonderful smile and she smiled back at him. And then he was speaking to another man who had come to join him, in a language that was unfamiliar to Alice. She wasn't surprised; she knew that there were men of all nationalities who stayed here and sailed in and out of the port of Liverpool. Tommy had told her all about them, during his many stories of life at sea.

By the time Alice had descended the cast-iron staircase, seeing mermaids as she went, the two young men had disappeared, but that smile had made a difference to her. It had brought her back to the present and her own life. Standing on the ground floor of the central hall, she looked up once more to the light above. She hoped that Tommy would be able to get up there to the roof that evening and see the river for one last time.

As she walked out of the building, she paused to stand on the top step for a few moments, feeling the cool breeze from the river on her face, and hearing the sounds of the harbour. It made her think of Maud and her leaving for New York, and, of course, the day on the river that she'd spent with Morgan. Startled by the cry of a gull directly above, Alice moved away, murmuring one final farewell to Tommy as she went.

Making her way through the city, Alice began to feel just how exhausted she was. She kept her legs moving, but her body felt heavy, like lead.

She just needed to get back to Stella's and Victoria; all she wanted was to sit in the back yard and rest her head against the wall.

She was relieved to find the house quiet and the baby sleeping soundly when she arrived home. Marie gave her a concerned glance when she dragged herself through, and she ordered her to go and lie down and get some rest. All she could do was nod, but Alice knew that she needed to sit first, out in the back yard, where she had room to breathe and space to think.

Without even removing her hat and cape, she sat down on the bench. At first she couldn't feel anything except numbness and then, as she rested her head back against the hard wall, she started to feel as if she was floating, like a leaf on water, at the mercy of every ripple. Then she started to tremble. Her teeth were chattering. It felt like all of the pent-up misery and anxiety of the last few days, weeks, months and year, was seeping out of her, bit by bit.

Alice pushed her head back harder against the wall and then she started to cry, tears streaming down her cheeks. She saw Marie pop her head out of the door, just to check, and Alice gave her a nod to indicate that she was all right. And then, she was holding on to her own body, trying to calm herself down, but there was no stopping the tears now. Alice knew that this had to be done. She needed to get rid of it all. So she let herself shake and she let herself cry, until she could cry no more.

When the worst was over, she removed her hat and placed it on the bench, like a friend, beside her. Then she took a clean handkerchief and wiped around her face. I must look dreadful, she thought, feeling how hot she was, knowing that her eyes were swollen. Just as she leant her head back against the wall again, she heard the creak of the back gate opening. She expected to see Lizzie. But instead, there stood Sue Cassidy.

'Are you all right, Alice?' she said, her eyes wide, and her matted hair sticking out at all angles.

Alice nodded.

For some reason, seeing Sue standing there like that made her smile. It must have been a strange smile because Sue came over immediately and took her hand. 'Are you sure you're all right?' she said. 'You look like Mam does, when she's been having trouble with a fella.'

If Alice had had the energy, she would have cracked up laughing. Instead she just smiled some more and patted the bench next to her for Sue to sit down.

As they sat together Sue told her about what she'd been doing, and that they'd had good news — her mam had a job now, as a flower seller on the market. And then she fished in her pocket and brought out an object.

'What's this?' said Alice, seeing what looked like an empty perfume bottle, with a simple pattern etched into the glass.

'I found it for you,' said Sue. 'It's a very special one.'

'It is pretty,' said Alice, picking it up and angling it to the light. 'Are you sure?'

'Yes, it's for you,' Sue said, swinging her legs

as she sat on the bench. 'The money you gave us that day I came, it bought food, and it helped Mam get better. That's when she got strong enough to look for work. So this is to say thank you, that's all.'

'Thank you very much,' said Alice, holding the bottle up to catch the light once more, before slipping it in her pocket and hearing the clink of it against the scissors that Tommy had given her.

'Do you need any more money, Sue?'

'Not now,' she said. 'We can manage now that Mam's working. I need to go soon, to get some food and make a meal for when she gets home. Are you feeling better now?'

'Yes, I am,' said Alice. 'You've made me feel much better.'

'Well, Mam always says, when she's feeling better, that none of them fellas compare to having a daughter like me; so the whole lot of 'em can go hang.'

Alice couldn't help but laugh, and she put her arm around Sue and they both laughed together.

'I need to go,' said the girl, slipping off the bench. 'Bye, Alice.'

'Bye, Sue. Come back again, won't you?' But the back gate was already swinging to, and Alice was alone again. She stretched and then stood, shaking and loosening her body, and then slipping her hand in her pocket to feel the shape of the small bottle and the pair of scissors in their silver sheath.

'The whole lot of 'em can go hang,' she muttered, laughing quietly to herself. Then she

279

picked up her hat and headed back inside, just in time to hear the sound of her daughter waking from her afternoon nap.

17

'It is not knowledge only: it is practice
we want. We only *know* a thing if we
can do it.'

Florence Nightingale

A whole week went by, and Alice heard no news
of Tommy. She'd spoken to Eddy, and been
reassured that he had an excellent district nurse.
All she could do was trust. And he'd been so
adamant that he didn't want her to visit that she
had no choice but to respect his wishes, even
though it was her half-day and she was sorely
tempted to go along and see him.

That morning on the ward, Sister Law had
pulled Alice aside to congratulate her on the
sterling work that she'd done with the iodine
dressings on Mr Swain's leg.

'I took down the dressing first thing and it
looks very clean and it's almost healed. We just
need Mr Jones to have a look, and if he's
satisfied, then I think we can look at discharging
our veteran very soon.'

Alice tried to control her smile, she knew how
Sister disapproved, but she felt it through her
whole body. How very satisfying. When the man
had been admitted, it had been touch and go as
to whether the leg could be saved at all. And
today there was a possibility that he could be on
his way back to his boarding house in the city.

'And what about the dog?' she asked.

'Stanley is fine,' said Sister. 'I've been popping in to see him at Mr Delaney's house, with some extra meat and a few bones. But he's been pining for his owner, so that's another reason why we need to get Mr Swain on the move as soon as possible. When we get to his bed on the ward round, I'll call you over.'

'I believe you've done a very fine job here, Nurse Sampson,' said Mr Jones, as he pulled back the sheet and removed the dressing pad to reveal Mr Swain's leg.

Alice didn't reply; she leant in with everyone else to view the wound. She held her breath as Mr Jones made his assessment then straightened up and looked directly at her.

'Excellent, Nurse Sampson,' he said. 'Excellent work. And please, Sister, make sure you convey the news to Miss Houston, I know that it was her idea to use the iodine soaks.'

Sister nodded, they all seemed pleased. Except Mr Stafford, who stood pursing his lips. Maybe he can't bear the thought of the nurses doing good work, thought Alice. And she felt like kicking him. What difference does it make, she thought, if it's a nurse or a doctor? More often than not it's the both of them working together. What difference does it make, as long as the patient recovers?

'When Miss Houston comes, Nurse Sampson, you do the dressing with her. She wants to see the result as well, for herself,' said Sister Law as she moved with Mr Jones and Mr Stafford to the next bed.

Miss Houston was soon there on the ward and working with Alice to re-dress the leg. 'My word, this has done well,' she beamed.

'Thanks to you, miss, and Nurse Sampson here. Yes, it has,' said the veteran.

'How is the pain?' asked Miss Houston, as she held the leg steady and scrutinized every inch of it.

'It's still sore, there's no getting round that. But it's been that way ever since I got hit by that shell. But it's not the very bad pain. I can manage it like this.'

'I know it's easy for me to say,' Ada continued, 'but this time, when you go back out, if things start to get worse again, try not to dull the pain with drink. Come back to the dispensary, see if we can give you some medicine first.'

'Oh, I will,' said Mr Swain. 'I've got Stanley to consider now, I can't start getting blind drunk again. Not when I've got him to look after.'

'Good, that's good, and what about other things, do you sleep all right?'

'Sleep's not good, and I get the nightmares. And I sometimes get the shakes. Anything can set them off. You were out there, you know what it's like.'

'I wasn't in the thick of battle or in the trenches like you soldiers, but I do understand. I've seen other men like you. The war doesn't stop for you soldiers once the ceasefire is called, does it?'

The man shook his head and Miss Houston put a hand on his shoulder, just for a few moments.

'Right then, Mr Swain,' she said, 'we don't need to use the iodine soaks on here any more. We'll put a dry dressing on and a bandage, and off you go. We can give the district nurse the address of your boarding house, and she can take it from there. We just need to get you up on some crutches and make sure you're steady enough. You know the score, you've done this many times.'

'I'll go and get the crutches,' Alice offered. 'I know where they are.' Within minutes she was back brandishing a new pair. 'Time to get you moving, Mr Swain,' she said. 'Let's just get you sitting up at the side of the bed first, and then Miss Houston and I will help you to a standing position.'

Alice soon had the patient standing, although after weeks in bed his legs were weak. 'Mmm,' said Miss Houston, 'I think we maybe need to give you a couple of days to strengthen up, so that you're more steady.'

'No, sorry,' said Mr Swain firmly, 'I'm going today, I need to see my dog.'

Alice saw Miss Houston square her shoulders and open her mouth to say something, but then she seemed to think better of it. 'All right then, Mr Swain,' she said at last. 'But I still need to check with Sister Law and you will have to take a carriage from the door of this hospital, do you hear?'

'Yes, miss,' said the man, grinning.

When Stanley was brought to the ward, he pulled Michael across the floor, wagging his tail and panting with joy, desperate to be reunited with his master. The whole ward cheered. Michael couldn't hold the dog back; all he could do was gasp, 'He's very strong, especially after all the meat and bones he's been havin'. He's been eating us out of house and home, he 'as.'

Once the dog reached Mr Swain's bed, he was beside himself, licking his master's face and barking, and the veteran was in tears, stroking him and kissing him, and trying to get him to settle. It really was a wonderful sight, to see the two of them reunited.

Once they were ready to move, Alice escorted them through the hospital to the waiting carriage. Sister Law had thought it too far for Mr Swain to walk to the door, so Michael and Stephen brought the stretcher and the whole party proceeded through the hospital with the dog trotting at the side.

Alice helped Mr Swain off the stretcher and the orderlies made sure that he was carefully loaded into the carriage with his dog. Whilst they were giving the driver strict instructions to pull up directly outside his lodgings, Alice leant into the carriage to say a final goodbye.

'I just want to say thank you again, Nurse Sampson,' he said, 'especially to you, for all the work with the dressings and for really looking after me. I know you've been on the ward previously, and you've seen me in some states. I must have been such hard work then. But you never let that stand in the way of giving me a fair chance this time around.'

'We never know what we're going to face in life, do we, Mr Swain?' said Alice, giving his hand a squeeze. 'You just try to keep as well as you can this time. And let's hope that we don't see you back on the ward again, hey?'

'I'll try my best,' he said, as Michael called that they were ready to move.

Alice waited for the carriage to set off before turning to make her way back into the hospital. Just in that moment she caught a glimpse of a man in a brown jacket stepping into the shadow of a building. She felt a shock go through her; from where she was standing, he looked like Jamie. She held her breath, watching, waiting for him to step out. But there was nothing but the shadow.

As she walked towards the hospital entrance, Alice felt as if someone was breathing down her neck. She had to make an effort to shrug it off. And then she saw an ancient woman, wrapped in a thick shawl, walking painfully slowly, aided by a girl with blond hair falling straight down her back. For a moment she couldn't place them and then she realized who they were. It was the old lady, Mrs Marchbank, who'd fallen over outside St George's Hall, on the day of Maud's wedding.

I'll walk quietly by, she thought, not wanting to distract the woman and risk her falling again.

But Alice had been seen. Mrs Marchbank and her granddaughter called to her instantly.

'So you have become a nurse after all,' declared Mrs Marchbank, looking Alice up and down and smiling.

'I have,' said Alice, returning the smile. 'And how are you? How's the rheumatics?'

'A bit better,' she said. 'We've just been in to

the dispensary, to get some more salts. But I'm fair riddled with it. It's just how it is. I'm surviving, that's the main thing.'

'That's good,' said Alice. 'It's so nice to see you again. I hope you didn't have any ill effects from that fall.'

'Nah,' the old lady said. 'We Marchbanks are made of strong stuff.'

Alice knew that she couldn't have walked by and ignored them once she'd been recognized, but she couldn't spend too much time with them outside the hospital. She needed to get back to the ward, so she was just about to say her goodbyes and turn away when Mrs Marchbank asked after Victoria. 'And how's that bonny baby girl of yours? She must be growing . . . '

'She is growing and she's keeping very well,' said Alice, glancing around, to make sure that they weren't in earshot of any hospital staff. Clearly Mrs Marchbank didn't realize that it wasn't usual for a trained nurse to have a child.

'Well, you give her a kiss from me, will you? What's her name again?'

'Victoria,' said Alice, as quietly as she could, drawing in a sharp breath when she saw the shape of a man hovering in the shadow of the building again.

'What's that?' said Mrs Marchbank, putting a hand to her ear.

'The baby's called Victoria,' repeated her granddaughter loudly.

'It's lovely to see you again, Mrs Marchbank,' said Alice, her heart pounding in her chest, 'but I need to get back to the ward now . . . '

287

'Of course you do, my dear,' said the old lady, 'and you keep up with the good work.'

'I will,' called Alice, already running towards the door. Surely if it had been Jamie he would have stepped out, he would be following her right now, but when she glanced back one more time, there was no one.

Once in through the door, she slowed her pace and started to take deep breaths to steady herself. She was almost there now, she nearly had her certificate, she couldn't risk Jamie or anyone other than the small group of senior staff who understood her situation finding out about the baby, not at this late stage.

She walked down the corridor, her heart still pounding in her chest. And as she came back down the ward, she saw Millicent Langtry glance up, then she instantly averted her eyes.

Alice knew that Millicent had been avoiding her on the ward and she suspected it was because she had been there with Nancy when she'd confronted her about Morgan. And she'd had no wish to engage with her either. But looking at her now, seeing the weariness of her, Alice's heart went out to Nurse Langtry. She, of all people, should know what it was like to be controlled by Nancy. After all, it had happened to her. If Maud had been around, she would certainly have advised Alice to make her peace with Millicent.

Seeing Millicent making her way into the sluice, Alice followed. She found her standing with her back turned and her head bowed.

'There's no need to worry, Millicent,' said

Alice quietly, 'I haven't come in here to have a go at you. I just want to make peace, that's all.'

She saw Millicent's shoulders rise and fall as she gave a sigh. And then she could hear her starting to sniffle.

She took a step towards her and gently placed a hand on her shoulder. 'Look here, Millicent,' she said gently, 'I know what Nancy's like, I know what she does to people. You just need to make a break with her, that's all.'

Millicent turned to face her and when she looked up, her eyes were brimming with tears.

'I don't need to make a break,' she said. 'I haven't heard from her since that day we saw you, and she told you about that thing.'

'Well, that's good then,' said Alice, rooting in her pocket for a clean handkerchief. 'Now dry your eyes and don't think any more about it. We need to work together on the ward — we have the patients to consider first and foremost, don't we?'

Millicent nodded and then wiped her nose.

'And if Nancy comes back, don't get involved with her again is my advice. She's only interested in herself, what Nancy wants. She will bleed you dry, if you let her.'

Millicent was still nodding.

'I need you to know that I hold nothing against you, Millicent. So stop worrying and let's get on with the work.'

'Thank you,' she said, grabbing hold of Alice and squeezing her tight. Alice didn't think that slow, weary Millicent had that much strength in her body. And what was that smell? It was some mixture of lavender and camphor. Alice had to break free in the end, and, when she did so, she patted Millicent on the arm. 'Don't you worry. We're friends now, and if Nancy bothers you again, you come straight to me.'

'I will,' said Millicent, starting to smile.

Alice came out of the sluice a little out of breath, and walked straight into the Reverend Seed.

'Oops,' he said. 'We seem to be making a habit out of this, don't we, Nurse Sampson?' Then his cheeks flushed red and he was straightening his dog collar and walking purposefully down the ward. Alice stared after him, her brow furrowed, then she realized that he must have been referring to her first night shift when she walked into him by a patient's bed. But that was ages ago, she thought. I hope there isn't anything in what Eddy was saying about him liking me. I'm done with men for good.

There was absolutely nothing more that Alice wanted that afternoon than to get back to Stella's place and spend time with her baby. That was the best thing in the world, now, to Alice. But she was cautious walking home and she didn't take any chances, going out through the back of the Nurses' Home, checking around her, looking for a glimpse of a brown jacket. She felt even more alert to danger because Eddy had needed to go home straight from work. Her father was a carter on the docks and one of his horses had stepped on his foot, making a bit of a mess of it. Eddy had given her the full detail that morning and it didn't sound like any bones were broken but Eddy needed to keep an eye on the wound.

When she arrived at the alley, Alice gave one final glance either side before proceeding. And as she rounded the corner, she saw Marie coming out of the door with Victoria in her arms.

'There she is,' cried Alice. 'There's my girl!' And she almost ran towards them, delighted by the baby's screech of laughter and the way she reached out to be held. All fears were dispelled in that moment. There was no creeping around and glancing behind her now.

'I'm glad you're back in good time,' said Marie. 'I was going to take her with me to the corner shop, but now I can carry on and see my old friend in the next street — she's bad with her legs . . . '

'Yes, you go, and is there anything I can be doing after I get this one settled?'

'Well, there is some laundry, but we'll do that together when I get back. You get some rest, Alice, spend some time with your daughter.'

★   ★   ★

It was quiet in the kitchen and unusual for Alice to have the place to herself at this time of day. Often during the evening she had the space, but then the rest of the house was usually alive with noise and raucous laughter. Often men would bump into the wall of the corridor or the kitchen door as they made their way towards the stairs. It had startled Alice in the first few weeks but now she'd got used to the bumps and the bangs and the singing and the laughing.

Being alone like this gave her some feeling for what it might be like living in her own place. She wasn't sure if she altogether liked the idea, it felt odd, but she knew that it would be nice to have some peace and quiet.

Holding Victoria on one hip, she removed her cape and hat, then sat with her daughter by the fire, and she was content, feeling the warmth of the baby's small body and the rhythm of her breathing. She ran a hand over her head, feeling her silky hair, snuggling her close to her cheek and breathing her in. Stretching out in the chair, Alice's foot caught the cat as he slept in his usual place by the fire. He lifted his head for a second and Alice reached down to give him a stroke. He stretched out further with one front paw and then he was back to sleep.

'Lazy, good-for-nothing cat,' murmured Alice.

Without knowing it, she was rocking gently backwards and forwards in the chair and she could feel the baby settling against her as the heaviness of sleep crept through her small body. Alice felt it too and wondered if she should just sit and doze with her in the chair. But no, Victoria was getting too big for that now, and they were too close to the fire. She roused herself and carried the baby across to settle her in her crib.

Alice filled the kettle and put it on the hob. As soon as steam began to come from the spout, the door opened and Stella came through, closely followed by Lizzie, and it became one of those half-hours that regularly happened in a house full of women, where it was good to sip tea and talk. Put the world to rights.

'Did we tell you, Alice, about going to the Midnight Supper?'

'No, what's that?'

'Well, these events are laid on by the church and the constabulary, a way of making contact with us 'fallen women' and trying to persuade us to give up our wicked ways and return to the bosom of our families. Mrs Butler would, ideally, like all of us working women to find redemption. Change our line of work. She's often mentioned these suppers and she's been trying to persuade us to go along for some time. So, out of respect for her, we did just that.

'Well, many of the women turned up in their best hats and their finery; they were in silks and crinolines. The place was packed. And they'd laid on a lovely spread for us: bread and butter, meat pies, fine cakes, pots of tea. All served up by lady volunteers. Ooh, and I tell you who we saw there — that housekeeper of Maud's, the one who was at the wedding, she was giving out plates and napkins.'

'You mean Miss Fairchild?' said Alice.

'Yes, that's the one,' said Stella, starting to laugh. 'I think she was a bit surprised to see me there; I don't think she knew about my line of work . . . But she said hello, and it was all very nice. She seemed to come over a bit faint later on, though, and she left early. But bear in mind the party only started about eleven p.m., so it was two o'clock in the morning before we were finished. Well, we had a good natter and plenty of laughs, and one or two had brought a flask of strong liquor to spice up the cups of tea. So the night was going really well. But then the Reverend got up to speak, and the lady volunteers were singing hymns, and what they wanted was for as many women as they could persuade to go along to the Home for Fallen Women.

'These suppers have been going on for years and most of us know the score, so as soon as the hymns started we all got up and left. One of the lady volunteers followed us out on to the street with her tea cloth, to make absolutely sure that we didn't want to change our minds — '

'So we lifted our skirts and scarpered as quick as we could,' added Lizzie, jumping up from the table and running around the kitchen with her skirt above her knees.

Alice laughed out loud and soon she was holding her ribs with tears running down her cheeks. As she was washing up the tea things after the others had gone, she heard a light tap on the kitchen door. 'Come in,' she called.

'Hello,' said Ada, walking into the room, smiling.

'Miss Houston,' said Alice tentatively, wondering what could possibly have brought her all the way out here on a Thursday afternoon.

'I came along to the ward to see you, Alice. But I didn't realize it was your afternoon off.'

'Right,' said Alice, still wary for some reason, even though Ada was smiling.

'I've brought something for you. I probably should have mentioned it to you, but as you know, we said that you only needed to do one more placement . . . ' She fished around in her bag and pulled out a piece of paper.

Alice still didn't cotton on until she read it, and then she doubled over and had to hold on to the kitchen table for support. It was a certificate. A certificate saying that she had now completed her course of training. She was a qualified nurse.

Alice couldn't speak. All she could do was read it over and over again, glancing up every now and then to Miss Houston who stood there still smiling.

As Alice held on to the piece of paper, everything that had happened to her since she'd arrived in Liverpool to start her training came flooding back to her. All the things that she'd got through. But now she was a trained nurse. And as she held that piece of paper, her hand began to tremble, and then she was laughing, and then laughing and crying, all at the same time.

'Well done, Alice,' said Miss Houston. 'You have worked hard and you have been through a great deal. You deserve it.'

'Does Sister Law know?' gasped Alice, when she could finally speak.

'Yes, of course. She was the first to propose that we consider your training complete. She put your case very strongly, saying that she'd seen a huge improvement in your performance since your 'return to the fold'. She told me that you were competent with dressings, bed-making, poultices, leeches, temperatures and enemas, and that you had a natural aptitude and willingness to tackle anything. She praised your recent work with Mr Swain's dressings in particular and singled out your devoted work with an incurable cancer patient, Mr Knox. Exemplary, was the word she used. Exemplary. She said that she could see you in charge of a ward in no time at all. She had no doubt at all that you have not only reached but *excelled* the required standard.'

'Sister Law,' croaked Alice. 'She said that?'

'Yes, she did, and not only that, she told me that Sister Tweedy on nights had told her that you were the best probationer that she had ever worked with.'

'That's probably because I got her a pillow to kneel on, whilst she said her prayers,' Alice laughed.

'Don't tell me she still kneels on the floor! I've told her so many times not to do that, her legs are so bad these days. But that's Sister Tweedy for you . . . Anyway, Alice, you ought to be very proud of what you've achieved. Especially with everything else that's been going on. You've simply soldiered on, haven't you?'

'I suppose so, but, then again, what choice did I have, apart from go home with a baby born out of wedlock and stay in the village, shunned by my family, for the rest of my life?'

'You've kept your nerve, Alice, and that takes a lot of doing.'

'Well, I wouldn't have if it hadn't been for you and Maud and Eddy and Stella and Marie. Even Miss Merryweather and Sister Law, you've all played your part. Without you women, doing what you do, I'd have gone under. And if that had happened, I don't know where Victoria and I would have ended up.'

'Well, every credit to you, Alice. This is cause for real celebration. We wanted to try and do something special at the hospital; the Reverend Seed was very keen to do one of his teas. But in the end, because of your circumstances, we thought it best not to draw any undue attention.'

'That's true . . . this is the best way,' said Alice, reading again the precious piece of paper that she held in her hand. 'I'll wait till they all come in this evening, and Eddy is here, and then I'll make an announcement. I am so happy with this, Ada. So happy.'

'And so you should be. I trust you haven't heard any more from the young man who turned up on the ward?'

'No, nothing. I have no idea if he's still in the city or he's headed home. And no doubt, if he has gone home, he will have told my whole family what I said. I've been expecting a letter from my mother, demanding that I marry him. But I've been thinking about this, and even though I hadn't seen him for all that time, when he turned up, right there on the ward, I didn't feel 'it', if you know what I mean. That special something that makes your heart race. Even before he turned nasty, I was just shocked and terrified that he might find out about the baby.'

'I do know what you mean, Alice,' said Ada wistfully. 'And I have some idea what you're facing now, with the baby and your work, all of that. What's important is that everything is stable for the baby and that you have someone that you trust to look after her.'

'Well, I'm lucky, I've got Marie. But I just

297

don't know if I should stay here or find my own place. I can't decide. I love it here with these women.'

'I know,' said Ada, 'this place is very special. I was a fool to keep my distance from my half-sister for so many years. Stella is an exceptional woman. And if someone had said to me that I'd be standing here in Marie's kitchen — the woman I resented for years for taking my father away from my mother — I would never have believed it.'

'Yes, life can be strange, can't it?' said Alice, looking around the kitchen, as if seeing it for the first time. 'If it's any comfort, Ada, Marie curses that cat,' she said, laughing and pointing to Hugo stretched out in front of the stove. 'She curses him every morning because he reminds her of your father, Francis, that lazy, good-for-nothing husband of hers.'

Ada laughed. 'Well, I've never met him, but from what my brother, Frank, told me of him, that's a very fair assessment.'

'None of that could have been easy for you . . . ' said Alice, reaching out a hand towards her.

Ada just shook her head and then smiled. 'Life isn't easy, is it? We just have to manage in the best way we can . . .

'So, the important thing is, Alice, now that you have your qualification you will have an increase of pay with immediate effect and we can guarantee you a job as a trained nurse. I'm waiting for the decision as to where you'll be placed. It all depends on where the most need is, so for the next few days I want you to continue on Male Surgical. Take time to think through everything carefully. There's no rush to make any decisions. You are perfectly fine here for the time being and it's important that you do the right thing for yourself, and for the baby . . . '

Alice noted a hesitance in Ada. She could sense that she wanted to say something else. She looked directly at her, willing her to say more. But Ada just shook her head and murmured, 'One day I might tell you my story,' and then she was smiling, and walking across to give Alice a hug.

'Well done,' she said.

And instantly, Alice could hear Sister Law's voice in her head: 'But don't you get above yourself, Nurse Sampson. You still have a lot to learn.'

18

'I do see the difference now between me and other men. When a disaster happens, *I* act and *they* make excuses.'

Florence Nightingale

Alice laughed to herself as she walked to work the next day. She'd imagined that she'd be feeling different, now that she had her certificate safely stashed in the wooden box beneath her bed. That she'd have an air about her as she walked through the city, to show that she was now a trained nurse. But she didn't feel one jot different as she hurried along in her hat and cape.

She hadn't gone far when she stopped short, catching sight of Mr Swain on the other side of the street. She was shocked that he was out and about so soon after returning home, and moving so slowly and so precariously on his crutches, the dog at his side.

She crossed over immediately, and easily caught up with him.

'Mr Swain?' she said quietly, not wanting to startle him and set him off balance. 'Are you all right?'

He stopped dead, swaying a little on the crutches, his dog looking up at Alice.

'Nurse Sampson,' he said, breaking into a smile. 'I didn't expect to see you all the way out here. Have you got a new job?'

Alice didn't reply but countered with her own question: 'Is it safe for you to be out and about like this so soon?'

'I don't really know,' he said, starting to chuckle. 'As you can see, I'm not exactly all that good on my feet. But Stanley here, well, he likes to get out for a bit of a walk in the morning and then each evening. And I couldn't stand to see him sat by the door, looking at me with a sad face . . . what could I do?'

'I see,' said Alice, beginning to understand. 'Well, you go very carefully. I'll be back this way later on; I could call and see you at your place if you want.'

'No, no, Nurse Sampson,' he said, 'no need for that. The district nurse will be coming anyway to do the dressing. Don't you worry, I know my way to the hospital. I'll soon be back to Sister Law if things don't go right. Now you go. Get on with your duties. There are others far worse off than me, I know that for sure.'

'You take care then,' called Alice as she continued on her way, almost running now, to make up time.

Eddy was there, waiting on the step for her, and she had some news. 'I've just seen Mr Knox's district nurse,' she said, her face solemn. 'He died peacefully last night.'

Alice drew in a sharp breath. Eddy's words had hit her like a punch. She was surprised at how much it affected her. After all, she'd known that Tommy was dying, it was just a question of time.

Eddy linked her arm as they made their way into the Nurses' Home. 'The district nurse said his friend, Davy, and a few of the others were there with him. They laid him out and sewed him in his blanket, like they do at sea. Tommy's ship is leaving tomorrow, so Davy won't be there for the funeral, but they're having a wake tonight and then the others will be there for his funeral tomorrow morning. They're having the ceremony at St Nicholas's, the sailors' church, which overlooks the harbour.'

Alice nodded, holding on to herself.

'I won't be able to go to the funeral,' she said. 'I'll be at work. But Eddy, could you take me along to the church some time, so I can pay my respects to him? Would that be all right?'

'Of course I can do that,' Eddy said.

'Thank you.' Alice removed her nurse's hat and placed it on the shelf. 'I've seen any number of deaths, like we all have, but this one feels different . . . I feel like I need to mark it in some way.'

'I think that's a very good idea,' said Eddy. 'Right, I need to dash — ooh, and I won't be here again this evening. I need to put another dressing on my dad's foot.'

'Oh Eddy, is he all right?'

'He would be if he'd keep his foot up on a stool and stop hobbling out to the stables. He's driving my mother spare . . . I'll see you in the morning,' called Eddy as she ran out of the door.

★   ★   ★

'Ah, Nurse Sampson,' proclaimed Sister Law, as she saw her scurrying up the ward with her cap slightly askew, 'glad you could join us. I was beginning to think that you might have taken to a higher calling, now that you have your qualification.'

Alice just smiled and then smiled even more as the whole group of nurses gave her a round of applause.

'Thank you,' she said, flushing pink. Now she did feel different, and this did feel like the beginning of something.

'Lest we forget, though, nurses,' said Sister, scanning the group with narrowed eyes, 'the certificate *does not* make the nurse. It is doing the work, spending the time with the patients, that makes the nurse. So let's get on. And, Fry and Bradshaw, no tittle-tattling in the sluice today, I've got my eye on you two.'

'Yes, Sister,' said the probationers, glancing at Alice for reassurance.

Taking Alice aside, Sister took a few moments to congratulate her but quickly moved to practical considerations. 'So, Nurse Sampson, there will be a new uniform, the uniform of a trained nurse, waiting for you in the Nurses' Home tomorrow — make sure you are wearing it. And get yourself a new cap, that one is limp. We need things to be in the proper order.'

The ward was busy, so there was no time for Alice to think about her different status, never mind act upon it. She did have a vague notion, however, that Sister Law wasn't calling her name quite as much, but she could have been mistaken.

Nurse Fry and Nurse Bradshaw were very excited by the news. They'd made a special congratulation card with a silk flower stuck to the front, and Alice was moved to tears by how pleased they were for her. And then, after afternoon visiting, the Reverend Seed appeared with a small bouquet of flowers clutched in both hands. Alice saw him coming down the ward and felt her face flush when she saw that he was heading in her direction. She half wondered if she should scoot off to the sluice, but he had already seen her and he was beaming broadly. It almost warmed her heart.

'Thank you,' she said, taking the posy of flowers from his grasp. 'That is so kind of you, Reverend.'

'You are welcome, Nurse Sampson,' he said, blushing. 'And please call me Lawrence.'

'Thank you, Law . . . rence,' she said, her voice faltering. It just didn't seem natural. 'Now, I need to get on with my duties, but I'll put these in a vase and place them on the ward table where everyone can see them.'

He nodded, and as she turned she couldn't help but smile. He really was a very sweet man.

★   ★   ★

Alice missed seeing Eddy waving and smiling from the step after work. It was always nice to link arms and listen to her light-hearted chatter. She could always make her laugh, and the journey home felt like it took no time at all when she was walking with Eddy.

As she walked through the streets that evening, making her way back to Stella's place, she moved quickly and stayed alert, as always. But while she walked she let thoughts from her day run through her head: the cases she'd seen, what she could have done better, and how strange that the Reverend Seed had come to the ward with that posy of flowers . . .

Alice had no way of knowing that her every step was being shadowed by a man, a few paces behind.

Jamie knew exactly where she was going, of course. He'd followed her that day, after he'd overheard the old woman outside the hospital asking about her baby. It had struck him to the heart. He'd known Alice his whole life; he'd known she'd been hiding something that day he saw her on the ward. But to hide a child, *his* child . . . He had no doubt it was his, even before he saw the woman at that place where Alice lived, holding the baby at the door. He knew she was his baby. But how Alice could keep her child in that place of sin — taint his child by living there with those common prostitutes — he couldn't imagine. That's why he'd tracked her ever since. Waiting outside. Following her home. Devising a plan. He needed to rescue his child, and take her far away to where she'd be safe from the evil influence of her mother.

He would have his daughter soon, he'd simply been biding his time.

It was quiet in the alley when Alice walked through. This time of day marked the space between the bustling activity of the day and the onset of night in the city, when the rooms in the brothel started to fill and the life of the night commenced. When she was happy to be settled in the kitchen with her daughter on her knee and the cat stretched out in front of the stove.

'Hello, my beautiful,' she said, seeing Victoria happily sitting on Marie's knee, playing with a cloth dog with lopsided button eyes — a new toy that Lizzie had made for her.

The baby screeched with delight when she saw her mother and Alice threw off her cape and quickly walked across the kitchen to take her daughter in her arms, immediately feeling the softness of her hair against her cheek, and breathing in that special smell of her.

'Sit yourself down,' said Marie, removing Alice's hat for her. 'I'll make you a cup of tea. And then I need to go up and see one of the girls. She's poorly with some fever.'

But Alice wasn't really listening. She was talking to Victoria, already making up stories about the toy dog, already lost in that special world that they had together.

Victoria was changed and wrapped in a shawl and starting to look a little sleepy when Alice heard the sound of the kitchen door opening, and she looked up, expecting to see Marie.

It was not Marie. And when she saw who stood in the kitchen, with his hands balled into fists, Alice froze. She wanted to scream, but she couldn't.

'Jamie,' she gasped, turning the baby away, trying to cover her with the shawl.

He walked towards her, across the kitchen, as

if hypnotized by the baby.

'No need to do that, Alice,' he said, 'I know all about it. Everything.'

'How do you know?'

'I've been watching you, all of this time. I smelt a rat.'

Alice gasped and clung more tightly to her child.

'Oh, don't worry,' he said, holding up both hands. 'I don't mean any harm. I just wanted to see my daughter one time, before I went home. Just once. And then I'll leave you in peace.'

Alice watched him warily as he came closer. She felt like they were playing a game from their childhood. How close could he get? Could he touch her before she ran away?

'Stop there,' she said, holding up one hand. 'Don't come any closer.'

She didn't trust him, not one bit. Not after what had happened on the ward. She'd seen something in him that day that made her realize that she had no idea what he might be capable of.

'All right, all right,' he said, squatting down on his heels, three feet away. 'Just loosen the shawl a little, Alice. Just let me see her face, and then I'll be on my way, I promise.'

Alice spoke softly to Victoria and turned her to face him, pulling away the shawl. She saw his face soften, the tears springing to his eyes. It made her feel sad and a bit guilty. But she knew that he'd never been the man for her, and there was no way on earth that she would let him take her daughter. 'She's got the same colour hair as me,' he said hoarsely.

'Yes,' said Alice, her breath catching in her throat.

Jamie stretched out a hand towards the baby. 'Yes, you have, haven't you, yes, you have.'

Victoria leant forward a little; she was reaching out a hand towards him, starting to make a noise. Alice couldn't see her face but she thought she was probably smiling. Her baby was smiling as Alice's heart pounded in her ears.

Jamie smiled, and Alice felt the baby lean closer. For a few moments all that she could hear was the spit of the wood on the fire.

Then, before she had a split second to react, he leapt forward and grabbed Victoria from her arms. She started to cry and Alice screamed, 'No, no!'

And then Jamie was running, the baby screaming now, in his arms. He stumbled as he came to the door, and the cat shot in front of him.

Alice almost caught up with him, grabbing the hem of his jacket. But then he was gone, pounding down the hallway with Alice after him and calling his name so loudly it was hurting her throat.

He was out through the door and running fast now down the alley. Alice picked up her skirt and ran. She had such strength, but his legs were longer and she couldn't keep up. All she could hear was the thin scream of her daughter. She was losing sight of them now, and then they were out on Lime Street.

'Help, help!' she shouted out, as she ran. 'Stop

him, he's stealing my baby.' But people just stared at her, trying to make sense of the situation. Alice knew she had to keep track of him. She couldn't take her eyes off him for a second, so she pushed past people, knocking into them as she went.

She was catching him up; he'd stopped now, waiting to cross Lime Street. Alice's heart was pounding so hard that she thought it might burst, and her breath was rasping in her chest.

She saw him glance back, and then he spied his chance and ran over the road, Victoria still howling in his arms. Alice felt like her heart was breaking wide open inside her chest, but she needed to keep after them. She would follow to the ends of the earth if need be.

She could see him glancing back as he made the other side of the street. She was on the edge, dodging forward, holding back, needing to find her way across, still keeping an eye on him as he headed towards St George's Hall.

Seeing her chance, Alice ran, the driver of a carriage hurling abuse as he yanked his horses to a halt. Alice didn't care; all she needed was to keep her baby in sight.

Her legs were burning with pain, but still she ran. She tripped a little, then, pulling up her skirt even higher, she continued her chase.

She could see him now, bounding up the stone steps of the Hall. She could hear Victoria's thin wail. As if she couldn't scream any more, as if she was weakening. That thought spurred Alice on even faster. Now she was pounding up the steps after him, climbing higher and higher.

Completely fearless.

When she reached the top, she stood for a moment, gasping for air, straining to hear the sound of her baby. She couldn't hear Victoria wailing now. What if she'd lost them? Where had they gone? Alice threw herself against the locked doors, not knowing which direction to turn. If she chose the wrong one, she could lose them completely. She needed to be careful. She made her breathing calm, forced herself to listen, above the pounding of her heart. And then she heard it, the ragged sob of her baby. And she knew exactly which direction it was coming from.

She guessed that he was resting, getting his breath back, thinking he could hide up here, in the shadows behind one of the pillars. Maybe he didn't even know that she had followed him up. He certainly wouldn't know that a mother can hear the faintest sound that her baby makes. It doesn't have to be a cry, just the tiniest noise.

Alice knew they weren't far away. She had to control her breathing, and move very carefully. Quietly does it, she thought, trying to steady herself as she moved across the stone flags. Another tiny noise, a bit clearer this time, and she knew that she was heading in the right direction. Not far now.

She could see a shadowed area; she knew that was the only place they could be.

Jamie must have thought he was safe; she saw him step out of the shadow with the baby in his arms. She saw Victoria struggling against him, and she wanted to run straight there. But she needed to be careful, so she stepped back and

310

crept slowly towards them, along the wall, keeping in the shadow. The closer she got, the more she could hear her baby, sobbing quietly now. Keep going, keep going, get closer, Alice was saying in her head.

She judged the distance that would do. And then she ran at him headlong, grabbing the baby, trying to pull her free from his grasp. But he had her held tight now and Victoria was screaming. Alice could feel her small body, her small bones. How easy it would be to hurt her.

'Let go, let go,' she screamed, 'let go of my baby!'

'Your baby!' he shouted. 'Don't you think I have a say in this? Don't you think that as I'm her father, the law of the land would say that she's mine?'

'No,' snarled Alice, still clinging on to Victoria but knowing she was caught now, caught between them, and she couldn't use all of her strength to prise her free. If she did, Victoria would be hurt.

Alice could do nothing except let go of her. But she didn't move away; she stood right next to Jamie, staring at him fiercely.

'I'm not going anywhere,' she said. 'If you move, I move with you. I can keep up.'

She could see his mind turning things over. He was glancing around now, and then he moved closer to the top of the stone steps.

'Stop,' called Alice, not knowing what he was capable of, fearful of the height they were at. If he slipped, he could fall with the baby. Remembering how he'd looked at his child, she knew that he wouldn't do anything deliberately to hurt her. But if his foot slipped, if he fell all that way down, it didn't bear thinking about.

He stopped then, and gave her a strange smile, and, as if reading her mind, he moved again, right up to the edge of the step.

'No, no!' wailed Alice, having no choice but to follow.

They were standing at the edge now, at a dizzying height for Alice. She couldn't look down, but she would stand there for as long as it took.

'Give her to me,' she said firmly.

'She's mine,' said Jamie, pulling her closer.

'How will you look after her?' she asked, her voice shaking, desperate to try a new tack.

'I'll find a way,' he said. 'I'll tell people that I married in Australia, that she's mine and her mother is dead.'

'They wouldn't believe you, Jamie. And I would follow you, I'd tell them that you were lying. That Victoria is mine.'

'No, you wouldn't,' he growled, grabbing the front of her bodice with one arm and somehow managing to swing her round, so that in one terrifying second she was hanging over the edge of the top step.

Alice heard a scream, so loud it filled her body. It rose and fell like the waves of the sea. Her body was rigid, straining, and her heart was pounding so hard it felt like it was about to break through her ribs. The scream went on and on. And then she realized, it was coming from her own mouth.

She didn't know what happened next but she heard a growling and a scuffling on the steps below her, then she felt Jamie rear backwards, dragging her with him. A dog was barking and snarling and she could hear Victoria screaming. She saw her struggling against Jamie, still held by him, but only with one arm. Alice knew this was her chance. She threw herself forward and grabbed her baby, then immediately ran back, well away from the edge, desperately checking her as she ran, making sure that she was warm, that she wasn't injured. As she stood well away, she rocked the baby, and Victoria's screaming started to settle to broken, ragged sobs.

She could see that Jamie was being held at bay by a thick-set dog, a white dog with a menacing growl. And then Alice realized she recognized the dog: it was Stanley. And appearing now just above the top step was Mr Swain — panting for breath, doing his best to shout at Jamie, crawling up over the step on his hands and knees.

Alice ran forward to help him stand, but he had no crutches, so he propped himself into a sitting position. She could see that Jamie was still held at bay by the dog.

'Nurse Sampson!' cried Mr Swain, shocked to see his nurse struggling with a man outside St George's Hall. 'I heard a scream and I knew it was desperate, so I sent Stanley up and I followed on my hands and knees.'

'Get this dog off me,' shouted Jamie. 'Call it off!'

'Not yet,' said Mr Swain, the breath wheezing in his chest. 'Not till this young lady and her baby are safely out of the way.'

'Well, that young lady has had her baby, my baby, out of wedlock. She is living in a house of sin. I am trying to rescue my child.'

'You think it right to forcibly remove a child from its mother?' gasped Mr Swain, desperately trying to regain his breath. 'And so what if she has a child out of wedlock? Well, from what you've just told me, the same goes for you. And there are far worse things in this world, believe me.'

Jamie growled an inaudible response and lashed out at the dog with his foot.

Stanley yelped, and then flew back at him, sinking his teeth in further this time. Jamie was screaming in pain now, desperately trying to shake the dog from his leg.

'He won't release you until I give the word,' gasped the veteran.

'Get it off me, get it off!' screamed Jamie, trying to kick the dog with his other leg but losing his balance.

'If I give the command, my dog will let go, but if you make one move towards this woman and her child, I will send him back, and he will have you again; he will bring you down to the floor if need be. Once he smells blood, there's no stopping him.'

'Get him off,' begged Jamie, desperate now. 'I'll go, I'll leave straight away, as soon as I'm free.'

'Stanley. Leave,' said Mr Swain firmly, and, immediately, the dog let go. As he trotted back to his master Alice could see a glint in his dark eyes.

Jamie shot a look of pure hatred across to Alice before limping away, leaving a trail of blood behind him. Before he disappeared down the steps, he shouted back over his shoulder: 'I'm going home, Alice. I'm going home and I'm going to tell your family *everything*.'

'Tell them what you want,' Alice yelled back, with every last ounce of her strength.

19

'Every feeling, every thought we have,
stamps a character upon us, especially
in our year of training, and in the next
year or two.'
Florence Nightingale

Alice leant against the wall, clinging to Victoria,
who was whimpering in her arms. Her whole
body was shaking uncontrollably and she had to
take deep breaths to try and get back some
control.

'Are you all right?' she called over to Mr Swain
who sat, slumped now, beside his dog.

'I am,' he said. 'I just need a bit of time to get
back some strength so I can lower myself down
those steps.'

'I can't believe you managed to get up them,'
she said, her teeth starting to chatter.

'Neither can I,' he said. 'I just heard a scream
and acted instinctively. It's a good job I could
send Stanley up, though. I wouldn't have stood a
chance against a young man like that on my
own.'

Alice couldn't answer, she was still shaking
and chattering, but already she was starting to
form a plan in her head. She needed to get
herself, the baby, Mr Swain and the dog all back
down to the bottom of the steps safely, which
would not be easy.

'I think you should go down in a sitting position, one step at a time,' she said, and he nodded. 'I'll wait till you're down and then I'll follow. I might be less shaky by then.'

'Good plan,' said the veteran, already shuffling himself along to sit on the top step. Alice watched as he disappeared from view, and then she walked slowly to the edge to make sure that he was safe. She saw him using his arms to lever himself on to each step as he went down, one at a time, the dog keeping pace beside him.

Alice was recovering fast now. She was wrapping the baby firmly in her shawl and speaking soothingly to her, then she crouched down and slipped her legs over the top step. Her legs were still a bit weak, so she used the same method of descent and went down on her bottom, one step at a time, cradling Victoria on her knee as she went. Standing up as soon as she reached the last step, Alice was then able to haul Mr Swain up and help him retrieve his crutches.

'I'm so glad that you heard me, Mr Swain. I don't know what would have happened without you and Stanley. You saved me from God knows what. I am so grateful.'

'All part of the service,' he said, smiling. 'From patient to nurse. I was just glad that it all worked out. Whatever was he thinking, snatching a child away like that? Now, I need to make sure that you get back to your lodgings safe and sound . . . '

'I don't think there's any need,' said Alice, looking over to spot Marie and Lizzie frantically looking around in all directions as they stood across the street. 'It looks like they've come for me.'

'Oh my God, Alice,' cried Marie, grabbing hold of her. 'Whatever has happened? I just heard a man's voice, a scream and the pounding of feet. And you were both gone! I thought we might find you dead.' Marie was crying now and Lizzie was fussing over Victoria. 'Is she all right? Who was it? Who took her?'

'It was Jamie,' croaked Alice, his name sticking in her throat.

'Has he harmed her? Is she all right?'

'She's all right. Thanks to Mr Swain, she's all right . . . ' repeated Alice.

Marie took the man's hand and shook it vigorously, almost knocking him off his crutches. 'I know you, don't I? You used to be a regular at our place?'

'I did, yes, but not for some time now.'

'Let me and Lizzie help you. Where do you live? We'll help you back.'

'No, no . . . please,' he said. 'All I want is that you make sure that Nurse Sampson gets back home safely with the baby. My dog will look after me. Please, just go.'

'Thank you again, Mr Swain,' said Alice. 'I won't ever forget what you did for me and Victoria.'

★   ★   ★

Back home, Marie put more fuel on the fire. 'You're still shaking, Alice,' she said, bringing a warm blanket to wrap around her. 'Now, just let

318

me have Victoria, that's it,' but Alice clung more tightly to her baby. 'Let me have her, Alice, she's safe with me. I just want to check her over, and then I'll give her a bottle. I'll sit right by you, right here.'

Alice nodded, handing her daughter over, and then she brought her knees up to her chest and sat with her arms wrapped around them, like she used to as a child.

When the feed was done, Marie pulled the crib across and placed Victoria in it, right next to Alice. 'She seems fine now,' she said gently. 'No harm done. We'll let her get some sleep.'

Alice nodded again and then reached a hand over and rested it on her precious daughter as she slept in the crib. She didn't want to move. She would have sat up all night if it hadn't been for Marie insisting that she get changed, have a hot drink and go to bed. Alice saw Stella and Lizzie there as well, but everything seemed to be in a haze. She saw them carrying Victoria's crib through and then Marie led her to her bed and tucked her in as though she was a little girl, giving her a kiss and saying goodnight.

'Now don't forget, Alice,' she said. 'Stella will go up to see Ada, first thing, and explain what's happened here. They won't be expecting you back at the hospital tomorrow.'

Alice nodded her head, but she wasn't really sure what Marie was going on about. Of course she would go to work the next day. Sister Law was expecting her; the patients needed her.

That night, as Alice lay in her bed, with Victoria sleeping quietly beside her, she entered

319

a strange, unearthly state that was neither sleeping nor waking. She turned from side to side, lay flat on her back and then shot straight up in bed, gasping for air. Checking that her daughter was still beside her. Lying back down again, only to wake with a start, feeling somebody clutching at her. When she did finally sink into sleep it was only to dream that some black creature had crawled from the side of the room and it was lying across her chest, crushing her. She needed to fight and scream and kick to get it off. Over and over she needed to wrestle with it, until at last it was gone and she could breathe. And then, when she opened her eyes, not sure if she was awake or still dreaming, she glanced to check her baby in the crib and then she looked up to the whitewashed ceiling of her bedroom and saw shimmering circles of reflected light, breaking into a rainbow of colours. As she lay, she started to smile, she breathed in the light and the colour. And then Victoria made a small noise, as if crying out in her sleep, and Alice sat bolt upright again in bed, her heart pounding.

Muttering to herself, she swung her legs over the side of the bed so that she could sit and gaze at the dark outline of her sleeping child, and listen to her rhythmic breathing. Alice sat like that until the light of day began to peep through her window, until she could be sure that they had both come through the night safely. When she lay back on her pillows again, she felt the remembered weight of that dark shape that had plagued her, and felt it start to creep back over her. But she would not have it. She pushed it straight away, out of her mind, determined to bring the circles of warm colour back to mind.

★ ★ ★

Eddy was straight there to see her the next day. Without even stopping to remove her cape and hat, she came directly into Alice's small room and crouched down beside the bed.

'What time is it, Eddy? I need to be getting to work.'

'You don't need to worry about anything, Alice,' she said. 'We got the message from Stella. Miss Houston is aware, she's spoken to Sister, and they're not expecting you back until the day after tomorrow.'

'But what about the patients? The ward is busy . . . '

'The ward is always busy, Alice. And really, it's all fine. Besides, you're not in any fit state to go in today, are you?'

'I suppose you're right,' said Alice wearily, barely able to sit herself up in bed.

She rested back against the pillows and then her body was shaking and she started to cry, big sobs that wracked her body. Eddy held on to her, cradling her. 'There, there,' she said, 'just let it all out, let it out.'

Alice sobbed until her eyes were sore. And then Eddy dipped a flannel into a bowl of water that Marie had brought through and she carefully wiped her forehead, and then her eyes and then her lips. 'There, there,' she said, over and over, 'you'll feel better soon.'

'Do that again,' said Alice, enjoying the feel of the cloth and the warm water on her face. 'It feels so soothing.' Eddy dipped the cloth again and repeated it, and then she immersed the flannel, wrung it out and placed the whole thing across Alice's forehead.

'That feels so good,' she said. 'Thank you, Eddy.'

And then Alice started to giggle.

'What?' said Eddy, but Alice couldn't speak at first; all she could do was giggle and then she was laughing and then she managed to get the words out. 'I was just thinking about poor Millicent Langtry and her wet flannel, going round the ward, looking for customers. Maybe she's on to something after all. It really is very soothing.'

'Millicent the ministering,' laughed Eddy.

They were still laughing when they heard Victoria starting to wake up. Eddy was straight there, pulling her out of the crib and handing her to Alice.

'Hello, my darling, what a time we've been having. It's a good job we're tough, isn't it?' murmured Alice, leaning in to give her daughter a kiss on the cheek. 'We'll just keep going, us two, won't we? Me and you together?'

'Is it likely he'll come back?' asked Eddy.

'I don't think so,' said Alice. 'I know Jamie — if he loses face, he doesn't come back, and I'm pretty sure he will have gone straight home. I can't be certain, but that dog gave him a very nasty bite. I don't think he'll be back.'

'We'll be vigilant, just in case,' said Eddy. 'And Marie said that Stella's spoken to some of the fellas she knows hereabouts and they'll keep a look-out.'

'You are all so good,' said Alice, on the verge of tears again.

'We are, aren't we?' replied Eddy, laughing and putting an arm around Alice's shoulders. 'But we all work together here, don't we, with each other and for each other. Right?'

'Right,' said Alice quietly.

'So dry your tears, Alice Sampson, because one day you might be the one who's helping me or Maud or Stella or Marie or any of the women that we know.'

Alice nodded and wiped her tears with the flat of her hand.

'I'll see you again this evening, but right now,' said Eddy, jumping up from the bed, 'I need to get back to my daily round. And when you're feeling strong enough, we'll go out to the sailors' church and you can pay your respects to that patient of yours.'

'Yes,' said Alice.

'Let me take the baby now, you get some more rest,' said Marie, coming into the room as soon as Eddy had gone.

Alice lay back on her pillows but she couldn't settle in the bed; she needed to breathe some air. She got up, still in her nightgown, and walked out to the back. There was no washing on the line today to catch the breeze, so she felt that she had some space. Sitting on the bench, she rested her head back against the solid wall of the house. Her head felt tight and sore, and she realized that her hair was still pinned back from the day before. Leaning her head forward, she took out the pins, one by one, and laid them on the bench beside her. Once her hair was loose, she leant further forward and ran her hands through it, enjoying the feel of it between her fingers, rhythmically running her hands through it, catching the faint scent of the soft soap she used as shampoo. She felt like a child again, on bath night. She'd always been the first, the youngest, so she had the water before her brothers got in. She'd loved the warmth of it, in the bath in front of the fire. And it had been the only time that her mother had seemed calm with her. She wished that she could bring her bed out here, to the back yard.

As she sat up straight on the bench and stretched out her arms, she caught sight of the book, *Wuthering Heights*, and realized that she must have left it there, face down. She picked it up and drew in a sharp breath of pleasure as she read the words, telling her of moors, great swells of long grass, woods and sounding water, and the whole world awake and wild with joy. She felt an ache in her chest and leant her head back against the wall. In her mind she was back home, walking the fields and the fells, with nothing but the sky above and the cry of a curlew to pierce her heart.

Alice continued to read the book for the rest of the afternoon, in between tending to Victoria and making pots of tea, and by evening time, apart from a slightly hollow feeling inside and two shadows under her eyes, she was very much herself again.

But when the kitchen door burst open as she sat by the fire with Victoria already sleeping in her crib, Alice jumped up from her seat as though she'd been scalded and the cat shot off with a yowl.

'Sorry,' shouted Eddy from across the room, crouching down to try and make herself smaller. 'I should have made a much quieter entrance, given what happened to you last night. Sorry.'

Alice couldn't help but smile, even though her heart was still pounding.

'Come in and sit down, will you?' she said. 'I'll make a cup of tea . . . and lace it with brandy.'

Eddy had already removed her cape and draped it over a chair back and then she chucked her hat on to the table and took the pins out of her hair.

'Phew, thank goodness,' she said, running her fingers through her thick hair until it stuck out at all angles. 'I've been chased through the street tonight by a patient I attended weeks ago. He had a bad leg and it got better, but I think he liked the attention. Anyway, he saw me going about my business and he's shouting across, 'Nurse, Nurse, me leg's bad again.' I'd only just seen him hopping and skipping along like a baby lamb, so I knew that he was making it up. So I pretended not to hear him and started to walk fast. When I glanced back, he'd broken into a trot and he was chasing me . . . Well, I went faster, and then he did, and then I had to duck into an alley and hide in a doorway until I saw him running by. When I stepped out I was covered in cobwebs and a nasty little dog had tried to cock its leg on my nurses' bag . . . '

Alice was laughing her head off by now, rocking in her seat. Eddy was the best medicine that anyone could have.

Once they'd had their tea and Eddy had pulled a chair up to the fire, the cat sidled back in and stretched out at their feet. Now both of them could relax and sit quietly.

Quiet time never lasted long with Eddy in the room, however. 'Oh, I forgot to tell you, Alice. When I went back to the hospital for supplies, I saw Miss Houston and she sent you her regards. She said not to think about coming back tomorrow and she'll be along to see you late afternoon.'

Alice nodded. She wanted to go back, but she knew that once Ada had spoken, she had no choice.

'So the plan is . . . ' said Eddy, with a glint in her eye, 'I've got an afternoon off tomorrow so I'll come straight here and we'll go along to the sailors' church. I'll get you back in time to see Miss Houston and if she's satisfied that you're ready to go back to work, you will go the next day.'

'I'll be ready,' said Alice firmly.

★   ★   ★

She still felt a little hollow inside as they walked out on to Lime Street the next afternoon. And every person rushing by, every cry of a gull or shout from across the street seemed to jangle her and make her feel a bit breathless. She was glad

326

that Eddy had offered to carry Victoria. She seemed to be getting heavier every single day and Alice wanted to be sure that she was steady enough to carry her any distance.

Once they saw the church, Alice started to feel better. It was right by the river, looking over the water. And as Eddy pointed out the gilded weather vane in the form of a ship on top of the tower, it made Alice focus on Tommy, and even thinking about him made her feel warm inside. She could almost hear the sound of his laugh. As soon as she walked through the door, she felt the stillness and the calm of the church envelop her. It gave her peace.

'Let's sit for a bit,' said Eddy quietly.

So the two women sat together in a pew, with Victoria, who'd fallen asleep on the way there, breathing gently in Eddy's arms. Alice leant against Eddy and let her body relax as she gazed up at a stained-glass window and saw the light coming through the coloured glass. It made her feel as though she was being restored in some way.

'This reminds me of Maud's wedding,' she said, sounding a bit sleepy.

'Yes, of course,' replied Eddy. 'I hope we're not going to turn around and see Nancy at the back of the church.'

'If we do, you'll have to deal with her, Eddy. I haven't got the strength. Not yet.'

'I'll take her on, no problem,' said Eddy, shifting the weight of the baby on her lap.

'I'm glad that they had Tommy's funeral here. I bet he came to this church sometimes,' said

Alice, straightening up now and starting to have a look around.

'Many of the sailors do,' said Eddy. 'After all, St Nicholas is their patron saint and the men often come here to offer prayers or leave tokens for a safe passage. My dad says there's been a church on this site for hundreds of years; sailors have always come to this spot.'

'He must have loved it,' said Alice. 'It's a perfect place to have a sailor's funeral.'

'It is,' murmured Eddy. 'It's a shame, though, that it's closed to burials now. But we'll go up to the public cemetery to see his grave sometime, if you want.'

Alice nodded, and then she stood up from the pew and Eddy followed suit, the two of them walking together out into the world again.

'Just take her for a minute, will you?' said Eddy, handing her the baby before disappearing round the corner of the church.

'I brought these along earlier,' she said, returning with an armful of bright red carnations. 'Glad nobody's nicked off with them . . . You can throw them down into the water.'

'Thanks, Eddy,' smiled Alice. 'These are lovely, so thoughtful of you.'

She threw the red blooms, one by one, into the river. 'These are for you, Tommy,' she murmured. 'And I won't forget, I'll be looking up to the stars one of these nights. I will remember you.'

The women stood for a few minutes, watching the flowers bob around on the water. 'They probably won't go till the tide changes,' said

Eddy. 'But they should head out to sea, eventually.'

★   ★   ★

When Ada knocked on the kitchen door later that day, Alice was straight there, letting her in and offering her a seat.

'I can see already,' said Ada, 'that you are recovering from what must have been a very difficult experience.'

'I am, and it was, but in the end, I've just got to get on with things. I mean, we've been living with the threat here in the alley of being picked up by the police for some time now, and then, I knew that Jamie might be lurking somewhere in the city, so there was that as well . . . '

Ada nodded. 'Let's hope that with time, you will feel more secure. Although I'm not sure that the police will be backing off any time soon. The campaign for the repeal of the Contagious Diseases Acts continues, but so far there's no change . . . Women's voices are simply not heard. Even Miss Nightingale has told them that the forced examination of women makes absolutely no difference to the rates of venereal disease amongst men. She's studied the statistics from earlier attempts to use forced examination of women on the continent. It simply does not work. So why continue? But they will not listen, and it makes my blood boil . . . '

Alice could feel the passion of Ada's conviction and it sent a warm glow through her body.

'Anyway, Alice,' said Ada, taking a sip of her tea, 'back to the matter in hand . . . I can see that you look ready to return to work, but there's just one thing. I think you need to go out into the city and leave Victoria here with Marie. Just to see how that feels. It will help prepare you for tomorrow.'

'Sounds like a good idea,' said Alice.

'Well, shall we do that now, then?' said Ada. 'When we've finished our tea. We can go together. Marie said she'll watch the baby whilst you're away.'

Alice trotted beside Ada as they made their way through the city. She hadn't realized how fast the assistant superintendent could walk.

'I hope you don't mind, Alice,' said Ada, over her shoulder, 'but we're calling by the home of a friend of mine. Someone that I've known my whole life.'

'No, of course not,' panted Alice, trying to keep up. 'That's absolutely fine.'

When they arrived outside the door of the house, Alice could see that Ada looked suddenly awkward, as if she might change her mind and run back to the hospital. She raised her hand to knock on the door, but seemed to think better of it, and then she turned to Alice.

'I've brought you here, so that you might understand something,' she said quietly. 'I think that it might help you, if you know my situation. But I need you to promise that you won't tell another soul — not even Maud or Eddy or Stella. This has to be kept absolutely secret.'

'Of course, I promise,' said Alice, intrigued by

330

what might lie on the other side of that door.

Ada knocked, and the door was opened by a woman with a careworn face, probably a bit older than Ada. Alice saw Ada take a deep breath and then she spoke clearly. 'Mary, this is Alice Sampson, a friend of mine from the hospital. I've brought her to meet Leah.'

Alice saw mild shock on Mary's face. 'Of course,' she said, 'if you're sure.'

'I'm sure,' said Ada and then Mary led them through to the kitchen.

A tousle-haired girl of about three years old looked up immediately from a pile of building blocks on the floor. 'Ada!' she cried, running and flinging herself at her, pushing her face into her skirt.

Alice gasped. There was no mistaking the resemblance. The beautiful little girl who had just run across the floor, she was the spitting image of Ada. She could only be her daughter.

She looked on as the curly-haired child continued to bury her face in Ada's skirt, and Ada met her gaze calmly.

'I did once tell you that we had a lot in common,' said Ada.

'Much more than I could have ever imagined,' replied Alice, with a wry smile. And then, crouching down, she tapped the little girl on the shoulder. When she turned, not really shy, but pretending to hide her face in the folds of Ada's skirt, Alice was struck once more by the striking resemblance. If it hadn't been for the child's bright blue eyes, mother and daughter would have been an exact match.

'What's your name, then?' asked Alice, speaking quietly.

'I'm Leah Rose,' she said, stepping away from Ada's skirt, with her feet planted square as she repeated her own name.

'Well, Leah Rose, I'm very pleased to meet you.'

'Pleased to meet you too,' said the girl, stretching out her arm to shake Alice's hand.

'You're very formal today, Leah,' said Ada, laughing, then reaching down and pulling the girl up so that she could hold her close. Alice could see her, burying her face in her daughter's hair, breathing in the scent of her.

As soon as they were out in the street, Ada linked Alice's arm and then she started to talk. Hesitantly at first, and then as if a river of words that had been dammed up for years had suddenly been released. She told her that she'd been an assistant superintendent for four years when it happened . . .

'I was devastated,' she said. 'I loved my work, I'd just properly got the measure of things and the hospital is my life. I pushed it aside, tried not to think about it. Thinking that maybe I was mistaken, maybe I would miscarry. I hoped that might happen . . . '

Alice was nodding. 'I know, I felt the same,' she said quietly.

'But as the weeks went by, there was no mistaking my situation. And then I started to feel the first flutterings of movement . . . but still I tried to carry on with my work as if there was nothing wrong, and I didn't tell a soul. But then,

332

one day, Miss Merryweather called me into her office and she told me what she'd noticed. There was no way that I could deny it. I cried and cried with her that afternoon, and then we came up with a plan . . .

'I'd seen my childhood friend, Mary, go through the grief of losing her only child to diphtheria when he was about the same age that Leah is now. She'd always wanted more children, but none came. So I asked her if she'd take my child as her own. And she agreed.

'In the meantime, Miss Merryweather informed the rest of the staff that I was being posted to a London hospital, extra experience for a full year. No one questioned it and they all wished me well. But I was actually going to stay with a dear friend, Rose, someone I nursed with out in the Crimea. She was recently separated from her husband and glad of the company and she is someone that I trust with my life. She made sure that I had the best medical care and stayed with me through a long labour.'

'And you named your daughter after her . . . '

'Yes, I wanted the baby to be just Rose . . . but she persuaded me to let Mary choose a first name and that's why she's Leah, after Mary's grandmother. What could be better, a child named after my two oldest and dearest friends . . . '

'A child that you could have legitimately kept and raised as your own?' offered Alice gently, giving Ada's arm a squeeze.

'There is that,' replied Ada quietly. 'And I wrestled with the decision, but each time I came back to the same thing. A nurse in a senior position has to live at the hospital, there is no way around that. And I wasn't prepared to give up all that I had worked for, all of the hopes that I have for the future of nursing and the care of the sick. I knew that if I did that, I would feel bitter, betrayed somehow. And I didn't want that for my daughter.

'Mary is a wonderful mother and she's like a sister to me. I can see Leah as often as I want and be involved with everything. And as you can see, my daughter is the happiest little girl in the world. She thinks Mary is her mother and I'm her aunt. And the whole thing works very well.'

'But she looks so much like you, surely . . . '

'Well, there is that, but Mary's husband is dark-haired, so unless someone knew me, then probably no one would ever be able to tell.'

'What about the father of the baby, was it — '

'I can't talk about that,' said Ada firmly. 'But he lives away and I haven't seen him since she was born. He has no clue . . . '

Alice drew in a breath. She could feel the tension emanating from Ada and she knew that she was not going to get any more information out of her. But she couldn't help but feel concern, knowing, as she did, from her own experience, how the truth had a way of coming out . . .

20

'If you wish to be trained to do *all*
Nursing well, even what you do not
like — trained to perfection in little
things — that is Nursing for the
sake of Nursing.'
Florence Nightingale

As Alice stepped through the door of the Nurses'
Home the next morning, the door to the superin-
tendent's room clicked open and there stood
Miss Merryweather.

'I hope you are fully recovered, Nurse Sampson,' she said. 'And I would like to congratulate
you most wholeheartedly on the completion of
your training.'

'Thank you,' said Alice.

Miss Merryweather moved swiftly on to other
matters: 'Your first appointment as a trained
nurse will be on the Female Medical Ward.'

Alice's heart sank — that was Sister Fox's
ward. The dreaded Sister Fox.

'When do I start?' she said tentatively.

'You start straight away, Nurse Sampson,
today. A trained nurse has gone, left the ward,
only yesterday. Sister Fox is one down.'

Nurses are always leaving that ward, thought
Alice; they never last long.

'This is a temporary placement,' Miss
Merryweather continued, 'until we establish fully

where your true talent lies.'

Alice relaxed a little. She didn't exactly sigh with relief, but once she knew that the position would not be considered permanent, she was sure that she would be able to manage. After all that she'd been through in the last year, she felt like she could manage most things.

'This is your new uniform,' said Miss Merryweather, walking over to the coat hooks and removing a hanger holding a brand-new gown. 'You can use my room to get changed. Please leave your old probationer uniform in there. And if you look to the table at the side, you will find a fresh cap and an apron.'

Alice paused momentarily with her new uniform in her arms, a bit reluctant to head into the superintendent's office and remove her clothes.

'Get on, Nurse Sampson, get on. The ward awaits.'

Alice got changed quickly, feeling very strange in there on her own as she slipped out of her frock right next to the superintendent's desk. Even though the blind was down in the room and she knew for a fact that Miss Merryweather would be guarding the door, she still felt as though she was being watched.

A snowy white cap and clean apron were waiting, as promised, and Alice felt very proud as she pinned the cap in place. 'You have worked hard for this, Alice, it is well deserved,' she murmured to herself.

Stepping out of Miss Merryweather's room in the new uniform, Alice felt clean and bright.

'You look very fine, Nurse Sampson,' said Miss Merryweather, standing back to admire her, just for a moment. 'But we have no time to lose.'

Alice had butterflies in her stomach as she walked down the corridor to the Female Medical Ward. Even as she approached the door, she could hear the high-pitched sound of Sister as she laid into someone over some issue.

'Here I go,' she muttered to herself, squaring her shoulders before walking through the door. 'A lamb to the slaughter.'

Sister Fox stood, thin and unsmiling, at the top of the ward. She narrowed her eyes as Alice crossed the space between them.

'So you're the replacement,' she said, almost spitting out the words. 'Well, let's see if you have any mettle. Today, you will be in charge of all dressings and I want you to supervise bed-making. I will be along to *check*.'

Of course you will, thought Alice, looking the woman straight in the eye without flinching. But I'm ready for you, make no mistake.

'Now, nurses, gather round, and I will give you a summary of our patients and allocate the rest of you your duties.'

Alice felt a strange energy course through her body as Sister Fox spat out her instructions and tried to belittle the nurses who stood huddled before her. She knew that she could rise above all of this; she wouldn't let this woman in a uniform get to her. All that mattered, on any ward, was looking after the patients. No one could take that skill away from her, and from what Eddy had said about Sister Fox, she liked to give out her

337

orders and then disappear off somewhere, only emerging again for the doctors' round. So Alice knew she could manage this. She would do her absolute best and if that wasn't good enough for Sister Fox, then that was Sister Fox's problem.

Even before they started the work, Alice had already given a reassuring smile to a couple of probationers who stood, petrified, before Sister. She would do what she could to help them. She would try to make a difference.

Eddy had been right: Sister Fox did disappear, but when she came back, just before the doctors' round, she was ready to inspect. Alice saw her walking stiffly down the rows of beds, first one side, and then back up the other. Picking up a sheet on one, leaning down to scrutinize the hospital corners on another. Alice had done her best to supervise the bed-making, but all that she'd really had time to do was demonstrate what was expected to the probationers. And be kind to them, telling them to just do the best that they could.

'Nurse Sampson,' called Sister Fox, as she turned to face the ward. 'It would seem that the bed-making is adequate.'

Phew, thought Alice, knowing not to show any visible relief. She simply nodded her head. Once the doctors had arrived, she went over to congratulate her probationers. 'Well done, you two, well done.'

The whole thing was exhausting, and Alice felt like she was playing some kind of game, but she was able to come away from the ward at the end of her first day feeling that she had managed.

And at least she'd been able to supervise the proper care of her patients. Most of the women on the ward were respiratory or heart cases. They were weakened and very poorly. They needed what Miss Houston had once described as tender care. Tender, loving care.

Alice would make sure that they got as much of that as possible for as long as she was on their ward.

'How did you get on, first day back?' called Eddy as Alice approached the door to the Nurses' Home at the end of her shift.

Seeing her friend's smiling face, Alice's knees started to feel a bit weak, and she began to laugh, a strange, mildly hysterical laugh.

'I hope Sister Law treated you kindly. I hope she drew you to the bosom of all trained staff.'

Alice was laughing even more now, and she could hardly get her words out.

'What?' said Eddy impatiently.

'I haven't been with Sister Law,' hiccupped Alice. 'I was sent to Female Medical.'

'Sister Fox! Oh, my lord!' Eddy almost shouted. 'No wonder you look deranged.'

Alice held on to Eddy's arm as they went in through the door, still laughing. 'Yes, it was challenging, but I remembered what you once said about her bark being worse than her bite. And do you know what, you were wrong. She barks and she bites, and it's all the same!'

Eddy was laughing too now as she helped Alice off with her apron and cap and on with her cape and hat.

'I'll tell you everything as we walk home,' Alice

said. 'What a day. But just let me check the pigeonholes first. I wrote back to Maud from both of us, but there hasn't been a reply. I just need to check — '

Alice stopped dead when she got to the pigeonholes and saw all the letters, neatly placed in their alphabetical slots. She recognized the envelope straight away. There sat a letter from her mother.

'What's up?' asked Eddy, coming to stand beside her.

Alice withdrew the envelope slowly, and then turned it over.

'It's a letter from my mother,' she said, glancing at Eddy.

'Don't open it,' said Eddy, taking it out of her hand. 'You don't need to be reading that, Alice. You know exactly what she's going to say.'

Alice paused for a moment, weighing it up, and then she held out her hand. 'No, I want to read it,' she said. 'I'm prepared.'

Eddy handed the letter back, shaking her head, and Alice took a deep breath and then ripped the envelope open.

Alice,

Jamie has told us the story. We know everything. You are no longer a daughter of mine. The doors of this house are closed to you, for ever.

Jemima Sampson

'Well, at least it's short and sweet,' said Eddy, putting an arm around Alice's shoulders as she stood rigid, the letter still in her hand. 'But how strange that she used her own name, her full name.'

'I think she just wanted to make sure that I understood. I no longer have a mother.'

Eddy didn't seem to know what else to say; she just gave Alice's shoulders a squeeze.

The letter was exactly what Alice had expected, but she'd somehow wanted more detail, more outrage. And she'd wanted to know what her brothers thought, and most of all, what her father thought about her situation. All of the detail was missing. And for Alice it was a cruel absence. She thought of her father, sitting in his favourite chair by the fire, his head in his hands. She could see him crying. It made Alice want to cry too, and then she pictured him looking up at her, with the tears streaming down his face. And her heart felt as if it was breaking. She couldn't bear the thought of never being able to see him again, but that might be exactly what this letter held in its brief words.

'Alice?' said Eddy gently. 'Do you want me to take the letter?'

'No,' she said, wiping the tears that brimmed in her eyes with the flat of her hand, and then crumpling it and pushing it into her pocket.

'I just need to go and see my daughter, that's all.'

★   ★   ★

Alice slipped easily into the routine of her new ward. At least there was one thing to be said about Sister Fox: she never varied, which meant that once the routine was learnt, then so it went on day after day. That made Alice's management of her situation on what was commonly referred to as 'the worst ward at the hospital' a little easier.

She devoted any spare moments that she had to working with the probationers, Nurse Kelly and Nurse Parker. They were from the same set as Fry and Bradshaw. They were single young girls, living in the Nurses' Home, both coming out of domestic service, so at least they knew what was what when it came to hard work and strict routine. Alice thought that the pair of them were showing excellent qualities; they just needed to learn, that's all. She was almost glad now that she'd been given the opportunity to support these two. It would have been such a shame if they'd given up and returned to maids' work, just because of one ward, and one sister with a vicious temperament. Alice made it her task to guide the pair of them through. After all, these girls were the future of modern nursing, something that they should all be proud of.

She was pleased to see that the probationers also had some kindly support from the Reverend Seed. He seemed to spend a good deal of his time on Female Medical, sitting with the patients, reading prayers and passages from the Bible. He had a gentle way with him, a way of making the female patients on the ward smile. Alice could see that even Sister Fox had a bit of a soft spot for the Reverend. Day by day, Alice was beginning to feel increasingly warm towards the young man with the pale face who, despite his bumbling ways, always tried to do his absolute best for everyone.

'Nurse Sampson,' he said one day, approaching her in the middle of the ward, 'I wanted to say — I need to ask — how is your situation — is everything settled? I mean, with that young man who came on to the ward that day. The one who I . . . ' he said, balling his fist and miming a punch.

'Yes, all settled,' she said, smiling at him and seeing how his cheeks flushed bright pink.

'Well, maybe one day, Nurse Sampson, when you're ready, maybe you might want to take a cup of tea with me on one of your afternoons off.'

'Yes, that would be very nice, Reverend,' she said.

She could see the flush on his cheeks extending now across his whole face. He didn't seem to know what else to say, so he bowed and walked away, bumping into the bottom of a bed as he went.

'He's so nice, isn't he?' said Nurse Kelly, as she came over to help Alice make up an empty bed. 'And I think he really likes you, Nurse Sampson.'

'Stop it now,' said Alice, 'and help me with this bed before Sister comes back down the ward and gives us both a telling off.'

But Alice suspected that Nurse Kelly was right, and what's more, she was beginning to like him as well. But that was all, she liked him. She didn't know if that was enough and she certainly didn't have any time to ponder over it. Besides which, he didn't know about Victoria — he didn't know she had a child out of wedlock.

The bed was made up just in time, for the orderlies were coming through with a new admission. All Alice could see was an older woman with her grey hair piled high on her head. When they were up close, she registered with shock exactly who it was: Miss Fairchild, and she was gasping for breath.

'Oh Alice,' she said, reaching out a hand to her. 'I can't get my breath. I woke last night and I thought I was dying . . . '

Alice noticed immediately that the woman's lips and the tips of her fingers were blue, and her face a deathly white. She grabbed her hand and held on with firm pressure.

'Now, Miss Fairchild, I don't want you to try and speak right now. We need to get you in bed and into a sitting position, so that your breathing will ease.'

Miss Fairchild nodded, and Alice felt a tightness in her own chest when she saw the woman's eyes filling with tears.

'Listen to me, Miss Fairchild,' Alice said steadily. 'You have been admitted to the hospital so that we can help you. There are medicines here that we can use, things that we can do to make you feel better.'

She gave Miss Fairchild's hand an extra squeeze before turning to Nurse Kelly.

'Run and get this patient some extra pillows,

she needs to be propped up in bed. And then go directly to find one of the doctors — we need to get her assessed as soon as possible.'

Alice was still holding on to her patient's hand.

'Right, we're going to transfer you on to the bed now. The orderlies will put the stretcher on the bed and then I want you to roll to me, and then they can slip it out from underneath you.'

'I . . . understand,' said Miss Fairchild, still gasping for air. Alice noted that the bluish discolouration of her lips was darkening.

'Try not to speak, not till we get you settled,' she said. 'I want you to save your breath.'

Miss Fairchild nodded.

By the time Alice and Nurse Kelly had their patient propped up in bed, as high as they could, the doctor had appeared, ready to examine her.

'Well done, Nurse Sampson,' said the ward physician, Dr Logan, a man of older age and a very agreeable disposition. 'I caught sight of this lady coming in on the stretcher but I was with another urgent case. You have already done most of what I would have recommended in the first instance. And I can see that our patient's breathing is much improved. Now, Miss Fairchild, let's have a listen to your chest.'

'Go for the screen, Nurse Kelly, please,' said Alice, and then she stayed right by the bed as the doctor first checked the pulse and then listened to his patient's chest with his stethoscope.

'You seem to have some irregularity of the heart and that's why you are out of breath,' he said.

Miss Fairchild seemed to fold in on herself. Clearly, she was preparing for the worst.

'The good thing is, my dear,' said Dr Logan, seeing the look on his patient's face, 'we have some medicine here at the hospital that might help your heart. It's derived from a plant, the purple foxglove; it's called digitalis. If we use it correctly, it will slow and strengthen the heart rate. We have been using it here for quite some time, so we know what we're doing . . . If we get the dose right and if your heart responds to the medicine, then we can make things a lot better for you.'

'Thank you, Doctor,' panted Miss Fairchild.

'Nurse Sampson,' said the doctor, turning with a smile, 'are you familiar with the radial pulse?'

'Yes, I am,' she said.

'Well, if you palpate it now, that's it, feel at her wrist . . . can you feel how fast, how erratic, how jumpy it is?'

'Yes, I can,' she said.

'Now I want you to remember that. And I want you to check that pulse every single day and make a note of it — will you do that?'

'Yes, of course,' said Alice.

'And if she gets a bad attack again, we'll ask Dr McKendrick to try a hypodermic injection of morphine. We've been having some success with using it, just a tiny dose . . . it really settles the patient and it eases breathing.'

'I'll remember,' said Alice, 'and I'll pass the information on to Sister Fox and the night sister.'

After Dr Logan had retreated, Miss Fairchild beckoned for Alice to come closer. 'Alice,' she whispered, 'thank you for looking after me. There is one more thing . . . I don't want Maud to know, please don't tell her . . . '

'But she would want to know, Miss Fairchild, you know she would.'

'No,' she said quietly, starting to pant for breath again. 'I don't . . . want to worry her when she's so far away and can't do anything.'

'That's all right, Miss Fairchild,' said Alice, concerned that her patient would start gasping for air again. 'I understand.'

Alice was quick to tell Eddy about Miss Fairchild, though, as soon as the two of them met up after work.

'Who?'

'You know, Maud's housekeeper, the one who gave you a handkerchief at the harbour that day.'

'Of course,' said Eddy. 'What's wrong with her? I hope she's going to be all right. And Maud is so far away.'

'She has heart failure but she doesn't want Maud to know anything, that's what she said.'

'Yes, but don't you think we should — '

'No, Eddy,' said Alice firmly. 'And don't you go blabbing to anyone about it, do you hear? I promised the woman that we would say nothing.'

'Maud won't be happy.'

'I know she won't, but a patient's request is a patient's request.'

'Fair enough, Alice,' said Eddy. 'I daren't contradict you, not now you're working on that ward with Sister Fox . . . I think you might be becoming a bit like her, all stern and bossy. Nurse Sampson, the very next scourge of the Infirmary. Feared by all . . . '

'Stop it, Eddy,' said Alice cackling with laughter, and pretending to slap her around the back of the head. 'Stop that or I'll dismiss you on the spot.'

21

'Every Nurse must grow. No Nurse
can stand still. She must go forward
or she will go backward every year.'

Florence Nightingale

Three days later, as Alice stood by Miss
Fairchild's bed dutifully checking her pulse, she
gave a contented sigh.

'Is everything all right?' asked her patient.

'Yes, it is,' said Alice warmly, turning to the
chart that sat by the bed so that she could make
a note of her reading. 'Your pulse is much
steadier. You still have some irregular beats but
it's slowed down nicely. I'm so glad that I've
been able to monitor this all the way through.
How are you feeling now?'

'As you can see, much better,' said Miss
Fairchild, smiling. 'I'm hoping that Dr Logan
might let me walk soon. I've been getting up to
stand at the side of the bed, but I think I'm going
to seize up altogether if I don't start walking
soon.'

'Let's see what he says on the ward round in
the morning,' said Alice. 'But from what I can
see, you are much improved. Your colour is
better, your lips are pink. So I think he will be in
agreement.'

'I hope I'll be able to do it, after all these days
in bed,' said Miss Fairchild, her voice suddenly

flat. 'I've already handed over all of my keys for the big house to another housekeeper . . . What if I'm going to be stuck in this bed for the rest of my life? What if I'll never be able to get back to my post?'

'Look, Miss Fairchild,' said Alice gently, crouching down by the side of her bed. 'We have no way of knowing until you try. So it makes no sense for us to start fretting over something that might not be a concern. Think about it this way — all's well until proved otherwise. And if it doesn't work out the way we want, then we'll just have to put our heads together and try to find a way of managing, making the best of it.'

'Alice, you are the sweetest, kindest person I think I've ever known, but I'm not sure if I can stop fretting. One minute I'm thinking everything will be fine, the next I'm plunged into complete despair . . . I don't seem to have any control over it.'

Alice stood up and put an arm around the woman's shoulders. 'You are bound to feel like that, of course you are. And it seems to me that you just need to know, one way or the other. And that's another reason for you trying to walk.'

'But I'm afraid,' said Miss Fairchild, her lip starting to tremble.

Alice reached for her hand. 'Of course you are. Anyone would be. But I'll be with you in the morning, right by your side, and we'll face whatever's coming together.'

Miss Fairchild nodded and then slipped a hand up the sleeve of her nightgown and removed a handkerchief.

'Now, I need to go back up to the other end of the ward but I'll come back down here in about half an hour, to check on you . . . I'm off this afternoon but I'll be back in tomorrow for a full day. I'll be there if Dr Logan says that you can get out of bed.'

Miss Fairchild nodded again and then sniffed a little. 'Thank you, Alice,' she said, her voice husky. 'I do not know *what* I'd have done without you.'

Alice was really looking forward to her afternoon off. She'd been so busy with the patients and the probationers and keeping out of the way of Sister Fox that even as she walked away from the ward, she still had all the details of her work running through her head — all she had done and the issues that she would need to follow up tomorrow. Miss Fairchild was at the top of her list.

She knew that she was ready for some time off and she was anxious to be away, but she had to stop in her tracks for a few moments as the hospital visitors poured in through the door. As she stood in the corridor watching them all flow by, she hoped that Miss Fairchild would be getting a visitor, someone who could offer some cheer. Not all visitors can do that, she thought, with a wry smile, remembering some of the conversations she'd overheard at a patient's bedside.

She wasn't, in fact, going straight home that day. The Reverend Seed had finally plucked up enough courage to ask her out for afternoon tea. He'd seemed very excited about the whole thing, and he'd told her that he'd located a suitable establishment and booked a table. He was meeting her outside the hospital at two p.m.

The fateful hour, Alice thought, as she walked along, desperately trying to push any trace of Roderick Morgan to the back of her mind. Infuriatingly, ever since the Reverend had started paying her some attention, she had started thinking about Morgan again. For so long, every time a hint of a thought had come into her head, she'd pushed it away. She'd been able to do that. But now, for some reason, there he was again. And increasingly she found herself thinking about their day at the park and the lazy glide of the swans on the water as they sat by the lake. All of it. She had to keep reminding herself of how she'd felt when Nancy told her that he was married, how devastated she was. But she couldn't make it outweigh the other feelings: the memories of their day out, the smell of him, the look in his eyes, and that kiss as they stood under the clock on Lime Street Station.

'Stop it, Alice, stop it right now,' she muttered as she walked down the corridor. No good could possibly come from having those thoughts. And he hadn't even written or tried to make any contact. She just needed to see how things went with the Reverend Seed, see a bit more of him . . . But that's it, she thought, I can only think of him as the Reverend. I can't even think of calling him Lawrence.

'You just need to see how it goes,' she muttered to herself, more firmly, as she came out through the main door. 'Give him a chance.'

'Alice?' said a gentle voice from behind her. 'Alice!'

She stopped in her tracks immediately. She knew that voice, she would have known it anywhere.

'Father?' she cried, turning to face him. 'Father!'

Frederick Sampson had removed his hat and he stood with it in his hands, fiddling at the brim, as he stared at Alice, with tufts of his hair sticking out at all angles and tears in his eyes.

'Alice,' he said again, his voice breaking, and she was immediately there, holding him in her arms, as he cried on her shoulder.

She was sobbing now too. 'I thought I'd never see you again.'

'What, leave my Alice? Forget about her? Never in a million years.'

'How are you? How is everyone?' she asked. Then, drawing back from him, she remembered the reality of her situation, and her body stiffened as she saw the pained expression on his face.

'I'm so sorry,' she said, reaching out a hand and gently touching his forearm.

She knew that she had to act swiftly, she had to make things right between them, or they never would be, ever again.

'Wait here,' she said, taking his hand. 'I need to go and get changed, but then I'll take you home with me to see Victoria, your granddaughter.'

Frederick nodded and then he wiped his eyes with the flat of his hand and put his hat on.

Alice glanced back as she walked towards the Nurses' Home, just to make sure that her father was still there and that he was waiting for her. When she turned around, there was the Reverend smiling at her.

'I'm so sorry,' she said. 'My father has just turned up unexpectedly, we will have to rearrange. I'm really sorry.'

Alice saw his face drop instantly and she felt for him.

'There he is, waiting,' she said, pointing to Frederick. 'I had no idea he was coming today.'

The Reverend nodded but she could see how disappointed he was.

'Until next time,' he said, taking her hand gently and forcing himself to smile. 'I can wait for another time.'

Alice smiled warmly and then she was running into the Nurses' Home, her heart fluttering and her mind flying all over the place with the excitement of introducing her father to Victoria.

She changed into her cape and hat quickly and then ran down the steps, eager to rejoin the lone figure standing quietly in his tweed jacket and woollen waistcoat. 'That's the Nurses' Home where I used to live,' she said, as she walked back towards him, turning so that she could point out the fine building.

'My word, Alice,' he said, starting to smile. 'What a grand place it is!'

She smiled and linked arms with him. 'And I did manage to finish my training and I've got a position as a trained nurse on the Female Medical Ward.'

He nodded his approval.

'We'll head back through the city now towards Lime Street. There's just one thing, though, that I might need to explain about where I live . . . '

'No need, Alice,' he said quietly. 'Jamie furnished us with all the details . . . he told us everything.'

Alice nodded. 'Sorry about that . . . but you do understand that I only worked there as a housemaid? I've never engaged with any other kind of activity . . . I needed somewhere to live, and without the women there, me and the baby, we'd have been out on the street.'

Frederick nodded. 'I guessed that, Alice. And I'm so sorry that you weren't able to come to us, at home. I would never have turned my back on you.'

'I know. But you know what Mother's like, she would have thrown me out. I daren't come home. I wanted to keep my baby, I wasn't even thinking straight at the time. But I feared for my child. I couldn't risk coming home.'

'What a world we live in,' said Frederick, shaking his head. 'We all know that women have babies outside of marriage. And instead of helping them, we shun them, turn our backs on our own kin, out of some sense of right and wrong handed down by other people. Well, I won't have any of it, Alice, not any more. From now on, I'll do all that I can for you and my granddaughter.'

'Thank you,' smiled Alice, holding on to his arm even more tightly. 'But I somehow think that Mother would not agree with you and I bet

355

she doesn't even know that you're here.'

'No, she doesn't,' said Frederick with a wry smile. 'Right now, she thinks I'm in Manchester, looking for new halters for the cows.'

Alice couldn't help but laugh when she saw the twinkle in his eye. She would never have thought he would dare to break free.

★　★　★

'Marie, Marie,' called Alice as soon as she was in through the front door, with Frederick in tow. 'We have a visitor.'

Marie turned with the baby in her arms and opened her mouth to speak, but when she saw the look on the face of the man who had just entered the room with Alice, no words would come. She had no need to ask who it was. As the man removed his hat, she could see that he still had enough strands of red hair amongst the grey to secure a strong family resemblance. And the way he looked at Victoria . . .

'Hello, precious,' murmured Frederick, walking towards his granddaughter as if hypnotized.

Alice stood still and held her breath. Her heart felt like it was fit to burst in her chest.

'Hello there,' he said again. 'You are a beautiful girl, aren't you, and is that a streak of red in your hair?'

Victoria looked at him, her eyes wide, then she glanced back to Marie.

'Will you come to me?' he said, placing his hat down on the table, and offering his hands out to her. 'Will you come to me?'

Alice felt a lump rise in her throat as Victoria beamed back at her grandfather, holding her arms out. He took her and held her close for a moment before looking at her again and continuing to talk to her. 'My lovely girl, you don't need to worry. I'm just your old grandad, that's who I am . . . '

Frederick, Alice and Marie were all crying now, together.

Frederick sat carefully in the chair by the stove after Victoria had settled for her nap. She'd stayed with him, playing with her cloth dog and listening to his stories and his songs, until she'd got tired. And then she'd wanted Alice.

As Alice busied herself cutting some cake and pouring the tea, she looked over to see Hugo lift his head from where he lay in front of the stove. To her surprise, he got up and the next minute he was rubbing himself against her father's legs and starting to purr as Frederick reached down to stroke him.

'There you go, puss cat,' murmured Frederick. 'You are a strange fella, aren't you? And it looks like you spend all day lying in front of that fire . . . '

'He does,' said Alice, laughing. 'And he doesn't usually pay anybody any attention. I think you're the first. He just ignores me and Marie, all day long.'

'It must be my country ways he likes,' smiled Frederick. 'Don't you, fella?' he said, giving him one last stroke.

Alice pulled up a chair and sat opposite him. She still couldn't believe that he was here, sitting with her in the kitchen. Her father.

'I'm so glad that you came to see me,' she said. 'I hope you will come and see us again.'

'You try stopping me,' he grinned, and Alice reached out a hand to him — this gentle man, her father, who had never once, to her knowledge, spoken out of turn to his wife.

'And what's more, when I go home, I'm going to tell your mother exactly where I've been. I'm going to tell her about Victoria and make it clear that I *will* be coming down to Liverpool to see our granddaughter as often as I can.'

Alice stared at him, her eyes wide.

'Yes, I know, the fury of hell itself will rain down on me for some time to come. But I can withstand that, Alice. What I can't withstand is thinking that I will never see you or my precious granddaughter ever again.'

'Thank you for that,' said Alice. 'And if you do need a place of safety then you could always come and live here in the city with us.'

'I'll bear that in mind, Alice,' he smiled, 'but you know what I'm like. I'm a countryman with country ways, I need to be on the land. And who'd look after the herd? I've left Tim Cowley in charge today — who knows what I'll find when I get back? Last time, he forgot to milk four of 'em.'

Alice laughed out loud, and then her face clouded a little. 'I hope that things don't get too difficult for you, though, back home.'

'Don't you worry about that, Alice. And there is something as well that I can fall back on, something about me and your mother that might work in our favour.'

'What's that?'

'You have to swear, Alice, not to tell anyone, even your brothers. If this got out, then it'd really put the cat among the pigeons . . . '

'I won't tell a soul. What is it?'

'Well, the thing is, your mother, well, she was in the same situation that you were in, when we got married.'

'You mean she was . . . '

'Yes, she most certainly was. She was expecting your eldest brother. We had to get married and sharpish. Well, your grandfather was a lay preacher at the Methodist chapel. He was blazing with fury. The whole thing was terrible.'

Alice didn't know what to say. She was stunned. To think that her mother's severity, her endless ranting about the work of the devil and avoiding sin, might have been some kind of reaction to what had happened to her as a young woman . . . Jemima Sampson had, herself, committed what she had always insisted was 'the greatest sin of all'.

'Well,' she said at last, 'I never thought that's what you were going to say . . . '

'What's more, your grandfather threatened me with a shotgun.'

'Really?'

'He did, and the thing was, I wanted to marry Jemima anyway, she'd always been the one for me. So, there are ways and means that I have for managing your mother. Try not to worry too much. I'm not saying she'll be down here with me, to see you and the baby. You know what she's like, she's her own worst enemy sometimes. We both know that she won't back down from this. But what I am saying is, she won't be able to stop me from coming.'

'So that's good then,' breathed Alice. 'Victoria needs to see her grandfather.'

'And then, when enough time has gone by, maybe you'll be able to come and visit us at home. But I can't make any promises there . . . '

'I understand,' said Alice, not wanting to rush back anyway, not even knowing if she would ever want to see her mother again.

'And now she's not hankering after you and Jamie getting together, not since he upped and got engaged as soon as he came back — '

'Did he?' said Alice. 'Who to?'

'To Mavis Webster, from Valley Farm.'

Alice couldn't think who it was at first and then she remembered pale-faced Mavis, George Webster's girl, from Sunday school.

'She's the only child, she'll inherit the lot when he's gone.'

Alice felt nothing but relief. That made everything clearer and she could be more certain now that Jamie wouldn't be coming back to haunt her. She wished him luck there, though — Mavis had always been a sour-faced misery, even as a child.

22

'... the friendships that have begun at this School may last through life ...'
Florence Nightingale

There was a note waiting for Alice on the kitchen table the next morning, lying beside a beautiful bouquet of flowers. 'Who are they from?' asked Marie as she stood waiting impatiently for the details.

'Oh, I know who they'll be from,' replied Alice. There was only one man she could think of who would send her flowers. How sweet of him to take the trouble ... He must have asked Miss Houston for her address.

'They arrived first thing,' said Marie. 'They must have come freshly cut from the flower seller. I've never seen such flowers, they smell wonderful.'

The Reverend Seed has really excelled himself, thought Alice, smiling to herself as she picked up the envelope and noted the handwriting. He writes with a real flourish as well, she thought, expecting to see a rather cramped, stilted style.

As she pulled the folded letter out of the envelope, she felt the quality of the paper. He likes the best, she thought. The Reverend Seed is a man full of surprises.

As soon as Alice saw the words on the paper,

361

she felt winded, and needed to clutch the back of a kitchen chair for support.

'Goodness,' cried Marie. 'Are you all right?'

Alice nodded. She felt ridiculous, but she couldn't speak for a moment.

'These flowers aren't from who I expected,' she said eventually, staring at Marie. 'They're from that married man, Roderick Morgan.'

'Read it, read it,' implored Marie.

Alice sat down at the table and as she read the words her heart was racing.

My dearest Alice,

Please accept my sincere apologies. I have no right to expect anything from you as I send these flowers. All I want is for you to know that I had absolutely no intention of causing you any distress.

I hope your work is going well. And I also hope that, one day, you will agree to accompany me on another walk in the park.

Yours, affectionately,
R.M.

Alice made to crumple the note; she wanted to throw it to the back of the fire. But as she held it, she caught the merest scent of his cologne and it stirred some feeling in the pit of her stomach.

'Oh, for goodness' sake,' she muttered. 'I can't be getting into that again.'

'I think you never got out of it, Alice

362

. . . seeing your face when you opened that letter . . . '

Alice was furious with herself. Angrily folding the letter, she pushed it back into the envelope. She could smell the flowers, the scent was wonderful, but she wouldn't look at them. Grabbing her cape and hat, she leant over Victoria's crib and kissed her lightly on the cheek.

'Bye, Marie,' she called, anxious to be out of the room. 'Chuck those flowers away for me, will you?'

But Marie was shaking her head and already looking for a suitable vase so that she could arrange them for Alice to see when she came back from work.

Alice marched to the hospital, her legs aching with the exertion by the time she got there. She needed to try and walk it off, stop that feeling that she got when she thought about the lazy glide of the swans on the lake at the park, the smell of his cologne, his dark eyes. She would manage this, she could keep her feelings at bay.

'Morning, Alice,' she heard Eddy call from the other side of the street as she made her way to her work in the city.

'Morning,' she called back, seeing Eddy give her a curious glance. She always knows when something's up, thought Alice. But by the time I meet her after work, this will all be sorted and I'll have no need to explain anything.

On the ward, Alice had no energy to spare for countering Sister Fox's snide remarks; she let them flow over her like water. She had her probationers organized and the morning's work ticking along nicely. She had accompanied Dr Logan on the ward round and her next duty would be to assist Miss Fairchild with her trial of walking.

'Nurse Kelly, Nurse Parker, please could you help me with the patient in bed seven. We need to try her with a few steps this morning. See how she copes.'

Standing by Miss Fairchild's bed with her two probationers, Alice smiled encouragingly. 'Are you ready?'

'I'm ready,' said the housekeeper. 'Let's get on with it.'

'Right then, Miss Fairchild, let's just help you to sit at the side of the bed first. Nurse Kelly and Nurse Parker will help you. Yes, like that. That's good . . . Now just sit a few minutes and get your breath back, there is absolutely no need to rush . . . Nurse Kelly, please go and find a chair and bring it here, will you?'

As soon as Nurse Kelly had returned with the chair, Alice spoke to Miss Fairchild. 'Nurse Parker and I will be at either side of you and then you can stand, like you have been doing, to stretch your legs. When you're ready you can try a few steps. Nurse Kelly will wait with the chair, ready for you to sit down, just in case.'

'Good plan, Nurse Sampson,' said Miss Fairchild.

'So when you're ready . . . right, yes, up you come.'

Alice was pleased to see Miss Fairchild standing tall with her back straight. In that one simple move she seemed to get all of her former dignity back.

'That is very good indeed,' said Alice. 'Now as soon as you're ready, take one step, and then another . . . Nurse Kelly and I will be right by you, you are perfectly safe.'

Miss Fairchild took two steps, and then she paused, slightly out of breath, but managing.

'This is your first time,' soothed Alice. 'You need to get used to walking again.'

Miss Fairchild nodded and then she took another step, and another . . . and now she was even more out of breath.

'Just try one more,' said Alice quietly. 'Just one more.'

Miss Fairchild took the step but then, in seconds, she was gasping for air. Alice saw the distress on her face, she felt her body sag and her knees were starting to give way.

'Chair, please, now,' said Alice firmly, and Nurse Kelly was straight there, neatly placing the seat beneath Miss Fairchild.

Alice saw the anguish on her patient's face, as she sat there helpless, fighting for breath.

'Right, Miss Fairchild,' she said, her voice gentle but firm. 'You have become a bit more out of breath than we expected, but you are perfectly safe on this chair. I need you to take some deep breaths now and try to steady up. It will settle, just try not to fight against it. That's it, yes, just one more deep breath.'

Once her breathing had settled, Miss Fairchild sat, her shoulders slumped forward and her head bowed. Alice waited.

'So now we know what we're dealing with,' she murmured at last. 'I won't ever get any better than this.'

'I'm so sorry,' said Alice, placing a gentle hand on the woman's shoulder. 'But it might just be that we haven't reached the right concentration of digitalis yet . . . Let's see what Dr Logan has to say, when he sees you again later. Try not to lose hope.'

'I know what he will say, Nurse Sampson,' said Miss Fairchild, her breathing much easier now. 'I could feel it when I was walking; my heart was hammering inside me, like something broken.'

'Well, let's see,' said Alice, giving her shoulder a squeeze. 'Now, we need to get you settled . . . Nurse Parker, please go and find the orderlies to lift Miss Fairchild back into bed.'

Sadly for Miss Fairchild, there was no better news from Dr Logan. He asked more questions, held her wrist and timed her pulse, and listened to her chest with his stethoscope. And then he shook his head. 'Mmm,' he said, 'I can tell that there has been improvement, a good deal of improvement with the treatment . . . '

'But?' said Miss Fairchild.

'But I'm afraid to say that the improvement is only there when you are at rest. This does happen. Sometimes, once the heart shows signs of failure, it can't manage any added strain . . . '

'Does that mean that I won't ever be able to walk again?'

'There might be that possibility,' said Dr Logan solemnly. 'I am very sorry. We do have some more capacity for increasing the dose of digitalis, but if there is no further improvement, then I'm afraid to say that you may not get back to anywhere near your previous level of activity.'

'I see,' said Miss Fairchild, pursing her lips.

After the doctor had gone, Alice stayed by her bed. 'Let's see what happens over the next couple of weeks,' she said gently. 'As Dr Logan said, there is still some capacity for more improvement.'

Miss Fairchild was shaking her head. 'You are a very dear girl,' she said, 'but I very much doubt if things are going to get any better.'

'Well,' said Alice, pausing for a moment as if lost in thought, 'I suppose in that case, the only thing that we can hope for, is that things don't get any worse.'

Miss Fairchild couldn't help but smile, and she squeezed Alice's hand. 'Alice, you seem to have a way of finding glimmers of hope in any situation, don't you?'

Alice shrugged her shoulders. 'You could call it that, I suppose. But what else is there for patients like you, with chronic conditions? All you can hope for is to hold your ground. And if you can do that, well, that has to be good news, doesn't it?'

Miss Fairchild nodded, still smiling.

'Just one thing, though,' said Alice, 'and I have a feeling I already know what you're going to say. Do you think we should write to Maud now and tell her about your situation?'

'No, definitely not,' said Miss Fairchild, pressing her lips into a firm line.

'But Maud would want to know. We'll all be in trouble if she finds out about it from someone else . . .'

'That may be the case, Alice, but I don't want her worrying over me when she's got her work to do and she's looking after Alfred. I won't have it and that's that.'

'Well, as I've said before, I will respect your wishes. But I don't agree. I think Maud can cope with most things. Please think about it, will you?'

Miss Fairchild nodded and said that she would give it more thought. But Alice knew her well enough by now to know that when she straightened her back and lifted her chin in a certain way, she had definitely made up her mind.

Come visiting time, however, the matter was decided for them. Hearing the sound of raised voices from Miss Fairchild's bed, Alice moved straight there.

'I know you said not to, Constance, and I'm sorry about this, but I needed to take things into my own hands.' Mrs Watson, a friend of Miss Fairchild's who visited regularly, was standing, red-faced, by Miss Fairchild's bed.

'But I gave express instructions,' said Miss Fairchild, her voice hoarse.

'I know that,' said the other woman. 'But sometimes, it is our duty, as senior staff, to countermand those instructions. Seeing you here, week by week, still struggling, not looking like things are going to properly get better, I took it on myself. Maud needed to know.'

Alice moved to the side of the bed and tried to hold Miss Fairchild's hand, but she pulled it away irritably.

'You had no right,' she countered, struggling to sit up straighter, starting to gasp for air.

'She needed to know, Constance, her and that boy Alfred, they're like family to you. It just didn't seem right that she didn't know. So the letter went last week, after I visited you. I didn't ask, I knew what you'd say. But it's done.'

Miss Fairchild let out a weary sound, and then she looked up at Alice. 'I'm too weak to resist,' she said quietly.

'Just take a bit of time to steady your breathing, that's it, let's calm everything down.'

By this time the visitor had found herself a stool and brought it over so she could sit by the bed, and then Miss Fairchild was starting to breathe more easily.

'You know this woman, don't you? My head cook, Mrs Watson,' she said. 'What do you think about what she's done?'

'Well, as you already know, I'm inclined to agree with her,' said Alice. 'I don't think Maud would forgive us if we hadn't let her know.'

She saw Mrs Watson nodding vigorously.

'And sometimes,' she continued, 'it's the sign of a true friend. Someone who will recognize what's in your best interest and risk getting into trouble to make sure that it gets done. I think that's exactly what Mrs Watson has done for you here, Miss Fairchild.'

Alice saw Miss Fairchild purse her lips again and she reached up to touch her neatly piled grey hair. And then she turned to Mrs Watson. 'So it looks like you are a true friend, then, Mrs Watson, what do you think about that?'

'I think that's just grand,' said the woman, patting Miss Fairchild's hand as she sat in the bed with her back straight and her head held high.

★ ★ ★

'Ooh, you know what that might mean,' said Eddy excitedly, when Alice met up with her after work. 'Maud might come home.'

'I don't know about that,' said Alice. 'I'll write to her now, and reassure her that although Miss Fairchild's condition is serious, she is being well cared for and I will monitor the situation.'

'I see what you mean,' said Eddy, more quietly. 'She's gone such a long way and she's hardly been there any time at all. She might not even be able to come back, and what about her work out there?'

'Well, let's see, shall we?' Alice said. 'I just wanted Maud to have the exact information, that's all. So that she can make a reasoned decision.'

'Reasoned decision, hey, as if you're familiar with that kind of thing,' teased Eddy. 'And anyway, Sampson, what the heck was up with you this morning? I saw your face when you were walking to work and I feared for the patients on the ward . . . '

As the two of them walked back through the streets, past shops and carts and horses and stray dogs, threading their way through the people of Liverpool, Alice told Eddy about the letter from Morgan and then the visit from her father.

'Crikey, Alice,' said Eddy. 'You've had a lot going on since I last saw you. You've had a lot going on for a full year, in fact. Do you remember when we first walked this route together? You and Maud, following along behind me as I led the way in my big hat.'

'Of course I remember,' said Alice, pulling closer to Eddy as they walked. 'I won't ever forget that night. You were walking fast, and we hadn't a clue where we were going. If it hadn't been for the red flowers on that hat of yours, we would probably have lost our way. Just imagine if we'd never found Stella's place.'

'But your face, Alice, and Maud's when they showed us in. You two looked like Sunday school teachers who'd taken a wrong turning. You wouldn't even sit down on that velvet settee.'

'I know,' laughed Alice. 'And then when we went through to talk in private with Stella, everything started piling up in my head, and I cried my eyes out. Maud looked so worried, but Stella, she just kept talking and told me everything that I needed to know. And all you seemed to be interested in, Eddy, was having a feel of my belly . . . and that was the first time that I felt Victoria move, that fluttering inside.'

As they went by Lime Street Station, Alice continued to think about that first night when the three of them had walked past together: the steam rising up into the air, the clanking of metal, the crowds of people around them. She'd felt lost, then, overwhelmed, as if she didn't have any direction. Now, she picked up on the excitement of passengers heading into the station, and she thought about the last time she had stood under the station clock with Morgan.

How she had kissed him. Her skin prickled, and she could almost feel him against her; she knew that she still wanted him.

'Come on, slow coach,' said Eddy, dragging Alice past, and then they both dived down the alley together, almost running, holding their hats on as they went.

'Evening, Sisters,' said a man, touching his cap as he slouched against the wall with a smoke. 'You keep up the good work.'

'We will,' they both called, before turning the next corner and bursting into giggles. 'Little does he know that we're heading to a brothel,' laughed Alice. 'And that under this cape and hat, I've got a body that fairly recently gave birth to a baby girl out of wedlock.'

'Little does he know,' murmured Eddy. 'But you know what, Alice, I'm sure that the people of Liverpool are some of the best. When you think about it, there are many people here, from all over the world. My father even knows an escaped American slave . . . We are so lucky to live in this modern world of ours, in a city that's so full of life.'

'Yes, we are,' smiled Alice, looking at her friend as she stood on the step, with her eyes shining, her hair all over the place and her hat so skew-whiff it looked set to slide off her head. 'We are very lucky indeed. Now come on, let's get inside and put the kettle on.'

Alice saw the flowers that Morgan had sent resting in the middle of the table. 'Oooh, these are nice,' said Eddy, burying her face into the middle of them and having a good sniff, which immediately set her off sneezing.

Marie walked through with Victoria.

'Hello, my darling,' said Alice, scowling at the vase of flowers before shrugging off her cape. 'What have you been doing today?'

'You've being trying to pull yourself up, haven't you, big girl?' said Marie, handing the baby over to Alice. 'She's growing and changing so much now, Alice. She'll be running this place before long.'

Alice laughed. 'Who knows what you'll be doing, hey?'

'Nice flowers,' said Lizzie, wandering in and flopping down in a chair, ready to apply her evening make-up. Alice had got used to her routine, and loved watching the way she held a hand mirror with one hand and carefully smoothed the paint on her lips and expertly drew a black kohl line along her eyelids.

Marie brewed the tea in the pot, and they all sat together in happy companionship whilst Eddy told them the story of the man that she'd seen on the way to her first case that morning, chasing a pig down the street.

And then Stella was in, telling them about the protest march that her and some of the women that she'd met at the midnight suppers were organizing. 'We'll walk down Lime Street with our banners flying, we won't be beaten by the police and their moral enforcement. Ada and Miss Merryweather said they'll come along. And we're going to ask Josephine Butler if she'll lead the way.' She leant forward across the table towards Alice, and added, 'You come too, and bring the baby. We're marching for all women, everywhere, even the tiny, baby ones.'

As she sat with Victoria on her knee, giving her little sips of tea and feeding her crumbs of cake, Alice looked around that table, from one face to another. All of these women are special to me, she thought. If only Maud were here, right now, my world would be almost perfect.

After Eddy had gone, and the baby was sleeping soundly in her crib in the small room that they shared, Alice sat alone in the kitchen by the fire, listening to the spit of the wood and letting her mind drift. The book that she'd almost finished lay face down on the kitchen table. She picked it up and started to read and soon, she had reached the next to last page and the ghosts of Cathy and Heathcliff out on the moor . . . Alice had tears in her eyes.

There was a murmur of voices in the corridor, and she heard Lizzie's voice with someone she assumed was a client. Then there was a gentle tap on the door.

'Come in,' called Alice softly, wondering why whoever it was needed permission.

The door opened and a broad-shouldered man in a black coat stepped in and stood with his hat clutched in both hands.

Alice gasped and jumped up from her chair, letting the book fall to the floor.

'I hope you are well, Alice,' said Morgan. 'I'd heard that there'd been some kind of difficulty in recent weeks.'

'I am fine, thank you,' she said pointedly, enunciating each word with cut-glass precision.

He stood perfectly still, never taking his eyes off her. She felt like he was holding his breath, waiting for her to say something else.

'Did you like the flowers?' he asked, gesturing to the vase which had pride of place on the kitchen table.

'Why did you send them? Why?' she cried suddenly, forgetting her attempt to keep her feelings hidden.

Annoyingly, she saw what looked like a ray of hope light his face. He infuriated her even further, standing there with the ghost of a smile on his face.

'I sent them, Alice, because I was thinking about you. In fact, I think about you all of the time, I can't help it.'

'Yes, but that doesn't mean that I think about you,' she snapped back at him, her mouth tightening.

'Then I am lost,' he said, holding out both arms, still holding his hat.

She sensed that he was going to move, she could see him poised. His eyes burned into her as she held his gaze without flinching.

He took a step towards her.

'Don't come any closer,' she shouted, stepping back and causing her chair to screech along the floor. 'Leave me alone. I don't want to see you. I don't want to speak to you . . . ' but her voice was wavering, and when she looked down, her hands were shaking. She stepped forward and grabbed the table to steady herself.

'Alice,' he said softly, and when she looked up he had placed his hat on the table and was gazing at her, his dark eyes pleading.

'I've agonized for all these weeks about coming to see you. I didn't mean to deceive you; it's just that the opportunity never seemed to come up to tell you about my circumstances . . . The fact is, yes, I am married, but it was more of an arrangement than anything. I live mainly at my business address — you remember, that card I gave you, that night in the hospital.'

He paused, still gazing at her, looking for affirmation, but Alice merely shrugged.

'My wife is a stranger to me, and yes, we have a child, but there is no closeness in our relationship. Please forgive me, Alice, for not telling you about all of this. It's just that I knew that you wouldn't even consider me if you knew that I was married. I wanted to spend time with you so desperately . . . '

Alice looked down. She could feel her resolve softening and she had a lump in her throat.

Don't give in, don't give in, she was saying over and over in her head, but she could feel her knees weakening and her heart was pounding in her chest, drowning out all sense of anything else.

He was moving towards her, he was standing by her. She could smell him now, the cologne that he always wore. He was right there and all she could do was reach for him and bury her face in his shoulder, breathing in the scent of him.

'This is absolutely the wrong thing,' she whispered, when she was able to speak. 'I should *not* be doing this . . . '

But it was too late, she was kissing him, the sensation of it coursing right through her body.

'Maybe not,' he murmured, between kisses. 'But it seems that neither of us have any choice.'

Then Alice drew back and took a deep breath, straining her ears. Yes, she was right, she could hear a faint whimper coming from the bedroom.

She took a step away from him, listening again, her body still aching, craving for him, her breath coming quick.

'Alice . . . ' he said, his eyes pleading with her, reaching an arm out towards her.

'It's my daughter,' she said. 'I think she's waking.'

'Go and see to her,' he said. 'I can wait here . . . '

'I don't know if you should,' she said, shaking her head now. 'It's just that, yes, I feel drawn to you, this thing between us is so strong. But you have a child of your own. And you have a wife. What about them? How old is your child — is it a boy or a girl?'

'A girl, Elizabeth, and she is three years old.'

Alice felt a tightening in her chest. She knew in that moment, now that she had a name for his child and a sense of who the girl was, she knew what she needed to do, but it ran against what her body was screaming for her to do.

'That's what I hate about this,' she made herself say, her voice almost a whisper. 'That's why I can't continue with whatever this is between us. You have a child and a wife, and I can't bear to think what this would do to them, if they found out.'

377

'But they won't — '

Alice held up her hand. 'Even if they don't find out, I know, I still know about *them*. Your wife is a woman with feelings, and like me, she has a daughter.'

'Alice, please . . . '

'No,' she said emphatically, grabbing the bread board from the table, and holding it in front of her like a shield. 'I need you to leave.'

In that space that had opened up between them, Alice felt her heart wrung out with longing. Her whole body was screaming, wanting to hold him, go back to where they were minutes earlier. She couldn't even trust herself to look at him, she wanted him so much.

That's when Victoria started crying, properly now, and it gave her the extra energy that she needed.

'Just go,' she said firmly. 'And don't try to see me again.'

She still couldn't look at him, but she sensed him picking up his hat and then she heard the snap of the door behind him. She stood, frozen, all alone in the kitchen, and then she realized that her baby was still crying in the next room.

As Alice picked her daughter up from the crib, she felt her body convulse with sorrow — or was it pain? She didn't even know what it was. She sat down heavily on the bed with Victoria in her arms. And then she was crying as well, alongside her daughter. For a few minutes they were both howling together.

Alice could feel her daughter becoming more distressed, picking up on her own sorrow. She knew that she couldn't just sit there with her, weeping. She made herself stand up, and then she pulled a small towel off her dresser and wiped it around her face, wiping over and over again until she had made herself stop crying and dried all of the tears. Looking down to her daughter, she tried to smile at her, but her face felt tight and swollen. She made herself smile and then she started whispering. 'You are all I need, my darling, you are mine, my daughter,' her voice punctuated by small sobs.

At last she could see the baby starting to settle and she sat back down on the bed with her, singing a simple lullaby that her father had taught her. Her voice was husky and out of tune as she sang, but the words and the act of giving voice started to soothe her own spirits and very soon, she could see her daughter's eyelids starting to close as she went back to sleep.

Alice did cry again after she got herself into bed, softly this time, into her pillow. And she woke a number of times during the night, crying. But each time she woke she told herself over and over, that she had made the right decision. That what she'd done was the best for everyone . . .

★ ★ ★

'You did what?' repeated Eddy, for the second time, as Alice told her hurriedly on the way to work what had happened the night before.

'Well, I know you'd said you never wanted to see that lying so-and-so ever again. But Alice, clearly, you adore him.'

379

'I do, I want him so much, I've never met a man like that,' stated Alice, feeling her chest tighten and the tears springing to her eyes. 'But it's not the right thing, Eddy. Not when he has a wife and child.'

'Crikey, Alice,' said Eddy, putting an arm around her shoulders and pulling her close. 'I knew you could be stubborn at times, but I never thought you could be so determined. Not like this. I am very proud of you. I don't think I would ever have the will power to do what you're doing.'

'I'm not really sure that I have the will power either,' sniffed Alice, wiping the tears away with the flat of her hand.

She did find the will power, however, and week after week she poured more and more into her work at the hospital. And every day as she spent time with Victoria she thought about his daughter, Elizabeth, and she told herself that she'd done the right thing.

She went for afternoon tea with the Reverend Seed on a regular basis and she was increasingly drawn to his kindness. She knew what he was thinking — it was easy to see in his eyes — but for the time being, she didn't want anything more than friendship. She still thought about Morgan, of course she did, but each time she remembered him she made herself think about how devastated she'd been that day she'd found out that he was married. How she'd sat and wept in the back yard.

And then she remembered what Sue Cassidy had told her that day about what her mam always said when she was having trouble with a fella . . . 'The whole lot of 'em can go hang.'

★   ★   ★

Weeks later Alice stood at the top of Female Medical, checking that all was in order before Sister's inspection. She couldn't help but admire the tidiness and cleanliness of the ward as the patients sat up in their beds, neatly awaiting the doctor's round. Alice was sure that Florence Nightingale herself would give them the highest commendation to Sister Fox.

However, Alice knew that despite how well she'd actually managed on this ward, the medical wards were steady, predictable, compared to surgical. The patients could be very poorly on admission, and some of the cases were complex and long-term, but you didn't get the orderlies running in with a patient covered in blood; you didn't see that patient go to theatre and return 'fixed'.

'Nurse Sampson, are we ready?' said Sister Fox, her voice cutting through Alice's thoughts like a knife.

'Yes, Sister,' replied Alice, and then she was required to walk along behind as Sister scrutinized each bed in turn.

'Sloppy work,' stated Sister, stopping at a particular bed. Alice beckoned to Nurse Kelly and Nurse Parker to come and remake the bed.

'And what's *that*, under this bed?' she screeched, bending down and peering underneath the next one.

'It appears to be a bed sock,' said Alice, trying

to stop herself from smiling. Anyone would think that Sister had seen a live rat under there.

Alice fished it out and as she straightened up she caught the eye of Miss Fairchild two beds down. She could see the amusement in the woman's eyes. Sister Fox's ward rounds were terrifying for new patients, but the ones who'd been in for a while soon got used to it.

Alice saw that Miss Fairchild was holding a letter and indicating that she wanted to speak to her as soon as possible.

Alice was straight there after the ward round and Miss Fairchild handed her the letter. 'It's from Maud,' she said. 'She's coming back. I do hope that she's making the right decision, what with her work out there and everything, but I have to say that I'm so glad now that Mrs Watson wrote to her. She will be back as soon as she can make arrangements. And she wants me to make enquiries at the Blue Coat School for Alfred, to see if we can get a place for him back there. So she must be thinking of coming back for good ... Oh, Alice, I am so excited about them coming home. So excited.'

As Alice read the letter she hoped that Maud had taken everything into account when she'd made her decision and she wasn't acting impulsively. But then, this was Maud, it was her nature to consider things carefully. So she must be doing the right thing. And then Alice felt tears springing to her eyes when she thought of her, Eddy and Maud being reunited.

'This is good news,' she said, returning Miss Fairchild's smile. 'Now take a deep breath,' she added gently, noting that her patient was starting to struggle a bit. 'Just get your breathing back into a steady rhythm.'

Earlier that day, Dr Logan had discussed the prospect of discharge with Miss Fairchild. He'd told her that they'd reached the limit with her treatment; there was nothing more that they could do.

'I won't be able to go back to work. It sounds like I'll be bed-bound for the rest of my life,' said the housekeeper. 'But, again, Mrs Watson has proved her weight in gold. She's spoken to the lady of the house on my behalf, and given that I've worked there for thirty years, they want to keep me on to do the books and supervise a new person. They've even offered to pay for a private nurse, so that's more than I expected. Much more.

'And I've remembered what you said to me, Alice, all those weeks ago, about sometimes the most you can hope for is that things don't get any worse, and that has really helped me get things in perspective.'

Alice smiled and gave her hand a squeeze. 'Well, I'm glad of that, at least,' she said.

She smiled all the way from the hospital door to Eddy perched on the steps of the Nurses' Home.

'Well, well,' said Eddy. 'It looks like you've had a good day.'

'It's Maud — she's coming back, Miss Fairchild's had a letter.'

'Really? Is that all right?' said Eddy, jumping up from the step. 'Is she doing the right thing?'

'Well, I wondered that, but you know what Maud's like — she always weighs things up properly, she's not like you and me. She's Maud.'

'She is, indeed,' said Eddy, starting to grin. 'And she's coming home!'

★ ★ ★

When Alice checked her pigeonhole there was a letter waiting for her from Maud too. She turned to Eddy, and as soon as she had the envelope open, Eddy was pulling out the letter and reading it aloud.

'*Dear Alice and Eddy,*

Just a short note to let you know that I will be back to Liverpool as soon as I can. It has really helped to have your letters, Alice, about Miss Fairchild's condition and I know that you will be giving her the best of care on the ward. But I need to see her, and it's important for Alfred too. So we will be home just as soon as arrangements can be made. This will take at least one month but I will write again when I have the details.

I have learnt so much here at the hospital in New York, but I can't wait to be back with you two in Liverpool.

Warmest wishes from your dearest friend, Maud'

Alice was smiling all through the letter, but then her brow furrowed. 'No mention of Harry again, and it doesn't sound like she's thinking of going back. There's something not right there, I'm sure there is . . . '

'Well, we can ask her soon, can't we?' said Eddy, starting to jump up and down with excitement. And then she was clinging to Alice and they were both jumping up and down and singing, 'Maud's coming home, Maud's coming home!', dancing around and around, their feet beating a steady rhythm over the coloured floor tiles of the entrance to the Nurses' Home.

As they sang, Millicent Langtry walked by, looking lost in her own world. They both called hello as they continued to dance. Millicent stopped for a moment, tilted her head to one side as she watched them, and then, with a shake of her head, she continued on her way.

A few moments later, Miss Merryweather peeped out of her door, a small smile on her face. 'Nurse Sampson, Nurse Pacey . . . It's a very good job that the night superintendent has already gone to the wards. It's time for you both to be heading off, I think?' Not waiting for a reply, she retreated back inside her room and clicked the door to.

Eddy pulled a face, making Alice cackle with laughter, the sound bouncing off the walls of the entrance and back up to the skylight in the space behind them. Then Alice grabbed Eddy's hand and pulled her out through the door and down the steps. 'Come on, you,' she said, linking her friend's arm and pulling her close. 'I've been in enough bother over the last year without you getting me a reprimand for excess noise and frivolous behaviour. It's a good job Maud's coming back soon — she'll keep you in the proper order.'

Eddy just laughed and continued to talk as they walked away, down the street. And as they disappeared into the evening light, they continued to chatter, their murmuring voices soon lost amidst the clamour of the city.

We do hope that you have enjoyed reading this large print book.

Did you know that all of our titles are available for purchase?

We publish a wide range of high quality large print books including:
Romances, Mysteries, Classics
General Fiction
Non Fiction and Westerns

Special interest titles available in large print are:
The Little Oxford Dictionary
Music Book
Song Book
Hymn Book
Service Book

Also available from us courtesy of Oxford University Press:
Young Readers' Dictionary
(large print edition)
Young Readers' Thesaurus
(large print edition)

For further information or a free brochure, please contact us at:
Ulverscroft Large Print Books Ltd.,
The Green, Bradgate Road, Anstey,
Leicester, LE7 7FU, England.
Tel: (00 44) 0116 236 4325
Fax: (00 44) 0116 234 0205

Other titles published by Ulverscroft:

THE LIVERPOOL NIGHTINGALES

Kate Eastham

Liverpool, 1870. In the dirty backstreets, housemaid Maud Linklater witnesses an appalling accident. Rushing young chimney sweep Alfred to hospital, she helps nurse the boy on the overcrowded ward — and finds herself with a new job. Maud cannot believe her luck at joining trainees Alice and Eddy at the new Nurses' Training School and they form the closest of bonds. Then one day Alfred is abducted. Maud and the girls know the alleyways and slums of Liverpool are no place for a lost little boy. Can these determined women find Alfred before it's too late?